BOOK 1

BOOK 1

ARGUS

To Raven and Quetz, whom I love very much.

All rights reserved. No part of this publication may be reproduced, stored in a retrieval system, or transmitted in any form or by any means electronic, mechanical, photocopying, recording, or otherwise without prior written permission from Podium Publishing.

This a work of fiction. Names, characters, places, and incidents are either products of the author's imagination or used fictitiously. Any resemblance to actual events, locales, or persons, living, dead, or undead, is entirely coincidental.

Copyright © 2023 by Forrest Taylor

Cover design by Podium Publishing

ISBN: 978-1-0394-2688-7

Published in 2023 by Podium Publishing, ULC
www.podiumaudio.com

BOOK 1

CHAPTER 1

James's life had been getting weird lately. Actually, that was probably the wrong way to say it. James's life had *gotten* weird lately, going from normal to something he didn't understand at high speed.

It started almost exactly a month ago. His work schedule had changed, and he got stuck on the night shift. Tech support at one a.m. is almost brutally boring, and it took a lot of effort to not just doze off. He was just getting into the pattern of it when something went horribly wrong. One Tuesday night that was technically early morning, the elevator was out when he clocked out. So rather than go all the way around the building for the other one, it seemed easier to take the stairs. Makes sense, right? The big bulky security door for the stairwell is right there. So throw it open and see . . . not the stairs.

Cubicles. Hundreds of them. Thousands, maybe. Stretching so far off that they faded into the horizon. He'd panicked then, and slammed the door. Clearly, this was sleep deprivation and hallucination. So he took a minute, then opened it up again, and of course, there the stairs sat, normal as could be.

It wasn't until it happened again the next week that he realized the crazy wasn't in his own head at all, but in the real world all along. The week after that, he did it on purpose, and with a little less panic, and he started to get a picture of what was going on.

On Tuesday, between 3:44 and 3:46 a.m., the door to the east stairwell of his call center led to . . . somewhere else.

That third time, he went in a bit. Careful to keep the door propped open slightly, of course.

All the desks nearby were occupied, but he didn't recognize the names on any of the tags. And the little knickknacks were all sort of . . . random. There were pictures of cats, office toys, plants, all the usual stuff, but they all felt kind of jumbled, like they were just dropped there to fill some kind of junk quota. It wasn't until he'd passed the fourth or fifth desk that he thought to check a drawer and made two major discoveries.

One, some of the desks had candy bars in them. And the candy bars seemed just as "random number generator" as everything else. He was well aware of the fact that humanity had put chocolate, nougat, caramel, and nuts together in just about every possible combination, but that didn't mean he'd seen any of them. And he was pretty sure that "Baby Things" weren't available at his local supermarket.

They did taste good, though.

The second discovery was when he found a wallet in a coat hanging on the back of a chair. The ID in it didn't match the name tag on the cubicle, it had a loyalty card to a coffee shop he was pretty sure didn't exist, and it also contained a hundred and seventeen dollars and fifteen cents in cash.

That last part was important, because the cash sure didn't look randomized.

As he was busy wondering what kind of person would carry almost exclusively two- and five-dollar bills, a thought in the back of his mind was racing. If this was what he could find a few feet through the door, how much more stuff was in here? A hundred bucks, even in weird denominations, was a hundred bucks. He'd just made in five minutes what would normally take most of a workday.

James wasn't an idiot, and he'd played more than one RPG in his life. Even if he hadn't been a massive nerd in his downtime, he worked in tech support. Hard to avoid that kind of incidental knowledge. He could see what was going on here, and his thoughts turned to spawn rates and drop tables. Was this place farmable? Hell, if he could just pick up a few hundred bucks and some novelty candy every week, that was more than enough to justify it, right?

So busy was he caught up in wondering if this place was his personal treasure trove that James didn't notice the skittering thing creeping up on him until it was already upon him. With a yelp of pain, he jerked his hand off the desk, a pained "Holy shit!" coming from him as he looked at the two tiny bleeding points on the back of his hand. On the desk, clicking at him in an angry tone, was a stapler.

It was black. Heavy. He could tell just by looking at it that it was one of those solid bricks that they don't seem to make anymore but that keep showing up in offices. It clattered at him, moving under some unseen power, and skittered toward him across the desk, not letting up its tiny furious assault. As for how it was actually moving, that was more obvious. Ten to twenty "legs," made of what looked like ballpoint pens, gave the impression of a matte-black crab.

Before he knew what was really happening, it launched itself at his face, and James could only flail backward in panic. The stapler got a few good punches in on his left cheek, leaving dripping trails of blood running down onto his shoulder, before he got a good grip on it and pulled it off. It was heavy, but not really any heavier than a stapler. Gripping the top of it, he ripped open the feed chamber for the staples, getting a surprising amount of resistance and a fleshy popping sound as he pried it back. Dumping the staples out onto the floor, along with some dripping fleshy strings that tied the stapler's internals together, he threw the creature into the far wall of the cubicle before slumping back into the swivel chair and taking panicked breaths as the adrenaline left his system.

It took him more than a few minutes to regain his breath, and longer to stop his hands from shaking. He'd just been attacked. By a stapler. God, he was bleeding! It wasn't threatening, but the wounds hurt like hell, and blood was dripping onto his shirt, and how was he supposed to explain this to his boss? As he sat there, trying to regain some calm, he noticed something about the corpse of the office tool he'd just fought off.

"Are you kidding me? It even has a loot drop. This is insane," he muttered to himself, kneeling down to pick up the small, slightly glowing, golden orb hovering above the body of the monstrous stapler.

Holding it between his thumb and forefinger, he brought it up to his eye. "Doesn't look like an actual gem," he muttered, slightly squeezing the soft sphere. "What am I even supposed to do with—" It popped in his grip, suddenly and almost violently, though he didn't really feel a thing.

In his mind, however, a single thought that was recognizably not his own echoed.

[+1 Skill Rank : Templating - Phone Book - New York]

"What." Without really meaning to, he thought about a New York phone book, and a series of data points jumped to mind. Column widths, ad spacing and costs, font size; it was like he'd spent the last couple months working a job printing the giant brick texts that no one used anymore.

"What the hell kind of reward is *that*? I think I am actually a more boring person for having done that! No, this is bullshit! No! The candy, okay, I get that. Money? Sure! But this? This is insane! Who the fuck wants to know how to format phone books?" he yelled into the empty, endless office.

Well, the mostly empty office.

A series of skittering noises answered the yell. Like a thousand dry ballpoint pens being scritched across paper, digging for ink that had long since run out. A waterfall of noise and motion. It took him a second to realize what he'd just done, and then the first stapler crested the cubicle wall.

A second series of noises joined the first; this time, it was mostly the word *fuck* yelled at high volume, punctuated by the sound of feet pounding the floor as James dashed for the exit at high speed. *How fast can those things go? What if they catch me? What if the door isn't there? How long have I been in here? Was I stupid enough to miss the exit window?* Thoughts ran through his head at high speed, and he ran through the office just as fast.

The door was still there, though. And it still led to the east stairwell. James was through it faster than he'd ever opened a door before, and he slammed the thick metal security door behind him, bracing himself against it to stop the incoming flood of stapler-crabs. But the impacts never came; no skittering noises or scratchings echoed from the other side. It was just a silent hallway. He checked his watch. 3:47. He opened the door. Stairs.

Heart still racing, he decided to take the time to walk around the building and use the other elevator down that night.

CHAPTER 2

So all of this happened two weeks ago. It took about a day for him to really start to believe it had even happened, though the aching scabs on his cheek and hand were pretty good proof. Another few days to really process the whole thing and stop double-checking every door before going through it. About five days to pretend his life was going back to normal—and pointedly *not* "taking the stairs" that Tuesday— with one day off for hanging out with some friends on the weekend and saying nothing about it in case he really was just going crazy.

And then a few days to consider the implications of everything.

The stapler, he decided, was not a huge threat. Oh, sure, if he'd let it, it could have taken out an eye, and the swarm could have bled him out in a probably horrifyingly painful way. But one of them wasn't a problem. For a few hundred bucks and some novelty candy, he could fight a few staplers. But that was just near the door; he hadn't gone too far in, so who knew if it got worse?

And, more importantly, who knew what other skill balls he could find?

As absurdly useless as knowing how to size a column for a list of phone numbers was, he'd basically just gotten two months of job training for free in a few seconds. Sure, it was a hyperspecific job, and he didn't live anywhere close to New York, but still. It was a fair bet that not every stapler dropped that exact same chunk of knowledge. It was also a fair bet that at least a few staplers would drop *some* chunk of knowledge. How long would he have to spend in there to learn something valuable? An hour? Two?

And so, that Sunday night, James spent his time at work spacing out, fantasizing about magically becoming a master chef, picking up judo like it was nothing, and, on a more practical level, maybe figuring out how to fix the internet when it went out at his apartment.

That Monday evening found him looking down at his bed, looking at the assortment of stuff laid out on his duvet. A backpack to hold most of it, an empty duffel bag for later. A handful of granola bars. Four bottles of water. About fifty feet of rope, which he hadn't realized would be as heavy as it was. A Maglite, of course; can't have an adventure without that. A notepad. A couple two-way radios, courtesy of a desperation sale at the last dying RadioShack. A smaller bag full of disinfectant and bandages. And, of course, a roll of duct tape. Because duct tape could solve a lot of problems.

All that went into the bag.

Oh, and a nine-millimeter pistol with two magazines and a box of spare rounds. That, begrudgingly, went into a locked matte-black hard plastic case on his desk. Too much of a risk tonight, given that he was about to walk into a job that did security checks for spare pens. James wasn't really sure why he'd even gotten it. Enthusiasm, maybe. Both from himself and from his dad, who was way too eager to lend James a handgun.

The heavy coat and fingerless gloves went on him. The crowbar he'd carry in one of the duffel bags until he got there. And voilà, one... well, one professional crazy criminal, thinking about it.

He'd prefer to be called an adventurer. But honestly, he couldn't rule out being crazy.

James himself wasn't exactly an adventuring type. Not physically, anyway. He was in his very late twenties, mildly overweight from spending more of his free time at a desk than actually doing physical exercise and *all* of his work time there too, and honestly pretty pale from spending all that collective time inside. He'd recently switched to contact lenses, and he still had marks on the side of his head from years of wearing glasses that were a little too tight, but those marks were covered by the hair he kept in a long ponytail that was probably the most well-cared-for part of his body. But, he figured as he set out the door, even *he* could deal with one, maybe two staplers without too much issue.

And then, after all that, work crawled by, almost unbearably slowly. James fielded a few intolerably stupid tech support calls, one from an older gentleman who, while friendly, had to be reminded that the CD tray wasn't a cupholder. At any other time, this would have amused him and been one of those tales from tech support to share with his friends and also Reddit, but right now, it just frayed his patience. And so by the time his shift ended, his nerves had him almost shaking.

Clocking out, spending the two-minute walk between his desk and his time card worrying that someone would notice the crowbar, James just kept running over in his head what a stupid idea this was. How he was gonna get himself killed, how it wasn't worth it, how he should just go home now and not wait for the door. And yet, when he got back to his desk, he did a quick double check of his gear, took an exactly twelve-minute "bathroom break," and then headed for the east stairwell.

No one was around at the elevator landing, leaving the area with a strangely dead silent feeling. Or at least, strange to someone who was used to being there during the day. It was the little things; the potted plants didn't rustle in the breeze of people walking by, the carpet that normally kept things quiet now muffled sound to a stifling degree, and the elevator's *ding* wasn't sounding every two minutes as someone got on or off. It was just . . . empty. Devoid of humanity.

Trying hard not to notice this, or at least not to let it bother him, James checked his phone, confirmed that it was 3:44 a.m., and pushed open the door.

The solid metal door swung open silently on well-oiled hinges. And beyond it, instead of stairs, was an ocean of low-walled cubicles. Like a beige fractal, the aisles and walls and open spaces stretched out before him. Nothing moved, nothing threatened him, but he still felt ill at ease. It was, he realized, almost an identical feeling to being at the elevator landing: not a single human around to make small noises or provide a bit of company.

When the door swung shut behind him, he almost jumped out of his skin. As he gave a nervous laugh to try to steady his nerves, the noise drew his attention to a clock on the wall over the door. 3:44, it read. And continued to read. As he watched, he could barely see the second hand ticking forward, but it was at an almost non-existent pace. So then, he thought, he couldn't be here forever. But it would be a very, very long time before 3:47 and the door wouldn't open from the other side. Would it still let him out? Or would he be stuck here forever?

James did some quick math, then checked that math twice on his phone's calculator. It seemed like, based on the speed of the clock, he had maybe eight hours in here before that was even a problem. And he had no intention of staying longer than it took to fill up a duffel bag. So he set a timer on his phone as a backup measure and turned toward his goal.

Step one, he figured, was to just rummage through the immediate surroundings. He couldn't actually see too far into the distance, because some of the cubicle walls rose up to just over head height, and after enough distance and enough walls, there wasn't a clear line of sight for very far. But nearby, there were cubicles. Some of them should have been the ones he'd poked through before, but he didn't recognize any of them. The first one he got to had pictures of what looked like a stock model playing with her dog, except each picture contained a different woman. Same dog, though. It was the kind of thing that made James pause and put a little too much thought into how silent and inhuman it was in here.

Not enough of a pause to stop him from checking the purse on the desk, though. Or muttering a quick "Score!" under his breath as he pocketed the ten bucks in it, along with a small bottle of perfume. Anything that looked vaguely fancy, he figured, he might be able to sell at a pawn shop. Or just give to someone as a gift. Nice perfume was a good gift whether it came from a store or a monster-infested nightmare zone. He assumed. He *hoped*. After all, he thought, he was here to loot, and he might not come back anytime soon. Best grab whatever looked nice.

James went through a couple more desks, snapping up cash (though making a point to ignore the three-dollar bills), grabbing any nice-looking pens, nabbing a smartphone of some kind. And of course, bagging any candy bars with bizarre names that he could share as a novelty with his friends. So far, not much was topping Baby Things, but Flavor Rocks was pretty close. Then again, he figured, Butterfinger and Whatchamacallit were both actual, real names for food that someone must have, at some point, thought were good ideas, so who was he to complain about the creativity of the random name generator in this cubicle landscape?

It wasn't until about fifteen minutes into his looting spree that he got his first bout of trouble. As he ducked under a hanging plant that looked suspiciously like how someone who had only heard of ferns before would make a fern, his first enemy struck. The stapler-crab came out of the thick fern like a bolt, falling the half foot onto his backpack and immediately trying to punch its metal payload into his right shoulder. Fortunately, the thick leather coat that he'd worn today absorbed the actual stab. Still, being punched at high speed by a motivated and furious stapler was gonna hurt anyway, and the feeling of its pen-legs scrabbling at his back almost made James panic right there.

He didn't, though. He kept calm, or at least calm enough, and slammed his back against the cubicle wall. It held up surprisingly well, and he both heard and felt the stapler hit the floor. Before it could skitter away, or worse, into his ankles, he stomped on it hard enough that his teeth rattled. Keeping it pinned, some of its legs bending under it, he brought the crowbar down on it like a golfer teeing off. Once. Twice. The third time, something gave, and the front of the creature tore off with a fleshy pop, lines of staples flying across the floor along with a splash of inky black liquid.

Just as he was taking a breath, leaning back against the wall, he happened to catch sight of movement. It was that stroke of luck that saved him from a stapler-induced concussion, as not one but two more of the crabs crawled out of the cover of the potted plant, perched on the edge of the hanging pot for a few seconds, and then launched themselves at his head.

The first one caught a panicked swing of the crowbar as James hissed out profanities. He kept his voice low even as he became increasingly adrenaline pumped; he remembered what had happened the last time he made too much noise here. And he probably wasn't at risk of actually dying, he knew that. Not after the ambush was spoiled, at least. But still, these things fucking hurt, and he didn't want to go through the process of pulling staples out of his fucking face again.

To that end, he decided to make just a little more noise, specifically by grabbing the second stapler off his shoulder where it was hauling itself toward his neck, winding up, and pitching it as hard as possible over the cubicle wall, off into the distance. Now, James was not athletic. He was the kind of person who worked tech support because it afforded him the opportunity to read more books while sitting down all day, which was a continuation of what he did at home. He wasn't lazy, or fat, but he wasn't overly strong or fit. Even so, he currently had enough adrenaline in his blood to kill a large dog, or perhaps a small horse, and so his throw was a bit more vigorous than normal. The creature arced up toward the ceiling, silently twitching its legs, and quickly went out of sight over the cubicle wall in front of him.

He didn't hear it land.

Turning back to the desk and the other crab, James swapped the crowbar back to his right hand and took a swing. But this time, he was starting to feel the shakes from his adrenaline-fueled fight, and he whiffed over the head of the thing and crunched the computer monitor instead, snapping the plastic frame and ruining the screen as the heavy bar of metal got stuck in it. He tried to yank it back for another try, but it really was stuck, and the office supply nightmare rushed him and sank its "teeth" into his wrist before he could jerk backward.

A solid stapler *ka-chunk* was followed instantly by a burst of pain as a staple punched down to the bone on the back of his wrist. About half the staple was still sticking out as the monster pulled back for another strike, and James reacted to instinctive fear. He dropped the crowbar entirely, grabbed the stapler around its midpoint, ignoring the abnormally sharp points of the legs, and as with his first kill here, he grabbed it with both hands and simply pulled until the top ripped off with a wet splattering sound, staples pouring out along with inky blood across the desk.

And then everything was quiet again.

As his body started to tremble from the aftereffects of what certainly *felt* like life-or-death combat, James pulled the office chair over and fell into the black padding of the seat. He took a few deep breaths to steady himself and to psych himself up to pull a centimeter of metal out of his wrist.

Pulling out his tube of disinfectant and a bandage from his bag, he was struck with the sudden realization of just how loud the rustling sounded in the otherwise dead air. Even in the office in the real world, when he was alone at night, there was at least the air conditioning constantly humming. But here, nothing. Not even the sounds of clicking as enemies closed in. It took him more than a couple minutes to get the medical supplies out, as he kept stopping and checking to make sure he didn't hear something, constantly looking around at the walls of the cubicle to see if anything was crawling over them.

But the coast was clear, and he couldn't delay any longer. With gritted teeth, he took a grip on the staple in him with sweaty fingers and jerked it out. Two small points of red blood started welling up and dripping down onto the carpet almost immediately as he tossed the metal away and clamped his hand over the wound. James cursed himself for not thinking to bring a towel or something to clean blood with as he fumbled with a single hand to put some disinfectant on the bandage and get the adhesive onto his skin in a way that didn't just slide off in the now quite slick layer of blood.

Eventually, he got himself no longer bleeding and took a few minutes to just try to calm down, process what happened, and get his crowbar out of the computer monitor as quietly as possible. After taking a few drinks of water and settling down, he decided it was time to check what he'd really come here for.

Over both of the dead stapler-crabs, a small yellow orb hovered. Mostly opaque skin around some kind of liquid or gas or maybe just congealed yellow magic, James didn't know exactly what. It was smooth, like a bath bead, and to him in that moment, it was the most precious of treasure. He had fought for this, literally bled for this, for a chance to, right now, be something more than just a dull IT guy in a dead-end job he hated.

"Yessssssss," he whispered to the empty office, doing a small fist pump in the air.

Time to see to the prize, he decided. Two small orbs popped neatly in his fingers. Two small thoughts ran through his mind, very obviously intruders, making their presence known clearly and politely.

[+1 Skill Rank : History - Boogieboarding]

[+1 Skill Rank : Repair - Fax Machine]

"Nooooooooo," he whispered, equally unheard by the chairs and desks around him.

But in truth, he wasn't mad. Not even a little upset or disappointed. As he ducked back out of the aisle and followed the pen marks he'd left back to the door, he had a sense of satisfaction and triumph burning in his chest. He'd done it; he'd made a successful incursion into this place. He'd tested himself on something that was trying to kill him, and he'd won and been rewarded.

His rewards were . . . lackluster. James was almost certain that his office actually had a fax machine somewhere, but damned if he'd ever had to fix it. But they were also different from the first one. As he walked, he made some notes on the pad he'd brought along, scribbling down the words as he kept his eyes on the walls around him. First, he marked the skills he'd gotten. It was actually pretty weird to suddenly know things he hadn't even considered before, and the lack of context or emotion on those chunks of knowledge made them a bit surreal to think about. He also made some notes on the things he'd learned about the diversity of orbs found so far, then started jotting down questions he had. The questions, and possible tests to answer them, took up a lot more space.

Before he was actually done, he'd arrived back at the door. It was almost absent-mindedly that he pushed it open, stepped out, and casually waited for the elevator to take him down. He'd gotten lost in the thought of what questions he had, and he suddenly realized how lucky he was that he didn't get jumped again on the way out, even though he wasn't that far in.

The big questions, things like "What is that place?" and "Who-and-or-what made it, and why?," were obviously off the table. But other questions, like "Does it get more dangerous?" and "Do the more dangerous parts drop better skills?," and even "What constitutes a single point in a skill?," were all things he could maybe start testing.

Of course, as he headed out of the building to his car, he also remembered that he had some much more fun questions to answer when he got home. Questions like "Can I afford to order pizza tonight because I just looted a few hundred bucks from an extra-dimensional office dungeon?"

He was pretty sure the answer was "Yes. And that's why I'll be back."

CHAPTER 3

"James!" The call was firm, but not shouted too loudly through the small apartment he shared with his roommates. "What the hell is this candy on the table?"

James reluctantly hauled himself out of his desk chair and plodded down the hallway to the messy living room. His roommate and relatively recent friend, Anesh, was in the futile process of trying to clean off their kitchen table. From experience, James knew that table wouldn't stay cleared off or in any reasonable way "clean" for more than a day or so. And knowing this, he'd emptied out his duffel bag several days ago when he'd come back from his first delve onto that very same table, hoping that he'd have plenty of time to sort it out later.

Of course, now Anesh had actually decided to do chores. This was unexpected, and now he had to explain something.

"They're from England?" was what he went with.

Anesh gave him a look. The sort of look you gave someone when you were absolutely sure they were full of shit. "James, I am from England. If these are from England, they're from a Poundland down a back alley that no one has been in since 1995. And they can't be that, because this one tastes pretty all right."

"You ate my candy?"

Anesh shifted his look to a more sheepish one. "That's not the point here. Where'd you get all this anyway? And, also, why'd you pile it on our table?"

James decided to go with the honest answer. "Well, I found an extradimensional cubicle dungeon at work, and it has cash and candy bars in it, among other things. This is what I had in my bag when I got home, but I needed the bag for groceries, because I didn't want to just carry milk home and freeze my fingers off, so I dumped it here. Also, here's rent for the month." He handed over a few hundred bucks in a range of different denominations.

"I . . . do *not* believe you," Anesh responded. "But whatever. If you don't want to tell me where you're getting your secret candy, I'm not actually that curious. Honestly, I care more about why you just paid rent in two-dollar bills. Did you mug someone's grandma?"

James raised an eyebrow. "Why a gran . . . ?"

"When have you ever gotten something like this except as a Christmas thing from your grandma?" Anesh asked with coyly raised eyebrows.

"That's a very good point. And no, I didn't mug anyone," James responded. "Probably. They're all from procedurally generated wallets."

Anesh sighed. "Well, again, whatever. It's rent. I'm gonna get back to this, so I'll probably shove your candy in the pantry." As he spoke, he casually unwrapped one of the bright neon-yellow-wrapped candy bars and started munching on it.

"Are you just . . . eating more of my candy? Dude, that took a lot of work to get." James moved to snatch the treat from Anesh, but his roommate dodged out of the way behind the table.

Keeping the table between the two of them, he shoved more chocolate in his mouth. "You left these here for almost a whole week! You forfeit your claim!"

James stopped trying to circle the table and grab his food back. "Okay, A, that is not how *property* works. B, wait, is it Sunday already? I have to go get some stuff."

Through the last mouthful of candy, Anesh said, "Ah, you work tomorrow, huh? Gotta get something before you're banished back to the night shift?"

"Yeah, going to the military surplus store. I want to see if they have, I dunno, some kind of armor." He raised his arms, showing the bandages, one of them actually a piece of gauze taped to his wrist. "I'm getting tired of how much these ache and itch."

Anesh just shook his head and turned back to what he was working on. "Sure, go get your head start on your Halloween costume," he said, casually dismissing his friend.

Jokes aside, James did have a plan for today. It was the last day of his three-day weekend, and he absolutely intended to go in again tomorrow. In to work, sure, but afterward, *In*. Capital *I*.

He'd been unsure about it at first. The visceral and insanely unpleasant feeling of a staple grinding against the bone of his wrist as he pulled it out had been . . . bad. Tooth-grindingly bad. And as soon as he'd actually gotten home, he'd sat down at his desk and, for about two hours, debated going to the hospital because of how bad it hurt. *Never*, he'd thought, *am I going to do something that stupid again. It's not worth it. It will never be worth it, especially if it gets more dangerous or more painful.*

The notepad he'd been jotting stuff down on lay where he'd tossed it on his desk, and he'd stared at it for half an hour, just considering whether he wanted to pitch it in the trash, cut his losses, and forget everything else that had happened.

And he'd had his whole workweek to remember how much he hated his job.

And then he'd paid Anesh rent with the cash and realized he could spend an extra three hundred dollars on whatever the hell he wanted. Probably random Kickstarter projects.

He'd gone in to work on Saturday, cursing his new schedule and already mad as hell that he was missing his apartment's D&D game, and his boss had told him he wasn't needed that night, and he'd wasted two hours on getting ready and the damn commute, and he was just . . .

Just perfectly ready to pick up the crowbar again, really.

And so, the local military surplus store. If there was one thing that James had learned from actually playing RPGs, it was that the three hundred dollars he'd gotten should be treated as an investment and instantly go into buying better gear. Gear that would allow him, and he could not repeat this enough, to not get painfully stapled.

As it turned out, though, military surplus stores, or at least, *this* military surplus store, did not sell functional combat armor. And James was hesitant to ask the bearded mountain of a man behind the counter who kept glaring at him if they had any vambraces in the back stockroom. So after about half an hour of trying to search through boxes and racks of old BDUs, ammo cans, machetes, and field manuals, he just gave up on that plan and decided to double down on the thick coat and maybe go full anime and just wrap exposed parts of his arms in bandages. That idea was abandoned as soon as he got home, tried it, and realized how surprisingly uncomfortable it actually was to move in.

Almost without warning, it was Monday again. James hadn't slept well; his nerves were actually starting to impact him this time. He'd stayed up staring at his ceiling for hours, mostly just thinking about how stupid he was and how he couldn't do this. Eventually, he'd drifted off, only to be shocked awake by his alarm, dragged out of the warm haze of sleep that only really comes when one has been battling insomnia. He'd pushed through his waking routine without thinking of anything in particular, but when the time came to go in to work . . .

Well, he'd thrown the duffel bag in his car.

Work was a series of sharp edges and near snaps. He'd almost punched his manager when she'd surprised him by the door. He'd half yelled at more than one customer. On his break, he'd taken some time outside to catch his breath and calm down.

Am I seriously this worked up over it? I feel like a kid going into their first day of work all over again, he mused, looking up at the night sky. *Except, well, normal jobs don't try to murder you.* He took one last deep breath. *I should probably apologize to the boss so she's not pissed at me all night. I got this. It'll be an adventure. A good way to kick off the rest of the boring-ass week.*

Now that he was resolved, and a little more ready, work passed quickly. And once again, before he knew it, he was standing in front of a certain door, checking his phone's clock.

3:44. *Time to go.*

Rows of gray and beige, the muffled sound of nothing, strangely dimmed fluorescent lights. It was starting to become a bit more familiar.

Right inside the door was a T intersection in the cubicles. And on the floor, right there in front of him, was a stapler. It looked normal, but it was still quivering a bit, doing its best impression of something that was totally harmless, and failing.

"Really? Come on, little guy." All of James's tension bled out suddenly. He dropped his bag to the left with a *whump*; unzipped it, keeping an eye on the "harmless" stapler; and pulled out one of the long cardboard strips he'd brought tonight. Holding it against a nearby cubicle wall, he swiftly reached down, grabbed the stapler-crab, and *ka-chunked* the cardboard into the wall, affixing it. The stapler's scrabbling pen-legs licked against his hand as he did so, but it wasn't actually painful when he knew it was coming. Keeping his grip on it, he found a blank sheet of paper and a black marker, drew a big *A* on it, and stapled that to the top of his makeshift flag.

Tossing the stapler down, he shooed it away. "Get outta here, little fella. I'm after bigger fish today." The stapler did something a bit different and made a low hissing noise at him that he hadn't heard before. It took him a while to realize it sounded like soft rattling metal. It also didn't leave, but it didn't lunge for him either. "Go on! Shoo!" He prodded it with his foot a bit, and it scampered off. "Either I've only met the berserk ones so far, or that little guy was weird," he muttered to himself.

And now it was time to do some more exploring. Further up, and further in, as his favorite leonine stand-in for Jesus would say. So, making sure to keep his signpost in sight, James headed straight on into the maze of cubicles.

He stopped a few times to loot when he saw obvious targets. Wallets and purses out on desks, or fancy coats draped over chairs. He was here to explore, sure, and to better himself, of course, but he was also here to be able to pay for fancy food for his whole friend group, and he wasn't going to pass up twenties when they dropped in front of him.

It was during this looting spree that he finally realized that most of these desks had computers on them, and computers actually have real-world value. Slapping himself for not thinking of it sooner, he went to power one up and see what kind of specs it had, before stopping. His hand about two inches from the power button, he froze.

There was a feeling that he'd gotten a few times in his life, when something had almost gone cataclysmically wrong. He'd dropped a knife once at a shitty kitchen job, and it had landed about three "oh shits" away from a coworker's foot. He'd almost run over a dog once, just barely missing it by an almost accidental swerve. And he'd accidentally set his desk on fire once, putting it out before it got too bad but still leaving that scorch scar on it forever. And now, he felt something similar. That feeling of dread, like he could see the mistake coming, and didn't want anything to do with it, but couldn't stop it.

So he froze. Looked down. Saw the flashing blue LED on the front of the computer tower pointed up at him, slit down the middle like an iris. Saw the CD tray opened just a bit, and a row of circuit board teeth inside.

Slowly, ever so slowly, he pulled his hand away. Swearing inside, because he'd set his crowbar against the wall by the opening into this cubicle when he got excited about the computer. His heart rate spiked. How many of these things were there? Was every PC and laptop in this place hostile? Was he surrounded right now?

Maybe it hadn't seen him. Maybe it couldn't move. Maybe a lot of things. James only had a few seconds to decide what to do, so he decided to play it cool. He hadn't had any of these things go for his ankles yet, so either this was the first one or it wasn't going to attack him if he didn't touch it. "Ah, sorry, friend," he said in a shaky voice. "Didn't see you there." And he slowly rolled the chair back.

It didn't move. The CD tray closed. James sighed out a lifetime of tension. As he backed out of the cubicle, snagging his crowbar on the way, he muttered to himself, "There goes a year off my life span. This place is gonna give me a heart attack."

Now a good deal more paranoid, he kept going at a slower rate, through the endless beige cloth walls, at some points the taupe office fortifications linking together overhead to form ecru arches. When he realized he was just running through a list of synonyms for *beige* in his head, he started to calm down a bit and stop making his legs ache with his exhausting sneak-walk.

The area around him was more or less the same as it ever was, but he was starting to notice a few new features that were showing up as he progressed. Small banners or drapes of blank printer paper hanging from arched overhangs and walls, occasional blisters of sharpened pencils coming out of the tops of cubicles, things like that. They made the surroundings feel less . . . dead. Less stale. Like it was more of a living place.

He had to stop a couple times to put up signs when he felt like he was about to lose track of the last one he'd stuck up. He hadn't taken many turns, but this whole place seemed to just be a grid, with a few quirks, so as long as he had line of sight to at least one of the signs, he was pretty sure he could get back safely.

Of course, when he tried to put up the third sign, the stapler he grabbed wasn't inanimate, and *this one* went for his fingers. That same stapler got slammed into the wall, then hammered with his crowbar until it couldn't get up again.

A few days ago James had briefly considered the idea of trying to take skill orbs out into the real world. But now, having one in front of him again, with the bitter taste of a mild adrenaline rush in his mouth from something trying to stab him, he found he couldn't help himself and popped it before thinking about holding on to it.

[+1 Skill Rank : Recipe - Pancakes]

"That is . . . almost useful!" James exclaimed as he found another (real) stapler and finished putting up the sign. "I mean, I already knew how to make pancakes. Kind of. In theory. I could make pancakes in potentia, anyway. I wonder how much better at making pancakes this makes me?" He stepped out of the cubicle, took a deep breath, and looked down the hall.

It looked like the line of cubicles ended up ahead. Oh, sure, there were still intersections around him, forks in the path, but if he followed this line, he could see a large flat table in a more open space, fluorescent lighting pouring down onto it. The whole thing brought to his mind a scene of a single large rock in a forest clearing, sunlight pouring down onto a holy object, protected against humanity and nature.

Except here, it was shitty, overly bright white light, and instead of a holy object, it was a cup of coffee.

Which, given how tired he was from work, might as well be an object of divine power. Smiling, he set forward, keeping an eye out for any surprises. He was about ready for a change in scenery. Time to check out the break room.

CHAPTER 4

He'd called it a break room as a joke when he saw it from a distance, but that wasn't exactly wrong.

When James had pushed aside the hanging sheaf of dot-matrix paper that was dangling from an arch like some kind of vine, the sight that had greeted him had been immediately recognizable and vaguely uncomfortable. Every job he'd ever worked had possessed what was, essentially, a carbon copy of the same break room. A too-cramped space for the number of people it served, usually with no natural light, terrible ventilation, the time card reader crammed in the corner of the room alongside a billion *Know Your Rights as a Worker* signs that the company was required by law to post but never seemed to read themselves, and the faint smell of stale socks in the air. And the new "biome" of this place was basically just that.

The bright lights were a bit closer down here, the ceiling also lower, although it was still so tall James couldn't touch it if he jumped. So "lower" mostly meant that it was only twenty feet overhead and not forty. The air was stale, unlike the slightly-too-cool atmosphere of the cubicle hallways. Across the walls were a bunch of signs, and while he couldn't read them from here, he was almost certain that they were going to be creepily alien versions of OSHA postings and mandatory break laws.

A cluster of dinged-up old wood tables covered the center of the space, surrounded by padded chairs that looked less comfortable than some medieval torture devices, about half of them with scattered corporate-label coffee cups and open, half-full snack food bags on them.

Actually, that cluster of furniture seemed more like a labyrinth, the more James looked at it from the mouth of the cubicle hall. There were a few clear paths through it, and as he studied the floor plan, he started to think that it maybe wasn't an accident. Against the walls on the left and right were counters with sinks, vending machines, microwaves, and pots of coffee like he'd glimpsed on the way here, and on the other side of the room, another long beige wall with a single point leading off into more office boxes.

And in the back right of the room, sort of divided away from the exit door, was a big plastic potted plant, fronds bending over the coffee machine, and a single, very large, very yellow glowing orb in its middle.

That sight almost made James drool.

Now, James wasn't the kind of person who would have *dangerously genre savvy* written on his TV Tropes page. But he was enough of the sort of person who browsed TV Tropes on a regular basis to recognize a trap when he saw one. He just couldn't really figure out what it was yet. Because there were so many options.

The vending machines weren't moving, but he could easily envision them spitting cans of bizarrely named soda at high velocity at him. The microwaves might actually shoot microwaves. The sink could spawn some kind of water elemental. The chairs . . . oh man, the chairs could be any number of problems.

And then he heard the hissing noise.

The real problem, he thought, could also be the nightmare ball of tangled cables crawling over the cubicle wall on the left side. Shrinking back as far as he could into the entrance while still keeping an eye on it, he watched with a pumping heart as dozens of power, Ethernet, and audio cables slithered down the wall, latching onto cabinets and flooring and dragging the mass of wires forward. It moved far, far faster than it looked like it could, for something that was large enough to shove James into itself two times over. And its cables poured like water across the counter as it moved. Frozen in fear, James could only watch with an electric buzz in his blood as the cords, many of which had what looked like teeth or needles on the end, stabbed out over and over to pull the main mass forward, rolling it like a ball or a tumbleweed. The thing made a noise like rain as it flowed by, moving under or over furniture as it crossed the break room and James's vision.

As it moved, it bumped into the leg of a table a little too hard and one of the not-Starbucks cups on it tipped over, off the edge, and onto the back of the monster. Then it exploded. Coffee hot enough that James could see heat waves coming off it sprayed out in an arc, splattering across the back of the wirebeast, but the thing didn't care or didn't even notice the popping shock wave and liquid hot enough to melt skin. It just kept going, triggering another coffee bomb as it went, before scaling the opposing wall and hissing away into the distance.

"I fucking knew something in this room was a trap," James said as he gasped in a breath he hadn't realized he was holding.

James was realizing, as he thought through possible traps, that he'd been going about this in a really stupid manner. He wasn't some fantasy hero who could react to anything; he was a soft boy IT employee who could quite literally get stapled to death here. He needed more than a crowbar and a prayer to get through here; he needed a plan. A lot of plans, a lot more resources, and maybe a few months of a gym membership. He poked the muscles of his arm; maybe a few *years* of a gym membership.

He was wandering around a death maze, and he hadn't made a plan. He'd let himself be blinded by free candy and wads of cash, and he was *pretty* sure this was about as dumb an idea as getting into a van with someone who was promising the same. He needed to back out, slowly, and start using his brain instead of his desire for loot.

As he started making his way back, keeping an ear out for the noise that IT nightmare had made, he got his first idea for a plan. Being in here alone was, more often than not, terrifying. So what he needed was backup. He needed someone in here with him, watching his back. Of course, he hadn't really, actually tried to convince anyone this was real, though when he'd been up front with Anesh, he'd gotten a *Yeah, sure*, which was about how he expected anyone would react.

What he needed for step one was, of course, proof.

He stopped outside a cubicle he'd tagged earlier with one of his signs. Peering in through the door, he made a quick scan of the desk with its clutter of family photos and crumpled papers. Spotting no stapler-crabs or anything else that looked dangerous, he slung his duffel bag onto the floor. Taking a deep breath, he gripped his crowbar and took a second to psych himself up by remembering how easy it was for him to accidentally brick a computer when he wasn't trying.

James took two big steps forward, planted his feet in a batter's stance, and swung the crowbar in an upward arc as hard as he could into the faceplate of the computer creature lurking under the desk. A noise somewhere between a failing cooling fan and a hard drive exploding responded to the assault, as chunks of plastic snapped off and the case bent inward a little bit. The beast seemed to unfold under the desk, a slithering base of power strips and loose wires bursting out from under it and propelling it forward as it lurched toward its attacker.

It was not that fast.

James was still a bit panicked by it, though, and he startled backward, dragging the office chair between him and the now mobile computer. It slammed into the wheeled chair, and in the time it took to figure out how to maneuver the obstacle out of its way, James brought the crowbar down on it another two times, aiming for the openings for the fans on the side. The first one just dented it, but the second strike bent the metal far enough inward that it caught in one of the fans, making a rattling screech as it ground to a halt. He planted his feet and prepared for another swing but didn't realize that his hits hadn't really slowed it down, and as he was bringing the solid steel bar down again, the front of the machine split open into four segments, fracturing outward like some kind of high-tech flower, revealing several rows of teeth made up of what looked like jagged and broken circuit board. James screamed as it clamped down on his leg just below the knee, the vertical segments doing their best to saw through his pant leg and into flesh.

Kicking it off, he fell backward, and it lunged again. He kept slamming the crowbar into its now open front, weak hits bouncing off the casing, until one finally landed right inside the snapping maw. The monster paused for a second, then made a noise that sounded for all the world like a computer choking on something, which, well, it was. Pushing himself backward, he got a bit of distance on the thing, which was now trying to use its cable base to pull the crowbar out of its insides. When he was sure it wasn't going to lunge again, he aimed a kick for the head of the crowbar still sticking out and, with a sound of tearing metal that made his skin crawl, punched it straight through the hostile machine.

In the aftermath of the skirmish, it took James about twenty minutes to get moving again. First, he had to come down from his adrenaline high. Then he had to make sure he wasn't seriously hurt and, when he learned that his pants were sort of shredded and he was leaking blood everywhere, bandage his leg. And in the process of doing that, he had to deal with several stapler-crabs that came scuttling in, probably to investigate his totally masculine battle cry, and not at all because his scream was high-pitched enough to be heard by dogs in low Earth orbit.

But eventually he got himself situated, loaded some stuff into his bag, and left that cubicle with a handful of new candy (Heckums), a magazine on auks that looked almost certainly factually incorrect, several sticks of RAM that were possibly still functional, and six skill orbs—one of which was quite a bit larger than the small fingertip-sized ones that he'd been getting from the stapler-crabs.

Following his signs back, wincing a bit when he had to put weight on his injured leg, James considered his options for people to tell about this. Coworkers seemed like an awful idea, considering one wrong word and he'd never be allowed back here again. His closest friend was already his roommate, and he trusted him, but he didn't work here, so getting him in would be hard. His slightly less close non-roommate friends still had the same problem of access. It was tricky, but even if he decided that it was too risky to really try to bring anyone in, he still had the skill orbs. Assuming they could leave this place, he could use them as novelty gifts. Or, of course, use them himself.

Fortunately, his signposts worked perfectly, and he found his way out pretty easily. Of course, he wasn't really that far in anyway and had mostly been going in a straight line, but he still felt a bit of satisfaction that he didn't have to stress too much about getting lost.

As he approached the main door, he noticed something. Sitting in the hallway in front of the exit door, in plain sight, was a stapler. It wasn't moving, but it was clearly one of the living ones. Matte black, heavy, and stationary. As he started to raise the crowbar for an easy kill, James remembered the one that he'd encountered at the outset of the night. It hadn't been too hostile, and he'd feel kind of bad killing it if it was the same one. So, skirting around it, he made for the door. As he did, it moved, because of course it did, but it didn't just charge for him. This one moved a bit like a cat: stepping side to side as it approached cautiously. He knelt down, sticking out a hand to it, curious if it wanted to be friendly. Of course, he kept one hand on the crowbar just in case.

But as it moved up, it nuzzled into his fingers, again reminding him of nothing more than a strangely metallic cat. He scratched the top of its ... head? Wondering if it could even feel it. But as he did so, it made a strange little chirping noise before pulling back and scuttling off.

"Well ... have a good night, little guy," he called after it before standing up. But before he could turn to the door, the thing came rushing back from around the corner of the cubicle it had retreated into. Except this time, as it ran up to his feet, it deposited from its pincer jaws a single, small, glowing yellow orb. And then, before he could react, it was off again, scampering off back into the labyrinth. "Th-thank you?" he yelled after it, confused.

After a moment, he decided that trying to think about it was too much of a burden, so he just smiled, grabbed the orb, and chose to enjoy the benefits of random kindness.

Now, he thought as he swung the metal security door open to reality, *if all the other ones could stop being so psychotically violent, that would be great.*

CHAPTER 5

Anesh walked into the kitchen at what was not, if James was going to be totally honest, his personal best moment.

"James," he started in a flat voice. "My friend. Esteemed roommate. Hypothetical godfather of my non-existent son." He paused and looked around the room.

James gave him a look, trying his best not to display emotion. Emotion like shame, or explosive laughter. "Oh, please, go on. I'm enjoying the compliments."

His favorite roommate looked back and made hard eye contact. "Why, James, why in the world does the kitchen look like it qualifies for humanitarian aid?"

"Hey now, that's not entirely fair!" James threw back, his voice pitched a bit awkwardly, slightly higher than he'd intended, as he struggled to defend his position from a direct verbal assault.

It was entirely fair. The kitchen looked like it'd been hit by a minimum of two separate tornadoes. At least four or five mixing bowls and pans were scattered around the sink, with another one currently on the stove in use. James's noble attempt at making breakfast had left splotches of flour, melted butter, and droplets of completed pancake batter splattered across the counters, floor, and, in a small area, wall.

He took a moment to look around at his handiwork. "Okay, it's entirely fair. But in my defense, I was doing science."

Anesh raised an eyebrow. "Breakfast science?"

"No, I was trying to figure out exactly what it meant to know a pancake recipe. Turns out, it doesn't do fuck-all for actually making pancakes." James tried to flip the pancake currently burning on the pan and ended up splattering more batter on the counter. "Okay, screw it. I give up. These would have been delicious, but I have no idea what I'm doing here."

His roommate stared for a minute. "James, are you doing okay? This is abnormal." Anesh got a surprised look, complete with raised eyebrows, in response. "Okay, yes, abnormal even for you. But come on, you're actually awake in the morning, and trying to cook. I don't think I've ever seen you cook anything more complex than rice."

"I actually don't do rice, since that one time I set it on fire."

Anesh paused briefly. "Like, burned the rice?"

"No, actually set the whole thing... Look, there's a reason I work a job that gives overtime, and that reason is so that I can eat out more." He started piling batter-covered bowls and utensils into the sink. "I am terminally stupid when it comes to making food. I was sorta hoping to fix that. Hey, on that note, I have something to ask you!"

Anesh snorted briefly. "I am not teaching you how to cook. If you tried to make a curry, you'd probably kill yourself. Or everyone in a two-block radius. I am unwilling to shoulder that burden of guilt."

This earned him a nervous laugh from James and a smile that got less nervous as he bantered with his friend. *Here,* James thought, *is someone who gets me. Someone I can trust.* After taking a minute, he asked, "Funny, but no. Okay, you remember the other day when you ate my candy?"

"I will not—"

James cut him off with a wave of a hand covered in what was probably flour. "It's fine, look, the point is, I told you where I got it."

Anesh rolled his eyes. "You said some wank I wasn't really paying attention to, because it was stupid."

"Right," James said, "insanely stupid, and also true. I found... I mean, honestly, it's a fucking dungeon. It's just, like, a billion cubicles and a beige horizon, but it's got loot drops in it. Like candy. And rent."

His roommate laughed. "Didn't we have this conversation, like, two years ago? 'What would you do if you found a real-life dungeon' or something? Or was that a podcast I listen to?" James's smile turned into more of a smirk. "It doesn't matter. The correct answer was pillaging, I think. But it's kind of a moot point . . ."

"No, but, like, really. I found an actual, for-real dungeon."

Anesh turned to walk back down the hall to his room. "Okay, I'm not really buying it, and I'm not sure I have the energy for this right now. I'm gonna go wedge some video games into my life before homework makes a comeback." He got about halfway down when something bounced off the back of his head.

Spinning around, he got *whumped* on the forehead by another projectile that James had lobbed at him. A small yellow-gold ball, almost like a bath bead. "Dude, come on!" James pitched another one his way, grinning, and this time Anesh caught it and squeezed it just a little too much. "Oh, shit!" he yelped as the thing popped. "I didn't mean to . . ." And he trailed off as an intrusive thought burrowed its way through his mind. It was clearly alien and yet didn't feel hostile. It just rummaged around a bit, and made it perfectly clear to him that it was doing so, before blaring a phrase into his consciousness and fading out.

[+1 Skill Rank : Naval Warship Classifications - Norwegian]

"What."

James leaned back against the couch, now certain he'd gotten his friend's attention. "Yeah, that was about my reaction too," he said with projected confidence.

Anesh just stood there, staring at his hands. "What?"

James chuckled again. "It's kinda weird, isn't it? Like, it takes you a while to remember what you remember now."

His friend looked up and made eye contact, possibilities running through his mind. "You found a dungeon?"

"I found a dungeon." James couldn't keep the wide grin off his face.

"Well, first of all, I'm taking these two that you hit me with, as is my right," Anesh stated, to which James nodded and made a magnanimous gesture with his hands. "And second of all, that's the most useless thing I've ever learned."

"I know, right?" James yelled.

Anesh popped the other two orbs as he asked, "Is there anything, I dunno, better in there?"

[+1 Skill Rank : Tax Law - American - Retirement Funds]

[+1 Skill Rank : History - Pizza]

"Not that I'm against knowing about pizza, but, well . . ." He looked back at James to see him holding a much larger ball. Not huge, but closer to a human palm than the fingernail-sized orbs that he'd given Anesh. "What's that one do?"

"I have no idea," James told him. "I'm mostly flying blind here. I was sort of hoping this would interest you enough to get you to help me out." He crushed the skill orb, taking a moment to breathe as his mind was mildly rewritten.

[+2 Skill Ranks : Origami]

"Hm. Origami. That's . . . actually probably the closest to something awesome that I've gotten so far. Not to discourage you or anything, just that it might take a little effort to get, like, good stuff." Inside, James was doing a little dance. He was trying hard to not discourage Anesh at all, but this was seriously the coolest thing he'd gotten from an orb, and it made him feel vindicated in his desire to use the dungeon to improve himself.

Anesh thought for a second, then nodded. "Okay," he said. "I'm in." He went over to their living room table and started clearing it off while gathering some other stuff from around the apartment. As he did so, he kept talking to James. "But first, I'm gonna want you to tell me everything you can remember. A general map, if possible, too." He thumped a sheaf of paper and notecards onto the coffee table. "Also, now that I've committed to this, like an idiot, maybe I should ask you exactly how dangerous this place is?"

James shuffled his feet as he stood over the table, picking up a pen. "Ah . . . now, okay, remember that you already agreed . . ."

CHAPTER 6

"No, ma'am, I don't think I can help you with that." James's voice was strained as he spoke into his headset. It was about 2:30 on Tuesday morning, his shift was almost over, and somehow, the main source of his stress was not sneaking his roommate into the building or the possibly lethal adventure they were about to go on, but instead, someone who didn't understand what a warranty was.

He nodded sagely, despite the caller not being able to see, as she let loose a verbal assault that could probably have injured him more than any exploding coffee cup ever would, if he'd really been listening. "Yes, ma'am, I understand the problem." He took a deep breath, kept his voice level as his supervisor walked by. Now would be the wrong time to snap. "But . . ."

He trailed off as Anesh plopped a duffel bag down in his cubicle and sat himself down in another swivel chair that he pulled over. "But we . . . One minute, ma'am, let me check something." He looked up at Anesh's wide grin and mouthed, *What are you doing here?* as he frantically muted the call.

Anesh just grinned and leaned back. "Oh, the front desk guy let me in. I said I was your ride home, and then we talked about *Star Wars* for five minutes. How's your night going? You on a call?" He leaned over and started reading the screen.

In his head, James started screaming. What if his supervisor came back? What if he got fired for this? Out loud, though, he cut off the torrent of anger being yelled down the customer's phone and simply said, "I'm sorry, ma'am. If you took your phone in the shower just to see what would happen, then it is both intentional and water damage, and neither of those are covered by warranty. I would be happy to help you find a local repair shop, but—" The sound of his enemy hanging up was one of the best things he'd ever heard.

"Okay," he said, pulling off the headset. "The call queue is empty, so I've got a minute. Why are you here early? What about the plan?" He half looked at Anesh as he typed up the after-call report.

Now spinning casually in the chair, his roommate replied, "I figured that I'd get here early. And the plan was bollocks. I'm not sneaking in the fire escape when I can just ask politely and be let in." James's boss chose that moment to walk back to his own cubicle, and as James's heart leapt into his chest, Anesh just gave him a polite nod.

"Ah, you found your friend. Good!" his boss said and got a thank-you and a thumbs-up from Anesh before he turned back to James with a thin line to his mouth. "Mr. Lyle. Remember not to leave the system until you're actually done." His mildly condescending tone was soothed only slightly by not sticking around and immediately moving on.

"How did you get my *boss* to let you in? He's always kind of awful to me," James asked. In his head, all he could see as a profile of the man was a series of inconveniences and petty threats.

Anesh just laughed. "It was pretty easy. I asked nicely, and when he mentioned that you annoyed him, I laughed and did that thing where I failed to disagree so that he'd think I was on his side. Works on everyone."

"Wait, have you done that to me?" James asked.

Anesh placed a hand on his chest. "Does that seem like the kind of thing I'd do to a friend?"

James narrowed his eyes at his roommate. "Okay, now see, that was . . . Oh, you're screwing with me. Okay. Got it." This got a laugh, which turned back into a laugh from him as well. The two of them spent the last twenty minutes while James was on the clock making light conversation, complaining about their jobs, and pointedly not at all discussing the breach in reality that they were planning on diving through within the hour. Finally, after what seemed like forever to James, his shift ended, he clocked out, and then they had to spend another half hour dicking around in the break room before the two of them headed for the stairs.

"Okay," James said as the two of them stood at the heavy security doors. "I know we kind of have a plan, but just so we're clear, we can leave whenever, got it? Like, we're not saving the world. The stakes have never been lower. We don't need to push ourselves."

Anesh snorted. "Yes, yes, the stakes have never been lower, the stakes are on the floor. Now come on, I want to see this. I'm still not totally convinced this isn't just the most elaborate practical joke ever."

James checked his watch, smiled, and stepped forward, pushing open the big heavy door to show his friend a vision of . . . stairs.

"You bloody wanker! I knew it! I knew you were fucking with me!" Anesh looked torn between uncontrolled laughter and uncontrolled punching-James-repeatedly.

Now laughing his ass off at the reaction, James pulled the door closed. "Nah, it's real." He opened it again, this time showing standardized beige cubicles that faded into the mist of the horizon and too many hallway turns before he and Anesh could see where they started to mutate into different geometry. "I just really wanted to see the look on your face when I did that."

If the look on Anesh's face was priceless when he'd thought he was being pranked, James was certain that the look now was even more valuable than that. His mouth was actually hanging open, which James was pretty sure was only a sitcom thing.

He went in first, doing a quick check around for anything hostile. Anesh followed him in, staring around at this new world.

It was very . . . beige. Cubicle after cubicle. The ones here near the entrance only had walls going up to about his chest, so he could clearly see over them. And the area he could see, well, it went on for a long time. There were a lot of hallways, and a lot, a *lot* of desks and chairs and cubes. "How big is this place . . . ?" he whispered, partially to James and partially to himself.

"Pretty fucking big," James replied. "Haven't found the other side yet, like I said. Though I haven't really gone that far in. It's bigger than the building out there, though. And yeah, seeing it is probably different than being told about it. Also, keep your voice low. I shouted once, and a few hundred of the stapler things came after me."

"We need a better name for them than 'stapler things,'" Anesh replied as the two of them dragged a desk out into the open near the door.

They plopped their duffel bags down onto it, and as James unzipped his and pulled out his crowbar, he said, "Look, they're staplers, and they're constantly angry. I don't really know what you want for a clever name there."

"Hatelers?" Anesh threw out as he opened his own bag.

"No," James cut back, pulling out the two-way radios; he clipped one to his belt and handed the other one over.

"Stapliders. Because they're kind of like spiders, right?" Anesh started unloading a set of football padding from his bag, then a second set next to it for his friend.

"Denied." The last thing to come out was a decent-quality hunting knife he'd bought at their local sporting goods store's eternal "going out of business for real this time" sale; he strapped it to his belt while Anesh pulled his own crowbar out.

"Well, I'm out of ideas." A couple light backpacks came out last. They'd leave the duffel bags here for now.

The two of them started pulling on the football pads, checking straps and making sure they were comfortable. "I know, that's why I'm calling them stapler things. Now. Ready?"

"Oh, goodness no. But I'm also intensely curious. Lead on, Macduff."

James noted with some interest that the signposts he'd made were still up and looking pretty good for something that should have been months old from the time dilation between the real world and in here. He gestured about this to Anesh, who made a small note on it for later. Then the two of them geared up and, ready for anything, hearts beating a mile a minute, took their first steps together into the maze.

With two people, active looting went a lot faster. They'd spot a cubicle that looked like it had something worth anything, and one of them would stand guard while the other went through drawers and coat pockets. Much to James's dismay, the stuff along the path he'd followed last time hadn't refreshed from his looting. So Anesh made them a supplementary signpost, and they diverted a couple of hallways left. Their plan didn't call for getting all the way to the break room anyway, so they didn't need to keep track of that.

Periodically, Anesh would ask James to stop for a moment while he sketched out a rough map of their path so far. This, too, was something they'd planned on, so James would stand sentinel, keeping an eye out for anything hostile while his partner drew.

So far, they'd been here for about half an hour and hadn't run into anything more dangerous than a flickering fluorescent light. Which, to be fair, had startled them both enough that Anesh had almost brained James with a flailing crowbar, and they'd added *helmets* to the list of things they needed.

"I'm beginning to think you scared everything away," Anesh whispered as they came to another almost-empty three-way intersection. This one happened to have a vending machine and a potted plant.

"Maybe, but at least we're getting decent mundane stuff. Also, I am super curious what this vending machine has, and I bet you are too, because I've seen you eat one of every single candy bar we've found."

"Baby Things are delicious! I don't understand why we don't just have these in reality!" Anesh retorted as the pair approached the machine.

It was tall. By this point in their journey, they were well into the territory where the cubicle walls were over head height, and this machine was, perhaps intentionally, exactly as tall as the surrounding cube walls. One of the old-style ones, too, with the big plastic dome buttons and a cash slot that would probably only take the most pristine of one-dollar bills. *DRINKS*, read the big glowing red-and-yellow text on the front. James took custody of the notepad with the map on it to get an idea of how far in they were while Anesh started looking over the options.

From the map, and how tired his feet were, they were twenty-six rows in. Each row averaged about ten cubes, which put them at about four times the length of his actual office building. James's head hurt thinking about that, but he shook it off. As he was about to tell Anesh that they should consider turning back today, his friend spoke. "Dude, check this out."

Looking over, he saw Anesh running his finger down the row of buttons. "What?"

"No, really, watch." Anesh pulled his hand away and then moved his finger to the first button, as if to select it. Then he moved it to the next one. Then the next. James watched, curious, as Anesh repeated this process about thirty times, each time moving down one spot to a new drink button, each time covering space, and each time, there was always more below. "We found a non-Euclidean vending machine."

"Oh, man, that's trippy, and there's no way in hell I'm drinking anything out of—*hurk!*" James was cut off abruptly as something wrapped around his ankle and yanked, hard.

Anesh was yelling something he didn't hear as his head slammed into the floor. Had he not just had the thoughts knocked out of him, he would have definitely doubled down on the helmets idea. As it was, it took most of his effort to kick his leg and look down to see what was trying to kill him.

It was the potted plant. They'd both zeroed in on the drinks, and he'd personally gotten complacent since they hadn't run into anything, and James had thought that maybe with two of them, it'd be fine. But no, they'd ignored the plant—it was mostly his fault, since he was the one with experience here—and now it had ambushed him and was slamming him into the floor with a rather long vine that had trailed out of it. And now the nearby cubicle wall, which he impacted the corner of with his shoulder. This thing was *way* stronger than he'd expected.

Anesh wasn't standing idle, though. After a brief pause to fully process the fact that his roommate was being murdered by vegetation, he took a big step forward and brought his own crowbar down on the middle of the plant's mass. One of the big fronds broke off and one of the smaller vines bent in half, but the rest of it didn't seem bothered. The main body stopped brutalizing James for a minute and brought a couple of side vines up to slap at Anesh.

The hits had enough force that the one he ducked under bowed in the front of the vending machine briefly. The second one caught him right on the arm guard he raised, and Anesh felt his whole left arm turn into a mushy bruise in an instant of painful impact. Swinging wildly with the crowbar, he landed hit after hit on the thing's trunk and vines, snapping off leaves and small twigs before a weaving vine caught his arm and slapped the weapon away.

James wasn't wasting the reprieve, though. He wasn't sure where his own crowbar went, but he had that knife, and he yanked it out, grabbed a handful of vine, and started sawing through it. The plant thrashed, but it only took him a few seconds and his leg was free. Dropping the knife, he lunged forward for his crowbar and, prone on the ground, started slamming it into the ceramic pot itself. It cracked on the first hit, then spiderwebbed on the second hit, and James punched a gloved fist into it to drag away chunks of pot. Inside, instead of dirt or more plant, there was only a single glowing red mass with a black slit down the middle: a malicious eye that turned to stare at him as soon as it was exposed. He was about to smash it when a pair of vines grabbed his legs again and threw him back down the hall.

To do that, though, they'd had to stop their dance with Anesh. And he'd seen what James was doing. Grabbing the one vine still on him, he took a half step back, lined up, and kicked as hard as he could into the hole, jabbing with his foot in a move that would make his year-five martial arts teacher furious, but a move that still worked. He felt something wet and sticky ooze into his boot, and all the vines and leaves suddenly fell flat.

"Hoooooly shit, are you okay?" was the first thing James could say as he caught his breath and stood back up.

Anesh looked at him. "Am I okay? Are *you* okay? You got thrown into a wall!"

"The pads are surprisingly good. I owe you whatever not having cracked ribs is worth. But dude, you're bleeding. Here, get away from the fucking thing, I think the leaves are sharp."

Anesh hadn't noticed it, but he was bleeding. A long, shallow line right above his left eyebrow. The blood started dripping around his eye, tickling and feeling generally awful, as soon as James mentioned it. Looking at him, James could only think that the blood looked more like oil as it tinted against his darker skin. It took him several tries and a few furious rounds of blinking before he could think straight enough to pull out their medical gear and help Anesh clean and bandage himself.

"Okay, well, that was different."

"Is it always like this?" Anesh asked. "I didn't really like the part where I got hit and cut all that much." He hissed as James applied disinfectant, his friend's hand lingering slightly on his forehead as he gently dabbed at Anesh's injury.

"Don't worry. This next part is a whole hell of a lot better." James pointed over to the plant's now-shattered pot, to where a palm-sized golden orb had manifested, along with three smaller ones. "That's also different!" James smiled. "Okay, you feeling good to go? We should get out of here before anything that heard that comes looking for us. I think we're well past the 'easy stuff' territory."

"Yeah, I'm good. You want to grab the things? My bag is kinda full of candy."

James almost sighed but chose to give a small snort of laughter instead. "You know, you could at least *pretend* like you weren't just here for the food."

Anesh grinned back. "Let me tell you, I am entirely here for the food. But yes, also because I'm secretly hoping for one of those to give me, I dunno, a full calculus course or something."

"Overachiever."

"Nerd." The words shot back and forth between them with familiar smiles.

"I will not apologize." James stood up, shouldering his pack, now slightly more full of mass and far more full of value. "Hey, on the way out, I want to try something. You good for one more fight?"

They trekked back to near the entrance, and at one of the cubicles, James stopped and held up a hand. "Okay, so, see the PC under the desk?" He pointed, and Anesh nodded. Both of them slipped into the cubicle, took up positions with their crowbars, and, at James's nod, brought them into the sides of the computer together.

"James," Anesh said after a lengthy pause in which nothing happened.

"Ah. Yes, good friend of mine?" The response from James was tinted with embarrassment.

Anesh looked at the pile of scrap parts on the floor. "James, how many of the computers in here are actually alive and hostile?"

"Well, the good news is, we now know that answer is 'not all of them.'" He shrugged in an exaggerated fashion.

One sigh later, and after James had convinced Anesh that tonight was not the best time to actually start checking the computers to see if they'd be worth taking, they made it back to their base.

"Okay," Anesh said in a more relaxed voice as they crossed the imaginary line between "inside the battlefield" and "safe." "I was going to suggest we leave our stuff here, but I'm reconsidering that right now."

"Why's that?" James asked.

"Well, do you remember bringing a stapler with us?" Anesh pointed with his crowbar at the piece of office equipment sitting next to one of the larger duffel bags. "I'm gonna take care of it; I want to see if these things are as bad as you say."

"Wait!" James half yelled. "That one's okay! I've been calling him Rufus in my head. He's got the different coloring, with the red, see?" He walked over and casually picked up the stapler, which deployed its pen-legs as he did so. It didn't lunge for him or struggle too much, though, so he put it up on the shoulder of his football pads, where it bumped its—snout? James wasn't sure what to call it—into his cheek. "See? He's friendly."

Anesh sighed and dropped the crowbar on the desk. "I have no idea how you could so easily forget to mention to me that not everything here is hostile. That raises a lot of ethical concerns, you know."

"Dude, I forget friends' names all the time. Don't tell me you're surprised that I forgot that someone *wasn't* mad at me."

"Fair. Now, do you want to pop these now or later? I have a few things I want to test, but I'm also really impatient right now." He motioned to the skill orbs in their growing pile of loot as they sorted everything out.

"How about one of the small ones each? We can save the others."

Anesh nodded, and they each picked one up. "I feel like we should have some sort of good-luck prayer for this," James said.

"How about—"

James cut him off. "Anesh, you are my friend, but if you tell me to 'get good,' I am never bringing you back here."

"I am out of ideas," his friend said.

"Well, how about this, then." He raised his hand and popped the orb. "To a higher level!"

Anesh grinned. "I can get behind that," he said as he triggered his own small orb. "I'm not gonna say it with you, though."

[+1 Skill Rank : Programming - JavaScript]

It was the best thing James had ever heard.

CHAPTER 7

James ducked as a blade went over his head, missing by mere millimeters. It embedded itself in the stone wall behind him. An arrow whizzed past, and behind him, his friend Alanna took it in the arm. All around their group, the ground ruptured and sprays of liquid rock splashed out into the open air, a little too close to them and their foes. Dave flicked out his fingers, sending a spear of ice into two of their enemies, while Alanna took one of the remainder out with a sweep of her broadsword. Then, just as the way to the temple ahead of them seemed clear, out of the lava a massive multi-limbed creature began to form, barring their way and . . .

"No, no. Stop. This is bullshit," James said.

Anesh looked up from across the table they sat at. "How? Every one of you got some kind of specific warning about how there was a lava monster, and you all ignored them."

Alanna chimed in. "Nah, I'm with James on this one. Our characters wouldn't have had the ability to understand any of those warnings. We're not geologists!" she said with an enthusiastic grin.

"Wait, hold up," Anesh said, holding up a hand to the D&D table, "are you telling me you all intentionally role-played a group of people who are too dumb to understand lava? Is James talking in character here?"

They all nodded.

"Okay. Well. You're all cooked alive, and shortly thereafter, the world is consumed by fire, as you did not stop the Kortian high priest's ritual. Congratulations. How in the hell did I let you all talk me into running D&D for you?"

James sipped his drink and replied, "Peer pressure, mostly?"

"I asked nicely," Dave offered.

"All of you get out of my house," Anesh said as he walked out of the living room.

Behind him, James called out, "I live here!" before turning back to the other two. "Well, it's been fun, guys, but I gotta get a nap before work tonight." After some friendly banter and after-game talk, it wasn't long before Dave and Alanna said their goodbyes and headed out, leaving the apartment pleasantly quiet for a little while.

After they were gone, Anesh came back out to find James clearing off the table. "Well, nonsense aside, hope that was amusing, at least."

"Oh, yeah, it was a blast. We just wanted to see your reaction and if you'd actually kill us off. It was great, dude," James reassured him as he stacked up cups and character sheets.

Sighing, Anesh sat down and plopped a folder onto the table. "Okay, just checking." He flipped the folder open and started laying out what could easily be mistaken for another D&D game's maps onto the table. "So it's almost Tuesday . . ."

James cut him off. "Nooooope."

Anesh looked up with puppy-dog eyes. "What? Why not? Don't tell me you're already chickening out on this! I got beat up by decor, and I still want to go back in!"

James gave his friend a level look. "You got beat up by decor. It's been a whole week, dude. Show me your arm." Anesh sheepishly pulled up the sleeve of his shirt to reveal a forearm that was more bruise than anything else. "See? How can that not hurt?" James went to poke at Anesh's tender skin and got his hand slapped in retribution.

"That's not the point." Anesh started arranging maps. "Just because we had one surprise doesn't mean I want to give up, especially not when there could be better skorbs in there. I want to try—"

"Skorbs?" James almost choked on his drink as he coughed out the question.

"Skill orbs. The orbs that give us skill ranks. Which, by the way, you said you were going to test for me. What exactly did a rank in JavaScript give you?" Anesh pulled out a sheet labeled *Tests* that was currently mostly empty of information.

James leaned back. "Not a whole lot, really. It feels more foundational, like I know a lot about the basics of it, but not the particulars. I could, given a week and a manual, make you a simple adventure game, or a simple web page tool, but I'd need to keep checking back on stuff, and there'd be bugs." He looked at the list of skills he and Anesh had collected. "Do you have anything to report on . . . boats?"

"Ships," Anesh corrected. "And no. I pirated a copy of *Jane's Ships* and was looking through it. You know that feeling when you're reading something on Wikipedia and you already know the information, but you never would have been able to tell someone if they asked?"

"Like you're getting a refresher that you don't think you need but totally need?" James prompted.

Anesh nodded. "Exactly. Like, I can tell you that way more ships are minesweepers than you'd expect, but I can't actually tell you anything useful."

The two of them looked down at the notes for a minute, just thinking. "Okay," Anesh said, breaking the silence, "what we need to do, clearly, is get another rank in the same skill, without practicing it, so we can compare."

James glared at his friend while smothering a grin. He knew why Anesh was enthusiastic; it was the same reason that he was, after all. But he'd gotten more than just a few cuts this time. The ache he felt was across his whole body, and he was in no particular hurry to repeat the experience. "Man, I know you're into this, and I'm glad that you're on board with going diving with me, but I am just not up to it this week."

Anesh exaggerated his pout even further. James just shook his head. "No, seriously. Even with the extra preparation, we still got trashed by topiary. Victimized by vegetation. Pummeled by a potted plant."

His friend went back to sorting maps while he waited. "Got any more?"

"Fucked by foliage?"

"That one," Anesh said, "sounds more like what you don't mean. But I get your point. I'm pretty sore myself. I still want to go back, though. We don't have to go far in!" he quickly said in reaction to James's renewed hostile look. "We can just stay near the entrance! I just want to, you know, check on the stuff we left. Do a little mapping. I also want to look at some of the computers near the entrance, just to see if they're worth it."

James shook his head. He knew that if he caved on this point, Anesh would have them going back in every week no matter how much of a wreck he felt like. But it was a good point; there was still a lot of stuff to check out, and if there were two of them . . .

He realized that he was doing Anesh's job for him and trying to convince himself it was a good idea. No, this would not do. Time to put his foot down.

"All right, sure. We'll just stick near the entrance." Wait, hang on. That wasn't what he was supposed to say.

Anesh smiled. "Great! So this map we've got is pretty incomplete, and I want to fill it in more so that we can start checking off where we've looted. The place doesn't seem to refresh ever?"

"Not that I've noticed, no." James was marking points on the map where they had encountered the different entities.

Anesh noted that down too. "Okay, well, I'm gonna see if I can figure out anything else that we should be bringing with us. We need some way of dealing with the plants, and that cord thing you talked about, without . . ."

"Molotov."

". . . burning the whole place down with us in it, you prat."

James sulked. "Fine."

"Well. That aside. Is there anything you want to test while we're there?" Anesh asked.

James considered for a minute. He had a lot of generalized *Why aren't more things like an actual RPG?* questions that had been sort of nagging him since this had started. Why weren't there health potions? Why did he get sort-of status messages for the skill orbs? Were there other kinds of orbs, maybe for, say, stats? Did this mean he could level up? Really, why weren't there health potions? Was there a boss fight? Did this dungeon exist for a reason?

Actually, that was kind of the big point. He clearly wasn't the main character, and he had no illusions of heroism. Was he usurping destiny here? Taking away the important dungeon quest from someone who was actually supposed to be doing it?

"Hey, Anesh..." he started, then trailed off. "Do you worry that... Ah. I'm curious if there's health potions somewhere." He clipped his own question off, deciding that it was a bit too silly. They were well outside the territory of normality, but the idea that he, a more or less bored IT guy, could upset fate was a bit too much.

His friend either missed his hesitation or just allowed his awkwardness to go unremarked. "I'll put it on the list of things to look into. I'm also curious if there are non-skill orbs; I don't know about you, but I'm wondering if there's any that change us physically. And then also if we should maybe not touch those, because it's probably a trap. Anyway! We can talk more later. Go to bed. If you're late and get fired and we lose out on this, I will be irritated with you for at least a month."

James nodded. He'd been up for a while, and he did need to sleep for a little while before work. Anesh was right that he couldn't really afford to be fired here. As he'd told his friend, the stakes had never been lower, but that wasn't really true.

He had an opportunity. Something no one else had ever had. And he'd be damned if he was going to throw it away.

James flopped into his bed and drifted off to sleep under the soft glow of the larger skill orb that he and Anesh hadn't decided what to do with. The thing made a smugly comforting night-light, and while James knew that it probably wasn't going to be anything super useful, the delayed satisfaction of knowing that it would be *something* made him grin as he napped.

It was going to be a long night. And, sore or not, he couldn't help being excited.

Out in the living room, Anesh scratched down notes. After getting over his shock at the whole situation, he kind of got why James was so eager to have his help; he liked planning, and James didn't seem to like thinking things through that much. Anesh always thought things through, at least a little bit.

Right now, he had a shortlist of their other friends. People either he or James trusted. He didn't think James really saw the potential for wealth that that Door to Another Office represented. If even one in every five computers in there worked, that was something they could sell off. Those coats they'd been plucking wallets out of? Those were of more obvious value than a four-dollar bill. The furniture: could they manage to get that out? Getting a series of desks past security might be an issue, but a good desk was a couple hundred bucks.

They were going after the easy money, the soft targets. But with a few more people, they could strip that place to the walls. The skill orbs were what got him interested, but the potential for something more was what made him think.

Not that the orbs didn't also make him think. They needed more people so they could push deeper and get more impressive bonuses. If he could gain in one night enough knowledge to skip even a single three-hundred-level class in his degree program? That was huge. But it was so erratic. They'd need to be on the lookout for a way to derandomize it.

Of course, trusting people was one thing. Trusting them with a crowbar was another. That triggered another thought, and he made a note to buy a couple machetes from that creepy military surplus store that constantly advertised how many machetes they had for sale. He knew James was afraid of it, but he wanted to try taking down that cord monster. But, again, after they'd maybe gone to the gym for a few months.

And then there were the risks.

Death, obviously. Somewhere no one would ever know or notice. But Anesh was a pessimist; that was something that he'd been worried about ever since he had to pay rent on his own and realized just how financially crippled he was, saddled with student loans and feeling responsible for helping with medical bills for two siblings who hadn't been covered by insurance properly. No, what concerned him here was the existential threat. What happened if they took one of the stapliders out the door? Was it still going to be an impossible, hostile thing? What happened if the door got stuck open and something else came through?

What if that was the point? Were the skill orbs and food and money just bait for suckers exactly like them?

He made a note. He looked at the table of notes and made another note to organize this on his laptop where he could actually read it later.

It was going to be a long night, waiting for James's shift to end. Though, worried or not, he couldn't help but be excited.

CHAPTER 8

James woke up and instantly regretted his decision. He'd gotten about three hours of napping in, and his sleep schedule was absolutely fucked. His *eyes* were sore, and as he rolled out of bed, it felt like he was running on empty. Something tasted bitter. His arms were limp noodles while he pulled on his shirt and pants with automatic, jerky motions. Limp, sore noodles.

He had work in twenty minutes. It was a thirty-minute drive at this hour. His brain, in a kind of hollow fog, took about five minutes of staring at the door while he sat on the bed to fully do the math.

"Shit" was his reaction when the math caught up.

He stumbled out the door, jerking his feet into his shoes without bothering to untie them from when he'd kicked them off last night. There was no consideration given to food or listening to Anesh wish him a good evening and tell him not to get fired from the kitchen table. He was running on the most garbage of human autopilots: the kind that gets you to work in the morning when you'd rather be doing anything else. That stupid "sensible" voice that tells you that losing your job is a bad idea.

It wasn't until about halfway through the car ride there that he remembered his promise to Anesh that they'd go in tonight. And then the sensible voice, which was now telling him that he still felt like he'd lost a fight with a freight train, got to move over and shut up. Because now, the voice in his head that told him that he was going to get to crowbar a potted plant and get paid in level-ups was talking, and boy was that voice jazzed for this.

He spent the next seven and a half minutes of car travel fantasizing about finding skill orbs that would make him a warrior, teach him weapons and survival. Or give him powers beyond humanity. Or, failing that, he laughed to himself, at least teach him how to do basic car repairs without killing himself.

Then he arrived at work and went back to regretting his decision.

His shift started kinda late, but it was still irritating to see how many empty desks the call center he worked in had right now. People out sick or out drunk or out hungover, he didn't know or care. All that mattered was that the idiots like him who did come in had to shoulder the extra work. And if there was one piece of self-knowledge that James had, it was that he was a profoundly lazy person.

Oh, he'd get the job done. He'd find the most efficient way to do it, and do it correctly the first time, so that no one would bother him about it again. Lazy didn't mean stupid. But it did mean that over the next eight hours, as the sun set over the highway out the windows by his desk and the world dropped into the dark of nighttime, he got really sick of his job, really fast.

"I'm gonna quit, I swear," he muttered to himself as another call ended with abuse hurled his way.

But he wasn't, and he knew it. Previously, it was because he was too lazy to find anything else, and he knew what he was doing here. Now, it was because . . . well, still those reasons. But also there was a hole in reality over by the east stairwell, and he was interested.

Curiosity, and free candy, beat lazy any day.

So he kept his eyes from dropping shut, kept finishing calls, and kept not strangling his shift manager when she walked by and made "jokes" about how he needed to keep working hard. And when Anesh showed up an hour early, the two shared a quiet look full of nervous energy, and he finished the last dozen calls with a bit of a smile in his voice.

"Okay," James said in a voice with a lot more calm than he was feeling as the door shut behind them, "I am never going to really get used to the lack of a horizon, and the endless ranks of office walls fading into the mists. But man, is it cool to look at." He stood looking off down the aisle that their map had labeled Hallway One, enjoying the view of the endlessly repeating tan walls until intersections, rising wall heights, and distance took the view away.

Anesh nodded and hummed agreement, even as he ignored the vista James was fixated on. Instead of looking into the distance like his friend, he went right over to the pair of desks that the duo had dragged to sit near the door.

"I mean, are you seeing this?" Anesh heard James call from over his shoulder.

"Not really. I'm seeing the gear instead." The left-side desk had the stuff they used. Crowbars, football pads, a couple backpacks, radios, flashlights, gloves. What James was starting to see as a standard kit and Anesh was starting to see as not good enough. The other desk had the duffels on it, one of them with a smattering of other stuff left in it, including rope and a bunch of candy they hadn't brought with them, along with some bottles of water. It was to that desk that Anesh added another backpack and started pulling stuff out.

James broke off from gazing into the distance to saunter over. "How much are we spending on backpacks? Real question: should we have accounting spreadsheets for this? And should that spreadsheet be honest? Because it would be weird if someone looked at my laptop and saw I was spending fifty dollars on machetes."

"I did pick up an accounting skill, I think," Anesh said as he pulled a pair of machetes out of the bag, setting them over with the crowbars. "But it's only gonna be twelve dollars for machetes. They are literally always on sale."

"How?" James gave him a puzzled look as he started messing around with one of the blades.

Anesh stopped and looked up. "I did not ask. I will not ask, ever. That place scares me." He looked back down, then froze as one of the duffel bags shifted a bit. Then he yelped out a panicked "Shit!" as he stumbled back a step, going for a crowbar as a pair of ballpoint legs dragged a black-and-red stapler frame into view.

James stepped up grinning as Anesh brandished the prying end at the small monster. "Hey, Rufus! How's my favorite mobile office tool? Who's a good stapler? It's you!" He started giving the thing pets down its back as it pulled itself fully out from under the bag, shaking itself on clicking pen-legs before giving James a slightly irate look at the baby talk.

"Holy hell, that thing gave me a heart attack. James, why are you keeping it here?" Anesh dropped the crowbar and went back to unpacking the bag, slowly dragging it farther away from where Rufus was getting his affection from his human buddy.

"I just think he's kinda cool. I'm not gonna kill something that isn't hostile, and he just kinda hangs out around here. Also, look, he brought me a skill orb!" James held up the tiny pip of gold that Rufus had deposited before him. He made sure Anesh saw before he cracked it. "As he is my friend, and you keep almost killing him, I do not think he would want me to share," James said with exaggerated sincerity, then raised his eyebrows at the prompt.

[+1 Skill Rank : Drawing - Abstract Art]

"Okay, my friend. I've got this thing set up." Anesh had mostly ignored everything he'd just said and was looking down at the table where he'd unpacked, somehow without James noticing, a quadcopter. Also a pair of helmets, though that wasn't what interested James.

James walked over and looked at the phone app that Anesh had open, showing a view of the two of them, looking at a smartphone, from the perspective of the drone on the table. "This is cool and all, but how much did *this* set us back? These things are kinda pricey, right? Also, how do you have signal in here?"

Anesh sighed. "The Wi-Fi in here has no password and is also garbage. And this actually came from Neil. You remember him?"

A short nod. "Yeah, I remember him. Big guy, kinda?" Neil *was* a big guy. Not fat, just someone who towered over James despite his own height of just over six feet, and had a width to him to match. Anesh hung out with him a lot, and James was pretty sure he was single-handedly responsible for ten percent of all drone purchases in the country. "He just gave you this?"

The drone whirred, startling Rufus from his little backpack nest. The stapler hissed a bit at the intruder before James settled him down with a hand on his back. "He said he didn't need it, and he was glad I was finally interested," Anesh said as the blades started spinning. A small plume of dust kicked off the drone, and the two of them coughed for a second, James waving a hand in front of his face. "Looks like he … *ahem* … hasn't used it in a while, anyway."

As Anesh started practicing with the drone, James got himself geared up, just in case, and went back to playing with Rufus. It was while he was down at eye level with the little guy, and also coincidentally the desk, that he noticed something. "Hey, Anesh?"

"Yah?" Anesh answered over the whirr of the small motor as he figured out how to maneuver the quadcopter. Badly.

"Why is there no dust here?"

The quadcopter landed, gracelessly, and shut off. "What do you mean?"

"Well," James said, "when I first got here I checked the time dilation thing, right?"

Anesh nodded. "You said it was about eight hours to three minutes, right? That maths out to don't-want-to-be-here-when-the-doors-close long every week."

"Correct. So why isn't there dust? Three years, and no dust? This place has dust, right?" James patted one of the bags. There was, indeed, some dust. "I mean, there should be more dust, right? How does time even work here?"

Anesh rubbed his fingers across the table, then shook one of the sets of football padding. "Yeah, this isn't three years of dust. I remember when my nan died, it wasn't until about a year later that I ended up going to her house to collect everything. Now *that* was some dust. I'm talking 'leave footprints in it' dust. Maybe this place is just sterile, but it doesn't seem like this is anywhere close to three years' worth." He wiped off the padding and started putting it on. "But that's really not that bad, right? It just means that we don't have as good a grasp on time dilation as you thought, and okay, I just realized why it's not fine."

"Yeah, thanks. Maybe we limit our time here to four-hour chunks. Let's just not get stuck here overnight, yeah?"

"Yeah," Anesh agreed. "Well, the drone thing is probably gonna make exploration a lot easier in the future, but I kinda didn't realize that I don't know how to fly the fucker. So I'll get some practice on that this week. Want to just go wander around for a bit? Get some exploration, maybe an orb or two?"

"You're getting more addicted to those than I am." James smiled as the two of them finished picking up their gear. "Rufus, be good while I'm gone, okay?"

Anesh shook his head as he started down Hallway One. "That's creepy."

"Hush. He's harmless. Also, we should keep it down." They made their way through a few rows before Anesh spoke up again.

"So, how's work been going?" he asked.

James looked up from the desk he was going through. They'd poked at the computer in this cubicle, as well as the chair and the cup of pens on the desk, just to be totally sure nothing was alive in it, and now James was looking for anything they could take. "It's work," he whispered. "Shouldn't we be keeping quiet while we're out here?"

Anesh looked back through the door. "Maybe? I mean, I'm not yelling like you said caused the problem. It's just really quiet in here, and it's creeping me out, honestly."

James stood up and dusted his hands off. "Nothing here." He grabbed his crowbar and headed toward the door. "And we still haven't seen any—"

He tripped.

It wasn't anything serious; he just stumbled a bit and caught himself on Anesh's shoulder. But that small bit, combined with Anesh's nervous feeling and the unfamiliar weight of their armor, was enough to send him sprawling while James stayed upright. He watched as Anesh tumbled back into the cubicle wall across the hallway, sliding it inward a little bit with a burst of scraping and a *crack* as a bit of the plastic corner snapped. Nothing fell over, though, and Anesh scrambled to pull himself off his ass and back up.

Then everything was quiet again.

The two of them stood there for a second, beyond tense, looking around frantically for any sign of danger. After a few heartbeats, Anesh started to say, "Ah. See? Nothing around to hear . . ." He trailed off as James shushed him, and then his eyes started to get wide as both of them heard the sound of clicking. Lots and lots of clicking.

"Run. Fucking *run!*" James half shouted, still trying to keep his voice down. The two of them turned down the corridor back toward their signpost and the front door and bolted. The place wasn't so large that hallways were ever longer than a couple hundred feet, so running wasn't usually something they did to get from place to place, but now they needed to haul ass. The pair thudded down the flat carpeted floor toward the intersection, picking up momentum with the unfamiliar weight on their shoulders. At about twenty feet away, James saw the first of the stapler-crabs come over the wall they were headed straight for. As he skidded to a stop, Anesh behind him got a good view of the next six or seven. By the time the next three dozen had crested the barrier and started to crawl down or simply hopped to the ground to give chase, the friends had turned and started booking it in the opposite direction. "Fucking run the other way, then!" James hissed out between breaths.

They didn't jog, or even run, really. They sprinted. One of the crabs wasn't really a huge threat. A few of them had panicked James at first, but even then, he could take them without dying. Even the potted plant, which had terrified Anesh at first and had tested their strength, still never felt like a fight they couldn't win.

This, though? This was a fight they would always lose. A hundred, maybe two or three hundred, of those things? That was lethal every time. So they sprinted. They booked it. Cubicles flew past as they moved, with Anesh catching glimpses sometimes of one or two of the stapler-crabs crawling off desks to join the horde. And, once, the larger bulkier frame of one of the mobile computers doing the same thing. Ahead of him, James whipped his crowbar across the top of one of the walls to his right, taking out an attempted ambush with a loud hiss as the multi-legged monster fell back. He could feel his blood pumping, fear racing through his veins. "There!" He pointed left at an upcoming turn, and James took it. Anesh followed, the two of them hoping to lose some of their pursuit.

They kept going, losing stamina fast, taking another turn a minute later. After a third turn, with no sign of the horde behind, they paused to catch their breath. James leaned on the inside of a cube wall, panting, and as Anesh went to do the same, he stopped, having seen a trio of staplers skittering down the hall behind them. They were alone, maybe scouts, or maybe just on the move now that the whole of their civilization was riled up. Either way, he acted without thinking about it.

The first one he just stepped on, pinning it down while he slammed the crowbar into the follower. Then again in rapid succession before the third could even react with more than a hiss. It crumpled a bit, enough black goo squirting out that Anesh was sure he'd gotten it. As the one beneath his foot struggled, he lunged forward and sideswiped the third, slapping it into a filing cabinet with a dull thud. Stunned, it had no chance to dodge the overhead swing that killed it. After that, he picked up the hissing, skittering nightmare from an office supply closet that was underfoot and pulled it apart like James had mentioned doing on his first trip.

It was harder than he'd expected.

The whole fight took less than a minute. That was, Anesh supposed, the difference when you were the one doing the ambushing. Silently, he tossed the three corpses into a nearby cubicle doorway, grabbed the orbs, and stepped back in to take a breather with James.

"What was that? We gotta go?" his friend asked when he came in.

He shook his head. "I got it. Here." He passed James one of the orbs. "If we're gonna get ate here, I at least want to see if I can get something good first." James nodded and cracked his while still trying to drag in great big breaths of air.

[+1 Skill Rank : Etiquette - Internet - Dating Sites]

James almost choked laughing. "Well, so much for that. What about . . ." He stopped, seeing Anesh's surprised face. "What?"

"I thought all these were normal!" his friend exclaimed.

James cocked his head. "Normal how?" His mind went through a list of ways that none of this was normal, but it hardly seemed relevant now. If "extradimensional office dungeon" was their baseline, "normal" could mean a lot of things.

Anesh shook his head. "It's not useful right now, but I just leveled up in rapiers."

"Bullshit," James exclaimed. "That is not fair. I refuse to believe that. I got internet dating politeness and you got swords. This is just . . . fucking . . . bah." He tripped on his words and trailed off. "Well, congrats. You got the good stuff first. And I'll treat you to a sword when we get out of here. But . . . uh . . ."

Anesh and James both peeked out of the cubicle they were in. There was no sign of the horde; they appeared to have lost their pursuit. But that did leave one very serious question that they had to ask.

"Where the hell are we?" James's voice echoed a bit in the still air.

There wasn't a signpost in sight, and they hadn't been able to track after the first turn. They must be close, but their map didn't cover out here, and they had run almost directly away from the door without counting cubicles. Which made Anesh think of one other big problem.

"How long do we have to find out?" he asked, mirroring James's worried look.

CHAPTER 9

"Okay, we need to move, now." James hauled himself back upright and took a few shaky steps, still breathing heavily. Anesh reached out and put a hand on his shoulder pad to stop him, which turned into him just leaning on James as his own adrenaline rush died off and he found his limbs unstable, his breath coming in short gasps. "Okay, maybe we need to sit for a minute."

"Yeah, yeah." Anesh slumped down into the swivel chair, while James slid down the wall to sit on the floor.

The two of them sat like that for a while, just focusing on trying to breathe and stop shaking. James let his mind just go blank; he wasn't panicked, really, but he was kind of at a mental dead end. He didn't know where to go from here. They were lost, exhausted, hunted, and also really quite lost, and James was feeling lost in his own head to match it. After a little too long of an uncomfortable silence in the chilly dead air, Anesh asked, "Is this how you felt when this happened to you the first time?"

James looked over at his friend, holding his head up with his hands against his forehead, an expression on his face he'd never seen before. He supposed this was how someone who'd just nearly died looked, and wondered if that expression was similar to what Anesh was seeing on him. "Yeah," he said, "that seems about right. Though this time there's a little more long-term panic thrown in, since I got out that time."

Anesh looked at him for a long while; his mouth started to move several times, but no words came out. Eventually he found his voice and quietly asked, "Why did you ever come back in?"

"Well..." He started to say it was obvious. For the money, for the skill upgrades, for that little bit of power that translated to the real world, of course. Then he reconsidered. Maybe it wasn't that at all, but just because this was the only place in his life where he'd ever really felt like he was tested. He started to say that too, but he looked up at his friend's face from his spot on the floor. That wasn't what Anesh needed to hear. That wasn't what either of them needed to hear right now. "Lemme tell you, I don't think we've even begun to get into the *good* candy in this place."

That earned him an incredulous look. But a second later, the words sank into Anesh's mind, and a smile cracked through. And then the two of them were laughing. Softly, but earnestly, sharing something that they'd never be able to find outside this place. It wasn't just themselves that were being tested, but their friendship. And while it sounded cheesy enough that they'd never say it out loud, they knew they were getting out of here together, or not at all.

James and Anesh were Good Friends. They didn't need a dungeon to tell them that.

"Well," James finally said after they'd relaxed a bit and finally stabilized their slightly terrified emotions, "this whole thing does vindicate my decision to not bring my gun in here."

This startled Anesh a bit. "You own a gun? Bloody hell, mate, when did that happen? Didn't you say literally last week that guns were, and I'm quoting, 'cool, but no one should ever be allowed to own one'?" He used air quotes around James's own words.

"Well, yeah, but I'm clearly a massive hypocrite," James said. "Also, I picked one up from my dad before coming here the first time on purpose. Then I chickened out because I was paranoid that I'd get pulled over on the way to work, or my boss would do a bag check at the door to make sure I wasn't stealing mouse pads or something."

"We should steal mouse pads from here," Anesh muttered. "I'll make a note."

"The *point*," James said, "was that unless the problem is 'I would rather shoot myself than be eaten by staplers,' a gun doesn't actually solve any problems in here. I can't actually imagine myself even hitting a stapler-crab, and even if I did, would it even do anything?"

Anesh shook his head. "I could hit a stapler. And it would probably do something. I mean, hitting them with a crowbar has worked well so far. That's gotta do less damage than a bullet would. I don't think they're actually as durable as real staplers."

James hauled himself up. "Bullshit, you could hit a stapler."

Anesh didn't even bother answering as he stood up, leaving the chair to lazily spin behind him. "Hey, before we try to navigate back, do you have a bottle of water? I forgot mine by the door."

"No, I didn't plan on being out this long, so I left it, because I'm a bit dumb," James responded. "Was there anything else we forgot that we probably should have brought, aside from guns and food?"

"We forgot our helmets," Anesh dryly commented. "Oh, and also to make a better map. And I didn't really 'forget' it, but I did leave the drone . . ." His eyes got wide. A second later, James watched as Anesh scrambled to extract his phone from a pocket covered in football padding.

James started stretching his arms a bit as he waited. "Why are you looking like the drone half a mile away is relevant?"

"Because it might be!" Anesh said.

"There's no way the controller works from this far." James paused. "Is there? I don't fully understand how those things work."

Anesh held up his phone, tapping through options. "No no, I left that behind too. But the camera works on Wi-Fi, and there *is* Wi-Fi here."

"I know I've been saying this a lot lately," James said, "but that's bullshit. Why is there Wi-Fi in here? Does the internet even work through time dilation?"

"Oh, oh no." Anesh waved him off. "There's no actual internet, it's all LAN. But there's devices on the network. Or, well, one device my phone can find, because I didn't think to install apps that search for security cameras or whatever. I'm not working from *The Anarchist Cookbook* here."

"That was written in the seventies and has basically nothing to do with the actual political ideology of anarchy as expressed by . . ." This earned James a glare from his partner. Anesh was patient with a lot of things, but he was losing his dry resistance to banter and political history lessons quickly. "Okay, okay! We get signal. So?"

"So the drone has a camera. Aaaaaaand . . ." Anesh held up his phone so James could see. "It's facing the cubicles." He waited a second for James to make the connection as he looked at the screen. About half of it was just the lower walls of the first row of cubes, but the upper half had a pretty decent view of the vaguely sloped "sky" between the cube walls and the fluorescent lights far above. It took James a second of considering mentioning how useless this was before he looked up above their heads. "Yeah, that's right. Throw something straight up."

James grabbed a desk lamp and went to lob it over their heads, and Anesh almost instantly slapped a hand on his wrist. "Throw something less stupid, please?" James would have been offended if he'd had any intention of actually flinging a lamp. Instead, he just smiled and grabbed a pen off the desk.

"Is this gonna be big enough?" he asked.

Anesh nodded, eyes on the screen. "Should be. I just need to see movement." He signaled James, and the pen went up, and James caught it on the way back down.

"Anything?"

"No, try again."

Once more, James tossed the pen up, and Anesh felt his heart sink. "Fucking hell, I was hoping this could get us out of here."

James came over and looked at the screen. "Wait, hang on. We went all over the place. If we're too far back, that's one thing, but what if we're to the sides? Let me try something." He started rustling through desk drawers until he found a manila folder full of documents. The pages all appeared to be charts, though not a single one of the axes was labeled. James ignored all of that, pulled one out, and started folding it.

A half minute later, Anesh looked over at his work. "That's a surprisingly intricate paper airplane."

"Yeah, turns out, I actually did get an applicable skill. Though don't tell anyone I'm using origami knowledge for this; I think it would legitimately offend Alanna's otaku sensibilities."

"Noted." Anesh smiled a bit, mostly relieved that his plan might still have a chance. "Also Alanna is . . . way less of a weeb than *you*, so that seems . . . oh, never mind."

A couple minutes and a few more paper airplanes later, James gave him a nod. "Okay, ready? I'm gonna throw them in different directions, and if you see one, we'll know at least what way we need to go. Assuming you can figure out the relative directions. I don't think I've ever once gotten those right when using my GPS, and that's without things trying to kill me."

Anesh gave him a thumbs-up, and James threw the first one over the front wall. "Nothing." A few seconds later, he turned ninety degrees and threw the second one. "Still nothing."

Both of them started to feel that seed of doubt in their hearts as James turned again and looked at his friend. "Two more. Ready? Sure it's getting signal?"

"Yeah, it's working," Anesh said. He didn't look up, eyes on his phone. "Go ahead. Cross your fingers."

James threw.

Anesh jumped out of the chair. "Fuck! Yes!" he almost shouted, before remembering how they got into this mess in the first place. He coughed a bit, half covering up his excitement, half just because his throat felt like sandpaper. He took a minute, and a few more dry coughs, to clear his throat, and then spoke again. "Okay, I saw that one. It came in at a weird angle. Throw another one in the same direction; we can figure this out."

It took three more airplanes and both of them looking at the screen, with Anesh trying to explain how the angles correlated, before James finally relented. "Okay, I get it. You know this stuff. I believe you." He did not believe him. But at this point, it was better than waiting around. They'd taken what felt like at least half an hour here trying to rest and work out their position, and he couldn't help but feel like they were running out of time. According to the clock on his phone, they still had an hour left before their four-hour limit, and that was playing it safe. They could afford to take their time and make sure they did this right.

They took another ten minutes coming up with a plan, and ten more for Anesh to convince James it wasn't that bad.

"All right," James said. "I found a roll of quarters and a granola bar, so this wasn't a total bust. We're not hurt, we've got more or less all our gear, and now we know we can set up our own camera network in here. All told, this has been a good learning experience. I'm pretty sure we leveled up. Go us." He set his crowbar off to the side of the curved desk in the cubicle and drew his machete. "You sure about this?"

Anesh sighed. "For the last time, yes." James shrugged, crawled under the desk, and punched through the back wall with his machete. Using the blade, and way more effort than he'd hoped, he sawed a trio of neat lines through the carpet and the plaster barrier before scooting back and kicking the new improvised door out.

"After you," James said as he stood up and readjusted his backpack and machete so he could retrieve his crowbar. Anesh nodded and got down on his hands and knees, crawling through. The idea was that they could shortcut to the row on the other side, and then all they needed to do was take a left and head in a straight line. If there wasn't anything to stop them, they could cut "doors" as needed to keep going forward and make their way back without any problems.

There were problems almost instantly.

As James knelt down so he could crawl through, there was the sound of metal on plastic on the other side. He hauled himself through as fast as he could and swiveled his head around frantically to see Anesh pinned down against the far wall in a sitting position and a heavy matte-black desktop computer tower, the mass of cables it used as propulsion writhing beneath it as it tried to drag itself up onto the struggling math major.

Anesh had dropped the crowbar when the computer came at him. His mind briefly made a note that he needed to name these things, too, before it had shoved him back and was trying to rip his face off. Fortunately, his football pads were enough to stop its teeth, for now, but the thing was gouging great big strips out of them as he kept throwing his forearm into its way when it lunged forward—like a big friendly black dog, except not friendly, and with way sharper teeth.

He was on the defensive, but he wasn't hurt yet, except for a small gash on his palm. The problem was he had no leverage, and even though this thing was slow, it was already on him, and he had to just trust in James to deal with it while he held it off. The problem was . . .

The problem was that James missed with his first swing.

The crowbar came in and hit the side of the boxy beast, and instead of bowing it inward and smashing the internals, it slid along the outside and smashed right into Anesh's left hand where he was holding it.

Anesh's vision went blurry as his pinky and ring fingers snapped in half. His left hand slipped off the casing where he was holding it back, and it lunged forward enough to sink circuit board teeth into the upper part of his thigh, shredding through his jeans and starting to leave shallow cuts. He didn't quite pass out, though, and started frantically punching the side of it, to no effect, as he heard James swearing loudly above him.

The next thing Anesh knew, the weight was off and he wasn't being mutilated anymore. Looking over, he registered James pinning the box to the ground even as its cables tried to right it, holding his crowbar like a shovel over it. There was a grinding noise, and then a series of electronic *pops*, and then more crashing as James brought the prybar end of his makeshift weapon down again and again, until he was certain the thing wasn't ever getting back up.

"Oh hey," Anesh gasped out. "That's where the bigger orbs come from, huh?"

"Shit shit shit shit shit," James frantically repeated as he threw his backpack off and started digging through it.

Anesh woozily stood up, holding his left hand in front of him, cupped in its uninjured partner. "Wow, thisssss hurts . . . a lot more than ex . . . ex . . . exhphected." He coughed, and spit a bit on the floor. "Ow."

"*Shit shit shit shit shit.*" James threw their medkit on the desk, pulled Anesh by his arm into the chair, and started pulling out supplies. Medical tape, tongue depressors, painkillers, and gauze. He pressed a trio of high-dose ibuprofen capsules into Anesh's hand. "Swallow these. I know we don't have water, but they're gels, so just swallow them anyway. Give me your other hand, don't move."

Anesh almost gagged a few times trying to swallow the pills but eventually got them down. "Thaaaat doesn't feel better."

James ignored him, busy splinting Anesh's fingers, wrapping them in gauze. It was about that time that the stapler-crab that had been lurking behind the monitor on the desk chose its moment to strike. The hellion lunged out, intent on inflicting damage to the fleshy hand going for the strip of tape near it.

Absolutely uninterested in playing that game right now, James grabbed it midlunge with his right hand, not letting go of the splinted fingers he was holding with his left. Deftly snapping the chitin switch that let the stapler swing freely, he raised his arm and slammed the tiny enemy into the desk three times, until a splash of black ichor sprayed out onto the floor and the leg of his pants. Then he flipped the unmoving shell into the pile of computer wreckage and went back to trying to fix Anesh's hand.

Between gasps of breath, Anesh, trying to regain his composure through the throbbing pain of having his bones broken and his flesh bulging at odd angles, asked, "Where did you even learn how to do this?" as James put the finishing seal of tape on the temporary splint.

"I took a first-aid class over the last couple weeks, in case one of us got hurt in here. You know we're allowed to learn things without skill orbs, man." He stood up, repacked the medkit, and threw it along with a pack of sticky notes off the desk and the dropped orbs into the backpack. "Okay, we gotta go. We need to get you to the hospital as soon as possible. Can you move? Let's go, come on."

His voice was shaking; he was worried, but Anesh wasn't. He wasn't mad at the injury. It was bound to happen eventually. But he trusted his friend. He stood up, kept his legs steady. "Okay. Let's go."

The two of them moved, not slowly, but not running, down the new hall. Anesh pointed them in the right direction, and James took point. Up ahead, a T intersection awaited them, with another of the vending machine and plant setups. James wasted no time, breaking into a sprint as soon as he made sure Anesh was okay. He slammed at full speed into the plant, knocking it to the ground; he punched his gloved hand into the faux-ceramic pot, hitting it while keeping the plastic vines and fronds pinned with his feet. When he cratered it enough to rip chunks away and look inside he saw . . . nothing.

Oh.

This one wasn't hostile. Or alive at all. Okay.

He walked back to Anesh. "Crisis averted. Let's go." And he turned to keep moving.

Even in extreme pain, Anesh still had the presence of mind to woozily mutter out, "My hero . . ." with a wavering smile at James's back.

They took a quick turn, but only because they saw another hallway that let them move in the right direction. And on down that hall they went. James took out two ambush staplers from the tops of the cube walls, on high alert and in no mood for their shit. Anesh was in just enough of a mood for this shit to stop to grab the orbs they dropped with his good hand.

Finally, finally they spotted a landmark James recognized. "I know this place. I know this," he said out loud, speaking to himself.

Anesh didn't catch the tremor in his voice. "Oh, thank the stars. Get us out of here. I would like to hospital now, yes."

"No. No, this isn't good. We need to find another way. Cut some tunnels around it," James said, starting to back up.

Anesh pushed a hand onto his back. "Why? What's up?" He looked past James and saw the floor change from hard office carpet into smooth white linoleum tile. Ahead of them, a small maze of chairs and tables filled the room between a set of refrigerators and vending machines on one wall and a counter with a sink on the other. A few scattered cardboard coffee cups sat around on some of the tables. "Oh, coffee. Is this a break room?"

"No no no. We've gotta go. We need to move, *now*." James was panicked now. He was legitimately worried, and Anesh wasn't out of it enough to miss it this time.

He started looking around. "What's going on? What are you . . ." He stopped as he heard a cascading hissing noise. Jerking his head around, over the wall at the end of the hallway behind them, he saw what looked like a car-sized tangled mess of Cat 5 cables drag itself down the wall and then down the hall. It didn't speed up, it didn't acknowledge them at all, but he had a sinking feeling in his gut that this thing was a predator and they were its chosen prey today. "Oh, fuck me running." He cut a quick look at James, fear pushing the pain away. "You said you haven't fought this thing, right? Anything I should know?"

"The coffee cups explode."

Anesh blinked at James, twice, rapidly. "I am so angry right now, you have no idea."

CHAPTER 10

James was frozen in place. Well, not quite frozen. He'd drawn his machete and slung his backpack to the floor off to the side, and he was more or less looking like he was prepared to go down swinging. This was one of many things Anesh noticed through the haze of pain, and it was one that he wasn't that interested in mirroring.

Anesh knew a lot of things. One of those things was what kind of person James was. He was a smart guy: lazy, but smart. But every time they played a board game together, James was the one who took a long time to finish his turns. Analysis paralysis, it was called. He could see the angles but couldn't make conclusions without thinking every single one through to its end.

The thing was, Anesh could empathize with that. He had the same thing, really. The main difference was, Anesh never stopped running through his options, never stopped noticing things and letting his brain autopilot its way to the conclusions. James was clever; he had a wit to him that Anesh couldn't always match, but Anesh was a Smart Guy.

By the time the cord monster, which he'd decided to call a tumblefeed, had hit the ground, he was already looking for options. While James was resigned to a quite possibly fatal battle, Anesh was checking escape routes.

The cube walls around them were well over head height; vaulting them was out of the question. Knocking them over? No; he'd crashed into one earlier today, and it took a lot of force to even move one of the unbraced walls a little bit. Cutting through? Too long.

Okay, escape to the left or right was out. What other terrain features were around that could be exploited? There were "vines" of dot-matrix printer paper; they'd have to make sure to duck through doorways or risk paper cuts. Not relevant, though; dismiss that for now. There were three cubicle doors still open on either side of the hallway that the tumblefeed hadn't passed yet at its leisurely pace. Hide? No, he could *feel* its focus on them. They weren't getting away.

In the distance, a flock of sheets of white paper fluttered across the sky. The smell of slightly burnt plastic drifted past them. Behind him, one of the refrigerators clicked its compressor.

Options. His mind didn't stop absorbing details. They needed options.

This wasn't the same tumblefeed James had seen; it was too big. James paid attention; Anesh trusted him. This one was older. Its cords were crumbling. It would be easier to kill. *That's a nice thought*, he told his pain-addled brain, *but it doesn't save us. Easier doesn't mean possible right now.*

Three options he came up with. First thought, last choice, the sacrifice play. One of them stand and fight, the other one make a break for it. Not good. Low odds of either of them getting away, honestly. Second thought, second choice, try to vault the wall to the left. The classic boost up from one of them, then haul that person over. He dismissed this idea pretty quickly, since, well, he was a math student and James was an IT guy, and neither of them was a big fan of the gym. He wasn't out of shape, but he wasn't making that happen easily, especially with broken fingers.

The pain was making thinking hard.

Last thought, choice made. Get through the break room. The minesweeper plan. Total elapsed time, four seconds longer than he'd like.

"Well, it was fun while it . . ." James was starting to say. Anesh wasn't listening. He took a long step behind James, swooped down, hooked the backpack in his good hand, turned, and flung it into the break room at all the speed he could muster with a leveraged swing. He then pivoted back toward the break room door, covering James from the ensuing calamity. ". . . What . . ." James got out before hell broke loose.

A series of four hissing *pops* resounded from behind the duo. Unseen, James's backpack swept across the first table, knocking into a pair of the rigged coffee cups. The detonations from them sent scalding black liquid and fairly significant pressure waves rippling through the air, and that, mixed with the backpack sliding into the base of the next table in line, knocked the next two enough that they added their concussive force to the mix.

Anesh was braced for it and only got knocked forward a little bit by the expanding blast wave. James wasn't paying attention, though, and turned to try to see and figure out what was going on, and he caught a nice splattering of molten coffee right down the side of his face.

He started to scream, wiping frantically at his face with his off hand. Anesh didn't give him time to recover, though, grabbing at his arm and pushing him onto the tiled floor of the break room. The tables had actual chunks torn out of them where the trapped cups had exploded, but it seemed like the force tapered off pretty quickly. A chair was knocked over and coffee was splattered everywhere, hissing and steaming. But everything else was intact, and Anesh guided James with a hand on his arm as he kicked chairs out of the way and rushed through the open area.

James got the worst of the hot liquid off his face as Anesh started pulling him along. He opened his eyes, clamped shut to make sure they didn't burn, to see that he'd been dragged into the break room area. *Work Hard and Also Work Hard* were the words on the poster his eyes opened to. He almost started laughing. Almost.

Breaking free of Anesh's grip, he kept up the pace, not wanting to be here too long in case it held more surprises. He looked back and instantly regretted it. "Man, we gotta go! It's moving faster!"

And it was. The tumblefeed was throwing out clusters of cables, grabbing onto the walls and floors and yanking itself along in great big spurts. It might have been huge and old, but it was burning energy fast to try to catch up to its prey. And now that they were running, it would do its best to catch them before they could take too many corners and escape.

Anesh started running, a clear line to the door. "There's signposts up from here! Just go!" he shouted. James called back assent, but his voice cut off halfway through as something punched him in the left side, hard enough to send him tumbling over the still-standing table and into one of the chairs.

Anesh turned at the clattering noise to see one of the large potted plants, this one hanging from a trio of chains that led all the way up to the ceiling. This one had lots and lots of heavy fronds, none of the vines that the last one had given them so much trouble with. But it looked like it had branches as well, and fake or not, it looked like it hit like a truck. As James staggered to his feet, reshouldering the tattered remnants of the backpack Anesh had hurled in here, he wiped a trail of blood from the side of his mouth. Glancing at his friend, Anesh saw a look in James's eye that worried him. He looked excited.

It took Anesh about half a second to spot the melon-sized skill orb, and another half second to start to say, "Don't you fucking . . . !" But it was too late, and James was moving in for the fight.

James ducked the next branch coming for his head. His machete, which he had somehow held on to through getting roughed up, slammed into the next incoming attack. He and the plant locked weapons, his blade digging into the wood, before he pulled back, grabbed the branch, and snapped it while it wasn't moving. Shouting wordlessly in triumph, he brought the oversized knife back for another swing, ignoring Anesh's frantic warning about running out of time. Unheeding, he slammed forward, hoping to shatter the pot, get the kill, and get the loot in one fell swoop.

The machete hit the pot, and the blade snapped off at the hilt.

Before he could even realize that he had a problem, the plant slapped him across the throat with the other branch, staggering him back and leaving James hunched over, holding his neck, coughing madly.

The next thing he knew, Anesh had him half over his shoulder and was running them out of there. Behind them, the wirebeast stormed itself into the break room, then settled down in a nest of loose cables and sparking wires to watch its prey take a corner. It could chase them down, it thought, but it was tired. There would be other chances. The creature gave a great heaving sigh, which manifested as several cable chunks unknotting themselves and the whole mass settling down. For now, it would rest. Later, it would hunt. They could only run for so long.

"You bloody idiot." Anesh dragged James around another corner. "You fucking bloody damned idiot," he half repeated as he tried to get his friend to move faster.

After another last, large cough, James spoke up in a rough voice. "That hardly seems fair."

This earned him a very pissed look from Anesh. "We were clear. We could have just left, and you turned around. Twice, actually, though the first one wasn't really your fault."

"Yeah, shouldn't I be mad at you for covering us in coffee?" James asked halfheartedly.

"No," Anesh answered. "Now, can you stand on your own? We need to go. I had to kick over one of those shellaxies a minute ago and I'm worried it's going to get up and come after us."

James sighed and looked at him. "You keep giving things weird names. What's a shellaxy?"

"Shell.exe, pronounced phonetically. It's what I'm calling the hermit crab computer things, because 'hermit crab computer thing' doesn't roll off the tongue." Anesh stepped up to the next intersection first, gave a quick check both ways, and waved James forward, face still pale and sweating. "Now let's go. I need to get to the hospital, even if this is kind of down to a dull roar of pain."

James nodded, frowning. "I'm really sorry." Anesh waved him off with his splinted hand. "No, really, I fucked up. I owe you a big apology." Before Anesh could say anything about how it was okay, James continued, "As my way of saying sorry, I will let you tell me what you've named the hairball back there and accept your name as canon."

Anesh glanced over his shoulder. "Hairball?"

"It's a big mass of Cat 5 cable. What else would I call it?"

"I've been calling it a tumblefeed," Anesh said, followed by a string of curses as one of the staplers tried to get the drop on him.

After the brief scrap, which in turn attracted a few more from nearby cubicles, James caught his breath, throat still aching. "'Tumblefeed' is . . . way better than mine. Fuck. Yeah, that's good."

The pair stumbled on in silence, just trying to conserve stamina in the home stretch. They could see the end of Hallway One, the exit door coming into sight.

"Hey," James said, holding his side as he paused for a second. "I bet you our whole haul that there's some bullshit there that we'll have to fight to make it out."

Anesh looked back at him. "You ass. Isn't that the one thing you could say that's guaranteed to make sure it happens?"

A shrug. "We're well outside the laws of the universe here; I think it's fine. What do you say? Double or nothing?" He drew his hunting knife and pulled himself upright.

"No deal," Anesh said, making sure everything was secure and gripping the crowbar tightly in his undamaged hand. He was pretty sure this one was James's. They'd gone through a few iterations of drop-and-retrieve with these things so far. One of them was lost forever, for sure.

The two of them took one deep breath at about the same time, which caused Anesh to snort with laughter. The tension eased away at that point, and they stepped toward the end of the hallway together, ready to face whatever was there.

Of course, it was nothing. Everything was as they left it. And then it was a mad scramble to get things sorted out and get out of there as fast as possible. They stripped off the pads and tossed them in a pile under one of their supply desks, then poured all the candy, cash, skill orbs, fancy pens, and unreal magazines that Anesh insisted on grabbing into one of the duffels, which James then took. And with one last pat on the head for Rufus, who was now burrowing in the scraps of James's tattered, coffee-stained backpack, they opened the big security door and stepped back into reality.

It was seven a.m. The emergency room had been a nightmare almost as bad as the Office Beyond The Doors. James was exhausted, Anesh was high on painkillers, but they were out. They'd made it.

They were currently sitting in a coffee shop.

There had been a long conversation in the car on the way back from the hospital. They'd talked about the danger, the risk, whether it was even worth it. Anesh had gotten the distinct impression that James was, even after all that, almost eager to go back in again. He could understand, but still. He'd had some *angry* words to say about James putting their lives in danger pointlessly like that. And James had apologized and promised not to do it again, yes, but he'd still been pissing mad up until the ER doctor had given him something for the pain and it got harder to be angry at anything.

They weren't doing this right. They needed more people, better gear, real maps, and maybe a hint of intel on what the dungeon even *was*. He'd talked to James about some ideas, but he wasn't sure if he'd said the words right, or if his roommate was awake enough to even hear.

What was important now, though, was that they'd survived. They had a pile of skill orbs. A *big* pile this time. And also money. Anesh was almost always broke; he was a college student in the United States scraping by on a scholarship, after all. And he knew James had trouble keeping himself fed sometimes too. But now they had almost two grand sitting in the bag under their table. That was rent, sure, but that could also be an investment. There was more, just waiting there. Waiting for someone to come and take it . . .

Okay, Anesh was eager to go back too.

As the two of them sat there, drained, injured, patched up, exhausted, they both knew, without having to say anything, what their future was going to hold. Just as soon as they were actually ready again.

"This," James said, "is the best bagel I have ever tasted."

Anesh sipped his drink. "I don't think I've ever felt like I've earned a mocha as much as this one."

They smiled. The risk wouldn't stop them, was never going to stop them. It was just the seasoning on the biggest opportunity, the biggest adventure, of their lives.

CHAPTER 11

Two swords came together with a light metallic rattle. The long thin blades, épées, met in the air between the two fighters, one of them lunging, the other casually turning the strike aside. They both pulled back, and again the aggressor stepped forward and aimed a thrust at his opponent. Again, it was casually turned aside, the sword point going too far to his left to recover before his opponent made a quick motion and took him in the chest.

The struck fighter took a staggering step back, caught off-guard. He frantically brought his blade up to try to launch a counterattack but misplaced it and instead let his opponent easily slap his weapon off to the side again before being hit in the shoulder.

Almost faster than he could keep track, his opponent, now on the offensive, lunged, coming in low under his counterswipe and stabbing right into his neck. And just like that, the fight was over.

"Okay, ow," James said as he was stabbed. Again.

Stepping off the piste, Anesh pulled off his fencing helmet. "You are surprisingly bad at this for someone who knew a *lot* about swords coming in here," he said as the pair went over to their bench to sit for a minute.

They'd been here for about an hour. Partly because James had been big on going to the gym lately, and this place where he'd gotten a membership happened to have a fencing piste with gear they could rent. Partly because both of them were aware that, if they were going to go deeper into the dungeon, they were going to need some serious self-improvement. And partly because Anesh wanted to experiment with his level-up.

Also, it was convenient that this activity didn't require the use of his left hand, which was still healing.

"I'm not bad at this," James said between panted breaths after downing half a bottle of water. "You are just unbelievably good at this."

Anesh shook his head as he sat. He was winded, sure, but throughout their bouts, he'd just been moving less than James. Putting in less effort. And yet. "I was expecting you to at least score a point. I mean, I'm literally fighting with one hand behind my back here."

"We both are! Fencing is one-handed!" James snapped back, still breathing heavy, chest heaving as he slouched over on the bench.

Anesh started making notes on his phone. "Okay, so, your griping aside, that's ten to zero, my favor." James growled a bit. "I'm not rubbing it in, mate, just saying. That's from a single skill point, in a skill with a weapon that isn't exactly an épée. I'm starting to get confused at exactly what a skill point represents."

"Well," James said, "in this case, it represents you absolutely demolishing me. It's a shame that it's midnight and no one else is here. We should come back sometime when there's random people you can challenge. See how long they've been doing this and training, right?"

"Right, makes sense. I'll make a note, do it sometime this week." Anesh nodded to his friend. "Oh, speaking of things we need to do, did you, um, talk to Alanna about . . . well, all this?"

The two had briefly talked a few days ago. Between Anesh's school and James's work, and opposite sleep schedules, they didn't actually get a lot of chances to sit down for long conversations these days. But in one of those moments when one of them was almost out the door and the other had just come home, Anesh had brought up the idea of more teammates, and James had agreed. They'd both had one of their friends to talk to, to see if they could get some more manpower. Well, Alanna was a lady, so *manpower* might not be the best word.

Power certainly was the right word, though. Alanna was stronger than him and Anesh put together, the perfect muscle for their party—in that she would add actual muscle to their party. A fact that James personally really liked about her.

Still . . . "No, actually," he said to Anesh. "I . . . um . . . couldn't? Did you talk to JP?"

Anesh, who a second ago had been looking kind of sheepish, suddenly lowered his eyebrows into a thoughtful expression. "No, I didn't. I couldn't either. I was going to, but then I kept finding reasons not to. Or just forgetting. And then I had a nightmare about it, but I think that's stress related."

"Me too," James said, suddenly curious. "What the hell?"

"You had a nightmare?" Anesh said, also curious but not in an alarmed way like James. "What about?"

James shook his head, thinking for a second before answering. "It was mostly nonsense, like every dream. Hard to put it into words. But the one thing that stands out is that I kept bringing people to the dungeon, and they kept dying. Just from knowing about it."

"That sounds too familiar." Anesh looked over at his friend, frowning now. "Okay, we never really talked about this properly, but what's our policy on secrecy here? You told me about this place, but now we're not telling anyone else? Why?"

"I didn't really think about it," James said. "I mean, I can think of a lot of reasons not to tell, like, the government, mostly selfish ones. I don't think there's any benefit to sharing with other people, and it doesn't feel like there's any potential to solve larger-scale problems in the world. Like, randomly spawned candy won't fix world hunger. But I didn't actively think of those. I just kind of didn't tell anyone. Except you, obviously."

"That bothers me. Is there something stopping us from sharing? Are we supposed to do this alone? Why? It doesn't make sense that you told me, but that's the limit."

This got a laugh from James. "Of course it doesn't make sense. Think about how many arbitrary things we've been exposed to so far. If it was properly explained, I'd be pissed." He shook his head. "No sense worrying about it now. You want to go home and sort out all the loot from last time? We can figure out what to do for gear too."

"Yeah, though I'm still angry at the mental coercion. We dive the dungeon, it's not supposed to dive us. But yes, I am sick of hitting things with a crowbar. How have you done this so often? My hands are still bruised."

"It is," James conceded, "an inefficient weapon. But I was pretty much just using it because I couldn't afford anything better. Oh, and then the machetes. Which, yeah, not great."

The two of them turned in their gear and headed to the car. By silent agreement, they spent the drive debating what fast food to get rather than anything heavier. They got sidetracked after getting burgers, and the remainder of the trip home turned into a heated argument about anime tropes.

"No, no. The ending of that one makes it creepy, and you're lucky I broke my machete or I'd disagree a lot more fervently," James yelled back as they took the stairs up.

Anesh laughed. "Calm down, friend. The neighbors don't wanna hear you murder me over your bad taste in media." As they got inside, he followed up by saying, "Anyway, speaking of machetes, you want to get the bag over to the table? We can sort through how much cash we got and decide what to spend it on, gearwise."

As Anesh moved their fast-food bags to the far end, James brought over the duffel with their unsorted loot, frantically piled in before their fast exit last time and left untouched since. At Anesh's prompt, he shrugged and dumped it out onto the table, a sprawling pile of money, candy, skill orbs, and other random stuff they'd picked up.

After catching all the skill orbs that rolled off the table, Anesh grabbed a fancy-looking pen that James had snagged, along with some scratch paper. From around a mouthful of fries, he said, "Okay, you sort out the stuff, I'll count up the cash."

They worked quickly, pausing every now and then for a bit of food. Since Anesh was counting, James didn't say anything, though he reminded himself to ask why his roommate had apparently grabbed a copy of *Yes Pony Things* magazine. A quick flip through showed that it was mostly gibberish; every third word, literally, was *horse*. The flip kept going, though, and James found himself getting a headache as more and more paper went by without the pages ever seeming to pile up in his hand. "Well, I found a non-Euclidean piece of media."

Anesh looked up from his notepad, then held it up for James to see. "Check this out."

"I can't read that, it's all in cursive," James said, frustrated trying to decipher his roommate's handwriting.

A nod in response. "Exactly. I wasn't writing in cursive." He tossed James the pen he'd taken from the bag. "Try it."

James pulled a notecard over and tried to write down *dickbutt*. It came out in flowing, elegant script that he had no way to actually read. "This is really cool, but ultimately useless. Why's it do that?"

"I mean, we were bound to find magic items eventually," Anesh said, taking the pen back. Curious, he unscrewed the back and pulled the pen apart, checking to see if there was anything weird about the inside. As he drew the ink tube out of the center, there was a strange snapping feeling. Not a noise, but judging by how James whipped his head up, he'd felt it too. In Anesh's fingers, the pen dissolved into fine sand, leaving only a small, blue, slightly glowing orb. "Ah. Well. I guess that's why," he said.

James's eyes were wide, locked on the new color of orb. "Oh boy," he said excitedly. "Well, I've got my tally if you do. We can . . . we can get to that one at the end, yeah?"

"Yeah," Anesh agreed, rolling the orb in his fingers before setting it down. "Yeah, we have . . ." He checked his cursive notes, piles of sorted bills around him. "One thousand, nine hundred twenty-four dollars in usable currency. Also about fifty dollars in notes that aren't real. I vote for throwing those in the fireplace before anyone asks us why we're shitty counterfeiters. How about on your end?"

James looked at the piles around him. "Well, we've got two big orbs, six smaller ones, and that blue one. I'll try not to drool," he snarked as Anesh gave him a look for his silly tone of voice. "Aside from that, a couple dozen candy bars, four mouse pads for some reason, a pretty nice leather jacket, your weird pony magazine, and a bottle of multivitamins. Wait, no, sorry, they're 'multivoltamins.' I'm not eating these."

The two of them looked at the pile of stuff. "Okay," Anesh said, "how about we put some of the cash into gear and then split the rest? Even split on the skill orbs. And . . . I'll let you have the blue one if I get the jacket."

"Deal." James didn't even think about it. "Want to crack 'em now?"

Anesh shook his head, smiling. "I mean, sure. But you sound like a kid who just got a new video game. Or, you know, someone who's actually addicted. Wait, these aren't addicting, are they?"

"Nah, I'm just really into this." James had already split the orbs into two piles. He held one up, and Anesh matched the gesture. "We get to *literally level up*," he said, grinning like a madman.

[+1 Skill Rank : Driving - Semi-Truck]
[+1 Skill Rank : Repair - Small Engine]
[+1 Skill Rank : History - Oregon]
[+2 Skill Ranks : Bureaucracy - Federal]

"Holy shit, some of these are actually really cool," Anesh said as he saw his own separate skills pour into his brain. And James couldn't help but agree with him. This was it. This was what he'd started this whole thing for. The money was great, the candy was delicious, assuming he didn't eat so much he ended up diabetic, but this? He could fix a lawn mower. Without even really trying, honestly. He could be a trucker. He wasn't *going* to, but he *could*.

Options. Flexibility. Knowledge. This was what he wanted. What it all came down to.

Power. The power to change his life, if he wanted to. A limited form of expressed freedom.

And he sure as hell wasn't going to stop here.

"Okay, Anesh, we've gotta replace the medkit I left in there. Probably upgrade that if we don't want to end up in serious trouble. We need weapons. And something to deal with the tumblefeed?"

Anesh gave him a manic grin. "Oh!" he almost shouted. "That reminds me!" He reached down to one of the chairs where he'd piled up a bunch of paper and pulled out a book. A few books, actually. He tossed them over to James, who checked out the titles.

"What the fuck are these books? *Ragnar Benson's Guide to Dragonfire? Ragnar Benson's Mantrapping Manual?* Where did you get these?"

"Ah, well, about that . . ."

"The back half of this book is just a list of *other* books! Wait, homemade C-4?" James looked up sharply at his roommate. "Are you secretly a government agent or something?"

"While I'm really glad you went to that and not 'terrorist,' given my skin complexion, no," Anesh said. "Turns out you can just buy these on Amazon. Anyway, there's one on improvised explosives. I'm thinking thermite. Which would require holding it down, which is why I got the one on traps as well. They're surprisingly informative."

James was half annoyed but also impressed. "You know, I know I said we should work on improving ourselves in preparation, but this is kind of beyond what I meant. I was talking about, like, going to the gym and learning how to shoot from Alanna or something."

"You're coming back around on guns now?" Anesh asked. "Isn't that gonna cause a huge problem?"

"Well, I don't really want guns, that was just an example. And an excuse to hang out with Alanna."

Anesh snorted at his friend. James had a fairly significant crush on their friend. Well, that wasn't exactly fair to make fun of him for; Anesh did too. It was hard not to, really. Alanna was one of those people who used charisma as a main stat at character creation before playing a mechanic and not a bard.

"Okay, okay." Anesh held up his hands. "Let's just make a list, yeah? Then we can sort out how much cash we'll have left over. Oh, are you gonna crack that one?" He pointed to the untouched blue orb on the table.

"I'm saving it for after this," James said. "Savoring it."

"Surrrrre . . . So, for weapons, I'm thinking . . ."

The list ended up being fairly lengthy. A professional first-aid kit, and then another one at Anesh's prompting that they needed redundancy for something that important. For primary weapons, the original proposition had been kukris, as both of them were weirdly excited about the Nepalese knives. But after checking the cost of an actual good kukri, that got put on hold for now. Instead, they opted for hand axes, having found one for sale online with good reviews from people who gave it heavy use. Also, one of them would have a compact construction sledgehammer. Basically for the same reason as the crowbar, but easier on the hands, and with a little more power behind it. They also each got a compact Taser. More for an experiment than anything else.

They also picked up some food. Quite a bit of food, really. Until they could test how long the time dilation actually lasted, they needed to maximize their chances of surviving for a long time cut off from the outside world. Well, "food" was a stretch. They were mostly just about fifty MREs. They both tried one each and decided they hated them, but that starving would be worse and that they were on a budget.

A lot of their money was going into buying a series of six wireless cameras. After Anesh's discovery that the dungeon had Wi-Fi, they'd talked about ways to exploit that. They were planning on testing for other devices on the network, but just for now, they could easily set up their own mini surveillance network to get in and out a little more safely.

Finally, after some googling, they settled on upgrading their football armor a bit. The helmets Anesh had bought were still good, and to those they added riot gloves, police-grade arm and leg guards, and combat boots.

They decided not to start buying bomb-making supplies off the internet. For now. But Anesh would see if he could pick up what they needed to make some pipe bombs later. They did get a weighted net, though, and, at James's insistence, a pair of industrial bolt cutters. When asked if that was necessary, he muttered something about poetic justice and then changed the subject.

"Is this maybe too much?" James asked after looking at their long list.

Anesh held up his broken hand, then started pointing to bruises on his arm and James's neck. "Is this enough?"

"Yeah, okay, good point," James said. "Oh, I was also thinking. It seems like the better stuff really is farther in. And so far, nothing has really respawned. Maybe we should use our next haul to get a couple bikes? We can cut down walls and move furniture and basically have a fast travel system."

"I'll put it on our future list," Anesh said. So far, they'd spent a lot more than expected, and Anesh was pretty overtly glad that they'd already covered rent for the month. It turned out that once the two of them started making a wish list, they could easily burn through their available funds in a hurry. As it was, they were splitting a grand total of thirty-four dollars after all the costs.

Anesh gave a final look over the notes. "All right, I'll start picking this up while you're at work tomorrow. We're taking this week off?"

"Yes" was the flat answer.

"Okay, I'm fine with that this time. I don't get this splint off for another week anyway. Now, before I get to bed, what're we going for next time?"

James thought for a minute. "Well, I dunno if we specifically need more cash. But I think that pen, and this orb, came from when we were lost a bit farther in. So yeah, I want to take out the tumblefeed, get through that little gauntlet area, and see what other weird stuff is in there for us."

Anesh nodded. "I agree. I want to see if we can find more magic items and then maybe not break them. Oh, are you gonna crack that last orb?"

James nodded, stuffing his share of the bills in his wallet. "Seems like the right time." He brought out the shining blue orb, glinting a bit in the contrasting dim light of their apartment's living room. Holding his breath, he held it up at eye level between two fingers, and then brought those fingers together.

[Problem Solved : Personal Banking]

[+1 Skill Rank : Program Use - AutoCAD]

After a second of James sitting there with his head cocked to the side in confusion, Anesh asked, "Well? What did it do?"

James silently pulled out his wallet and opened it up. The bills he'd just stuffed in there were gone, replaced by a deposit slip. "I think . . . it just went to the bank for me? The thought-prompt thing said 'problem solved,' so . . . I guess that's what these ones do? Fix problems?"

"Was going to the bank a problem for you?" Anesh asked dryly.

"Well," James said, "I didn't want to do it. So yes?"

Anesh looked down at his broken fingers, then back up at James. He repeated this gesture again. "I get the next blue—"

"Yeah, that's fair." James cut him off rapidly, laughing.

The two of them split off, Anesh to sleep and James to relax for a while on his own. Both of them felt energized, motivated. For James, who spent a lot of his daily life fighting depression, the motivation that he felt due to this dungeon was life changing. He knew that Anesh, already asleep one room over, was getting into this, but that was normal. His roommate was always motivated, always moving forward.

For him, though? He wasn't really kidding when he said that he didn't want to do his banking. And checking his bank account, it looked like the orb had paid his phone bill for him too. That weight off his mind, of something just done, felt like a thousand pounds off his chest. He knew he had to do it, but actually working up the energy to do so was . . . straining.

But here and now, with the dungeon beckoning to them every week, with new horizons and new loot and something that broke up the monotony of his shitty life?

Well, he felt it. He felt alive. More than that, he felt *normal*. He was diving into another dimension, or a warped piece of this one, fighting staplers with pen-legs and Cat 5 cables run amok; he was rewriting his brain with new information every chance he got. But he felt normal.

For that? He didn't mind spending every extra cent on gear. He wouldn't complain about being forced to keep silent. He'd fight any inhuman monster that came their way, just to hold on to that feeling.

Though, he thought, maybe he'd call in sick from his mind-numbing job tomorrow.

That feeling only went so far.

CHAPTER 12

The next week passed in a blur. The enthusiasm of the dungeon was powerful, but it wasn't really enough to carry him through a week of work on its own. James got up, went to work and sort of autopiloted through hundreds of support calls. He went home, he sat in front of his computer and watched stuff on YouTube, lost a few dozen hours playing RimWorld, and only got up to eat when he absolutely had to. Every few days, he mustered up the motivation to go to the gym.

He didn't see Anesh most days, since his roommate was busy dealing with exams, and James himself was spending most of his time shut away in his room. He ended up missing their group's weekly D&D night, which Anesh informed him later had shifted into a different game, since they'd gotten their D&D campaign world reduced to smoldering ash.

Over that time, the events that made James perk up and start to break out of his depressive slump mostly came over the last few days before their next planned dive. In addition to starting to feel that excitement building, that knowledge that soon he'd be risking his life for fortune and glory, they had started getting packages.

The wireless cameras came in first, and James got delegated the duty of setting them up, making sure that he could access them from his phone under hostile circumstances. That was Friday, and from that point on, their focus shifted to preparation.

While James was learning how to install and manage their surveillance grid, Anesh was teaching himself how to blow things up.

Since most commercial explosives were difficult to purchase, and their research into how exactly to *make* explosives wasn't really giving them precise instructions, they'd settled on thermite as their opening salvo in the upcoming tumblefeed fight. The reasoning was that they didn't need concussive force so much against something that didn't seem to have organs to liquefy or bones to break, but the heat from the ignition of a batch of iron thermite would, hopefully, be suitable to slag enough of its cables to stop it dead.

Actually making the stuff had been worryingly easy. Anesh had simply signed up for some lab time at his college and brought materials purchased legally at a hardware store or taken from the school's supply. An actual chemistry major had actually stopped by to give him tips on making it and keeping it stored safely, without prompting, and also without asking questions. This partly worried him, since Anesh still wasn't sure how far the dungeon's mental cloak extended, and he didn't know if the cavalier attitude toward making dangerous substances was a result of the other student not being able to ask, or if this was just how chemistry majors were in the wild.

Frankly, he wasn't sure which one scared him more.

Rigging them up with secure containers, ignition sources, and timers was a bit harder. He'd tested the timers and sparkers obsessively for days, and even after assuring himself he had something functional and mostly secure, he still decided not to put them together fully until they were actually in the dungeon.

The hand axes they'd ordered came in next and were added to the growing sprawl on the kitchen table, alongside the stuff they'd already purchased locally. They arrived with the weighted net, which James spent a good fifteen minutes screwing around with and getting tangled in. By Monday, they had just about everything loaded into the bags they'd be taking in, along with one whole extra duffel just for the "food" that they'd picked up: cases of humanitarian daily rations, functional for survival and also just the worst thing James had ever tasted.

And all of this served to get him excited. By the time he woke up Monday afternoon, he was as ramped up as a kid on Christmas Eve. The effect was a bit ruined because he had to stagger out the door to work, passing Anesh on the way, who was finishing getting everything loaded up and ready.

"See you tonight?" he asked as he shoved his shoes on.

"See you tonight," Anesh said solemnly.

The two of them made eye contact before nodding and going back to what they were doing. A bit of determination had passed between them. And then James was out the door, and Anesh went back to trying to fit the last bundle of rope into the bulging duffel bag.

James wasn't sure what hell was like, but if he had to guess, it would be his job.

He hadn't taken a break except to quickly hit the bathroom and drink some water. The calls just kept coming. Client after client, problem after problem. At a certain point, James realized that he had been answering questions above his support tier, mostly using Google and intuition to pull solutions out of his ass.

His shift lead was mysteriously absent tonight, and his floor manager was fielding just as many calls as he was, so he couldn't be annoyed at her. What he could be annoyed at, though, was the number of coworkers he had with him during his waking nightmare. There were a grand total of two other people on the phones with him. Two. Out of a shift that normally had twenty.

In between calls, and while half listening to complaints and rants, he messaged his boss, asking what was going on. All he got was a response that they'd had a lot of turnover lately, and hiring wasn't replacing people fast enough.

He didn't see Anesh, and time got away from him. It wasn't until his last call ended at 3:20 a.m. that he was finally able to leave. As he clocked out, his boss came by his cubicle while he packed up. "Your friend is waiting for you in the break room. Is he looking for a job?" she asked.

"Not that I know of," James said as he finished shutting down his station. "What's been going on with that anyway? Why are so many people getting fired?"

His boss, a generally pretty grim woman named Lisa, just scowled. "I haven't fired anyone. People are just not showing up. If they stopped not showing up, I wouldn't even fire them right now, that's how bad it is."

He made some sympathetic noises and extracted himself from the conversation quickly, heading to the break room. They weren't exactly late, but he didn't want to risk missing their only window.

When he got to the break room, he found Anesh sitting with their duffel bags at one of the tables, methodically shredding a magazine, a wastebasket next to him slowly filling up with paper. "What," James asked dryly, "are you doing?"

"Well," Anesh said as he stood up, shoving the magazine into his back pocket, "I had the thought the other day that if breaking the pen got us a blue orb, that maybe breaking this thing would do the same." The magazine he was shredding, James realized, was the endless pony-related zine they'd found in their loot pile over a week ago.

James looked at the ten pounds of paper in the wastebasket. "Is it working?"

"No," Anesh flatly remarked. "It won't break. It just keeps having more pages."

"Did you try tearing off the cover?" James asked as he shouldered one of the gear bags and the two of them headed for the door.

Anesh, following him out to the stairwell, said, "I tried, really. It just had more covers. I'm thinking of setting it on fire later. We'll see."

They stopped. In front of them was the door. It was impressive to James, really, that the door that he saw every day at work could transform into something with so much more gravitas when it counted. It was still an off-white-painted metal brick of a door, some of the paint chipped a bit at the bottom edge. It still led to plain concrete stairs. And yet, right now, it felt like the gates to El Dorado.

"One minute. You ready?" Anesh asked him.

James smiled. "I don't think I'm ever gonna be ready, but like hell am I missing this."

Somewhere in an unremarkable office building, an unremarkable door opened, and two friends stepped into a very remarkable world.

Step one, they'd planned out, was setup. Doing a quick check, it looked like nothing had been respawned, but there were a couple stapler-crabs moving around in the cubicles near the entrance. Nothing respawned, the desks they'd dragged over unmoved, but some of the incidental damage was repaired. One of the walls James had knocked a hole in during one of his first dives was patched up, as was the monitor that he'd smashed with a missed swing.

So, with that knowledge in mind, they had a plan for setting up a little defensive fortification that they could fall back to. And also maybe act as a bit of a beacon for when (not if) they got lost.

First, though, they needed to get geared up. And as they stashed their bags and started pulling out everything they needed, James got to say hello to an old friend.

"Hey there, Rufus! Hey! Who's a good little nightmarish spider thing? You are! It's you!"

Anesh scowled. "I wish you wouldn't encourage that thing," he said as James knelt under the desk. "Wait, what the hell is it nesting in? Is that one of our bags?"

It was, indeed, one of their bags, the scraps of which were currently hanging like a suspended hammock from a mass linking of paper clips embedded in the underside of the desk, looking like nothing less than a massive matte-black spider napping in its web.

James mock glared at his friend. "I'm not 'encouraging' him, I'm just giving him the love and affection he deserves!" He cuddled Rufus up to his face, smiling wildly as the little guy skittered his pen-legs through James's hair. "As a reward for not being murderous!"

Anesh was not amused. He couldn't decide, as he and James started strapping on armor, if he was more or less not-amused when the thing crawled back out of its web to bring his partner in dungeon exploration a pair of small golden skill orbs.

After they got their new armor on and took a minute to check their straps and fittings, he got another surprise.

James snapped his head up to a strangled scream from Anesh and a harsh buzzing on the other side of the desk. It took him a second to realize that what his friend was frantically swatting at around his head looked a little too similar to the quadcopter they'd brought in a few weeks ago.

"Whoa, whoa! Hang on!" James yelled as he ran over and deftly snagged the mobile drone out of the air. The rotors buzzed in his hand, but he gently set it on the desk, keeping it pinned firmly under this palm. "What the hell?" he asked, the question aimed at nothing in particular.

Anesh was frantically rubbing at his face, and James did a quick check-in with him. "You okay?"

"Fine, just . . . startled. I don't think it was trying to kill me."

James looked at the newly alive entity. "Yeah, no kidding." It had settled down a bit, and it looked like it could "walk" by bending its front two rotors down to crawl along the desk. It looked almost bat-like, except for the long needle-spike that extended from its front, the glass and metal of the camera reshaped into a wicked-looking weapon. "If it were trying to kill you, I think you'd be missing an eye. I think it just wanted to say hi."

Anesh shook his head. "Are we starting a farm here?" He reached down, pulling one of his gloves off to give a gentle scritch to the "head" of the drone. Well, maybe *drone* was the wrong word. It was a bit more alive now.

"Maybe," James said. "Either way, let's get things set up. These guys aren't gonna be a problem for now."

"Yeah, yeah. I guess I'm starting to see why you keep Rufus around. This little dude is . . . weirdly cute," Anesh said, letting the drone crawl up his arm to perch on his shoulder.

That resolved, they started with part one of the plan. The first four cubicles were carefully dismantled, clasps undone and reattached to make a new wall. They rearranged the local walls to build themselves a semicircular fortification around the entrance. It wouldn't keep anything serious out, but it gave them a little bit of stalling power when they needed to run from something. Also, stacking the walls up to double height, maybe halfway to the too-high ceiling, gave them something they could spot from farther away.

After that, they dragged the desks over, bracing them against the insides of the walls to give some extra stability. It also gave them a place where they could sort and stash stuff that they didn't feel comfortable bringing out into reality, and as with their original plan, it made for an easy spot to lay out weapons and armor and avoid the question "Why do you have a hand axe in your bag?"

Finally, James set up one of their cameras over the doorway, plugged it into the extended battery, and checked it on the Wi-Fi network.

"Good to go. You ready to move in?" James asked.

"All set," Anesh said, strapping the pair of thermite grenades he'd rigged up together and attaching them gently to his belt. "Let's go kill something overlevel."

The two of them set out, James on point with the sledgehammer out, Anesh behind him and off to the side, keeping watch on the walls to make sure nothing crawled over on them. The drone, still sitting on Anesh's shoulder, was scanning the walls as well, matching the movements of Anesh's head and eyes with its own jerky, mechanical twitches.

They had a goal in mind this time. They weren't here for loot or orbs, at least not at first. They were going to kill the tumblefeed and clear this area of anything lethally threatening. After that, they'd reassess. See how they felt, then decide if they wanted to go farther in.

As they passed through the tunnels of cubicles, getting to the point where the walls were curving overhead and vines of paper dangled from the walls, James spoke softly. "Do you ever get the feeling that we're all just tiny little things, barely holding on to a giant ball of furiously spinning rock?"

"You pick the weirdest times to open up emotionally," Anesh said wryly.

James snorted. "I mean, yeah, but also this was a lead-in to me saying that I think the gravity here is a little lower than normal."

"You pick the weirdest times to share useful tactical information," Anesh said in the same tone, and they both had to hold back laughter.

Ten minutes of careful travel later, they were within sight of the break room. Just down the hall, the breach into the brighter light, smell of coffee, and tile floor yawned. There was no sign of their prey. Nodding to each other, they moved to the cubicles on either side, drawing their axes.

Five minutes of work later, trying to be as quiet as possible, they had each cut a doorway through to the next cubicle hallway. Exit routes were on both their minds; neither of them wanted to be trapped again. In each of the hallways they cut into, and at the doorway looking into the break room, they placed one of the wireless cameras. Then they came back to the entrance and settled in one of the cubes slightly farther away to wait.

"Pen."

"Nope."

"Pencil."

"Noooope."

"... Piece of paper?"

James grinned. "You got it!"

Anesh sighed. "I am so mad at you right now." He leaned back and stretched his arms. "How is this boring? Shouldn't we be drowning in hordes of monsters by now?"

James just shrugged. "Maybe we got unlucky the last two times?" He was looking down at his phone, watching the cameras. "Gah. This is..."

He and Anesh both looked up. They heard the same thing before the cameras saw anything: a sound like pattering water, like a handful of beads being poured out onto wood. But on and on and on. The two of them tensed up, and James locked his eyes on the camera.

"Ready?" he asked.

Anesh nodded. "Ready."

A minute passed, and then another, and then, just when they were about to scream from the tension, James saw movement on the camera. Tendril cables, first a few, then a hundred, hauled themselves and the main mass over the wall into the break room. The previously repaired room got itself a new chunk taken out of a table as one of the coffee bombs was knocked a bit.

They waited as the tumblefeed curled up on the floor, nestling in under a table. James passed off his phone and stepped out into the hall. Anesh readied one of their grenades as James stepped up to the doorway.

"Hey, hentai tentacle monster! How's it going?"

The reaction was instant. In a split second, the coils of cables spread out into a viny web on the floor. Then the body started rolling, dragging itself toward James at a pace that reminded him more of a Japanese horror movie than anything else.

So he did what he really wanted to, and also what the plan called for. He turned and fucking booked it.

Sprinting down the hall, he flew past Anesh's hiding spot, passed a couple cubes more, then turned and slid to a crouching stop at the corner, axe out.

The tumblefeed drew its bulk down the hallway, also rolling right past Anesh. It paused about twenty feet in front of James, coiled tendrils of cords slamming into the floor, smaller cables latching onto the walls around them, as it hauled itself up to full height. It didn't quite dwarf the walls around them, but the walls around them were over twelve feet tall, and it came close to matching them.

"Okay, friend," James said softly, breathing steadily, "just sit nice and still for a second." They weren't sure if these things had forward-facing vision, but it shouldn't make too much of a difference.

Behind the beast, he caught a glimpse of Anesh in a pitcher's stance, and then a spray of fire.

The improvised grenade had landed right inside the tangled mass of the tumblefeed, and five seconds later, it lit off exactly as planned and started burning. It was like a forge come to life: a spray of sparks and temporarily molten metal that fountained down around the monster. It let out a scream, thousands of tiny mouths at the ends of cables hissing in unison as one by one they were cut off with fire and heat.

And then the thermite burned out, and it wasn't dead. Dozens, maybe hundreds of dead cables left a carpet of dross on the floor behind it, and it was thrashing wildly, but it was still alive.

Anesh didn't wait to prime the other grenade and throw it into the still-writhing mass of cords. And again, a few seconds later, a wave of heat poured forth as the left side of the tumblefeed sloughed off in a shower of melting metal and burning plastic.

A noxious odor filled the air, burnt plastic and carpet, the feeling of crackling electricity and ozone. And still, it wasn't dead.

But it wasn't moving nearly fast enough to stop its hunters. James and Anesh moved in, Anesh bringing down his axe on every clump of cables that strayed too far out from the central mass. James grabbed the pair of bolt cutters from where they'd left them at the end of the hall and waded in, pushing them into whatever point seemed most like the core and snapping them closed with arm-straining effort. Flailing Cat 5 cables with spined gnashing mouths tried to find purchase on either of the armored attackers, and James got a couple of gashes down his face before either he or Anesh could take out the troublesome parts. But their boots and hardened limb guards let them almost casually knock away anything that got too close.

And then, all of a sudden, James planted his boot on something solid in the middle of the mess. Aiming for the lump, he jammed the bolt cutters in and, with as much strength as he could muster, snapped them shut.

And it died.

The whole thing gave a shudder, stray cables sticking straight up in the air, and then nothing. It all went flat, curled up like a withered weed.

Silence.

"Well!" James said between labored breaths. "That went really well! We didn't even have to use the net!" He pointed up to the net they'd rigged up, ready to be dropped when the rope just to his left was cut.

Anesh knelt down in the smoldering remains of their target. "Oh yeah. And hey, how about this?" He stood up, holding something large in his left hand. His glove had gotten torn off at some point, and his hand was dripping blood from a bite mark. But what he was holding caught James's attention.

It was the size of a grapefruit, and it was glowing a fierce emerald green.

"Dibs," James said. Anesh laughed, then shrugged.

"You know what?" he said. "Go ahead." He lobbed the orb over to James, who caught it with a startled expression. Before James could ask, he explained, "I've got dibs on the next, like, dozen blue ones, okay?"

"Deal," James said, and broke the piece of power in his palm without a second thought.

[Local Area Shift : Internet speed increase, +32Mbps Down/ +18Mbps Up]

[+4 Skill Ranks : Artillery - Indirect Fire]

"Oh holy shit, the internet got better!" James yelped out.

Anesh looked at him with wide eyes. "What, like, everywhere? Did we just bootstrap humanity by one tech era?"

James got a disappointed look on his face. "Local area? Like . . . in here?" He looked around theatrically at the extradimensional office they were in. "Why? Why didn't I wait on that? Goddammit. Oh, also, I know how to hit a target two miles away with a mortar. But that's really not enough to stem the disappointment. We could've upgraded our internet!"

"Go back to the mortar thing?" Anesh asked.

James shook his head. "Another not-so-useful combat skill. Four ranks in field artillery."

"Four?"

"Four. Best so far."

The two of them took a second to breathe, just enjoying the feeling of victory singing in their veins. Anesh broke the silence a minute later. "Okay, it smells like a tire fire here. Are you up to moving on? I'm feeling okay, but I need to get a bandage on this." He held up his hand, showing off the bloody mark.

"Yeah," James said. "Let's get patched up and see if we can find anything good around here before we go deeper."

Twenty minutes later, James was finishing up putting medical tape on the bandages on his face, and Anesh was methodically snapping pens in half. They'd taken the chance to move through the break room while the minefield was clear, and James had, with Anesh's permission, taken the opportunity to surprise the petulant potted plant with a sledgehammer strike, securing another pair of skill orbs. After that, they'd set up in a cubicle, broken out a medkit, and started fixing their minor injuries.

And after James had gotten Anesh bandaged, Anesh had set about testing everything in the cube for magical properties.

But that was taking too long, and he didn't really want a pencil that only he could see or a pack of sticky notes that never ran out. So he went to the simpler solution: just start snapping things in half and see if anything came out.

By the time James finished with his cuts, Anesh had a pile of three tiny blue orbs. This earned him a snorted laugh and a smile. "I'm glad you're catching up to my debt to you so fast," James said, "but what if one of those was cool?"

"We were never gonna find out anyway," Anesh replied. "Now! Ready to go? Let's get moving. I wanna see what's farther in."

They got to their feet, stretched, rechecked their armor, and started moving. There were more corners here, more intersections. They left signposts stapled to the walls every turn they took, taking extra care to leave a trail of bread crumbs. As they moved, they took only the most obvious loot, prioritizing cash and leaving everything else. They could grab it on the way out; they didn't want to worry about extra weight on the way in.

Half an hour later, they hadn't encountered anything new. The worst they'd seen was a vending machine flanked by a pair of plants, which they'd decided to skip for now. They'd seen some stapler-crabs, but none of them had tried to ambush or challenge the team, instead making obvious movements and keeping their distance.

Anesh had wanted to go hunting, but James stopped him. As far as he figured, if something wasn't instantly hostile, he didn't want to break that peace. He'd played in too many D&D games where anything that looked even a little "evil" was fair game, and it never sat well with him. He might be a greedy bastard, out to loot this place for all it was worth, but he wasn't a monster.

The architecture around them continued to shift in small ways. The walls, now towering overhead, started to have small windows and parapets cut into them. They were seeing doorways covered in sheaves of sticky notes, and in some places, they were having to take time to disconnect the paper clip webs that the stapler-crabs used as their nests when they were strung across the hallway.

It was while James was bolt-cutting his way through one of those webs that Anesh, keeping watch, felt something at the edge of his senses. He tried looking around, but it wasn't anything he could see. It was then, as he felt a bump on his cheek, that he had an idea. He poked the little drone, still nestled on his shoulder. "Ganesh. Go give me a good view, 'kay, mate?"

The small mobile machine trilled a bit, then fired up its rotor blades and launched itself into the air. Anesh pulled his phone out and quickly found the Wi-Fi signal, pulling up the camera app that let him see what his drone was seeing. And it worked! He could see, almost at a higher quality, as it flew around corners and over walls, giving him a good aerial view.

And there ahead of them, past one of the four-way intersections, something changed. The ceiling suddenly cut down to a normal height, and the whole thing on the outside looked like blue-and-white tile. "Okay, you delightful little wasp, get back here," he muttered and was surprised to see the viewpoint change almost instantly as the drone responded and headed back. "James!" he called out. "I think I found something!"

As James finished off the last paper clip web line, they both heard a whispered voice float through the air above them. "Meeeeeetingggggggg..."

"Yeah," James said. "I think I found something too."

CHAPTER 13

"Okay, so, we're in agreement that this is stupid, right?"

Anesh was complaining. Not without reason, he thought. After all, when one hears a mysterious moaning voice droning out a word with long, tortured syllables, typically, you don't go toward it. If he'd learned anything from his exposure to American pop culture at the hands of James's DVD collection, it was that this is exactly how someone dies in a zombie movie.

After snapping their way through that thick mass of paper clip webs, they'd had a quick round of rock-paper-scissors. Since James won, he was currently leading them down a curved corridor, away from what Anesh and his drone pal had spotted, in search of the voice.

James, moving ahead in a low crouch, trying to be as quiet as possible, whispered back, "Look, if it's a zombie, we need to know before we walk into one blind. If it's not a zombie, well, we probably also need to know before we walk into it blind."

It was sound logic, and Anesh didn't really have any reason to argue with it. Beyond, of course, "Yeah, but it just seems stupid to walk into the zombie on purpose."

"Coffffeeeeeee . . ." came the response from up ahead, down the right side of the intersection they were walking up on.

"See, Anesh? Coffee. It's probably just an intern. They're like zombies anyway, and I deal with them every day," James said.

The two of them stopped for a minute. The intersection ahead of them was a three-way, like those they'd been leaving signs on this whole way through. But this one was the first in a while that wasn't empty. Ahead of them, against the back wall of this new hallway, was one of the large, nineties-style vending machines they'd previously seen, sitting right next to a cliché office water cooler. The walls around the intersection weren't curved overhead like they were in the hallway, creating a spot where the lights shone down without obstruction, banishing the gloom of the hallways behind them. Overhead, a flock of printer paper fluttered by, roughly crumpled shapes propelled through the air via unknown means.

James held up an arm, stopping Anesh from moving into the little courtyard. "What're you doing?"

"I want to see if the vending machine works. We never got to check the other one," Anesh said.

James turned to look at his friend, mouth hanging open, eyebrows askew. "And you didn't want to . . . check first? Like, throw some stuff at the water cooler, make sure it's not gonna explode?"

Anesh froze. "Ah, right. I saw there was no potted plant and assumed we were clear."

They rubbed faded bruises without thinking about it. Their first fight with a plant was still painful to remember. James wouldn't be at all fond of the memory of being slammed into the ground if it had happened once, and it had certainly happened more than once. Anesh knew that it had been weeks, and his arm was physically fine now, but he couldn't help feel the phantom of that soreness that stuck around for days and days after the fight.

James spent a second checking his pockets for something to throw but only came up with his own phone and wallet. Next to him, Anesh couldn't find anything aside from blue orbs, and he'd throw his own pants before losing those. "Okay," Anesh said, "I'm gonna check the cubes here. Make sure it doesn't grow tentacles and come after us."

"Why would it . . ."

"Have you seen this place, James? Two out of three . . . no, three out of four of the sodding monsters here have tentacles," Anesh muttered as he slung his backpack onto the floor next to the door of the cubicle to the left.

James kept his eyes on the intersection as he answered softly, "How are you counting your drone there? Is it a monster, or do you qualify the rotor blades as 'tentacles' somehow?"

As Anesh started their standard looting routine on the cubicle, he thought over the question. "Hrm." He grabbed a handful of coins out of a coat pocket as he checked for a wallet. "I didn't really count him as a monster. He seems generally too cheerful to be too bad." He gave a quick poke to the computer tower under the desk to make sure it wasn't a shellaxy before starting to open the desk drawers.

Out in the hall, James was keeping an eye mostly on the fluttering paper overhead. The strange not-birds seemed to move in jerks and starts, like a school of fish more than any actual avians. The sight of the fliers reminded him of something from a few minutes ago. "Hey, why'd you name the drone Ganesh, anyway? Isn't that going to get confusing?"

"Why would it do that?" his friend asked in return as he shoved a pair of candy bars into his bag; these were labeled *Stuff Chucklers*.

"Well," James said slowly as he tracked the paper flock, "I don't know if anyone's explained how language works to you, but that name is maybe one letter tops different from your name."

"I don't see how that would be a problem," Anesh called back. He opened up the large filing cabinet drawer and saw something that made him giggle packed among the stacks of folders and paperwork. "Oh, score!"

James looked over at the door as Anesh came out, preceded by a ratcheting sound. "What the hell did you . . . Oh *hell* no! Do not point that at me!" His voice went up an octave in pitch as he saw his friend come out, redoing the clips on his bag with one hand and holding a Nerf gun in the other.

"What?" Anesh asked. "It's not even one of the big ones," he said as he stepped out of the cube, brandishing the toy dart gun, freshly loaded and cocked.

James was well aware that he wasn't the most attentive guy in the world. He missed obvious details with regularity. Hell, he'd needed to bring Anesh in on this whole endeavor just to have it pointed out to him that sporting goods stores existed. He never would have thought, as Anesh did, that mass deconstruction of items would save time checking for magical traits. He also would probably have been dead to a tumblefeed, because he didn't make the connection that he could sweep traps the easy way.

That said, he wasn't *stupid*.

"Dude, so far, we've seen hostile staplers, moving sheafs of paper"—he pointed upward at the flock above them—"and actual for-real magic items." He glared at Anesh, putting a bit of actual anger and lot of shaky nerves into his next words. "Do not. Point. The Nerf gun. At. Me."

There was a moment of silence, and then Anesh pointed the gun at the ground, looking sheepish. "Yeah, didn't think of that. Sorry, mate."

James nodded, then clapped Anesh on the shoulder. "No worries. Just made me nervous there for a second. You wanna test that on the water cooler?"

"Sure, yeah," Anesh said, still shaking a bit. Fighting monsters so far hadn't been a problem for him, emotionally. He'd had a few adrenaline rushes, but with the exception of when they'd been staring down that tumblefeed, pinned between it and the booby-trapped break room, he hadn't really felt nervous in here. But the idea that he'd actually made his friend angry? Well, like James, he wasn't stupid, but he didn't have friends to spare.

But fortunately, James snapped back into casually cheerful in the blink of an eye, and Anesh internally sighed before lining up the dart gun and letting it fly with a plastic snap. Both of them felt a surge of excitement as it connected with the water cooler, and then an equal surge of disappointment as they sat there staring at the perfectly mundane orange dart sitting on the floor next to the unimpressed tank of water.

"Okay, so it's probably safe," James said, and Anesh bonked him on the head with two fingers. He laughed before saying, "I'll keep watch while you check out the machine, and then we'll go investigate, well, *that*."

As he was speaking, the softly droning voice returned, a quiet "Eeeemaiiilllll . . ." coming past them.

"Got it, I'll be quick about it," Anesh said as they approached the intersection. He moved up to the vending machine, taking a minute to have fun with the sensation of running his finger down a list of options that never seemed to end and that never seemed to visibly produce motion from his arm. He didn't waste too much time with that, though, and quickly jammed several of the coins he'd swiped into the slot. Two rumbling *thunks* later and he had a pair of randomly selected drinks, which got shoved into his bag without tasting.

James looked back at his friend's activities. "Not going to drink those?"

"I'm not thirsty right now, and they might be poison," Anesh retorted.

"The candy might be poison, but you eat enough of that."

Anesh had the good grace to look sheepish as they put up their improvised signpost and headed down the hallway, leaving the brightly lit drink machine behind and moving back into the semishaded gloom of the cubicle rows. "I like candy," he muttered. "Oh, and the drone is named Ganesh after the god. I thought it was clever, because it's like a scout."

James nodded as they kept moving. "Good choice. Just, you know, it's also almost your name. So don't blame me when I yell at you and the drone comes instead."

On Anesh's shoulder, Ganesh tilted its single spiked "eye" in a gesture that matched his own. Anesh looked sideways at it, then back at James. "Yeah, I agree with him. If you ever call me, he'll show up anyway."

"Stop agreeing with things that can't talk, Anesh."

"You're the one who has a pet spider thing that you coo at every time we come in," Anesh said as he did a quick check of the upcoming cube on their left. They were both moving in slow walks, not quite crouching but keeping a bit low, perhaps unconsciously due to the presence of what their brains registered as "spiderwebs." So he was in a pretty good position to peek through the windows cut into the walls rather than push his way through the layers of paper or sticky notes that made up the doors now.

He and James were using this less to look for good loot and more to look for threats. Just a quick check through the increasingly complicated linear and spiral holes, and then moving on. They were trying to move quickly and find the source of the words. Both of them figured they could loot on the way out, and so far, there hadn't been anything that really stood out as "new." Neither of them was going to complain about scrounging up a few thousand dollars, but at the same time, neither of them was going to go over every desk in detail in the hope that they might find a mouse that enhanced their video game skillshot prowess or spreadsheet-formatting ability or some other useless power.

This hallway was really long, too, with no real intersections they could see. James figured it probably stretched out at least fifty cubes long. He also figured he was spending too much time here if that felt like a natural unit of measurement. Regardless, the voice sounded like it was coming from this area, so he was on alert.

"Daaaaaamn iiiiit, Jaaaaaniceeeeee."

"Okay, that was definitely close," James said.

Anesh looked up from the window he was checking. "Really? That's what you're focusing on here? Not that there's a zombie pissed at Janice?"

"I'm not a Janice," James replied.

The voice had come from up ahead, though. Maybe two or three cubes up, on the right. Even as they were talking, they were also unslinging their backpacks, and Anesh was setting down his sledgehammer and new Nerf gun in favor of pulling his hand axe off its clip on his belt. They moved up close to each other and started very carefully checking the next few windows.

The first one was empty, of course. More so than normal. Just a single chair and filing cabinet, not even a computer or desk. A single cardboard box full of paperwork sitting on the chair. They gave that one a pass.

The second one, though, was more interesting. Through the spiral curves of the inset window, they saw a space that was a little more decorated than any they had previously seen. The monitor on the desk was on, with a screen saver of a rotating leaf. The desk itself was neatly organized, with a corded phone nestled among vertical rows of colored plastic binders. On one wall was what looked like a tapestry, a composition of folded colored sticky notes showing a bright, stylized sun. On the wall opposite it hung a paper mask, made out of some kind of construction paper, with its own mane of blue sticky notes trailing out of it to give the impression of either hair or fire. James couldn't tell which.

He nodded to Anesh, and they moved to flank either side of the door. Anesh pushed back the curtain of clean white printer paper, and James slipped inside.

"This one is weird . . ." he whispered to Anesh. "Is the dungeon vaguely racist?"

Anesh just shrugged. "Can't say. But hell, I've seen a couple desks at your office that look a bit like this."

The mask on the wall chimed, "Quiiiiiittinnng tiiiiime . . ."

Anesh and James nearly jumped out of their skins, whirling with beating hearts, axes up. Of course, it was the mask. Both of them felt a little stupid for not paying more attention to that.

"Cofffeeeeeeee breeeeeaaaaakkkk . . ." it groaned out as the two of them stared at it, frozen.

They could see the paper around its eyes narrow as it watched them, the sticky note fire that was its hair twitching in a non-existent breeze. "Is it . . . going to roll us?" Anesh whispered.

James replied out of the corner of his mouth, "I don't know. Play it safe, move for the door."

They began inching for the cubicle's exit, Anesh going first, neither of them taking their eyes off the mask. With his free hand, axe still held up in front of him like a cross against a vampire, Anesh pushed back the sheets of the door and tapped James through. James ducked past Anesh's axe and stepped out, also unwilling to break eye contact with the mask on the wall.

As Anesh was backing out, James stepped into the hallway and took a quick look around. And this was why, as Anesh was stepping through the paper, he heard a loud "Oh *fuck!*" from behind him.

Anesh snapped his head around at James's shout, and his eyes went wide at the sight at the end of the hall from where they came. Plodding forward on thick legs of corded cable, a single small LED shining red in the middle of its body, a tumblefeed hammered its way down the hall, its single "eye" fixed on James. "Where the fuck did that come from? I thought we killed it!" Anesh yelled.

He didn't have long to think about it, as a second later, with a scream of "Innnterrrrrnnsssss!" and a papery hiss, the mask impacted the back of Anesh's helmet, and he yelped as something hard started scratching along the top of his headgear, the mask dragging itself toward his face.

"Run!" James shouted.

"Help!" Anesh yelled at about the same time.

"Laaaate!" howled the mask shortly after.

James threw his own bag over his shoulder, grabbed Anesh's pack, and started shoving Anesh down the corridor away from the tumblefeed. Anesh was furiously swatting at his head, trying to knock the mask off. Throwing off a loud buzzing noise, Ganesh was also flitting around, diving down to try to stab at the mask's form as it crawled over his friend but being constantly swatted away by the strange tendrils of blue sticky notes.

"Just go! Worry about that later!" James snapped out as they ran down the hallway.

Anesh let a little panic creep into his voice as the mask found purchase over the edge of his helmet, and a small spur of what felt like bone or hard plastic drove into the skin on the side of his head above his eye. "I'm worried about it now! Just get it off!"

He skidded to a stop, and James almost tripped over him. Snarling, he grabbed at the mask, intending to just pin it to a wall. Instead, Anesh screamed as the spur in his skin tore a line down the side of his head, and a second later, holding the mask by its base, James got another surprise when a half dozen of those same spines sank into his own arm. They slid around the arm guard to almost effortlessly stab through the cloth and flesh underneath.

This, it turned out, was a bad idea. James was scared, running, worried about his friend, and now hurt. But above all else, this thing was making him *angry*. They'd spent almost an hour making their careful way to this voice, and he was hoping mostly for some kind of Big Damn Heroes moment, finding someone trapped here in need of help. Or, at the very least, a chance for some cool loot. But this? It was creeping him out, it was trying to eat his friend's face, and it was *wasting time*.

"Fuck! Yoooou!" James yelled. His hand slammed into the nearest wall, pinning the mask to it, face-first. From the rear, he could see that it had about a dozen of those spurs on either side of it, and the thought of it latching onto his face, sinking them in, sent a spike of horror through his chest. He didn't want to find out what happened after that.

A second later, he pinned it to the wall with his hand axe, the blade chunking into the wall behind the flimsy paper. "Reeetiiiirremeeeennnnttt . . ." it moaned as the paper relaxed, and the paper fire that surrounded it went limp and colorless.

Anesh breathed heavily, grabbing his bag from where James had dropped it, and then snapped up the fist-sized yellow orb from the pile of crumpled paper on the ground. "Thanks. *Now* we can run!" he said, checking how much ground the slower tumblefeed had gained. It was moving slowly but deliberately, and the motions reminded

Anesh a bit of how he and James were going. He saw cords probing through the doors to the cubes around it as it advanced, almost like it was checking. Had it learned from their ambush earlier? It wasn't the same one; this one was smaller and looked ... newer, almost.

But there was no time to talk about it or think about it. Its caution was their escape, and the office flew by as they ran, dripping blood behind them.

Forty cubicles later, they hit a wall and had to take a corner. It was another three-way intersection, and Anesh turned right almost without thinking about it. His lungs were screaming at him, his legs were throbbing, but there was no time to stop, only this flight for survival.

He almost screamed when he turned and saw a person in the hallway.

The walls here were lower up ahead, with clusters of four or six workspaces sitting together without visual impairment. And he thought he saw people sitting in a couple of them, either typing or on phones. What he was certain he saw, though, was someone walking down the hall away from himself and James.

Someone was the wrong word.

Something. It was shaped like a human. It had two arms and two legs. It was wearing a polo shirt and black slacks. It was carrying a coffee cup in its five-fingered hand. In every single detail, it was human, from the messy didn't-have-time-to-shower hair to the casual checking of the smartphone in its hand.

And then it turned at the noise of their running, and Anesh met its eyes.

And it was not human.

At all.

Anesh turned before James could catch up, grabbed his friend, and fled the other way. There was no explanation, there was no time. James would just have to trust him and they could talk when they were clear.

They took two more turns into this deeper part of the office before ducking into a mostly concealed cubicle. James got a sinking familiar feeling to this whole turn of events as he pinned up some open folders over the windows of their hiding spot. Overhead, about two-thirds of the cube was covered by the curving architecture of the wall, leaving a few spots open in strange patterns and leaving the two of them in almost darkness.

"Did we lose it?" James rasped out between breaths that tore at his throat.

Anesh just slumped into the chair, bag dropped to the floor, slowly spinning around without saying anything except his gasps for breath. He raised his hand to the side of his head, and it came back slick with blood.

James leaned forward, resting his head on the wall, trying to still his breath enough to hear. "Seriously, did we lose it?" he whispered.

"Oh hell, what now?" he heard Anesh mutter behind him. It didn't sound like the tumblefeed had caught up to them or tracked them down the hall, so he took a deep breath and turned.

Anesh had his feet up on the chair, and Ganesh on his shoulder was revving its small motor in fear, both of them looking down at the bag, which was currently being crawled on by some ... phones?

James knelt down and poked one. Yup, iPhones. "They're iPhones," he said.

To be fair, there was also one larger one that looked like an iPad. That and four smaller phone-sized devices were crawling across Anesh's bag. They didn't seem to have eyes, and their screens were all on and glowing in the fairly dark room. Dozens of copper pins served as their legs, and their bodies seemed to bend and flex in ways that a normal commercial phone would snap from.

"Jaaaaames," Anesh whispered in a shaky voice. "Don't poke the bugs! God, they look like fuckin' millipedes. I hate this so much."

James looked up at his friend, cowering on the chair. "Are you seriously telling me, after all that, what really gets you panicking is bugs? Also, they're not trying to murder us. I think they're just curious little things." He looked down at one of the ... "I'm gonna call them iLipedes," he said. "Spelled like 'iPhone,'" he clarified. Its screen was on, and as James watched, it pulled a coin out of one of the pouches on Anesh's bag, and an app on it opened.

"That's a stupid name for a stupid, bug-stupid thing," Anesh said, to a sharp *Shh* from James. Hushed, his fears being ignored by his partner, Anesh settled for pushing his chair back against the front wall, as far away from the colony of crawly things as possible, his skin itching at the thought that one of them might touch him.

At this point, James wasn't listening. He was leaning in, tilting his head to peer at the screen as the iLipede mulled over the quarter. And then, a series of lines of text started to appear. *Value : .25 USD. Composition : 8.3% Nickel, 91.7% Copper. Represented : George Washington.*

"Anesh, look at this! It's my own personal fantasy of a device that gives you statistics on things!" he said excitedly, holding up the squirming iLipede, still clutching its coin, to show the screen to Anesh.

Anesh was less than amused. "Get it the fuck away from me!" he shouted as he opened up the medkit from James's bag on the desk, one hand pressed against his head.

"It's not actually a bug, you know?" James set the thing back down, and it scampered over to its friends, which were still poking around Anesh's backpack.

"I don't care, it looks like one. And after the mask and the suits, I'm nervous about everything in here," Anesh said.

James paused in his attempts to get one of his new bug pals to tell him the chocolate content of one of the candy bars Anesh had in his bag and glanced over, looking worried. "Wait, suits?"

"Ah, yeah. So, as long as we're lost again and trapped deep within the dungeon, I guess now's as good a time as any to tell you . . ."

CHAPTER 14

"This pencil has another thirty-six thousand words in it!" James whispered excitedly.

The two of them were creeping along what felt like a secret tunnel. The cubicle walls here were so close together that they almost hadn't noticed it as they snuck out of their hidey-hole, hoping to circle around past the tumblefeed before it caught up to them. The rough semicarpet on the walls left a gap that was maybe a little less than a meter across, which meant that the two people in football pads, helmets, and arm and leg guards, with weapons and medical kits strapped around their belts and bodies and carrying travel packs, had a *bit* of a difficult time maneuvering through it.

"This binder is seven months old!" James said softly, trying to get Anesh's attention.

Anesh was taking point this time. He'd had to forfeit his claim on the next half dozen blue orbs in order to convince James that they shouldn't go back down the other hallway to where the empty people were. James, for his part, wasn't actually super interested in getting into another fight while being chased by a bundle of angry power cables, but he was having fun playing with the iLipedes and didn't exactly want to leave. He'd accepted almost at once the "compromise" that Anesh had hastily suggested, and he was only mildly offended that his friend thought he'd willingly rush a bunch of inhuman office drones unprepared.

"Anesh, this thing is so cool. You should get one and see if we can get a spectrometer app for it or something." He poked at his friend.

Up ahead, Anesh twitched with rage. "Why did you bring that? I hate those things, and we are enemies now." He said the last part flatly, not exactly angry, but certainly displeased. He'd been annoyed ever since his ploy to get James to move had sort of backfired, with his bug-loving now-enemy grabbing one of the iLipedes on his backpack before shaking the others off and declaring it his new pet.

James slid the iLipede, its twitching copper pin-legs facing out, into his pocket. "I'll tell you later. If it works, it'll be cool, and you'll be happy I grabbed one."

"I already know you're gonna try scanning one of the orbs. It's clever, but it feels like we're starting some kind of anime harem of office supplies around here now," Anesh griped as he squeezed his way underneath a small arced feature jutting out of the wall at head height. "Personally, I was hoping for some kind of inherent ability to just know things, but then, you can't always get what you want."

"It's not that bad, is it?" James asked, legitimately concerned that their collection of mobile devices was a problem.

As Anesh stopped at the end of their cramped little path, blocked by an array of paper clip webs, he reached a hand back and said, "Bolt cutters, please, assuming they're still non-sentient. Also no, it's not really a problem. It's just that you're way too excited about something that grosses me out, and also we're in dire peril, and yet you keep talking about meaningless statistics, instead of, I don't know, trying to find us a way out of here?"

James sighed. "Look," he said, trying to defuse the tension, "I don't know anything you don't; we both heard ourselves talking about what to do ten minutes ago." Ten minutes ago, they'd heard the slithering sound, so much like rain against metal, of a tumblefeed passing nearby. They'd decided then that holing up and hoping it went away was a bad plan.

So here they were, trying to keep the twists and turns of their path in mind and hoping to recross their old path. Or at least find a place far enough away that seemed safe where they could hunker down for a bit and let Anesh deploy his drone friend to take a quick look around for them.

As Anesh clipped his way through the mass of webs, James leaned against one of the cramped walls, trying to make enough space to feel like he could take a breath. Between the soreness in his legs from sprinting (an activity he didn't much care for normally), the pain of the cuts on his hand and arm, and his own short attention span, he found himself reaching into his pocket to start to pull out the phone creature and maybe figure out if his arm guard had an estimated life span. It was because of this lack of focus that he didn't notice anything amiss until he heard Anesh scream and a similar whining noise from the drone.

Snapping his view over to his friend and off the half-arch protrusion from the wall that he'd been staring at, James saw a stapler, this one with legs made of gleaming gold-and-black pens, attempting to give his delving partner a new ear piercing. The little drone on the other shoulder fired up its rotors and flitted back, still screeching, perching on one of the small brick-shaped chunks that made for perfect drone shelves on the wall near them. Letting go of the squirming phone in his pocket, he didn't even think as he lashed his hand out and grabbed the thing, jerking it off Anesh.

This turned out to be a bad idea. The pens of its legs weren't sharp enough to do anything but futilely scribble on the arm guard, but James hadn't really thought through *where* he'd grabbed it, and it drove a staple into the meat of his palm as it slammed itself back together, its metal "teeth" biting through the flesh of his ungloved hand.

Gritting his teeth, he shifted his grip, the metal tearing slightly larger holes in his hand. He couldn't get enough room to slam it into the floor, his weapons were stuck in his belt and weren't really designed for fighting this thing anyway, and he sure as hell wasn't tasering it while he held it, so he frantically looked around for some way to deal with it.

The waste of time got him stapled again, this time as it jerked slightly out of his grip and nicked him in the back of one of his fingers. Bleeding and furious, trying to not howl in pain, James grabbed the thing in both hands and felt a strange burst of nostalgia for the first time in here as he slowly pried the thing's "jaw" apart. Sticky black ichor spilled out of it, along with a pile of staples. The slit eye on the front of the stapler flicked back and forth in panic as James strained his arm muscles, ripping it in half.

As soon as it stopped moving, he plucked the skill orb out of the air where it spawned and dropped the corpse. "My hand is really starting to hurt," he muttered to Anesh, who was looking at him with wide eyes.

No, he realized, not at him. Past him. He turned his head a bit and saw with some apprehension another trio of the things crawling toward him, using the chunks of architecture sticking out of the walls to move at about head height.

"Get the damn web out of the way!" he snapped out, causing Anesh to jolt a bit and turn back to furiously snapping through chunks of paper clips. The clips weren't individually anything that could stop them, but they'd discovered earlier that the webs were hooked into the walls with something that seemed to defy physics. Not surprising, exactly, but also almost impossible to tear out quickly. So just running through them wasn't going to be a good way to get anything except a thousand tiny stabs as the ends bent and punctured cloth and flesh.

Facing down the incoming threats, James noticed that they all seemed to be a little sleeker than the ones he'd seen before. Fancier pens for legs, a glossier black hull. They were still clearly staplers, but they had a bit more of an organic feeling, and he had a sinking feeling that they were going to be a little more flexible when it came to landing bites.

His hand dropped to his belt, but he already knew he didn't have enough room to actually swing the hand axe in here. It was compact, but he could barely move his arms already. So he unclipped the Taser, flicking the switch on it and muttering a quick "Man, I hope this works."

As soon as the first one got a little too close, he shuffled his feet forward in a half step and lashed out with the device, thumbing the button. A pair of prongs popped out the end of the small metal box and made contact with the hissing stapler. James thought he could almost feel the electrical charge transfer, but…

The stapler didn't even flinch. Instead, it dove forward, seeking out the exposed flesh of James's hand. He dropped the stun gun without even thinking about it and jerked his hand away before darting back in to grab the stapler. Glancing back as he held its "mouth" shut like he was some kind of crocodile wrestler, he saw that Anesh almost had a person-sized hole cleared in the web. Only needing to buy a bit of time, he used what limited range of motion he had to fling the stapler-crab at the next nearest one that was encroaching on them, knocking it off its perch and sending both of them tumbling back in a metallic clatter.

"Okay, go!" he heard behind him, and he started moving backward down the tiny hall, just trying to outpace the things chasing him. He dragged himself past obstacles at a furious pace, knocking his elbows and ribs against chunks of cubicle wall that felt more like solid stone as he tried to get out and away from the now seven little demons swarming at them down the floor and walls.

And then he was free. A metal scraping noise burned his ears as his helmet brushed against the top of the webs, and then he could move again. As soon as his arms were clear, he yanked his hand axe off his belt, continuing to backpedal.

He saw Anesh crouched to the side of the tiny tunnel. And as soon as the first stapler cleared the breach, Anesh wasted no time smashing down with his axe. The compact blade was durable enough, and Anesh put enough force behind it that it caved in the top of the stapler right in the middle. A small spray of black liquid and a hissing screech that trailed off were the last things James really got to focus on before the others poured out into the light.

The next few minutes were a series of moments to James. One of the first things that happened was that he was jumped from behind by a shellaxy, this one looking almost like an Apple product. The smooth white shell must have been attracted by the sounds, as the cubicle from which it emerged was right next to the cramped tunnel he and Anesh had just come out of. Propelled forward by what looked like a writhing mass of USB and FireWire cables, it had slammed into James at the back of his knees, and he'd toppled forward, head cracking against the ground with the helmet doing little to negate the concussive force.

He remembered kicking the thing hard enough to crack the plastic casing. He remembered Anesh calling his name as several of the staplers swarmed over his prone form. He had a memory that made him snicker when he recalled it, of Ganesh swooping down over him, the little drone latching onto one of the staplers trying to take out James's eyes and lifting off carrying it, rotors screaming in protest as it hauled the weight away. He remembered hitting one repeatedly until he'd shattered the chitinous outside and almost severed it in half. There were several flashes of himself and Anesh throwing stapler-crabs away to clear space to finish off others. And he distinctly remembered trying to convince Anesh that they should call them stapler-spiders, because of the webs, in the middle of nicking the blade of his axe hammering through the innards of the shellaxy.

And then the next thing he remembered was opening his eyes to a panicked-looking Anesh shaking him. He was sitting on the floor, his back against one of the walls. Around them were the shattered remains of about two dozen hostile things, mostly stapler-crabs, though James also saw a second shellaxy corpse and a crumpled pile of paper that he would have missed if not for the orb over it.

"My head kinda hurts," he droned out in a dull, monotone voice. And Anesh sagged his shoulders in relief.

His friend had bandages on his cheeks and was missing one of his arm guards, which James found off to the side in chunks of plastic. "Oh good, you're okay. Bloody hell, I was so worried." A deep breath, almost a shaky sigh. "You've got a bit of a concussion, I think. Can you see? One of your eyes is super bloody."

James nodded and then regretted that a whole lot. "Yeah, I can see," he rasped. "Can I have some water?" he asked.

Anesh shook his head. "We went through that. All I've got is a couple 'drinks' from the vending machine. Want to try one, or has it not come to that yet?" James extended his hand and made a grabbing motion, and Anesh shrugged as he pulled one of the bottles out and gave it to his friend, opening the cap for him.

After a few gulps, James took the drink away from his lips with an "Aaaahhhhh." He rubbed at his head a bit before looking around again, only just now starting to feel like he was awake. Or alive. "That's surprisingly good. Tastes like a salty mango."

"That's not an endorsement at all," Anesh said, trying not to grin wildly in relief. "Are you okay? I want to gather up the orbs and do a quick check before we move. And we do need to move."

"Yeah," James said, "I need to sit for a bit, but I can walk for now. Let's find a spot once you get those." He watched Anesh grabbing orbs for a while before noticing something else. "Hey, why is my leg guard gone? And the bottom half of that pant leg? And what the fuck happened to my leg?"

Anesh came over and helped him to his feet, his bag now packed with well over twenty skill orbs. "Okay, what do you remember?" he asked, helping James walk as he realized how much pain putting pressure on his injured leg caused. James described the fight from his perspective but ran short of words at some point and didn't have any details for his friend. "Ah, the shellaxy. I need a new name for the iPhone-looking ones. So after you kicked it the first time it tried to bite you; I think it decided it wanted its food cooked. Turns out, those things have actual for-real lasers. Not *Star Wars* style, sadly, or I'd have cracked it open more carefully. But like one of those illegal laser pointer things. It had about five of them, and it just started slicing into you."

James bent down to rub at the burn lines on his lower leg, feeling the gel that Anesh had put on it. "No bandage for it?"

Anesh shook his head. "We ran out of the big ones. We need to get out of here, get you to an actual hospital."

"Okay," James said. "One step at a time. Let's get moving again. Is there any good news I missed while blacked out? Did Ganesh spot anything?"

"No," Anesh said, "though here's something we didn't know: he ate one of the skill orbs from the stapler he killed. We should maybe be feeding Rufus. I don't know where he's getting the ones he brings you."

James staggered down the hall, looking around for the cubicle that looked safest. "I was more hoping for good news. Like, extra loot. Not having to give up some of mine."

"The shellaxy dropped a green one, if that makes you feel better?" Anesh asked with a sideways glance at his friend as they checked an intersection.

James thought for a second, then nodded. "Yeah, yeah, it does."

CHAPTER 15

The two of them were sitting in a cubicle a little ways away from their battleground. Anesh was trying to repackage their medical bags into one single bag that was slightly more complete. They'd gone through their big bandages on James's hand and arm and another large cut on Anesh's arm. Their smaller bandages they'd used a ton of on face cuts, with Anesh having to discard several of them when shaky hands soaked them in blood and ruined the adhesive. So he was spreading stuff out, discarding garbage and things they'd brought too much of and muttering about how they'd screwed up their choices.

When James got bored with nursing his hand and watching Anesh throwing piles of wrappers and empty gel packs onto the floor, he started digging out and sorting the various orbs they'd both shoved into their bags over the last few hours. The green one in particular was his target, just to see what they'd gotten, and when he found it, he was a bit disappointed to see that it was only about two-thirds the size of the first one.

As for the rest, after Anesh emptied his pockets to add to the collection, they had eighteen of the smallest skill orbs, along with five more midsized ones, three tiny blue spheres, and the single brightemerald one that seemed to overshadow the others with its glow.

"This is a pretty good haul." James nodded in approval. Ganesh had come over to poke at the skill orbs with him, and James had started playing fetch with him by rolling one of the small ones away while they waited for the drone's master to finish up. "Hey! Do you mind if I test something with these?" he called over to Anesh, who was still muttering furiously while rearranging bags.

"Go ahead, do your experiments. We've got test subjects now, after all," Anesh said. He sounded a bit gruff, but James was pretty sure he was just exhausted and that was affecting his voice a little. So he shrugged and went ahead with his plan.

James pulled the iLipede out of his pocket, ignoring its fresh set of squirms in his hand. Setting it on the table, he gently held it down while poking at its back and firing up the statistics app. Unable to resist having a little fun before serious testing, he pulled off the glove he still had and put the phone bug on top of it.

A few seconds of the iLipede prodding with its microchip legs later, a notification popped up on its face: *Fabrics contained : Nylon, Polyester. Product rating : 4.8/5. Blood Loss Prevented : 32 ml.*

"That's a distressing amount of blood loss," James muttered. "What did I do, grab barbed wire while I wasn't paying attention?" He put the glove back on, pulling it away from Ganesh, who was now poking at the article of clothing. "Well, anyway, good job, little guy. Now I've got something a little more important for ya."

He took one of the fingernail-sized skill orbs and set it in a clear spot on the desk, right in front of the iLipede. It took a couple pokes to motivate the thing to move forward and latch onto the tiny little golden sphere, but eventually, James got it to do so. As soon as it was situated atop the skill orb, the screen on its back changed almost instantly.

To a loading bar.

"One percent done. Estimated time to completion, seventy-four minutes. Huh. Well, ain't that some shit," James said, half disappointed that he didn't have an identify scroll on a stick. Of course, the other half of him was pretty excited to see if this was going to work at all.

His imagination jumped to keeping a pen of these things near the entrance, a dozen or so little iLipedes in a nice nest of FireWire cables, constantly working toward his own personal goals, tirelessly scanning things for him, making his life incrementally easier in exchange for no reward...

James did a quick check of his own internal TV Tropes page, just to make sure he wasn't actually the bad guy here. "Hey, Anesh!" he called across the cubicle. "Are you okay if... maybe we don't do some kind of crazy exploitative iLipede farm? I'm kinda iffy on the whole 'starting a labor camp' thing, even if they are probably just animal-level intelligence."

"What the hell are you banging on about?" Anesh asked as he zipped up the now-organized bags. "Wait, more of those things? No. No more, thanks."

James nodded and gave the one he had a little pat. "Glad you agreed. Hey, before we go, do you want to use up some of these smaller ones? I don't really like the feeling of a bunch of slippery balls in my bag."

"... No, I'm sure you don't," Anesh said after a long, deliberate pause, staring at James. The two of them maintained neutral expressions for only a couple seconds before they burst out laughing. "But yeah, these things are a bloody pain in the ass to sort in an organized way. May as well go through some of the small ones. Let's say, five each? That way you can satisfy your addiction, and I can pretend that I'm not doing the same thing under the guise of some kind of backpack organization obsession."

"Deal," James said. He plucked up the top five from the pile. "Okay, this feels strangely satisfying," he commented as he held up his hand, brimming with skill orbs, and slowly made a fist, popping them one by one.

[+1 Skill Rank : Math - Algebra]
[+1 Skill Rank : Filmmaking - Camera Angles]
[+1 Skill Rank : History - Comics - Silver Age]
[+1 Skill Rank : Cooking - Knife Technique]
[+1 Skill Rank : Martial Arts - Jeet Kune Do]

So two things he already knew, one thing that would only be useful if he took up that career as a YouTuber, one thing that actually got him a step closer to his dream of not having to order takeout every night, and one that brought him one step closer to a completely different dream of *being Bruce fucking Lee.*

While James sat there rubbing his hands together, a wide, manic grin on his face, Anesh reached over and picked up a few of the orbs for himself. Unlike his friend, he didn't just scoop up a handful but spent some time rolling through them, picking out very specific ones.

"What're you doing?" James asked.

Anesh looked up from making his choices. "Looking for ones that speak to me."

"Literally?"

"No, that would be insa— Hm. Okay, maybe that would be normal around here. But no," Anesh responded. "Just trying to see if any of them, you know, resonate. Maybe I can find one that feels familiar and it'll give me more calculus knowledge."

James looked a little sheepish. "Oh, I got an algebra one. Shoulda let you pick first, I guess, if you were going to be discerning. Sorry, friend." Anesh just waved him away, not worried about it now, and went back to choosing his own. After a couple minutes, he made his final choices and snapped them off one by one. "Do I get to know what you got?" James asked.

Anesh just threw James's repackaged bag back onto his lap while pulling out his own actual phone. "Poetry, French, and three different wilderness survival things. Ganesh, you up for a little flyover?" The drone hummed in agreement, rotors firing up as the little device launched itself up into the air; it pushed backward at first before snapping its front "arms" back into a flat position, and then it pulled up through one of the holes in the overhanging walls that formed the ceiling. "James, you good to keep watch while we look for one of our signposts?"

"Yeah, I'm okay. My head still hurts like hell, but I can deal with any of the small stuff easy," James said. "Three survival things? That's kind of weirdly consistent."

Anesh shook his head. "I'm clumping them together. They're a bit more varied than you think. I know a little more than I want about varieties of snakes now." He made a gesture to the door. "Go make sure we aren't about to get ambushed."

"Oh, come on," James said as he peeked out of the curtain. "If the tumblefeed didn't hear us from that fight and the screaming—I assume there was screaming?" He raised his eyebrows at Anesh, who nodded. "Right, if the screaming didn't summon it, we should be okay. But yes, I shall be your valiant protector." He leaned on the wall as a burst of dizziness hit him. "Assuming I can stand upright," he muttered under his breath.

James watched Ganesh flit away down the hall while behind him his friend watched his phone screen and tried to sketch a rough map of the surroundings. For his part, he just kept an eye out on the hallway and tried not to fall over.

To distract himself, he started rifling through the filing cabinet near the door, pulling out files and trying to read them to himself while he waited. He gave up on the top drawer after getting halfway through a report on office heat use that, he took too long to realize, didn't use any verbs. Moving on to the second drawer after listening to make sure nothing was coming, he was thrilled to find a brown paper bag nestled in there with a purse and what looked like a medication bottle.

"Score, lunch!" James said to himself as he opened up the bag, finding a wrapped sandwich and banana. "Hey, Anesh, check it out. This . . . actually smells like my high school lunch period. Is 'unrelenting nostalgia' an enchanted property? Can I eat this sandwich to get a blue orb?" The only response from his friend was a grunt as he stayed absorbed in his scouting procedure. "Fine, fine. Oh hey, candy! Chocolate Chocolates. Hey, want to bet this contains no chocolate?" Again, no response. James huffed to himself and pocketed the money and headphones out of the purse.

It was because of this that he didn't really notice the noise of something moving until it was a little closer than comfortable. James peeked out the door just as the shuffling noise stopped, and he looked around in confusion. It took him a second to realize what had happened. The hallway, previously devoid of any features, now had a giant, bulky box of a copy machine sitting just across from the door to their cubicle. "Hey, Anesh . . ." he started to say in a whisper, but he was cut off as Anesh, not knowing what was going on, jumped up with a victorious shout.

"Found one of our signs! We can get outta here!" Anesh called over. And a second later, his face turned to one of panic as a series of whirrs and beeps sounded from the hall outside.

James threw his backpack on and snapped up his axe. "More bullshit. Come on, we gotta go. Get Ganesh back here." Anesh nodded and tapped at his phone screen before shoving it in his pocket.

"What this time?" he asked.

James strapped the one reorganized medkit onto his belt. "Copier. Let's hope it's not literal. Come on, before it blocks us in here."

The two of them steeled themselves and then rushed the door. Anesh went first, less weighed down, and James followed hot on his heels. They burst out into the hallway, and Anesh moved to take a hard right, ducking under something by reflex.

Behind him, James took the hit from the blast of ink that Anesh had dodged right in the face, and he yelped in pain as he lost his balance. The copier shifted in front of him as he fell forward, and when he reached out to brace his fall, what he actually caught himself on was the flat glass pane of the machine's scanner with both hands. There was a flash of light that James only barely saw as he wiped ink out of his eye, and then he was up and running again.

The copier made no move to chase, and after a couple hundred feet of running, they slowed and glanced back.

It sat there in the middle of the hall. James could hear it from this far away; it was whirring and making the soft chuffing of paper that all copiers made as they pumped out duplicates. But it also wasn't chasing them. He supposed it would be difficult for something that large to move fast, especially with no visible legs. It was just as he was about to poke Anesh and tell him they could take it easy with the sprinting that he saw the first copy come out.

It was a hand.

It ended with about four inches of arm behind it, though no blood dripped from the opening. It was a kind of pasty white color, and it had long slender fingers. Keyboard fingers, James always called them. He knew those fingers pretty well, considering they were his. And the copy was not, as he had desperately hoped, a piece of paper. It was a full chunk of flesh, as if it had been run off a 3D printer and not a regular one.

A couple seconds later, next to the hand, another limb dropped from the slot. This one was a mirror to the first but holding the haft of a short hand axe in a closed fist. James couldn't tell from here if it was all one single object or if the axe itself was a separate part of the whole object.

But either way, fuck everything about that. He shoved Anesh forward, yelling something about getting them out of here, and his friend obliged with minimal swearing. Both of them had probably yelled something obscene when they saw the first copy drop, but they tried to contain their profanity for now, both to save breath and to not attract any more attention. They could stockpile all the swearing and use it later when they talked about this nightmare over coffee.

James had a feeling he was going to ask Anesh to make a lot more thermite for them.

Right now, though, they just ran. Beige walls and paper vines flashed by as they beat feet. Anesh, seemingly from memory, took them around two corners that James thought might as well have been random. But somewhere along the line, Ganesh buzzed down from overhead and did a hard landing against Anesh's pack, so they must be close to on the right track.

And then, up ahead, a pink sticky note with an arrow on it, at about head height on a corner. Their signpost, their way out. Just one more right turn, and they were back on the correct path. They could take it easy, make it out safe, and not worry about whatever was chasing them.

James made the mistake of looking behind them to see about ten sets of his own hands crawling after them across the walls.

"I am sick of everything in here looking like fucking spiders!" he gasped out between breaths to Anesh.

Anesh didn't even say anything. He just grabbed James's arm and yanked him to a stop. James almost came crashing down but managed to keep his balance. He was about to give a shout of panic, tell his friend they needed to move, to *run*, but then he saw what Anesh had seen.

Above the archway of the intersection, perched on one of the overhanging walls where it transformed into a ceiling, watching the water cooler and vending machine that they'd seen what seemed like a month ago, was a tumblefeed. It wasn't camouflaged, but it was out of eyesight to anyone not paying attention to "up" as well as everything else. If James had just walked forward, he'd be dead now.

Behind them, there was a trio of beeps and another whirr. A copier rolled itself into position at the end of the hall. A legion of false hands lurched forward.

In front of them was a series of thuds as the coiled limbs of the tumblefeed impacted the floor, its single red LED trained on the pair.

There were four cubicles around them but nowhere to hide.

James looked forward; Anesh looked back. They stood there, trapped between two monsters, weapons ready, but their hearts and minds were totally unprepared.

"Okay," James said, "okay . . . let's everyone just . . . calm down . . ."

He didn't get any farther than that before both sides charged them.

CHAPTER 16

"Oh hey, candy! Gummy Shrocks. Hey, want to bet this does not contain anything gummy?"

Anesh snapped his head up from the desk where he had casually popped the orbs he'd picked. He'd figured that James wouldn't mind if he took the one blue one that sang to him, especially since James didn't seem to care and was busy digging through mystery lunch. As a small wisp of blue dissipated between his fingers, the invasive thought lingered in his head.

[Problem Solved : Exercised Foresight]
[+1 Skill Rank : Fishing - Fly Fishing]

In a burst of motion, Anesh was up. Dropping the bag and his phone onto the desk, he took two big steps over to James and deftly clamped a hand over James's mouth. "SHHHH!" he hissed out between clenched teeth.

From behind Anesh's hand, James spoke in a muffled voice. "If you wanted some candy, you just had to ask." Though it came out more as "Eef oo annnted aandy, oo ust aad oo ask."

At this point, James had an equal amount of confusion to match Anesh's panic. From his perspective, his friend had either heard or noticed something and snapped a hand over his mouth with no warning. It took his brain a second to catch up to the fact that he probably shouldn't actually be talking, but really, what did Anesh expect, trying to silence a known wiseass? In the history of James's life, he couldn't really think of a time when someone telling him to be quiet had ever actually worked.

Meanwhile, that one tiny blue orb had just let Anesh see the future. He was still trying to figure out the relative strength variances in each individual orb; for the blue ones, they only had two examples right now, but he felt like there was a *slight* difference between the one that took a trip four blocks to the bank on behalf of James and the one that let him rewind fucking time.

Well. He didn't have time to dwell on how that worked right now. But he also didn't really have time for James to sass him when he was trying to save their lives. "We need a hole in that wall, now," he whispered. "As quietly as possible and *yes I know that's difficult just do it.*"

James nodded, trusting his friend. He pocketed the cash from the purse he was rifling through and grabbed up his axe. While Anesh called back Ganesh, they both moved over to the back wall and were about to start cutting. Just then, both of them heard a soft shuffling from outside the door to the cubicle they were in.

"Okay, no time," Anesh said. "We're gonna have to climb over." He pointed up at the top of the wall.

James looked up. The cube wall here was well above head height, and a foot or so beyond that, several strips of the material curved inward, forming a staggered set of ceiling lines, maybe five to ten feet above their heads. "You are joking. I can barely climb *stairs*, even with all the gym time the last couple months. How the hell am I supposed to pull myself up there?"

Anesh ignored him, climbing onto the desk and trying to do exactly what James was complaining about and pull himself up. A cup of pencils went scattering onto the floor; a rack of neatly and randomly arranged folders and documents joined them a second later, victims to Anesh's scrambling feet as he tried to drag himself upward.

"Dude, neither of us has the upper-body strength for that, especially not with how beat up we are," James commented dryly, standing passively in the middle of the cubicle, watching his friend. "Do you wanna tell me what's got you spooked?"

"Saw the future in a blue orb," Anesh gasped out as he let himself drop back down. "There's a copy machine outside and an ambush waiting for us when we run."

James nodded. "Okay. So, first off, I'm upset that you used a blue without asking first." He wasn't really upset, but he also didn't want to encourage either of them to sneak orbs. "Second of all, I believe you, but calm down. I know that telling people to calm down never works, but, like . . . calm down."

A memory flashed through his head of all the times his mom had angrily told him that he was too upset and needed to relax or calm down. Much like being told to be quiet, having someone else tell you that you needed to be less angry was, in James's opinion, the worst possible way to actually make someone less angry. Though it was a fun trick to use on his younger coworkers when he wanted to get a rise out of them.

"And C, why don't we just kill the copier? How bad could it be? Wait, does it have tentacles?"

Anesh took a couple deep breaths before realizing he wasn't actually going to be able to clamber over this wall. "I . . . hadn't thought of that. Okay. Okay, let's . . . figure this out." A stray thought struck him. "Why is it you're always commenting on or asking if things here have tentacles? Is this a secret fetish I shouldn't probe too much into?"

"Nope!" He looked away from Anesh and muttered, "I'm not *that* into tentacles."

Anesh chuckled. "Heard that." He knew what James was doing. It was how his friend defused situations: get a laugh from someone, and you were halfway to getting them to stop being angry, stop being panicked, start acting more like a sane person and make a reasonable choice. He was mildly annoyed that this tactic was working on him after he'd previously seen it work on other people in their friend group or even just random strangers. But he was also glad that James was, even if just by accident, clever enough to help him manage the fear that his vision of the future had sparked off.

James smiled as Anesh got himself back together, but that faded a bit as he heard another shuffling noise from outside. "So what is that thing? How do we do this?"

He listened as Anesh outlined what he'd seen. Their attempt to run, finding the signpost, getting ambushed, the copier pinning them in with its army of James's hands.

"I'm not a fan of that at all," James said.

When he asked, though, Anesh didn't have any information on the machine itself. "It spit ink at us, that's how it blinded you and scanned your hands," he said. "Aside from that, I don't know. It can clearly move, but I didn't see how. It probably has some other way to drag us in to make copies. It didn't start churning out anything until after it got you."

"Okay, well, that's not a problem," James replied. "We've got a hammer, right?"

"I lost the hammer somewhere."

"Okay, okay, that's still fine. We can . . . probably still break it? I mean, is the plan of 'just hit it a lot' somehow not a good one?" he asked. "Like, there are things that look like staplers, but they're clearly not actually staplers once we start hitting them, right? Like it's some kind of chitin."

Anesh took a deep breath. "Yeah, okay. Want to give that a shot? I mean, we have nothing to lose but our lives."

"You know we can just go the other way, right?" James asked. "Like, we don't have to walk into the ambush now. We can just . . . go left instead of right and circle back on our circling back."

There was a long pause. Anesh had, in fact, not thought of that. Seeing his own death coming had shaken him quite a bit, and he didn't think that James really understood how hard it made it to think things through. "I . . . had not thought of that," he settled on saying. "Okay. Yeah. Let's break through, then." He let a little more energy creep into his voice.

They threw their packs back on and made sure all the orbs were secured in the side pouches. They did a quick check of their armor, making sure the straps were set and they weren't going to lose more pieces. As they were doing so, there was a buzzing as Ganesh flew back into the ceiling and crawled his way through to drop down and alight on Anesh's shoulder, his rightful place in the world. James took a couple practice swings with his axe as he and Anesh posted up on either side of the door.

"Ready?"

"Ready."

James reached out and pushed the curtain back a bit, peeking out. He slowly drew back, letting the paper fall back into place.

"Okay, I lied, I was not ready for that. It's right there. And it's got tentacles, because of course it fucking does," he whispered.

Anesh peeked out himself. "Yeah, those are tentacles. Looks like they're actually made of ink. What the hell does it make copies with, anyway? Like, where's it storing the material?"

James kept an eye on the machine as he answered. "We've been leveling up in random skills and pocketing extradimensional candy and this is the line where you start to question physics?" Anesh just shrugged by way of answer. "Heh. Okay. Well. I'm relaxed. My arms aren't that sore. No better time than now, right? I'll go first, after it shoots, you follow? Take the left, take it apart?"

"Aye, mon capitan," Anesh said. "Ganesh, wait in here. Don't come out until it's safe, okay?" The little drone whirred a reluctant assent.

The two of them shared a look for a few breaths. Both of them felt a tension in their muscles and in their chests. This was, to James, the moments that were really starting to resonate with him here. These silent pauses before risking his life, throwing himself into a situation where he would be tested and the stakes were literally as high as they could be. He grinned at Anesh, a real smile full of spirit.

He stepped out and ducked almost instantly.

A spray of ink splattered against the paper and wall behind him, and he lunged forward, moving to the right. The copier rotated to face him, and from down low, he could see that it looked like it was mounted on the base of a swivel office chair. That must be how it was getting around, he thought before there was no more time for thinking.

Rushing forward, he heard Anesh come through behind him, moving around behind the distracted foe. He brought his arms up in front of his face as one of the tendrils of congealed ink—and he could see now that there were eight of the things, all of them weaving out of the middle port of the copier—came crashing toward his face. The strike splattered ink across his arm guard, and the tentacle, much to his dismay, separated from the main body, the rest of the ink maintaining momentum and splashing across the side of his face.

He reopened his eyes after reflexively slamming them shut and saw more tentacles coming in. Throwing himself backward onto his ass, he slammed into the ground hard enough to bruise his tailbone and rolled to the side, flattening his body out as he covered the width of the hall and pressed himself up against the wall of the cubicle. As he rolled, behind him, lash after lash of ink struck out at the floor, leaving black splashes with the sound of sharp snaps. When he hit the wall, he prepared to fling himself back to his feet before he could get hit again, but as he started to jump up, the machine lost focus on him and the attacks stopped.

Anesh had pressed the advantage of a distracted enemy and struck at its other side. With only a couple of the tentacles focused on him, he'd shouldered his way through the first strike, letting the surprisingly forceful hit splatter across the side of his armor. Stepping through the spray of black ink, he spun forward, putting the full force of his body behind his axe and letting it smash into the power port on the rear side of the copier hard enough to bury the blade inside the plastic-and-chitin shell.

The reaction was almost instant. It let out a scream, like the sound of a document being scanned, only at a much higher pitch. The lid of the copier tilted open, exposing its glass pane radiating a brilliant white light.

James kept in a low crouch. He remembered what Anesh had said, and he didn't want that thing able to copy any part of him. As the machine started turning, whirling around on Anesh, he endured a trio of hits from it, stinging but not harming him. At least, until the third one clipped his helmet and sent him sprawling on his ass again. He scrambled up to his knees as the copier turned to face Anesh, intent on taking advantage of its lack of focus the same way Anesh had.

While James moved in, though, Anesh was having a problem. He was too close now, and with the disorientation of the light and noise, he was having trouble blocking or dodging anything. So James simply set about trying to shut off the problem at its source, bringing his arm up and cutting down with his axe repeatedly, leaving scratches and gouges on the lid and front, before the lid sprang up and knocked his hand, jarring the axe out of his grip and into the air.

Coming in behind it, James reached forward and grabbed one of the paper trays. At first, he was going to use it to drag himself up, but as soon as he touched the handle, it sprang out, splitting in half down the middle to reveal a distended maw filled with conical teeth and with a single red eye right in the middle. He let out a scream, which he would later explain to Anesh as a totally-not-fearful battle cry, and with a spike of adrenaline flooding his blood, he ripped the tray out in one smooth move, inky black ichor spraying and fleshy strands tearing as he tore it wholly from the main body and threw it backward away from him, the teeth leaving scores of torn skin down the back of his hand as it left his grip.

Anesh wasn't doing nearly as much damage, trying to clear his vision and find where his axe had fallen. He made a mistake at just the wrong moment, looking away from the still-weaving tentacles as one of them lashed in. James pulled himself up to see the ink wrapping around Anesh's head and, with a jerk, slamming him down into the flat surface of the copier, the lid hammering into his head once before James caught it on the upswing and dropped himself backward, snapping it off in a clean break.

The scanner fired off, white light bathing Anesh's face as it was held pinned down by the tentacles behind him. "James! Help!" he called out as his hands tried to find purchase on the tendrils. But every time he grabbed at one, his fingers just sank through the ink, clenching into a fist with no grip on anything.

Abruptly, the tendrils let go. Anesh scrambled backward, hand falling on his axe, which he brought up in a fast smash at the base of the machine. James, standing up on the other side, slammed his own axe down in a double-handed overhead strike, shattering the scanner glass into shards that the machine sprayed from side to side as it thrashed back and forth between them. Lashing out with a foot, Anesh kicked into the side of it, leaving a hairline crack in the plating and sending it rolling back into the far wall of the hallway.

James quickly reached down and lifted his friend to his feet. Bruised and dripping ink, breathing heavy, they faced off against the copier, which shuddered on its own against the wall. And then a whirring noise started from within it.

"Oh, hell no!" James spat out as he stepped forward, stomping on the small tray where copies should come out, bending the plastic down to the floor as he chopped in sideways with his weapon. Anesh moved to the other side and made repeated hits against it, even as his arms started to tire, but neither of them was able to stop the copier from opening the front panel and ejecting a mostly smooth copy of the right side of Anesh's face, expression locked in a snarl, onto the floor.

The copy was mostly smooth because of the dozens of tiny fangs that ran along the uncopied sides, which it used to pull itself upright and lunge forward at James's ankles. "James. Help," it flatly muttered as it tried to punch its fang-legs into his boot or find purchase with its actual teeth on his shin.

"Oh, *hell* no!" both James and Anesh chorused, James stomping down with a violent thud that shook his leg to the bone, pulping the copy of his friend's visage. He could already see another one being run off by the copier, the whirring never stopping. "Anesh! Tear it open!" he shouted.

Anesh didn't think twice, jamming his axe into one of the cuts on the side and using the blade to pry open the side. His arms strained, muscles screaming in protest, while the copier was more literally screaming in protest as he wedged back a large chunk of its exterior. And what he saw inside looked like what would happen if the director of *Hellraiser* had spent a lot more time at steampunk conventions as a kid. Hundreds of turning gears, dozens of tiny mechanical arms, all of them plucking pieces of skin, flesh, bone, and tooth from seemingly nowhere. Assembling with precision, layer by layer, the skin of his own face. One unblinking eye, swiveling madly in a bone socket uncovered by anything yet, turning to look at him. Deeper inside the machine, he could see another station just like this one. And another. And another. A dozen or so flesh manufactories, more than could possibly fit inside this space, all of them building replicas of himself.

And in the middle of it all, he saw, as he heard James getting slapped into a wall on the other side of the machine, a single glowing orange orb. Like the skill orbs they'd found before, it was like a perfectly smooth bath bead, supple and glowing. It was hooked into a black plastic claw, holding it above the whole production line.

Anesh tore back more of the covering, even as he saw another pair of half faces being run out the production slot and heard James turning one of them into flesh pulp. He snapped off a chunk of plastic, punching a few times to bend another panel of chitin out of place, and then, when the hole was just wide enough, he lunged forward into the guts of the machine.

His shoulders got half stuck on the outer shell, but he was able to twist and wedge one of them a little farther in. His hand reached forward, even as some of the mechanical arms moved with their knives and pins to stop him. He pushed in, inch by inch, slapped away an assembler, and brought his fingers up just far enough to brush the outside of the orb.

"Anesh! Hurry!" he heard from outside, even as he saw below him a row of a dozen iterations of his own face being shoved out the slot. He tried to move but couldn't. Stuck. Twisting a bit, he felt plastic gouge into his side, and he ignored the pain just long enough to push a bit farther. Just one more inch. Just a little bit more.

And then the orb was in his hand. And he ripped it backward, out of its mount, and pulled himself out of the machine. There was a stabbing in his side where the sharp plastic caught under the armor and left a bloody hole in his flesh, and his helmet caught on the exit wound of the copier, almost pinning him in place before he stopped himself from thrashing in panic and carefully dragged his head out.

Behind him, the insides folded in on themselves. Over and over, the extra copy stations no longer had the space to exist and smashed on top of their cohorts. Space that had previously been there suddenly was not, and edges sheared away as reality compressed inward. Anesh had a plummeting feeling in his stomach, like gravity suddenly pointed inward instead of down, and there was a blink of himself, bisected as the part he was in suddenly was not anymore.

Then he was out, and his body was intact.

James took the last of Anesh's face copies out of the air with his axe when the machine lunged at him. The thing had stopped pumping out duplicates a minute ago, and he assumed Anesh had something to do with it, but he was busy on crowd control. It wasn't until everything was cleared that he really registered the noise he was hearing. It was like the audio version of dust in your eyes. A grinding that didn't make any real sound but burned the ears and stretched what he felt was real.

He gave the copier, now immobile, another couple of good hits to its front face, just to be sure, burying his hand axe in the console, before Anesh crawled up and said, "All right, all right! It's dead, Jim!"

And it was. The thing had gone silent, and it looked . . . smaller. "What happened?" he asked Anesh.

"No idea. Some kinda space fold inside. It . . . um . . . broke when I pulled this out." He held up the orange orb in his gloved hand. "I call dibs on this one later," he said as he pushed it into the pouch on James's pack where they'd stored the other orbs.

James just nodded. "Yeah, fair. You ready to get out of here?"

"Hell yes. Ganesh! Come on!" he called, and the drone flew out of the cubicle where Anesh had told it to hide. It did a hard landing on

Anesh's helmet and started affectionately tapping on the piece of armor as it slid down the side onto his shoulder. "Yeah, I'm glad I didn't die too," Anesh muttered to it. "Now let's go."

"One sec," James said. A large, fist-sized green orb floated over the copier's corpse. "Double loot on this one?" he asked apprehensively.

Anesh just shrugged. "Take the bonus and let's get out of here."

James struck out down the hall, pocketing the new orb and retracing their steps on the way here. It took them some time to cram themselves back through the cramped tunnel, especially since they froze after James had to kill a stapler-crab. They stayed still for a few minutes, praying that nothing new was attracted, but fortunately, the noise didn't draw anything new.

"What's our time?" James asked as they pulled themselves out the other end.

Anesh checked his phone. "A bit over four and a half hours. We've been doing a lot of walking, and you were unconscious for a bit there. Should be about an hour's hike back. Not a whole lot of margin for error, but we can make it."

James just nodded. He wasn't worried. They could always make a mad dash if they needed to. His legs ached, but they weren't going to give out just yet. His throat was a bit raw from all the heavy breathing and running they'd been doing so far, but again, he could take more.

Hell, he could take anything if it meant survival. Especially when they had a new orb to look forward to.

James would go through a lot for a new toy like that.

Onward they pressed, and it didn't take long to double back across one of their signposts. "Okay, we're mostly clear from here, right?" Anesh asked.

James just shook his head. "We don't know where the tumblefeeds roam yet. That thing could come back this way at any time. Let's get a little farther, at least past the first break room, and then we can take a break."

"Oh, I'm fine with that," Anesh said as he poked Ganesh, sending him forward to check a corner. "I just want to take some time and pick up at least a few hundred bucks."

James nodded as the drone buzzed out and back. "Right, right. Thinking of any new gear?"

"What?" Anesh shook his head. "No, I'm thinking that I want to be able to afford food this month. I'm a mostly broke college guy living off student aid in America with working-class parents; there's a natural limit to how much I will ignore the fact that we can pay our bills using this place."

"Ah. Right. Fair," James muttered, feeling a bit awkward.

They moved on, with James keeping watch every few cubicles while Anesh quickly dipped in to rifle through wallets and purses. They were moving slowly, taking a lot of time to check corners and listen for motion but still making pretty decent time since they weren't doing deep searches of every potential loot box they came across.

In short order, they came across the break room, still cleared from their trip in: coffee puddles still steaming on the floor, a pile of shattered pottery and dirt over in the corner. James wanted nothing more than to cut straight through here and get out, but Anesh stopped him. "Hang on, I want to see if there's anything in the fridge."

"No. Hell no. Absolutely not," James said. "I will allow you to go through the cupboards. I will help you jam as many sugar packets into your bag as you want. I will even carry one of these alarmingly unmotivational posters back so we can put it in our living room. But today, I draw the line at opening the fridge."

There was a silent moment before Anesh sighed. "Yes, okay, good point. Can I take the coffee maker?"

James looked over at the fancy-looking coffee maker sitting on the counter. He eyed it for a minute, considering the options. He made a show of glancing around at the rubble of the room, the dead potted plant that had tried to murder him twice now, and then back at the coffee maker. "Okay, but you get that there's a fifty percent chance it's going to try to kill you, right?"

The duo stood there in front of it, looking at it for a while. "Okay," Anesh said, "we've seen vending machines and water coolers that haven't been overtly evil, right?"

"Right." James nodded.

"And everything that's tried to kill us has been normal office stuff," he continued.

James rubbed his chin. "Also correct, yes. So you're saying this should be safe since it's a food thing?"

Anesh snapped his fingers. "Exactly! I'm taking it!" He reached down to start unplugging the device.

"You're carrying that, for one," James said. "Because it looks like it weighs about forty pounds. This may not be your best idea. But more importantly, if any part of that thing, or the stuff it dispenses, comes to life? It's going to be your job to explain coffee elementals to people, okay?"

"Deal," Anesh said without hesitation.

It took about five minutes for Anesh to unplug the thing and figure out how to get a good grip on it. While he was doing so, James kept checking the far door, looking down the hall for any sign of the tumblefeed coming after them. He nearly jumped out of his skin when he heard cords hitting the counter behind him, and he turned to glare at Anesh, who hadn't even noticed the noise while he was busy unhooking the coffee maker's water tube. "Don't *do* that." He shot an angry whisper at his friend.

"Do what?" Anesh asked, hoisting the heavy brick of a machine up against his chest.

James just shook his head. "Never mind. Let's just move, okay? No more looting for today."

They weren't that far out now, and James was getting itchy to leave. The weight of his gear was really starting to pull on his back, even though it had lightened a bit as a few things got lost along the way. His feet dragged as he put in the effort to keep ahead of Anesh, who was now also struggling visibly under the burden he'd stupidly decided to carry.

He tried to hold his breath as they passed by the still-smoldering remains of the dead tumblefeed. The stench of melting plastic burned the back of his throat as he coughed out a breath. One of the still-melted cables stuck to his boot in a gooey mess as he stepped in it.

They went on through a few more turns, cubicles around them becoming shorter, more real. Paper vines gave way to plain walls, with only a few nameplates, pinned-up memos, or clipped-out newspaper comics adorning the exteriors. Anesh stopped them to take a brief break for his exhausted arms, and while he did a few stretches and tried to get ready for the final stretch, James ducked into the nearest cubicle and started grabbing anything that looked good, just filling up the last bit of space in his bag with something that might prove useful.

After a few deep breaths from each of them, and James laughing softly at Anesh's muttered "This is heavier than I wanted it to be," they were as ready as they were going to be.

"Come on, man. Just another block or so and we're at the door. We can go get a burger and go home," he said. "Or, you know, to a hospital!" He held up his hands placatingly as Anesh turned a glare on him that could melt steel.

His friend wasn't actually mad, just worried. "Your leg got sodding lasered. We're getting you to an ER. You, I know, have insurance, so it's not a problem."

"Oh right," James said as they pushed through the final hall of cubicles. "You still have that bill for your hand, right? I'm fine giving up my half of the cash if it helps."

"I'd appreciate that. I am, as mentioned, broke. Poor. Destitute. Bankrupt. Impoverished."

"One of those doesn't mean what you think it means, but I'm not sure which one," James said with a smile. "And oh joyous day, there's the door."

They made their way through the door to their little fort in near silence. Well, silent except for Anesh swearing and moaning as the coffee maker kept hitting him at an awkward angle.

"Okay!" James said. "You sit, because you're gonna have to carry that to the car. I'm gonna put all the loot into the duffels to take out.

I think we can safely leave the rest here. Our armor and medical stuff didn't animate last time. Not really sure why Ganesh did at all, honestly." As he plopped the bags onto the desk and started transferring everything that wasn't equipment, a familiar stapler crawled its way up. "Oh hey there, Rufus! Were you good while we were gone? What a good little chap!" He looked over at Anesh, who was draped over a chair, head rolled back to stare at the ceiling, "I can say 'chap,' right? That's not an English thing?"

"It *is* an English thing, but since you're stealing our language, you may as well do it properly," Anesh responded.

James chuckled as he threw orbs, money, candy, and all the miscellaneous stuff he and Anesh had grabbed to experiment with into their traveling bags. He didn't have an actual count of anything, but the pile of stuff glittered in his eyes like a dragon's hoard.

"All right. Time to go," he said. "See you next week, Rufus. Anesh, you ready to grab that thing and go?"

Anesh groaned as he stood up. "Bah. Fine." He moved to take the coffee maker.

"Don't complain to me, man, you're the one who wanted coffee that badly." James rolled his eyes at his friend's griping.

"I know, a decision I regret to this day," Anesh said flatly. "Ganesh, you want to stay here or come with us?"

"Now hang on . . ." James started to say. But he didn't need to think too much about that. Ganesh gave his human's helmet a friendly tap, then folded back into flight position and buzzed down to the desk to roll-land next to Rufus. The two of them started exchanging clicks like old friends. "Are they talking?" James asked the air.

Anesh just hefted the coffee maker after leaving his helmet and armor on the chair. "We can worry about that next time, after some food and sleep. Let's go," he said.

And then they were through the door, James giving one last wave to his first friend from the other side.

They were sitting in a twenty-four-hour diner near their apartment. On the table in front of them was a small black dice bag that James had emptied out to hold skill orbs.

"Okay, you get the orange, I get one green. What do you say we just evenly split the yellows? We can save the blues, and *clearly should*, for times when we need them."

"I'm okay with that," Anesh said, already halfway through the burger James had ordered him, as promised.

James rolled the emerald sphere around in his fingers. "Do you wonder what these things actually are?" he asked. "Like, why do they do what they do?"

"Of course I wonder," Anesh responded. "But if there's any answers, they're inside, right? No amount of thinking out here is going to help."

"Fair, I guess," James said, sipping at his milkshake. Four a.m. milkshakes after life-or-death situations, he decided, were probably just the best food. "But you said Ganesh ate one. Does that mean that everything in there is using these as, what, food? Where does Rufus keep getting them?"

Anesh thought for a second. "Maybe the small ones produce them, and the larger ones eat them and refine them into the bigger and different orbs? Like an ecosystem?"

James shook his head. "What do the little ones eat?"

"Well, nothing. I mean, it's 'like' an ecosystem, but still magic and bollocks," Anesh said.

There was a pair of *hmms* from their table. They ate a few bites in silence as they collected their thoughts.

"Have you noticed that the skills aren't really random?" Anesh broke the quiet from around a mouthful of fries. "I mean," he said as James gave him a disbelieving look, "they seem random. They're not, though. They're all normal things, all things from reality, even though the office space isn't. And they're all things that someone from an office would know."

"I have four ranks in field artillery," James retorted.

Anesh snorted out laughter. "Okay, yes, but you told me a while back that a couple of your coworkers were gone because of National Guard training, right?"

"Yeah, um ... they were both Nathans. There's a surprising number of Nathans at my work. They both quit, though, I think. Or were there three of them? Haven't seen them in a while, anyway. So you think as long as someone there knew it, it can show up?"

Anesh shrugged. "I mean, it's the only thing we can say hasn't been contradicted yet, right?"

"Fair." James shrugged as well. "What about the other colors?"

"Oh, fuck that, I have no theories. But at least we know where they're from. Green for big things, blue for 'magic' items. Orange for ... Okay, green for big things, blue for magic items. We'll worry about orange later."

"Speaking of which," James said, finishing off his sandwich, "want to use what we have?"

"Yes, please," Anesh replied. "Big ones first?"

James wordlessly pulled out one of the shining green balls and snapped it apart in his fingers.

[Local Area Shift : Hours of operation +1]

[+4 Skill Ranks : Chemistry - LSD Production]

"I have two questions," James said. "First of all, who the hell in my office was a drug lord?"

"What—" Anesh started to ask.

"LSD production. Also, I'm glad we did this out of the apartment, because the other effect was an extra hour of operation."

Anesh looked around at the twenty-four-hour diner. "This place is open twenty-four hours a day—?" He made the statement into a confused question.

"Yeah, I don't really ... know. I think that might be a serious problem, even if it's only for their payroll department."

"Huh." Anesh shook his head in confused amusement as he pulled out the orange orb. "All right, ready?"

"Go for it," James said and watched as his friend did so.

The thoughts that poured through Anesh's mind were like music to him. He could feel the exact strings they were rearranging, because it was something he was intimately familiar with, and he could feel himself gaining a depth of wisdom that was previously unknown to him. Then he realized what the first words said.

[Certification Added : Class-C Driver's License]

[+3.8 Skill Ranks : Math - Differential Geometry]

Silently, he pulled out his wallet and opened it up. Giving a surprised laugh that was a little louder than intended, he pulled out a driver's license that hadn't been there a second ago and handed it to James.

"So I can drive a truck now? Also, I got a fractional skill point. It was in something that I already know, though. So I think it bumped me up to the next 'rank'? Maybe? I don't know, but I do know I can go write my thesis now. Oh god, I can just . . . I can . . ." Anesh put his hands on his head as he lost his words. "This is exactly what I needed. This is perfect."

"Man, I hope the rest of these get me a reaction like that," James said, trying to break the awkwardness of seeing his friend almost crying. "Um . . . do you want to just . . ."

Anesh took a shaky breath. "Yeah, yeah! Go for it. You pick first. I just . . . you know, thank you. Thank you so much for trusting me on this, and bringing me in. I know I've been a wanker about it sometimes, but . . . thanks."

"Of course, man. You don't need to thank me, you've saved my stupid ass enough to make up for it, right?"

"Oh god, right. You'd be dead if not for me." Anesh laughed. "Okay, you owe me then. I take back the thanks."

James laughed as he pulled out orbs from the bag. "What? Too late for that, buddy. We're stuck with this nonsense now."

[+1 Skill Rank : Cooking]

[+1 Skill Rank : Programming - C++]

[+1 Skill Rank : Game Design - Rule Sets]

[+1 Skill Rank : Geography - Holland]

[+1 Skill Rank : Language - Spanish - Northern Mexican]
[+2 Skill Ranks : History - Roads - America]
[+2 Skill Ranks : Animals - Teju]

"Do you...um...want to get a pet lizard?" he asked Anesh as his friend drew out his own set of orbs from across the table.

"Why, what stupid skill are you going to try to adapt your life to?" Anesh asked.

James put on an exaggerated offended look. "It's not stupid! I will have you know that tejus are very smart creatures that have dog-level intelligence and are quality companions!"

"What the fuck is a teju?" Anesh paused, confused.

James laughed. "You know that picture of a lizard in a sweater? The one the size of a dog? It's that thing."

Anesh was laughing as he popped his own skill orbs.

[+1 Skill Rank : Yodeling]
[+1 Skill Rank : Anthropology - South America]
[+1 Skill Rank : Ventriloquism]
[+1 Skill Rank : History - Metallurgy]
[+1 Skill Rank : Seduction]
[+2 Skill Ranks : Ritual - Catholicism]
[+2 Skill Ranks : Longbow]

"Hey, um . . ." He looked over to James, who was updating their notebook of learned skills. "Do you . . . want to trade? I changed my mind. I want the lizard thing now."

They were both still laughing together when the check came.

CHAPTER 17

James stood in the middle of a massive room, polished tile floor beneath his feet. A circle around him illuminated him in brilliant white light, reflecting off the floor brightly enough to sting his eyes. Beyond the lit-up ring around him, there was only darkness, but he could feel the void stretching on, and on, and on . . .

He spun around, startled, and began running. The circle of light followed his steps, or perhaps he never actually made any progress at all. He ran, and ran, and ran, and eons passed by. James felt the time grinding by, months and then years and then centuries spent doing nothing more than fleeing. His heart pounded in his ears, raw terror screaming through him.

And then he stepped out of an office cubicle. Hard gray carpet under his feet. Around him, figures moved about their day, hollow shadow suits carrying too-real coffee cups and documents in multicolored folders. He froze up, trying to act normal, and started walking down the hallway. Around him, the people who weren't there greeted him by name, friendly, if a little tired.

James kept walking, the cubicles around him dripping and twisting in ways that hurt his skin to look at. As he walked past a water cooler, he saw a pair of the empty people drinking cups of water that never ran out, heads that weren't there drowning in water that wouldn't end.

To his right, down a side hall that went on for exactly two hundred twelve steps, each one of them curving upward until it was in the artificial clouds overhead, he saw a man being torn apart by computer cables. Unable to even shudder in revulsion, he moved on as the blood looped down the vertical spiral floor.

He passed more and more people dying. After the fourth or fifth one, he started to recognize them. He saw Anesh first, guillotined by a paper cutter. Then his boss, screaming, dragged back through a cubicle door by a hundred hissing staplers that walked on clawed human fingers.

His mother was swallowed by a tumblefeed. An old coworker harpooned by a dozen razor-tipped pencils to lie bleeding out under James's feet as he walked. His ex was ripped in half by a false copy of themselves that shone around the edges and sang while it moved.

And then he saw his younger sister hanging from the impossibly high ceiling by a phone cord; the handset for the phone itself lay against her chest. There were paper clips puncturing her skin where her dress didn't cover, and blood dripped into a pool beneath her. James could hear the phone ringing as he approached. His feet wouldn't stop, and soon he stood in that red circle on the floor.

The phone kept ringing. So he reached out and picked up.

A semimechanical woman's voice spoke through the old black plastic earpiece. "Hello. This is a courtesy reminder that *you need to come back.*" The voice cut midway through to a harsh grinding noise that slammed into James's ears.

The message pulsed in his head. The lights surged, then died abruptly, screaming. A thousand things that would never look like eyes, but would also never blink or stop staring, glared down at him. The walls, now unseen, receded into the distance. He felt them being pushed farther and farther away, dragged away by an unseen force. Whispered voices came through the phone, which had shattered in his hand and now hung around his head. *you need to come back james there are people waiting for you james . . .*

James looked down. He stood in a circle of bright white light, on a polished tile floor . . .

Some time later, James woke up screaming.

Anesh stumbled out of bed around one p.m. He hadn't slept well at all, and as the cobwebs cleared out of his head, he remembered vague fragments of fear and whispers from a dream. He tumbled himself onto his floor and lay there in a sleepy daze for a few beats before dragging himself up onto his desk chair. Throwing on his bathrobe, Anesh was careful not to scatter any of the stuff spread across the surface of his desk.

He'd pushed his computer monitor back out of its normal position and cleared pretty much everything else off. A pile of opened mail, some pens, a pair of legal pads, birthday cards, a fancy copper bowl he threw coins into, and keys, all sitting in a small cardboard box off to the side of his desk on the floor. This effort had nothing to do with being organized; Anesh wasn't an excessively organized person at all, though he did try not to let his room get too bad. No, in this case, he just needed to make sure that what he was working with didn't get mixed up with his own normal stuff.

Laid out across his desk were about fifty different pens and pencils, all of them carefully tagged. An annoyingly undamaged magazine about horses on the corner topped off a pile of manila envelopes and tan folders. Five wallets lined up on the opposite side of his desk created the impression of a contained but busy workspace.

Anesh was testing. He'd spent last night going through each of these, looking for any kind of magical properties. All of them had come from deeper inside the dungeon, so he'd figured at least one of them would have something going on. Thinking back, he remembered sitting in the corner cubicle while James bandaged himself, snapping pens in half just to harvest the orbs and getting a fairly high success ratio.

So it annoyed him that none of these seemed to do anything. Or, at least, nothing he could figure out or recognize.

He had some theories. Maybe the items had to be special in some way. Maybe he needed to pay attention to what random stuff their eyes seemed drawn to next time? So far, they hadn't encountered any kind of treasure chests or actual physical loot drops beyond the orbs. He didn't know exactly how the dungeon decided what was going to be enchanted, or even what the purpose behind it was, but it felt like something that was important.

Right now, though, he felt like getting to his computer was important. But that wasn't going to happen until he was awake enough to pack this stuff up properly. He sighed, which turned into a rough cough as his breath caught in his dry throat.

Heading out to the kitchen for something to drink before starting his task of sweeping everything on his desk into a bin, he heard an alarming sound from down the hallway of the apartment.

"No, no! Get down!" James's voice was coming from their kitchen and living room area, and it sounded annoyed. "Dammit, my shirt!" Anesh took a moment to decide whether it was worth it to go quench his thirst or if it would be better for his sanity to just go back into his room.

Unfortunately, curiosity got the better of him. Plodding out into the living room, he prepared himself for a worst-case scenario of disaster in their kitchen again.

He did not come close to preparing enough.

"James," he croaked out, before clearing his throat and finding his voice. "James. Friend. Brother in arms. My *favorite* raid member."

"Anesh!" James said, jumping a bit as his roommate started talking. The broom in his hands, which he was using to sweep at the ceiling, clattered to the floor as he dropped it. "How're you! Good morning! Nothing to worry about here, just making some breakfast! Hi!" He rattled off words at a rapid pace, slightly out of breath.

"James," Anesh repeated. "Why, James?" He swept his hand in a gesture that encompassed . . . everything.

The kitchen was actually more or less fine. James in fact was making breakfast, and as the smell of pancakes and bacon caught up to Anesh's nose, he started salivating. And unlike last time, there wasn't flour sprayed across the floor, batter burning on the stove, or an extra half dozen mixing bowls piled up on every surface.

There was batter on the floor, though. And on James. In fact, the batter was still dripping down on him from the ceiling. From that same battered point on the ceiling, soft jazz music was playing. Anesh just stared at the lump of raw pancake that was defying gravity for a second, before feeling his skin crawl as it started to move.

"James! Is that the fucking iLipede? You brought it home?" He crawled back over the arm of their couch, hunkering down and keeping it as an impromptu barrier between himself and the bug. It might be twenty feet away and on the ceiling, but Anesh couldn't take any chances.

James picked up the broom again and this time actually got the iLipede to crawl onto the head of it. He carefully swung it back around and picked up the little creature. "Yeah, I know you had some hesitation on letting Ganesh out, so I'm sorry I didn't ask you on this one. But I wanted to see how she identified the orb, and also if it has a music app." He set the iLipede back on the counter and started wiping it down with a towel.

"You brought a bug into our house, James; this isn't okay," Anesh growled out, now setting up pillows to make himself a small couch fort.

His roommate looked over at him. "Okay, tell you what. You can test the skill orb, since I didn't use it yet, and I will give you breakfast, and in exchange, *you* get to test the coffee maker that is currently occupying a third of our counter space up here, and also not give me shit about Lily for at least the rest of the week, until we can return them."

"Lily?"

"I named her Lily. She's a good little smartphone," James stated proudly, pouring pancake batter into the pan on the stove.

Anesh let out a groan. "You need to stop naming these things. They're not *pets*."

The only response he got was laughter, and then James said, "You're the one who took your interest in drones to a new level. Oh, hey, are you ever gonna show Ganesh to Neil? He'd probably love it."

Anesh and James both went silent for a second. "Um . . ." Anesh started, while James just let out a quiet "I mean . . ." And then they lapsed back into uncomfortable stillness. Both of them were feeling a twisting pressure in their hearts, something that told them this was a bad idea.

"Did you have a dream last night?" James asked suddenly, and Anesh snapped his head up.

"Yeah," he said. "I was... running, I think? And I took a phone call, and someone told me that..."

"You needed to come back?" James finished, and Anesh nodded. "Yeah, I think I had the same thing. I'm... supremely uncomfortable with the idea that the dungeon gets to control my emotions." James flipped a couple pancakes over in the pan, catching them more or less neatly. "I feel like I want to tell Alanna and JP just out of spite now. Hell, I'll tell *Dave* if I get the chance. Like, giving me bad dreams and mind control is not a good way to get me on your side."

Anesh laughed. "No kidding. I've seen how you play RPGs." The tension faded a bit, though it didn't fully recede. There was a lingering feeling in the air, and the jazz from the iLipede wasn't enough to make the lights feel bright enough right now on this cold cloudy day. "Hey, why was... ugh... Lily on the ceiling anyway?"

"Oh!" James chuckled. "She hijacked my phone charger! I don't know if these things need power to operate, but she got kind of hyper after that. That's also when I learned about the jazz. She does have a music app, but only for jazz. I think. It might not be an app; iLipedes might just be able to hum saxophone." He fired up the fancy coffee maker that Anesh had helped him lug out of his car when they'd gotten back last night. A hiss of steam and the sound of burbling liquid filled the apartment for a moment, and Anesh sank into the pillows of the couch. He felt at home here, even with the looming bad dreams.

It was weird to have James cooking and not burning anything to the ground or swearing. It was weird to have soft music floating through the air. But it wasn't unpleasant at all. And when his friend dropped a plate of pancakes and bacon with what looked like homemade blueberry syrup in front of him, he got a feeling in his chest of quiet peace. Like the moment could just stretch out forever.

Then James handed him a mug of liquid with an expectant, raised-eyebrow look. "Eh? Eh? You carried that thing through a thousand feet of hostile territory and then down three flights of stairs and then back *up* a flight of stairs, it's only fair you get the first one. You earned it, my friend."

Anesh snagged the cup out of James's hand and glared at him. "Don't mock my coffee. I already checked its insides after you went to bed; it's not poison. It's just a normal coffee maker."

"Could be magic poison," James grumbled as Anesh sipped the drink. "Anyway," he said, "I also promised you this thing." He held up a small yellow orb.

Nodding, Anesh reached for it, but James pulled it back. "Oh, come on," he muttered into his mug.

"I wanna tell you what Lily said about it first, you might be interested." Anesh was interested, yes. Unconditional information about the dungeon was a priceless commodity to him right now. Of course, he also wanted James to stop being such a wanker, at least within a few hours of when Anesh woke up. James rambled on, though, unconcerned. "I wrote it down here somewhere. Ah, here. 'Power unit type : Memory. Operational time : 622 hrs/1k. Contains traces of : Dramatic, Violent.'"

"What the hell?" Anesh asked as he pulled the paper that James was holding over. He read it a few times, frowning. "Power unit. Well, I get the 'memory' bit, it's clearly referring to the skill part of it. Contains traces of, probably refers to the skill inside. But what the hell is operational time?"

James bit his lip. "Good goddamned question. Feels like Lily's referring to these as batteries. And you said Ganesh ate one, yeah? What if that's all they are? Power sources?"

"Could be, probably." Anesh shrugged. "Could also be that it's got a shelf life. Or that 'hrs/1k' doesn't even refer to 'hours' or . . . '1k,' I guess. Fuckin' hell. This feels like an escape room puzzle where I picked up the clues in the wrong order. My head hurts." He took a long drink of his coffee. "Can I try the orb out?"

"What, this orb?" James said, grinning as he held it out across the table from his friend, taunting him. "Why, I suppose you—"

He got cut off suddenly as Anesh's arm blurred out and snapped it from between his fingers. The motion was so fast that James felt a breeze from it. He couldn't even blink before Anesh had the orb in his hand and popped it.

[+1 Skill Rank : Performance - Acting - Shakespeare]

"Ah! It was stage acting!" Anesh remarked as he cut into his pancakes. James just sat across the table from him, mouth hanging open, hand still up in the air. Empty. "That explains the drama and violence. Shakespeare. Heh." He shook his head.

James took a minute to breathe deeply, tapping the table. "Um . . . did you notice anything weird there, Anesh?"

"No, why?" Anesh responded from around a mouthful of pancakes.

There was, James decided, an easy way to test this. He grabbed a couple of d6s that were sitting on their living room table within arm's reach. "Here, think fast," he said, and snapped both of them at Anesh's head.

Anesh didn't duck the impromptu projectile attack. Nor did he knock it aside. One second, he was holding a fork eating breakfast, the next, he was simply holding the dice between his first three fingers on his left hand. James hadn't even seen him move, just barely registering that an action had taken place at all.

"Oh," Anesh said. "Oh!" He grabbed his coffee mug and looked into it, then tipped it toward James and pointed into the empty cup. "*Oh!*" he yelled out, joyously.

This was quite possibly the worst thing that could have happened, from James's perspective. Because now, for the rest of eternity, he was going to have to deal with Anesh reminding him that he had, one time, looted a magical coffee machine that gave stat buffs, and James was going to have to sit there and explain that while that was cool, maybe *this* time they should hurry the hell up. And Anesh was going to ignore him. Forever.

Well, he thought as Anesh practiced juggling increasing numbers of dice with a single furiously blurring hand, *at least we've got a magic coffee machine.*

CHAPTER 18

It was Friday. Which, to Anesh, meant that it was his Friday, while to James, it was merely Thursday. He jogged up the stairs to their shared home, relieved to be done with classes for the week. The commute into the city to actually get to his college was exhausting, especially since he adamantly refused to drive into that web of furious drivers and one-way streets. Public transit was just easier, even if it required more walking. Classes, too, were exhausting. Though this last week, at least one 400-level math class was almost *too* easy.

The boost from that one skill orb was worth everything. The broken hand, which he still didn't blame James for. The dozen cuts and scrapes and bruises. The lingering stinging soreness in his legs from all the running without proper stretching. The stupid fucking bug phone that James had brought home and that still creeped Anesh out. All of it was worth it, and he'd forgive his friend for anything for giving him the chance to bootstrap his knowledge forward a year or two.

"Oh hey, Anesh, you're home!" James greeted him as he came through the door.

"James, *why*. We talked about this!" The first thing out of Anesh's mouth was a statement of frustrated disbelief. His admiring musings were snapped in half when he saw what his roommate was doing.

Their living room, with its horseshoe of couches and armchairs focused around a big wooden dining table, was currently occupied by James. James, two cups of coffee, a laptop, Lily the iLipede, and a USB cable. The combination of those last three things had instantly caught Anesh's attention and was the focus of his ire.

James looked up, his eyes practically glowing with excitement. He spoke in a rapid pace, his tone excited and happy. "Okay, look, I know you said not to do this, but I disconnected the laptop from the internet and pulled the network card, so it should be fine. I've been trying to copy apps off Lily so I can maybe start making non-sentient scanners for things, because it'd be super cool to have a phone that isn't alive but can tell me how many cows went into the burger I'm eating. Also I've been testing out the coffee today, and a lot of it or at least a few drinks don't do anything, but I found one that I think makes us make logical deductions, or maybe that's just what caffeine does. And I wanted to see if it would still work if it sat for a while, because we would want to take thermoses of it into the dungeon and not take the entire coffee maker back, and it totally does! The only thing is that you have to drink kind of a bunch of it for it to work like several cups or something, and only one drink works at a time. Like, any drink. If you drink water, it cancels out the buff. I don't know why, but we can work around it. How was class?" He broke off suddenly with the question, staring wide-eyed at Anesh, his breathless string of information at an end.

The response he got was, at first, just a silent, blank look. It took Anesh a second to audibly clear his throat and say, "Okay, first of all, breathe. Deep breath. There ya go." He reflexively sighed as he saw James inhale deeply, pinching the bridge of his nose as he did so. "So you plugged it in."

"Yup," James confirmed.

"And then you downloaded stuff off it, despite us explicitly talking about how that was a bad idea."

"Yup!"

Anesh dropped his school backpack onto one of the chairs. "You know what? Fine. Did it work?"

James threw his arms into the air with vivid enthusiasm. "No!" he said with a disturbing amount of excitement.

There was another long pause, with James grinning, barely able to stop himself from bouncing in his seat, and Anesh just silently judging him. "Sure. So why're you still here? Skipping work today?"

His friend deflated a bit as his defiance went unnoticed, some of the wind taken out of his sails. "Oh. There was something about training new people tomorrow morning, so I'm going in and staying late. We still planning on Tuesday?"

Anesh threw himself into the chair next to his bag. "I think so. I'm just going to take the weekend to relax and heal a bit. Are you sure your leg is okay? You were a lot more fucked up than I was."

James nodded, even though he didn't really mean it. His leg hurt like hell, but the burn gel he'd kept on it was helping the angry red patches heal up more or less okay. So far, it hadn't stopped him from also going to the gym every other night, a fact that he was hoping to keep from Anesh. He didn't want his friend thinking he was pushing himself too far and calling off their delve next week. "Yeah, I'll be fine. I think that, especially with the coffee as a buff, we can probably just take the day as a mass loot session. Sweep the outer area, amass some cash and maybe a few orbs."

"Are you sure there's no downside to the coffee?" Anesh asked probingly. He didn't fully believe that James had done rigorous testing on the liquid, especially not in just the time that he'd been at class.

The answer was, of course, ambiguous. "Well, I mean, I felt slower when it wore off. But of course I did, right? I wasn't moving at super speed anymore. I'm sure you got the same. But no other side effects. Anyway, I want to get the money for a couple bikes that we can take in. It seems like damage gets repaired, but not redecorating, right? So I wanna do that thing where we make a path through, so we can just skip to the deeper areas without worrying about a thousand twists and turns."

Anesh nodded. "Good plan, though how are we supposed to take bikes into your building and then not take them back out? We already got a weird look from your night security guy when we lugged the coffee machine out."

"Ah, but he didn't stop us!" James said, smiling and waving a finger in the air. "Because he doesn't care!" he concluded.

Fundamentally, James knew that the heart of his company was rooted firmly in the idea that employees should show up, half-ass their jobs, and go home vaguely unsatisfied with their lives. It helped keep costs down, or something like that, but it also meant that no one really cared to be there. Even the security staff always felt like they were suffering fools when they checked badges and did patrols. As if they were well aware of the fact that they didn't really need to do any of it, because there wasn't anything worth stealing in the first place.

So when he and Anesh had just strolled past Frank, the one guy on duty at the front desk at four a.m., the man had looked up, said good night, and given not a single fuck about the expensive coffee maker they were in the process of walking off with.

"I believe you," Anesh said. "Really, actually. Which sort of scares me, if I'm being honest. Your building needs better security protocols." James just started frantically shaking his head. If the building upgraded security, that was a bit of a problem for both of them. "Ah, right," Anesh said, his brain catching up. "Well, regardless of all that, can you please unplug the iLipede? I know you said it didn't work, but I don't want to accidentally proliferate any of the stuff from the dungeon out into reality, and this seems like one missed keystroke away from doing just that."

James sighed as he popped the USB cable out. "I don't get that, really. I mean, even if I did accidentally upload a torrent file of an arcane scanning app that didn't follow the laws of physics . . ." He looked down at the array on the table before glancing back at Anesh. "Okay, that sounds bad when I say it out loud. But even if that did happen, what's the worst-case scenario? Everyone gets an amusing app? The police can solve murders a hell of a lot better?"

"I don't know, James, that's sort of the point," Anesh answered in a strained voice. "We don't actually know what the purpose or function of these things is. I mean, come on, you're the nerd who introduced me to the SCP Foundation. I'd think you'd understand the importance of not spreading this around."

"The foundation is the bad guys, though."

"That's subjective. *Just like for the police.* But it doesn't really matter," Anesh said, smirking at their side banter. "We're two late-twenty-somethings with minimal resources. Even if, like you said, it made murder investigations easier, that's not really our responsibility. And if we can't prevent abuse of it, it comes across as pretty bloody irresponsible to try to improve the whole world."

James rolled off the couch, closing the laptop as he did so. "Stay here, Lily. Just gotta get ready for work," he said as he walked off to his room, leaving Anesh to stare at the iLipede on the table with suspicion. It wasn't tethered to the laptop now, and he constantly felt like it was eyeing him with its camera. James called back, "You remember how we wanted to try to get Alanna in on this?"

Keeping his eyes on the phone bug, Anesh responded, "Yeah, sure. She'd probably love this. Also, she owns weapons and works out more than either of us."

"Right." James came back out, pulling on the only polo shirt in his wardrobe. "But you do realize that if you make that argument at her, she's going to yell at us for a few hours about the utopia fallacy?"

Anesh looked like he was about to say something, then cut himself off. Words hung unsaid in the air. "Right," he finally said. "She's going to be pissed. Hm."

"Yeah, see?" James said as he laced up his boots. "You can talk about civic responsibility all you want, but as soon as she finds out, and she *will find out*, she's going to be furious with us for not trying to do more to help the world with this."

"It's not that exploitable on a large scale!" Anesh threw up his hands in the air. "I've checked! Also, why are you so sure she's going to find out?" he asked as James grabbed his coat and opened the door.

James just chuckled. "Because we're both garbage-ass at keeping secrets, and you know it. I'm off to work, I'll see you later. Take care of Lily!"

"No, wait!" And then the door closed behind him, and Anesh slowly turned, avoiding sudden movements, to see the iLipede on the table, staring at him. "Fuck . . ."

James wasn't sure if he'd arrived late or early, given his weird schedule for today. He wasn't super concerned about it, though. No matter what happened, he didn't think he could get in trouble today, what with how his floor manager was supposed to be training new people and not focusing on when he was or wasn't showing up.

He'd just clocked in and sat down at his desk, about to set up his headset and start taking calls—or pretending to take calls—when that same floor manager walked up to his cubicle. "James, please see me in my office," she said before turning and walking away.

Well, shit, he thought. So much for that theory.

He got up from the small fortress of office chairs he'd built to serve as a makeshift couch. One of the benefits of working nights when he was one of three people who hadn't quit was that he got to mess around with furniture pretty much at will. The reverse of that was that when his boss did show up, he looked unprofessional, and was also trapped by chairs.

After maneuvering out of his walls, he headed through the empty cubicle space toward her office. The call center was always pretty dead around this time of night, but with the number of people who'd quit lately, it was a ghost town. He saw exactly one person on his walk through the floor, and that was just a brief glimpse of their back as they turned a corner.

If he hadn't known better, he would have been able to mistake this place for a slightly-better-color-palette version of the dungeon.

He found it weird that he could be so nervous. He'd literally faced death multiple times a few days ago. But now, here he was, walking slowly to put off a meeting with his manager. But, sadly, this floor wasn't an infinite dungeon, and in short order he found himself at her office door. He knocked once, heard a summons from inside, and went in.

"James. Have a seat." She gestured to the lone uncomfortable chair on the door side of her desk.

Theo, well, Theodora, was a fairly unimposing figure as a manager. She wasn't the kind of person, as far as James knew, who wore power suits or kept her hair in a tight bun. Instead, her order of business was keeping her brown hair in a short pixie cut that would have looked unprofessional a couple decades ago, and the same style of button-up that pretty much every tech support person in the office wore. Though she was either exercising her manager powers to defy the dress code or just getting in a small defiance of the head office by having hers be a raucous plaid pattern.

She also hated makeup. James knew this mostly because he'd heard coworkers making some pretty shitty comments about her imperfect face, and he had to admit, he'd been tempted to join in sometimes. She wasn't the best boss. But then, she was also one of those people who'd been promoted above her level of skill, and James could easily recognize how he could have ended up in the same position.

He was also pretty sure that she played casual rugby in her downtime, and he had absolutely no desire to piss off someone who could snap him in half.

He took in her office in a half second, mostly because there was nothing there to talk about. No pictures or decorations, just a flat desk and blank walls.

She cleared her throat. "I suppose you're wondering why I've called you here."

James stopped himself before he could make some wiseass remark about her confessing to secretly being an alien. "No?"

"Well, there's a couple of things. First of all, I'd like to give you a warning that there might be some layoffs coming." She said that in the most bitter, mocking voice he'd ever heard from his boss.

James struggled to keep from snapping, his face contorting into a half scowl against his will. "Why?" he finally said, his anger getting past his desire to not annoy anyone who could fire him. "Why the hell? We're already short on people, why are you firing more?"

If Theo was offended by his comment, she didn't show it. Her response made James think she was just as angry as he was. "The company has been losing contracts, and upper management isn't doing anything to fix it. So we can't afford people, but we can't cover the contracts we have."

"So we need to fire more people and tell everyone else to work harder?" he growled out.

Theo steepled her fingers and leaned forward on her desk. "Pretty much. Now, here's the other thing. You're a pretty good employee. You go through a lot of calls effectively, even though you spend twenty minutes at the start of every day doing nothing." James wanted to object, but she seemed to already be onto him, so he decided against it. "But I'm supposed to look at firing you first, because our security guy told another manager that you stole a coffee maker."

Ah.

"I didn't—" James was going to defend his honor. And also his job, which was less important to him. But he was cut off again.

She nodded as he started to speak and then overrode him. "I know you didn't. Well, I know there's no coffee makers missing from the building. The problem is, you and your friend are on security camera walking out with a coffee maker. So where'd it come from?"

And there was the sixty-four-thousand-dollar question. The one thing James couldn't actually manage to say the true words about. Because, of course, it came from the dungeon. It came from outside reality. It wasn't from Earth, or if it was, it had been changed into something else, and it was his—well, Anesh's—by right of victory.

But his mouth wouldn't let him say those words anymore. He was locked into lying, or saying nothing. And now, for the first time, he found himself furious with the dungeon itself.

So he just shrugged and lied as best he could. It wasn't like he hadn't planned for this moment in his head. "It was just in the stairwell." Technically true, in a weird way. "It was advertised as free, so we took it home." Also technically true. Everything in the dungeon was "advertised" as free, in that nothing stopped them from taking stuff.

His boss just gave him an appraising look before looking down at her computer. "When do you get off, James?"

Again he had to avoid wisecracking. "Three a.m., but usually I'm around until a half hour later finishing up calls. Why?"

"Just checking something." He watched her tap away at her computer and noticed as she turned her head in that direction that there was a long, angry red scab on the side of her neck. The hardened blood mark ran down from just under her ear to just past her jawline.

James pointed at her wound and asked, trying to deflect away from her judging him, "That looks pretty bad; are you okay? What happened?"

"Hm?" Her hand went up to her injury. "Oh, a sports thing. You wouldn't understand." Ouch. That stung a bit; James wasn't *that* ignorant of rugby, and he knew she played. She did a bit more typing, then looked back up. "Okay, look. I'm going to try to keep you around." James breathed a sigh of relief. "But just one thing first. Have you heard anything around here?"

He cocked his head to the side, thinking. "Wait, like, rumors?"

"Anything," she replied, staring at him.

He thought over what he heard over the course of the day. Most of the time he spent with his headset on, so he didn't get a lot of sound coverage of the office. "Nothing, really, I guess? The air conditioner gets weirdly loud at the same time every day, which is annoying, but not bad. Oh, and I think Other Luis is thinking of quitting. He's mad about management denying him a shift change. But that's all."

"Nothing else at all?" she asked, leaning forward a bit.

James wasn't sure why, but he felt like a rabbit facing down a wolf all of a sudden. He wasn't being tested, he was being hunted, or at least Theodora was hunting for some piece of knowledge she seemed to think he had. "No, no, nothing else. I mean, I don't talk to anyone enough to get the gossip, you know that."

She nodded a bit, though her expression looked disappointed. "Well, thank you for your time, and for explaining the coffee maker. Not sure who left it there, but there's too many holes in the security cameras anyway." She muttered the last bit offhandedly; perhaps James wasn't supposed to hear that. "You can go back to work now." She gestured him out of her office.

And he was happy to oblige, practically running back to his desk. He'd never liked the feeling of being in a boss's office.

I think my boss might be a good dungeon candidate was the message James sent to Anesh midway through his shift. There was a moment of downtime, and in between calls, there was only so much that James could get done aside from staring at the ceiling tiles as he spun around in his chair.

Why dat? was Anesh's poorly formatted reply.

James scowled at his phone as he read his friend's minimalist approach to communication. *She plays high-impact sports, so she's used to getting hurt. She's in our age bracket, which is nice, or it would be weird. And she just has a kind of combat-ready attitude.*

You at your desk? Anesh replied. James growled out loud at the ping from his phone as his mental text editor flagged half of his friend's message.

Yes, I 'at my desk.' Stop typing like you don't speak better English than I do.

At that point, his headset went off, and he had to take a call. After resolving an actual technical problem, which was a rarity for him, he turned back to his cell phone with a satisfied feeling to see a series of messages.

Your boss can probs see your screen

Don't talk about OD on text there

too risky

Well, at least for one of them, Anesh tried. That was good enough, James thought, as he replied, *No, I'm on my phone. Though that would have been a good way to tell someone if I hadn't thought of it. Now I don't feel like I even can, what with the weird mind control bullshit.*

Oh. Oops. The reply almost made James facepalm. Trust Anesh to use punctuation on his phone only when he was admitting to guilt. Ah well, that was the problem, wasn't it? James wouldn't be able to bring anyone in unless he was doing it more or less by accident. Maybe just start shopping online for an armory upgrade while at work, or get really careless with leaving skill orbs out in the open. Would that work?

They hadn't really tested the limits of the mental coercion. It certainly felt like he couldn't just tell anyone, or let anyone he knew was watching know. But James was pretty sure that if he, for example, left Lily lying around his house, and then his friends came over, he wouldn't be forced to hide her. Probably.

It was honestly quite confusing. He almost felt like he had a second set of thoughts in his head, and he didn't really like it. Hell, that was an understatement; he fucking hated it. It was awful. It really was the one major downside to this. Being physically hurt, he knew he could heal through, if he lived. But this? Humans didn't have defenses for this.

Or maybe they did. Maybe he should take up meditation or something. James leaned back into his desk as another call came in, but not before opening up a browser tab to look into local classes on that.

The shift kept going, on and on. It was only a half shift, but it still felt like a lifetime to James, especially once a wave of exhaustion from lack of sleep kicked in. He'd been waking up early to go to the gym and take martial arts classes, which felt great but left him bone weary at work.

It really didn't help that, for some reason, Friday nights were always dead. So in addition to being stuck at work and nearly asleep, he was also bored out of his mind. He spent most of his time browsing around the internet, but his company locked almost everything out, so his options were limited. Really, James was at a point in his life where he felt like he relied on the internet for entertainment but couldn't actually tell you what he did with it beyond read webcomics.

He did find out that his company had a fairly extensive employee reimbursement program for education. He wasn't really interested in going to college again, but they also inexplicably paid for classes from the local parks and rec district, and that was a pretty extensive catalog.

The business James worked for honestly confused him sometimes. They were nominally a call center, but he was also aware that sometimes people got transferred to all sorts of bizarre projects. He and Anesh had talked once about how it was probably a front company, designed to move money around without actually accomplishing anything of value. Anesh disagreed with that, instead positing that the whole thing was just a grand experiment in how far a company could push employees before they started asking questions.

And yet this organization that was apparently throwing away its biggest customers and paid its workers as little as possible would also pay for elective education.

Well, James wasn't going to question it. So the experiment could continue, he thought as he signed up for a course on guided meditation. And then another one-off class on Mediterranean cooking. That one was just for him.

He kept spinning in his chair for a while, whittling away the time. He almost fell off when he got surprised by two thirty. Two thirty a.m. was the time, every other day, when the air conditioner in the ceiling above his desk stopped working. Loudly.

The grinding *chunk* noise was usually something he anticipated, but he'd more or less zoned out, and the sudden sound was enough to almost make him jump out of his skin. He stared at the ceiling tiles for a while before shrugging to himself. No one was around, and he didn't have any work to do, *and* he was curious. It was a dangerous combination at the best of times, and even worse now that James was bored.

Setting his headset aside, he got up and started stretching, just looking around and seeing if there was anyone nearby. Theo was still in her office, and the only other coworker who was here tonight that was within view was at their desk, on a call, and around a corner that James could only see from one specific spot near his cubicle.

So he climbed up onto his desk.

The air conditioner had been an ongoing problem for him. It was always too loud, and it failed on a basis so regular he could set his watch to it. Old James had complained to building maintenance about it, and they'd never done anything. New James knew a little more about mechanics than he'd ever actually learned in his life.

So it seemed like the perfect solution for him to just open up one of the ceiling tiles, crawl over to the unit, and see if he could fix the ongoing problem. Assuming no one noticed him up on his desk peeking into the ceiling space.

Standing on his work platform, James crouched low, peeking one more time over the walls to check for anyone approaching before rising up and reaching up to the ceiling. Moving his hands up to push up one of the tiles, he suddenly got a strange feeling and froze.

He narrowed his eyes as he pushed his hands against the tile above him, trying to tune out the hum of fluorescent light to his left. He put his hands flat against the ceiling but didn't lift it up. Instead, he just focused on the feeling. And a second later, his eyes widened as he felt rapid tapping on the other side of the tile, moving farther down the ceiling.

"I should probably let Theo know that there's a raccoon or something living in our ceiling," he muttered, already having decided that he was *not* going to let her know if he had even a chance that he could add a raccoon friend to his growing list of "animal" companions. Standing up on the tips of his toes, he pushed upward and moved the tile to the side, laying it down in the ceiling compartment. Grabbing at the edge of the ceiling frame, he pulled himself up a bit, just enough so he could see into the dark space.

A second later, he got his phone out and brought it up to turn on the flashlight. He could hear the tapping now, soft and inconsistent, but still nearby. He rotated around and swung the light to try to get a good view. There was the air conditioner fan unit. Looked like it had the whole side panel removed, and he could see a little wisp of smoke in the air near it. That was almost certainly an engine problem, and James bet he could fix that. But first, more importantly, finding a raccoon.

He kept turning, and then he spotted it.

Except, as he should have expected by now, it wasn't anything as cool as a raccoon. There, off to the left of the AC vent, was a stapler. It wasn't a very fancy one, just a simple plastic-shelled model, fairly small and frail-looking. The octet of mechanical pencils underneath it, methodically propelling it forward, made a soft tapping noise as it moved.

James almost screamed, but instead he froze and kept himself from panicking. The stapler-crab, caught in his flashlight, also froze. The two of them sat there for some time before James lowered the light a little bit. The stapler backed up, inch by inch, taking each step very deliberately, as if trying intentionally not to spook James. James, for his part, was trying to decide if he should lunge for the potentially hostile target or just let it go. It hadn't manically attacked him, so maybe this one was more like Rufus. He'd told Anesh before, he didn't need or want to just slaughter everything in his path.

Decision made, he nodded a bit at the stapler-crab and let it go. It backed away slowly at first before deciding it was out of his reach and scrabbling off. James watched as it crawled into the HVAC vent and dropped down. He dropped from his perch in the ceiling, to see . . . nothing. Just the normal office he worked in. Nothing weird at all. Pulling himself back up, he tried to see where the stapler had gone, and he couldn't really tell. It looked, as he got a better angle with his light, like the bottom of the fan casing simply wasn't there and instead had been dropped into somewhere else.

"Ah, fuck," he muttered.

This was either really bad or really good, and he couldn't tell which one. Crawling down from the ceiling, James replaced the panel and casually dropped back into his desk chair. He took a minute to wipe off the boot prints he'd left on his desk before anyone could come by and ask him why he'd been walking up there. A quick check showed him that he'd missed exactly zero calls.

Above him, he heard the air conditioner fire up again. He checked the time. 2:39 a.m. He wondered about the maintenance report he'd have to file to get this fixed. *Part of HVAC system is temporarily a time-dilating wormhole. Please fix. Not urgent?*

James sighed. For all that his job was turning more and more into something bizarre and amazing, he still found that, dungeon or no, the night shift was boring as hell.

He went back to spinning in his chair, this time keeping a much closer eye on the ceiling.

CHAPTER 19

"Your manager, beyond a doubt, is absolutely doing this too," Anesh said.

He and James were spending their day before James went to work pushing a large flat cart around a Home Depot, and James hadn't stopped giggling to himself every time he looked down and saw what was on it. Their first pickup had been a hand truck, on Anesh's insistence that they should be doing more remodeling of their fortification by the door, and his further insistence that he'd be damned if he had to move another desk unassisted. So while Anesh rambled, James just saw a cart on a cart and was amused.

"Sorry, what? I wasn't really listening," James said. "Say all that again. But less paranoid this time."

Anesh just sighed as he added a replacement sledgehammer to their cart. "I said, I think that your manager is doing the same thing we are."

"Shopping at Home Depot?"

Anesh didn't even pause for the joke. "Going into the dungeon. It adds up, right? She's suspicious of you, you found another door, so we know why we haven't seen her on Tuesday nights, and she has mysterious hobbies to cover up her injuries."

James took on an incredulous tone. "I know that it's not the most common thing around here, but rugby isn't 'mysterious.' As far as I understand, it's mostly an excuse to tackle people? I don't know, I'm not Australian. Or athletic. Or . . . I guess . . . capable of googling rugby. But it's not super suspicious. Also, I think she's shown up looking way worse since before the dungeon was there."

"How do you know? We only know when you found it, not when it started existing. Also, which brand of bolt cutters?" Anesh held up two sets of the industrial cutting tool for James to pick.

"Get the Tekton. Longer clippers, seems slightly more offensive." James shook his head at the rest of what Anesh said, though. "I guess that's a good point. But she doesn't seem like the adventurer type, you know?"

"She plays rugby!" Anesh snapped back, pushing the cart on down the cold concrete aisle.

James took a second to check the signs before pointing them toward what they were looking for. "I thought you didn't believe she played at all? Now I'm suspicious that you're just a sports racist or something."

He'd been poking fun at Anesh for a few days since he'd caught his roommate watching cricket in the living room. Personally, James didn't really care that much, but Anesh seemed so determined to be embarrassed about it that James didn't feel like he had much choice but to make a few jokes every now and then.

"Okay, look, I just think you should talk to her about it. Since she *clearly already knows*, it's not sharing the secret to tell her, *right?*" Anesh emphasized that last part heavily, his English accent enunciating every word in a sharp tone. "Also, just because I like certain sports more does not make me a 'sports racist,' whatever the heck that is."

James sort of got what Anesh was doing, and as soon as he did, he felt like there was a set of reins on his mind, yanking his thoughts in a specific direction. *Stay silent*, it said. *Keep the secret at all costs*, it made him think. James gritted his teeth as part of his own mind rebelled against him, struggling to cut the reins off. And then he realized something else. Instinctively and in the back of his mind, away from where the controls were sitting, he had a thought. *What if Anesh is right?* His subconscious, with a light guiding touch from the rest of his persona, built a vivid picture of his boss.

Of course Theodora was a delver. She had to be. It was so simple, just like Anesh said. That was, of course, why she never sent anyone to fix the AC unit. It all added up! Not suspicious at all!

And just like that, James grabbed control of the reins in his mind. The shackles were still there; he knew he couldn't go up to the clerk down the aisle and tell him about the dungeon. But he also knew he could talk to his boss. Not ask her, of course, because she already knew, beyond a shadow of a doubt. But have a normal conversation with her.

The human mind is remarkably well equipped for self-deception.

"You know what? You're right," he said out loud to Anesh. It had been a couple minutes of mental gymnastics, and his feet had sort of autopiloted him to follow his friend and their cart. Anesh was stacking a trio of carboys on the platform and also saying something, which James cut off with his own comment.

Anesh *thonked* the third large jug into place. "I'm glad you agree."

James coughed a bit, stumbling over words and suspicious of Anesh's sudden acceptance. "Wait, wait. What did I just agree to? I wasn't paying attention. And why are you getting these? There's cheaper ones at the grocery store."

"You literally just agreed that this was a good idea." Anesh palmed his forehead in frustration. "That is what I was talking about. You know what? I'm not explaining again. Trust me on this one." He stalked off, dragging the cart behind him.

James nodded enthusiastically. "Okay! That's worked out for me so far, so I'm fine with just blanket trusting you." Anesh's face flushed at the sudden praise, the tips of his ears going a deep orange that he hoped James wouldn't be able to see against his darker skin. Fortunately for him, James was already walking farther on down the aisle. "Come on, let's find some pipe. I want to see if we can overclock a potato gun without killing ourselves."

Anesh let out a soft laugh to himself as James defused the tension without even trying, and followed after his friend.

The rest of Saturday afternoon was mostly unloading stuff into their apartment, then breaking off to do their own thing for a while. James sequestered himself in his room to see how many times he could google "potato gun thermite launcher" before the FBI showed up at their door, and Anesh occupied their living room to prep for their friend group's D&D game that James was going to miss again.

A few hours later, James came out to grab a slice of pizza and say hi to his friends before leaving. The smell of greasy food wafted through the apartment from the kitchen, while in their living room, people clustered around the table.

Anesh sat at the head of the table, occupying the big comfy chair. On the couch, with their backs to him as he came down the hallway, he spotted Alanna and JP, the former towering over the other, even as she was draped over the couch. And on the other side of the table, Dave had pulled up a kitchen chair to make a space for himself. The table itself was covered in a large embellished city map, printed out on glossy poster paper. James smirked as he saw it; Anesh was getting real value out of the extra cash they were bringing in.

"Hey, nerds," he said, announcing himself as he walked in, getting a chorus of "Hey," "Yo," and "You read that thing I sent you?" in response. James smiled, a pleasant feeling flowing in his chest. It was just a good scene for him: friends, games, and food. His own place, now a bit more secure in the rent. Well lit and warm and dry. The whole thing made him feel pretty happy. Of course, they didn't need to know that. They'd get smug and let it go to their heads. So instead of sharing, he just asked, "What're you guys up to tonight while I'm imprisoned in cubicle hell?"

He saw Anesh straighten up a bit at the last couple words before giving James a look. It was JP who answered first, though. "Character creation. We're switching to something new, since you're not here as much anymore because of work."

"That's cool. What system?" he asked, a little disappointed that he wasn't going to be involved but not begrudging his friends a good time.

Anesh answered, "Shadowrun. Playing as devious criminals pilfering from the megacorps. I'm going to run it like a heist movie." He motioned to the table. "It takes place in slightly future Seattle."

James groaned from around the pizza he'd shoved in his mouth. "That sounds awesome; why'd you wait for me to leave to do this? Also, wait, isn't this a little close to home?" he said without thinking.

From the strained look in Anesh's eyes, he'd clearly had the same thought already. "Your job isn't that bad." He covered for James with a half-hearted joke.

"Your job isn't that *fun*," Dave chimed in, getting a laugh from the room.

"All right, guys, have fun storming the castle. I need to get to work. We still on for Tuesday, Anesh?" he asked, just making sure in case they didn't see each other before then.

His friend nodded. "Yeah, yeah. Now go, don't get fired."

"See ya, kiddo," Alanna said as he made it to the door. "Now, Anesh, I'm thinking shark shaman." James just shook his head as he got a sympathizing look from Dave. Alanna called all of them by titles that were, fundamentally, wrong. Alanna was younger than James, but James got called "kiddo." Dave often got the less fortunate tag of "punchy," which was also something that better defined Alanna than himself, and also something that made new members of their friend group suspicious at first, until they figured out that she was just making these up and Dave was the furthest thing from violent you could find.

James shook his head at Dave, both of them sharing an eye roll as James opened up the door. "All right, guys, have fun," he said as he walked out into the night. Cold winds whipped around him as he walked to his car, but for some reason, he kept that warm feeling the whole way.

The rest of James's night passed as a normal shift. He tried to find time to talk to his boss, but by the time he had a gap in the call log, she'd already gone home. The problem with everyone having offset schedules, aside from literally everything, was that no one was ever around when he needed them to be.

The good news was that a few of the new employees had finished their training, and for the next few weeks, until the company decided to fire half their staff, James didn't have to deal with quite so many people who were furious at waiting for two hours on hold. The bad news was, well, now he had random firings to look forward to.

Still, he got through with no real problems. Though at a certain point, he became acutely aware of the ceiling above him, and every small noise from the building made him glance up in anticipation. Kind of hard to focus on work when you feel like something is watching you the whole time.

And then his job was over. He had a whole two days to himself. Anesh was occupied with a school thing—his friends did have their own lives—and James had no responsibilities or opportunities for a brief, relaxing window of time. Left to his own devices for his own personal weekend.

As he sat in his room, in a chair that was orders of magnitude more comfortable than the one at work, he considered just going out looking for trouble. Patrolling around and stopping crimes was probably the fantasy of everyone who'd ever heard of Batman, but James wasn't sure he was at all prepared to actually face down an armed human.

James also wasn't sure if there was even enough crime in his town to warrant it. It wasn't like he'd be "cleaning up the streets"; he lived in what was a modestly suburban place with a murder rate of a quarter of a person a year. If he decided to spend his weekend doing the caped crusader thing, he'd most likely get arrested before he stopped a single crime of any importance.

Also, it would cut into the precious free time he had set aside for eating chips and playing video games.

So that was right out.

Instead, he spent the day just relaxing. Like a daylong sigh, he just kicked around the apartment. Didn't get out of bed until he'd slept for ten hours. Got through half of his replay of Dark Cloud 2. At a certain point, he realized that humans actually needed some food to live and walked to a burger place a couple blocks from their apartment. The gaps he filled with doing some mild chores, and he felt a sense of self-satisfaction at just doing the dishes.

Overall, he reveled in his own motivation. He knew it wouldn't last. This level of enjoyment in his life never lasted. But while it was here, he was damn well going to enjoy having vacuumed, and he lounged around for a full day.

On Monday, he actually managed to get himself out of the house for more than a food run, and he spent a couple hours at the gym. But beyond getting a workout in, his day was more or less the same. He still didn't catch sight of Anesh, and by the time he heard the front door open and close, he was already exhausted and too comfortable in his bed to say hi.

Tuesday. Almost.

How easily James had let his life be transformed, he thought as he walked into work.

Once a week, through a process he didn't fully understand, the front door of his office suddenly looked inviting instead of mundane. The security desk, instead of being a common hassle, was a threat to his ability to really start profiting. The calls were... Well, actually, the customers weren't any different.

He said a short greeting to his boss as he walked in, though he didn't get a chance to say much before he had to clock in. He spent a slightly longer time trying to have a conversation with one of the few coworkers he still shared the night shift with when he got bored on break, but he gave up when he realized that they shared literally nothing in common.

By the time Anesh showed up, James was pretty sick of the whole "being at work" thing. "No, sir. There isn't an easy way to remove someone from the internet. There isn't a way to do it at all, actually. No, sir, bribes aren't going to help. That won't help either. Uh-huh. Uh-huh. I see." James nodded at Anesh as he walked up to the cubicle, mouthing a silent *Kill me* at his friend. "Sir, I'm sorry you don't like the comments section, but we don't own YouTube. We don't have jurisdiction there. Might I recommend you call Google? I can get you the number."

By the time that call was done, James was ready to throw his head back and let out a low scream. "Did that guy seriously offer you money to ban someone from YouTube?" Anesh asked as they headed to the break room so James could clock out.

"Yeah. Then he kept trying to find more convoluted ways to bribe me, instead of listening when I told him I didn't have that power. God, if I could ban people from YouTube, there wouldn't be anyone left to comment." James rubbed his eyes with the palms of his hands as they sat at one of the low tables. "Okay, six minutes left. Where'd you leave the hand cart?"

"By the stairwell. I figured it'd be less suspicious. Did you talk to your boss?" Anesh asked back as he handed James one of the travel mugs full of coffee.

James went to take a sip, but Anesh put a hand over the cup, glaring at him for jumping the gun. "Sorry, right. Forgot. And also forgot to talk to Theo. She was busy today, and so was I, honestly."

"Busy looting, eh?" Anesh elbowed James as they walked out.

This got an exasperated look in response. "Yes, sure. Looting customer accounts. You get that even if she's a delver, we both still actually work here and have a job to do?"

"I don't understand," Anesh responded flatly as they approached the stairwell and he checked his phone's clock.

"It's what happens when you finish college."

"Sudden and perpetual wealth?" Anesh said with puppy-dog eyes, and James didn't know whether to burst out laughing or give his friend a consolation hug. And then it was time. "Unto the gates of hell," Anesh muttered as James pushed the door open. Anesh grabbed the hand cart with the carboys on it and followed him in.

The inside was pretty much exactly as they left it. Their fort was still up, their gear still scattered around on the desks they'd set up. "Oh fuck, right, replacement armor!" James exclaimed as they walked in. "I actually forgot that one."

"It's fine," Anesh said, "I didn't lose any of mine."

"Dick," James muttered.

"Jerrrrrrrrrkkkk!" The howl reverberated through the air near them. James nearly jumped out of his skin at the otherworldly wail; the thermos of coffee flew out of his hand and flipped over once before he caught it. Anesh had already dropped the duffel bag he was carrying and snapped up one of the axes off the table as both men whipped their heads around, looking for the source.

James leaned over and whispered to Anesh, "Where is it?"

"Can't tell, let it say something else," his friend replied.

"Smellllll cooffffeeeeeee..." the voice sang mournfully. It sounded like it was coming from above them. They looked up but saw only their improvised roof. Stepping carefully out of the cubicle fort, James nearly died with relief. There, strung up around the outside of their fortification, were dozens of paper clip webs; they wound around the outsides of the walls but also hung in draping ropes from the ceiling. And in a pair of these hanging nets hung a bright paper mask.

The lines on its face almost looked inked with how crisp the folds were, and the mane of pink sticky notes radiating out behind it gave the impression of energetic fire. None of that helped it, though, as it thrashed in the web, several of the clips impaling its thin "flesh." Just above it, Rufus hung suspended by a single stretched paper clip, his front legs reaching down to strike at the mask, which twitched every time the stapler got too near.

"I have no idea how to process this," James said simply.

"Laaayyyyyoffffffs!" the mask screamed as Rufus lunged forward to bite down on a chunk of its forehead and tear it off.

James and Anesh watched in fascinated horror as, bit by bit, Rufus dismantled the mask, shredding it even as it screamed. The paper skin, James knew from experience, was harder than you'd expect, but Rufus went through it like butter. Just how strong was that little guy? Could he go through bone? James wasn't sure, and he didn't want to test it, but he was pretty sure Rufus would have to be an order of magnitude stronger than all the common staplercrabs they encountered.

Then, above them, a piece was torn off the mask's left side, and it suddenly found that it was no longer trapped. Howling in delight, it fluttered away, and Anesh made to throw his axe to stop it as he saw the bony fangs jut out of the inside of the mask. But before either he or James could take action, there was a furious buzzing, and Ganesh struck. Half covered by webs, the disguised drone had been invisible,, and the little stirge leapt on the wounded mask with a surprising fury.

The glass needle on Ganesh's front drilled into his prey over and over. Every time the mask tried to flee, the drone was there already, making another strike and pushing it farther back into the webbed zone. And then the mask made a slip, struck another web, and Rufus was there waiting.

Thirty seconds later, a flutter of pink sticky notes dusted away into the office, like cherry blossoms in the wind, and Rufus held a decent-sized golden orb in his mouth.

"Holy shit," James and Anesh said together. Spotting Anesh on the ground, Ganesh gave a happy-sounding hum and buzzed down to his . . . *Owner* seemed like the wrong word, James thought. Either way, the drone seemed happy to see Anesh again, and for all that he claimed he hated bugs, Anesh didn't seem too displeased himself.

"Hey, this reminds me," James said as he held up a hand for Rufus to climb into. "Did you bring Lily? We should put her back here with these two."

Anesh glared at him as he walked back into the fort to deposit Ganesh and his axe. "No, and if you think about that question, I think you'll figure out why."

"Okay, okay. Well, good job, Rufus! You two really fucked that thing up! Good little vicious killing machine! Who's a good horrifying spider monster? It's you!" Rufus, sitting in the palm of James's hand, made a delighted little hissing noise, the orb rolling out of his mouth as he did so. James caught the errant skill orb and set Rufus down on one of the desks, the stapler looking at him with hesitation. A second later, he grinned and put the orb down there too. "Yeah, you guys earned this one. Share with your friend, yeah?" Rufus hissed again before consuming the entire orb in one go. "Well, so much for that." James laughed.

But then the stapler shuddered for a minute, and golden smoke started to form around it. James watched, speechless, as in about fifteen seconds, the smoke coalesced into a solid-looking skill orb. A pair of them, actually, one of which Rufus grabbed and ran off with, over to the other desk that Ganesh was sitting on.

"Well, shit. Did you see that?" James asked Anesh, who was unloading their new gear.

"No, what?" he asked, pulling the oversized potato gun out of the bag and assembling it.

James stared down at the skill orb that was left behind, presumably for him. "Rufus just ... extruded? A skill orb. Just made it. I think he ate the big one and broke it into pieces, but still, that's cool."

"How?" Anesh asked, coming over and looking at the orb in James's hand. "Did he do anything special? I mean, anything that we could replicate? Because if *we* could extrude skill orbs, that would ... actually solve no real problems, would it?" He laughed at his own train of thought.

James chuckled along with him. "Not unless we get into a really contrived movie moment where one of us is trapped but the other person needs to know how to, I dunno, disarm a bomb or something."

"I don't think I look forward to that."

"Yeah, this isn't Hollywood. Anyway, what's on the agenda today?"

James put on a pompous, overblown British accent and clapped a hand on Anesh's shoulder. "Adventure, my good man!"

Anesh just snorted and patted James's hand pityingly until he removed it from his shoulder, then started pulling on pieces of armor. "Right, but really," he said as he strapped on his arm guards.

"Well, we're currently short on team funds. So I figure we take today to do some heavy looting of this outer area, and then after a couple hours of just stripping it of everything that isn't nailed down or on fire, we do a bit of exploration farther in. Maybe go check out that wall formation you found last time?"

His friend nodded. "Yeah, I'm okay with that. We should get some more fortification in here first, though. I want to reinforce the walls; I know that these things are strangely durable, but if we get chased back here by something the size of a truck, I want it to at least buy us one hit's worth of time."

James thought it might be a little paranoid, but then again, he was absolutely certain they hadn't seen everything of note in here. So he agreed, and he and Anesh spent the next twenty minutes or so using the hand truck to bring back the solid wood and metal desks, as well as a few filing cabinets that Anesh wanted for storage purposes.

"I just like being organized," he explained as James griped about being sent out for the third cabinet while Anesh neatly fit their stockpile of food, water, and extra medical supplies into the metal drawers. James just rolled his eyes and made a promise that the next time a stapler ambushed him during one of Anesh's errands, he wasn't going to kill it but lob at Anesh's head.

They spent the next half hour sweeping the outer edges of the cubicles for anything and everything. The large open space between the outer wall—the actual wall, not a cube wall—and the first row of cubes and desks seemed to stretch on forever. As far as they knew, it actually might. The gray walls seemed to have a curve to them, so that as far away as they could see down the outer line of the space here, there was only a blank nothingness, like fog, but more boring.

After the first half dozen outer cubes of their looting run, Anesh spoke up. "Hey, we've got radios. And there's nothing huge out here on the fringe, right? I'm gonna go the other way, and we can meet up when we're done. Cover more ground, right?"

"Right," James said. "Or meet on the other side. You see the curve, right? This is starting to feel like a giant ring."

"That'd take hours. It must be at least a mile to the artificial horizon here; that maths out to about an eighty-klick loop? Yeah, that sounds about right." Anesh grabbed some scrap paper and a pen from the cube near him and started writing numbers. "Ninety-eight kilometers, yeah. Oh, that's a bit over sixty miles, because . . ."

James snorted. "I'm American, not stupid. I know how long a kilometer is. Okay, so we're not meeting up on the other side. Probably a terrible idea anyway. Oh, *this* is what we need bikes for!" he exclaimed excitedly as the thought struck him. "All right. Go cover clockwise. I'll keep going this way. Stay in touch if you find anything, head back in an hour, and then we can rest for a bit before we go deeper?"

"Got it." The two friends shared a casual high five as they crossed paths and walked in opposite directions, before James ruined the moment by having to turn around and grab the backpack he'd forgotten to pick up.

James moved on alone, feeling the strange texture of the silence in here. Without Anesh, he didn't have anyone to banter with or to watch his back. He knew that out here, the worst he was going to find was a bad stapler infestation, but now it felt a lot more tense. The air was too still; the words he'd found so easy with a partner just sat in the back of his throat, wisecracks unused. The strange mixed scent of cleaning solution and despair that made up every office environment he'd ever worked in filled the air with a harsh chill.

In short, he was on edge almost instantly.

Of course, this didn't stop him from looting. Anesh was a lot more ambitious, and James was aware that his friend had taken the hand truck with him. He really hoped the guy didn't try to convince him to carry one of these desks down the stairs. But even with that, they'd come up with a plan to maximize value, mostly at Anesh's insistence.

Drawers first, then the cabinets if possible. Candy? Grab it. Novelty candy was just the tip of the iceberg, but it was still something they'd both come to love. And James sure as hell wasn't going to pass up Double Double Blastos. Money? Obviously. Food? Eat if you're hungry; they were going to be here a while, and dealing with that without having to eat one of the MREs was generally a good plan, as far as James was concerned. Next, check anything obvious on the desk; information gathering was, so far, totally useless, but they might get something, and they only needed to look for nonrandom information.

One stack of papers that just had nonsensical technical details on them later, James was done with that. He checked the computer and found it to be functional, if bizarrely formatted. He poked at what he thought were some programs and got . . . a lot of runtime errors. Okay, so it wasn't alien architecture, it was just *bad* architecture. Well, the insides still worked, and so the next step was to open it up and grab the most useful parts. RAM was the best size-to-value ratio, and along with the video card and CPU, went into separate static bags for safe transport.

Final step, anything else obvious. Consumer electronics, like the pair of headphones James nabbed. High-value items, though nothing stood out to him here. Any kind of clothing—usually coats, though also fresh dry cleaning—could also be folded up and stacked outside and taken on the way back. If nothing else, there were enough coats here to make sure that no one in this city ever had to go cold. That, or selling them off on Craigslist.

Opening up the computer was probably the most profitable part, since James had only found twelve dollars otherwise, but it also took the longest. Still, without interruption, it only took him about ten minutes. He could get another five done before turning around.

It was when he was midway into his fourth loot box of the day, as he'd started calling them in his head, when the walkie-talkie on his belt scratched to life. "James, you there?"

"You need to say 'over' at the end, man. Over," James said as he tried to open the network shared documents folder on the computer.

There was a brief pause. "Just letting you know, after a certain distance down the line, the lamps get a bit hostile." Another beat, and then, "Over. Jackas—"

James chuckled, then realized what Anesh had actually said. "The lamps? Over," he said as he clicked through connection menus.

"The lamps," Anesh confirmed. "Any little desk lamp, specifically ones that clamp to the side of the desk. They go briefly nuclear, and then..." The radio cut out.

After a couple seconds, James pushed the button. "Anesh? You there? Over." He suddenly felt a surge of curiosity that drowned out his worry, though, as he noticed that there was a single text file in the shared documents folder: XKUT.txt. Without thinking, he opened it.

"Empty. Damn. I was hoping for a survivor note, or some kind of supernatural document." He blinked as the file flickered, showing a dense screen full of text for a brief second until he finished his sentence, and then changing again to a much less dense document. "The hell?" James muttered, reading. "Dean, Castiel, these are character listings for *Supernatural*. Wait, hang the fuck on. Um... *Farscape*," he intoned, looking at the screen. An instant later, all the words on the screen changed, now listing out the plot synopsis of James's favorite Australian science fiction series. "This is the dumbest thing. I'm kind of angry this is wasting my time when I should be... Oh shit, Anesh!" He thumbed the radio. "Anesh, you alive? Over."

"Yes, I'm alive. Also ouch, also I'm claiming the orbs I've found by right of victory." Anesh's reply crackled with static.

"Fair. Also over," James said. "Also, undo that over. I found a magical text document. What should I do with it? I didn't bring a USB stick, for obvious reasons."

"What's it do?" Anesh asked. And then, as James waited, just reading his own personal *Farscape* wiki, a minute later he added, "Over."

James laughed quietly. This was filling his emotional yearning for sass. "It gives you the information on whatever television show you speak in front of it. Over."

"Have you tried saying things that aren't shows? Over."

This caused a moment of head slapping as James realized that he hadn't really tested this fully. Right, okay. Easily fixed. "*The Warded*

Man. The Bible. King Kong." He started off listing fiction that wasn't a TV series. Nothing. "Random wiki page? Oh! Google!" Nothing, damn. That last one would have been great. "Okay, yeah, I'm not finding anything else to yell at it. Over."

"Just delete it, then. See if you get an orb," Anesh replied. James didn't even mind the lack of an *over* this time, and he grinned as he dramatically applied the delete key to the silly little enchantment. A second later, a fingernail-sized blue orb appeared, floating steadily just above the keyboard.

"It worked!" he yelped, forgetting both the radio and the presence of stapler-crabs. The former he moved to rectify, reaching out to call Anesh. The latter he barely noticed sneaking up and jerked his hand away as it lunged forward and *chunk*ed a metal shard into the desk. "Son of a . . . !" he cried as it moved again, lunging to go for his arm.

James leaned forward, smashing it flat by applying pressure with his armored forearm. As its legs tried to find purchase while pinned, he grabbed the back half with his gloved hand and then quickly flipped his grip and pulled it in half.

"I think this is getting a little too easy," he muttered to himself as he grabbed the two different-colored orbs in his thin, spidery fingers. *Well, Anesh got some, only fair I have these to myself,* he thought as he cracked into his prize.

[Problem Solved : Reorganized]

[+1 Skill Rank : Medical - Pathogens]

[+1 Skill Rank : Gambling - Card Counting]

"Reorganized? Wait, why am I asking, these have been consistently confusing and no one ever answers me." James did a quick check but couldn't find anything amiss on his person. Shrugging, he decided to loot one or two more cubicles, specifically looking for cash, before heading back. Standing up, he grabbed for the loot duffel and stumbled as he realized that it was devoid of weight.

Unzipping it, he found it empty. "Fucking dammit, did the orb put everything back where I found it? That's not a problem solved, you fucking fuckers!" He swore under his breath. Angry and frustrated, he radioed Anesh and told him he was heading back, then started the quarter-hour stroll along the wall to get to the door fort.

He got back just after Anesh did and found his friend standing over the desks unloading his bag. "Hey. What'd you get?"

"Lots of stuff. More than you, it seems," Anesh said smugly. He dragged a hand through his shaggy black hair. "Tell me my wealth makes me beautiful."

James scowled at him. "Yeah, well, I didn't get anything because of the stupid blue orb," he muttered as he lobbed his bag onto the floor.

"Wait, what?" Anesh looked puzzled. "I thought you already dropped off your loot. What's all that stuff?" He pointed over at a desk, where neat rows of computer hardware, clothing, food, and electronics were arranged.

"Oh," James said. And then a wave of relief went through him, the sour taste in his mouth and chest banished by the sight of what he'd been working on. "Oh! Okay, so that's what it did! I thought it just stole everything back!"

"Doesn't matter, still got more," Anesh said, unloading boxes full of keyboards and monitors from the hand truck he'd taken.

James sighed. "Dude, how are we supposed to get those out? Much less sell them off."

"Easy," Anesh said, "just stash the box under your desk and take one or two a day in your bag. No one will suspect anything."

"Except the janitors, or the people who use that desk on other shifts. Anyway. You ready to go head out for some exploration?" James made sure his bag was empty except for a bottle of water and some duct tape and rope. Never knew when you might need duct tape. He'd had the axe on his belt already in its holster, and he picked up the potato gun that he and Anesh had built over the week and brandished it, hoping he looked like an action movie poster.

"Wait, hang on. You don't have personal desks?" Anesh looked insulted as he hoisted the sledgehammer into a comfortable carrying position, set Ganesh down on his shoulder, and moved out the door to give James room.

James shook his helmeted head. "Nope." Fitting the gun through the door was difficult. Six feet of thick PVC pipe, with a larger folding mount beneath it if they needed to set it down somewhere and still have access to it. Instead of hairspray, the two had opted for a compact propane tank to use as fuel, and Anesh had built an ignition trigger that looked a lot more professional than he felt.

"You should really consider looking for a new job," he told James as the two of them struck out down Hallway One, fluorescent lights burning overhead.

CHAPTER 20

"I've been thinking," James said as he and Anesh took a right corner.

They were currently headed toward the formation of blue-and-white tile that Ganesh had spotted for them. The visibility at ground level was pretty bad down on the floor where they were; the ceilings of curving overhead walls cut off their view of the real ceiling, and the panels of the cubicles were too high to see anything over them. Beams of bright white light filtered through from overhead, casting sharp-edged shadows. Overhead, Ganesh kept track of their path; the column of tile coming down in the distance was an easy landmark for him to keep track of. Anesh could always reference his phone for the feed when needed.

Anesh pushed aside a rope of sticky notes as they took the turn. "That's dangerous territory. How are you planning to get us in trouble now?"

James moved forward and checked the cubicles on the right side while Anesh took the left. This hall only extended a few desks before terminating in another turn. "Well," he said as he flipped through a wallet. "I found that hole in the vent, right? I think I told you about that."

"Yeah," Anesh said, keeping watch at the door, eyeing the lamp on the desk opposite them suspiciously.

"Okay, so . . . Hey, this one has a credit card. Have we ever tried one of these? Anyway, so, I think we should get one of those Wi-Fi cameras and stick it up there. Keep an eye on it."

"Are you worried about something coming through and attacking you while you're at your desk?" Anesh asked as they moved on to the next cubicle. "Also there's no way that card is going to work."

James held up his hand to stop Anesh as they got to the last cube in the row. "Hang on, 2.0 under the desk there. Look, see? It's twitching." Anesh nodded and took a grip on the sledgehammer, while James set down their cannon in the hallway and drew his axe. "I don't think that I'm in danger from staplers while at work, I just don't want to explain it. Mostly, I really want to know how long it's open for."

"Why? Oh, and ready when you are. Finish this conversation later," Anesh muttered quietly.

James nodded and tapped him on the shoulder. Anesh stepped into the cubicle, winding up for a wide swing at the sleek white computer case. Without waiting to be struck by surprise, the shellaxy burst into motion, a fractal pattern of cables beneath it flinging it to the side with a surge of speed that Anesh wasn't expecting. His hammer came down with a crunch as it punched a ragged hole in the desk drawer to the right of where the target had been a second ago.

Stepping in behind him, James had just enough time to mutter a quick "Aw shit" as the front panel on the shellaxy opened up and a series of bright blue beams of light lanced out, focusing on his friend, the lasers briefly visible in the dust kicked up from Anesh's hit on the desk. They flickered between visible and hidden as they burned through the small particles of matter. Anesh had just enough time to register the problem before the sleeve of his shirt caught fire and the heat on his face started to scald. Jerking the hammer out of the desk, he spun and tried to get the lasers focused on something other than his skin, but the lasers just kept tracking his sensitive areas, and he was forced to reflexively keep his arms up just to protect his eyes as the creature tried to steady its aim on his face.

James, meanwhile, was left basically unopposed. Stepping around Anesh on the left side, he just leaned in and kicked the thing in the side, hoping to knock it over and off target. His heavy steel-toed boot connected, and even cracked the plastic casing a bit, but a rapid pattering of organized cords from underneath the computer pushed it back into position like one of those inflatable clown things. He went to kick it again and stomp down on it, but as he did so, the side of it rippled like liquid, and the plastic shifted into a series of bristling spikes. His kick slid along one of them and tapped it sideways enough to send the frontal lasers sliding off target into the wall and off Anesh, but one of the spines went up his leg, digging a clean red line against the flesh.

Now clear of the beams for a bit, and only slightly on fire, Anesh maneuvered the hammer into an overhead position. "Move!" he barked at James, who jerked back, stumbling on his now-injured-again leg and having to brace himself on the desk behind him. Anesh howled in pain as the shellaxy righted itself again and brought its lasers into line with his stomach. As his shirt burned away and his flesh started to scorch, he brought the sledgehammer down as hard as he could onto the technological nightmare.

Its outer shell rippled and tried to harden in anticipation of the strike, but the industrial tool was simply too heavy, and Anesh was too motivated. The metal head of the hammer punched clean into the creature, and a spray of cold liquid plastic splattered in drops in a ring around the impact as the insides crunched into splintered fiberglass and warped copper.

As the lasers went out and the spikes dissolved into nothing, James snapped at Anesh, "Dude! Shirt! Fire!" His friend went scrabbling to extinguish the problem, but as James moved to help, he spotted movement. With wide eyes, he shoved Anesh to the side with one arm and snapped his other arm forward, flinging his axe at the lunging stapler that was diving off the wall. It impacted in midair but at an odd angle. Just enough to knock the thing to the ground, where James stomped on it while he picked up his weapon.

Anesh watched his friend dismantle the little demon, leaning on the desk. He patted the fire on his shirt out and was pulling his bag off to get a bottle of water out to cool the burned area. As he set the backpack on the desk, out of the corner of his eye, he saw something that made him snap out a "No!" The desk lamp, previously pointed at the keyboard, had swiveled over to focus on James and was now glowing hot with both light and heat. In an instant, Anesh knew, it was going to pop and spray molten glass shards forward.

So, with no time to think, he grabbed the coat from over the chair and flung it over the lamp. An instant later, there was a whining *pop* and a burst of white light that stung his eyes even through the material covering the lamp. James looked up, holding the small skill orb from the stapler as well as the larger green one from the 2.0 shellaxy. He'd been alerted by Anesh's shout, but by the time his vision fell on the scene, all he saw was a coat on the desk, a smoldering hole burning in the middle of it.

"What was that?" James asked, raising his eyebrows.

Anesh just sighed, dumping water on his shirt. "Lamp. I told you about them, remember?"

"Oh, I think you got cut off in that conversation. And I got distracted. We should probably get better radios if we're gonna split up again." James stood and resheathed his axe. "So, what do they drop?"

Anesh shrugged. "Nothing, actually. They're more like the coffee cups. They explode and that's it. I got the orbs earlier from staplers."

James shook his head. "Nah, I don't buy it. Everything here drops orbs." He started poking at the lamp on the desk, twisting and turning it to get a good look.

"Not these." Anesh shrugged, then winced. "Ow. Okay, next time Dave says that people with darker skin don't burn as easily, I can now clearly tell him that is a bunch of crap. Can you get some burn gel out for me? Hell, ow!"

As Anesh doffed his armor and put the gel and a covering bandage on his burned areas, and James tried to dismantle the remains of the desk lamp, they talked.

"So you were going to tell me about the doors?"

"Yeah," James said, "there's more, right? We don't know how many more, though. So maybe I just start taking my breaks at weird times and trying all the doors in the building. Maybe find some other ones."

Anesh smiled. "But none of this makes you not paranoid about the little guys dropping on your head."

"They look like spiders! I thought they were crab things, but now Rufus is setting webs everywhere! I don't like spiders." James muttered out the last bit.

"I understand, believe me," Anesh said. "But you like Rufus. Anyway, what are we doing with the green orb? I kind of want to use this one at home, just to see what it does."

"I'm fine with that," James said, finally giving up on the lamp, which he had by now hit several times with an axe and torn the power cable out of. "I can't figure out how to get anything out of this, but I'm absolutely sure that we can. Also, you know we have another green at home, right?"

"What?"

"Yeah, it's on the table. I intentionally forgot about it and hoped JP or Alanna would notice it. Didn't work, though." James shrugged as Anesh looked at him in shock, halfway through putting his pads back on.

"How do you intentionally forget something? Wait, are you trying to get around the oath-of-silence thing?" He grabbed up the hammer, filling the air with a scraping noise as he dragged it out of the now-hardened plastic. "That's kind of messed up."

James nodded. "Yup. I'm a master at lying to myself. It's how I got through high school."

"You wanker." Anesh broke down laughing as they stumbled back out into the hallway. "Okay, tell you what. If I can have that small one, and the green when we get home, I will give you first crack at whatever you find when you manage to disarm one of the lamps. I don't... a hundred percent agree with you? But I feel like I'm not going to tell you it's impossible that they've got something."

"Yeah, well, the coffee cups keep respawning, right? That seems kinda weird. Everything weird here has a power source," James reasoned. "Anyway, yeah, go ahead and crack that, and the next lamp we see, we'll try to, I dunno, smash it early?"

"Didn't work for the cups," Anesh quipped as he cracked the tiny skill orb.

[+1 Skill Rank - Basketball]

"Get anything good?"

"No. Let's go," Anesh grumbled. He sure as hell wasn't going give James any more ammo for their ongoing sports argument.

They fell into comfortable, companionable silence as they moved on. They weren't checking every cubicle, just ones with things that looked out of the ordinary. So they made pretty good time down the next hall.

This path also ended in a right turn at the end, they saw as soon as they turned the corner. James and Anesh froze and turned to each other, then back to the path in front of them. "Hey, James," Anesh said.

"Yeeeeeah?" James drawled, turning to check behind them, hand going to his axe.

Anesh took a few steps forward, waving his hand in the air in front of him. When nothing turned out to be an illusion, he moved all the way to the end of the corridor, James standing behind him. "James, we've taken three right turns. All the same length halls."

"Yeah," James said in a defeated, flat tone.

While James felt himself getting fast exasperated with the situation, Anesh came running back to him, eyes sparkling with enthusiasm and excitement. "James. Hey, James!"

"*Yeah*, I fucking know. I get it!" he snapped out.

"James it's a Möbius hallway! We're standing in fancy geometry!" Anesh grinned madly as he grabbed his friend's hand and started dragging him at a jogging pace down the hallway. "This is fantastic! I should take a video of this! In fact, hang on. Hold this hammer."

James just looked at Anesh, already holding an axe and lugging a weighty potato gun in his off hand, balanced over his shoulder. "How, exactly? Just get Ganesh to record it."

"He's . . . up there? Maybe?" They looked up to see the area completely covered. "Well, that's probably fine. If a physical Möbius strip weren't enclosed, it might seriously mess us up to look at."

"That's great, man, but how do we leave?" James asked dryly as Anesh led them around the sixth right turn, now with his phone out, taking a video of it all.

Anesh just shrugged. "No idea. Maybe we just need to go far enough. We can also try turning around and 'backtracking.' If this is common non-Euclidean geometry, then we might be repeating the same space over and over, but turning around is the only way 'forward.'"

"Then why aren't we doing that?" James asked as they took the ninth right turn.

"Because this is super cool!" Anesh shouted as they moved.

James just sighed. This was going to be a long walk for the lack of distance they weren't going to cover.

CHAPTER 21

After taking a dozen more right turns and never overlapping with their own path, Anesh had felt the novelty wear off. "Okay," he told James, "let's turn around, see if we can backtrack and get out of this trap."

They backtracked. After thirty left turns, they had not gotten anywhere, instead seeing the same four hallways repeating over and over. A quick discussion, and they started trying different movement patterns. Anesh started keeping notes, leaving up sticky note signposts that they never passed again. One of them would go to the end of the hall and wait while the other one looped around. They'd communicate by radio and find that they should have passed twice but never saw each other.

Undoing their steps and meeting up again after only a single turn, they put their heads together. "This is a bit awful," James said. "But not a big deal. We can try punching through the walls, right? Let's just cut our way out and meet up with Ganesh."

So they shifted one of the desks away and took their hatchets to the towering wall. After punching a perforated door pattern in it, they did a quick three count and kicked inward. Checking through the poof of dust from the shredded fabric of the wall, they looked into the cubicle on the far side. "That was easy," James said as he ducked his tall frame through.

Anesh just grunted as he thumped the sledgehammer through the breach and stepped in next to him. They went out to the hallway, and James had grumbled a bit as the ceiling still covered the "sky" above them. "Well, no Ganesh back yet. Let's get outta here."

They walked for exactly three hallways before both of them stopped again, and Anesh facepalmed. "It *was* too easy," he said accusingly. "You buggered it up by taunting the dungeon!"

"The dungeon isn't alive," James said with more confidence than he felt. "Probably. Okay, probably not. But whatever. Okay, fine. We're in twisted space. There's still a solution. We just need to find the orange orb and rip it out, right? That's what worked on the copier; this is just like that, but . . . you know, bigger. And we're inside it instead of being beaten to death by it. We can work with this."

They started being extra meticulous, scouring cubicle after cubicle, going through every drawer, searching behind furniture, in plant pots and folder holders. They even started opening up the mundane computers. But they didn't find anything aside from more exploding lamps, more staplers, and one very lethargic shellaxy that James simply patted and told to go back to sleep. The computer rumbled and settled back down, annoyed at being disturbed but willing to let it go.

James also tried more than once to "disarm" a lamp before it detonated, even going so far as to smash it before it could pop itself, but it never worked. "I think I need to try getting the bulb out without them seeing me," he told Anesh, which earned him a wide-eyed, raised-eyebrow look.

Still, their hunt didn't turn up one of the orange orbs or anything else that might be holding them in these cubicle-surrounded Penrose steps. Half an hour later, they stood at one of the corners, having earned nothing. Well, not exactly nothing: seven small skill orbs, one blue orb from a stick of RAM that Anesh had fried when he touched it, and three new small staple cuts on their hands. They were both annoyed that they'd never know what weird things the RAM did, but at least now they knew that computer components could be enchanted.

"Okay," James said for the tenth time, drinking the last of his water, "this isn't good."

"No, really?" Anesh said with a mock shocked gasp, hand on his chest like he'd just heard the world's most offensive joke. "How did you ever—"

James cut him off. "Okay, okay, yes, I get it." He dropped the potato gun he'd been lugging around this whole time and sighed, stretching his arms. "All right, new plan!" he announced.

But while James was busy getting cut off by Anesh, neither of them really noticed that, around them, in the cubicles, things were moving. Shifting slowly at first, but moving more directly as they started to get into position near the doors of their respective cubicles.

Anesh spotted the first one when its front panel clicked open. A smooth, rounded oval case, white plastic glimmering a bit in the dim light. An upgraded shellaxy, the kind that had mounted beam weaponry. He smacked James's shoulder and pointed, and his friend turned to look but stopped two cubicles before seeing where Anesh was pointing. "Shit, over there too," he muttered, causing Anesh to jerk his head back and forth between the targets.

The two of them backed slowly down the hallway, two or three steps at a time, standing shoulder to shoulder, angled to try to keep an eye on all of them. "Seven. Seven of them," Anesh said.

"Are they hostile?" James whispered back. The 2.0s had their weapon ports open, a dozen small metal orbs in each one rotating back and forth, tracking as a unit on the duo standing in the hallway. A few of the shellaxies scuttled out into the hallway, their cord-legs moving in meticulous patterns, but none of them opened fire.

"All right," Anesh said. "We just calmly and slowly back away, and turn the corner, and never see them again. Ready?" He shuffled a couple steps, and James moved with him, gripping the cannon tightly.

James flicked his eyes between the two foremost shellaxies. "I think we can just go. They don't look like they're—" Light flared and the wall to their left burst into flames, a cup-sized portion of it blackening to ash as the beam traced toward them.

"*Run*," Anesh barked, and they turned and bolted.

James felt his back heat up and a searing pain as the molten plastic of his armor dripped through the breach and onto the small of his back. Beside him, he heard Anesh scream and throw his helmet off behind him, the metal clanging onto the ground as they scrambled around the corner. "They're fucking hostile! I figured it out!" James shouted as they stormed down the hall and nearly tripped. "I'm a genius!" he yelled as they ran on.

The air smelled cold and dead. Not rotten or anything, just empty of life. James felt like he was suffocating, no matter how fine the oxygen was. He was breathing a bit heavy now, and sweat was starting to bead on his forehead before he wiped it away. Legs sore, arms burning. He hadn't had a break in five minutes, keeping at a constant jog.

They'd taken over twenty corners but still heard pursuit behind them. Their legs pounded, and James had yelled at Anesh to think of a way out of here ten turns ago. Every now and then, a beam would lance out from a cube door and nearly catch them as another shellaxy joined the chase.

After two more turns, Anesh panted out to James, "I don't fucking know what to do! The only place we haven't checked is through the walls farther in!"

"Then check there!"

"How?" Anesh screamed.

James skidded to a halt. They were, undoubtedly, faster than the computer shells chasing them. The benefit to legs, even ones that got tired, was that you got to cover a lot of ground pretty fast compared to anything with legs that could generously be called tiny. So he had at least two halls of distance before they caught up. "Take out the wall! Go!" He pointed into the cube to their left.

Then he flipped down the bipod on the potato cannon.

It wasn't exactly a masterpiece of construction. It was really just a simple pressure gun built out of stuff they could legally buy at Home Depot. The only thing that made it special was that it was easy to disassemble and move, that it was honestly pretty quiet compared to their other projectile weapon options, and that it could, probably, launch things.

"This thing better fucking work," he muttered as he pulled the pump trigger, flooding the base with propane from the tank. As he saw Anesh shove the desk to the side and plant the first hit from the sledgehammer in the wall, he pulled one of the upgraded thermite grenades that Anesh had made for him off his belt. Ripping the safety case off, he carefully slid it down the barrel of the cannon and then sighted it on the end of the hall. "Anesh, how's it going?" he called.

Another crunch, followed by "I'm working on it!"

James gritted his teeth and pulled the other two grenades out, pulling off the safety case on one of them, setting it gently to his side. Anesh said the impact triggers wouldn't just randomly go off, but Anesh wasn't a weapons engineer, so James was a bit wary. But as he glanced to the left and saw Anesh frantically punching his way through the wall in their last-ditch attempt, he felt a wave of protectiveness.

He turned back and waited. He didn't have to wait long.

The first shellaxy came around the corner and paused when it saw him. Before it could open its port, it was pushed sideways by another, and another, the first trio that led the pack blundering into the open corner in a neat cluster that made James think he couldn't have asked for a better target.

James looked down the sight of the cannon. "Please work," he whispered, and pulled the ignition trigger.

Fwummmmpph was roughly what the thing sounded like. James was braced for a lot more recoil than he got. Even with the long burst noise as the propane lit off and flung the canister downrange, it wasn't that loud either. Kind of like an echo; he noticed the strange detail as he fired. And then it impacted. His shot hit the front shellaxy perfectly and went straight through the case with a *much* louder sound, catching inside the vitals. The impact trigger set off the thermite, and a blaze of temporarily molten metal sprayed out the front of James's first kill with the cannon.

As the fire continued to spray, the shellaxy slumping as it melted, the other two made a screaming noise like multiple error messages going off all at once. They scrabbled away from the melting corpse of their brother but seemed panicked to James. They weren't opening their weapon ports, they weren't shifting their cases to a defensive form, they were just backing away, staring at the molten slag that he'd just turned one of them into.

James didn't wait. He was already filling the chamber with more fuel, and with his other hand he slid the second grenade down the tube. As soon as it was in position, he tracked at the shellaxy closest to the corner and fired again.

This shot caught it broadside and went straight through. Another shellaxy from the swarm that was moving in behind it took the canister, half sticking out of shattered plastic. More error window bells and chimes went off, escalating in volume as the thermite lit off and started burning through the newcomer, even as the sleek white monster that James had aimed at rocked back and forth, a chunk of its internals ripped away.

Smoke and a fountain of sparks now filled the hallway, and James couldn't even see what was going on, though he could certainly hear what sounded like a hundred furious screams from behind the billowing smokescreen. "Anesh, we are out of time, man!" he called over as he primed the third and final grenade. Shapes moved in the smoke as it filled up the hallway and started pouring closer and closer to James.

At least it would weaken the lasers, he thought grimly. And then the first one burst through, laser already tracking and firing. James pulled the trigger.

The *whump* this time was accompanied, almost instantly, by a second slamming crunch. James grinned with smug satisfaction as the lead shellaxy, the one that was bold enough to step forward first, died burning. And then the rest of the horde poured through the burning breach.

Then he looked down. A dozen tracking lasers zigzagged down the hallway. James saw one of them, burning a trail on the floor, track its way up to the propane tank. He dropped the cannon and bolted into the cubicle where Anesh was still hacking his way through the thick wall. "Out of time!" he yelled, and heard Anesh scream in frustration, slamming his hammer into the wall one last time.

The laser had melted a clean hole through the barrel of the cannon and burned into the small propane tank. The propane tank did what it was designed to do and split neatly in half as pressure and fire poured out. Half of the tank flew off to who knows where, while the other half clipped James in the back of the head as he ran, causing him to stumble into the shattered portion of wall and fall forward, taking the damaged cube wall with him.

Anesh jumped forward over James through the breach before the shellaxies caught up to them. And right there, hovering between two fluorescent metal pyramids that reached from the floor and ceiling to form a pinpoint grip, was an orange orb. A big one.

He didn't wait. Anesh just lunged forward, letting the hammer slam it out of place.

The orb popped out of its case and rolled onto the floor. And then there was a rumbling in the back of their heads. A pair of lasers cut through the dust and smoke, alighting on Anesh's torso as the rumbling increased in tone. As he spun around, he saw the shellaxies in the door to the cubicle lining up for full power shots. And then they were just . . . gone.

The cubicle was also gone. There was a blink of blank space, of nothing, and a snapping pressure that rebounded over and over in their heads. James slammed his eyes shut, and Anesh clapped his hands over his ears. Both of them screamed against the pressure that built and built, and then, just like that, it was over.

James opened one eye, and Anesh looked up. They were sitting in a hallway. James almost groaned, but then Anesh nudged his arm from where he was slumped against the wall to his right. He pointed, and James saw that the hallway ended with a vending machine and a T intersection.

He just lay back down, resting his head on his arm. "I'm gonna . . . I'm gonna take a nap. Here," he said, curling up a bit to rest his head on his backpack. And then he felt his spirits rise and his energy come back as he looked down the hall behind them and saw four glimmering green orbs sitting neatly on the ground, and a single orange one rolling out of the door of a cubicle.

Anesh reached over and picked up the orange one. "Dibs," he muttered, and James gave a weak laugh.

"Yeah, okay. All yours," he gasped out.

CHAPTER 22

"Oh, damn it all," James muttered a little too loudly.

Anesh looked over from the small side table where they'd dropped his football armor and laid out the medical supplies that he was using. He'd gone through so many packets of burn gel that his kit had run out and he'd asked to dip into James's; the scored red flesh from the shellaxy horde's concentrated laser fire demanded pretty immediate attention, no matter how tired they both were. Even for Anesh, whose skin was a rather dark brown to begin with, burns showed up as angry pink marks. Thankfully, the beams hadn't focused on either of them long enough to inflict third-degree burns, but even without the melted flesh and blackened blisters, James still felt pretty dramatic pain from where the plastic of his armor had melted away and poured down on his shirt.

"What's up?" Anesh asked in a weary voice as he shoveled the green orbs into the pack.

James pulled something out of the bottom of his backpack and thumped it onto the table with a metallic *clunk*. "You know what would have been super helpful? Magic coffee," he said, showing off the thermoses they'd both placed in the bottom of their bags along with their water bottles.

Anesh just looked over flatly, taking a good ten or twenty seconds to process what James had said. "Oh." He went back to taping a piece of gauze to himself. "Oh! Bloody hell, why didn't we use that?" he said as his brain caught up to James's words. "I mean, we were a bit busy, but this is sort of what we packed it for."

Shaking his head as he pulled out more burn gel to hand off to Anesh, James just sighed. "Well, I guess we'll have to use it next time. Unless... I mean, do you want to keep going?"

"I don't see why not," Anesh said as he put his armor back on over his scorched shirt, taking extra care when settling it onto his shoulder where the cloth had burned away and singed his skin. He winced a bit as he dropped it down a bit too hard. "I mean, this is right painful and all, but these are pretty mild burns. If we go to a hospital, they're going to tell us to keep it covered, apply burn gel every couple of days, and only come back to the ER if it gets infected because we didn't do those things. We don't need medical attention."

"We've only got four hours left, give or take a bit," James said as a rebuttal. "Also maybe I *like* medical attention." He stuck his nose in the air as he put on a haughty voice.

Anesh shrugged. "So we take another hour to explore and head back then. I mean, this is a great haul for the week, sure, but..." He looked over at James.

The look he had on told James all he needed to know, and he understood at once. Anesh felt the same way he did: this place, this dungeon, it promised them something. It offered a lot of things: money, power, knowledge, really weird candy, all the office supplies they could carry, and magical coffee machines. But it also offered something else entirely.

Adventure.

Here is what James knew, in that moment: that he was ordinary. That his life had never once been on a good track, and even now that he had a bit of stability from his job, he wasn't going anywhere exciting. He knew that he was, in a very real way, doomed. He was doomed to work a crappy job for most of his life, maybe getting promoted when he was forty to a management position he'd hate, or maybe dying of something stupid before that. He didn't have a plan for retirement and couldn't bring himself to care about his own well-being enough to make one. There were enough days when it took far too much effort to get out of bed and far too little effort to think it would be easier if he were simply dead.

And then there was this place. This, for lack of a better term, dungeon. It had burst into his life by accident, and it had taken over every moment of his thought processes since he'd realized what exactly he had on his hands. It was big, it was exciting, and it didn't just distract him from his problems. It gave him agency; it gave him control of his own destiny.

It was the thrill of exploration, the sense of excitement at seeing what was around the next corner. The satisfaction of testing themselves against all the dangers this place had to throw at them, and coming out alive. It was the feeling of being something more. Something that was just a little bigger than getting through life doing tech support or struggling with college.

He looked into Anesh's eyes and saw that reflected back at him. Maybe not exactly the same quiet desperation he felt, but certainly the spirit of adventure. The will to not just survive but thrive. "But you want to see what's next." James quietly finished the sentence that Anesh had started.

They stood there looking at each other for some time. There was a lot that could be said but nothing that needed to be spoken.

"So!" James broke the silence with an overly enthusiastic tone and a clap of his hands. "Want to go check out the suspicious towering tiled visage in the distance that looks an awful lot like it has a Dark Souls boss fight in it?"

"Fucking hell, I thought you'd never ask." Anesh grinned back at him.

The duo checked their armor, made sure their weapons were in place, and repacked their bags while Ganesh did some quick recon for them down the path forward. Anesh was pretty sure there wouldn't be any more space-time traps nearby, but James wasn't as confident.

"If it can make one, it can make a dozen," he said.

Anesh replied, "If it could make a dozen, you wouldn't have survived to invite me here, and I'd be mysteriously down a roommate."

James couldn't really argue with that. The James of even just two months ago was almost a different person entirely, in terms of what he was capable of. If he'd walked into that twisted hallway, he would have made right turns until he died. The thought made him shudder.

As he and Anesh rested for a bit, set up in an open area in a square of cubicles, they also discussed what to do with their rewards so far. It was, as Anesh had said, a great haul for the week. Five green orbs, though James couldn't help but think these were a bit smaller than the one from the tumblefeed. Still, he and Anesh planned to do some experiments with them.

"We use two at the park near our place, two at the coffee shop, and if none of those do anything horrible, the last two at our place. This one and the one we still have at home," Anesh said, laying out the groundwork.

James thought for a second as he reclined on a trio of rolling office chairs that he'd turned into a couch, putting skills from his job to use. "What if they're all just good? Wouldn't it make more sense to test fewer outside and use them on our place once we're sure they aren't going to, I dunno, set it on fire?"

This got him a glare from Anesh. "No. No chances. I like that apartment, and I'm not moving again. If I had the option, I'd make us use a hundred of these things before we even brought one into our city. We'd go out to the desert and use them all one at a time and see how long it took for things to go wrong."

"Does this state even have a desert?" James asked, tangenting off from the main topic.

"Of course it does. It's technically a 'high desert,' but it's still . . . How do you not know this? You've lived here your whole life, and I'm from another continent. Come on, mate," Anesh replied. To which James just let out a soft laugh before cutting himself off as he realized how sore his throat and lungs were.

They decided to use some of the smaller orbs right away. They had seven of the little yellow skill orbs piled up, and James was holding on to the blue one they'd found. Anesh had apparently left his own blue orbs at home, leaving one for Lily to analyze for him.

"You got over your fear of bugs!" James said, congratulating him. "This place *is* refining you!"

"No," Anesh snapped back, "I left it on the table and hoped the damn thing found it interesting. I'm . . . Look, I'm not afraid of bugs, it's just unsettling, and I don't want to touch it or interact with it at all, okay?"

James laughed as they sorted out the skill orbs. Two for himself, three for Anesh; James would also use the blue one now in case it could help, and Anesh had another orb to feed to his drone when he came back. The others they'd hang on to in case they found another iLipede in here, or when they got home to give to Lily. "I just want more information, more data points," Anesh muttered. "The only problem is I don't want to interact with anything that has that many legs to get it."

James stifled a smile and cracked into his orbs, not wanting to make his friend feel too picked on. As the soft-colored smoke escaped the popped beads, though, he let his grin show through. No need to hide the joy he felt from this part.

[+1 Skill Rank : Games - Chess]

[+1 Skill Rank : Gardening]

[Problem Solved : Decent Night's Rest]

[+1 Skill Rank : Lucid Dreaming]

"Well, that's . . ." James listened to the echoes in his thoughts for a second, then blinked a few times. The world seemed a little brighter around him. Experimentally, he stretched his arms, taking a deep and satisfying breath. He stood up, stretching further as he spoke to Anesh. "The skills aren't anything special, but the blue one gave me a night of sleep. I feel . . . pretty good. Throat isn't sore; legs are, though. But, like, in a good way. Anyway! What did you get?"

Anesh just let out an exasperated noise as he held up one of the skill orbs for Ganesh to pluck from his fingers. "Those blue ones are too convenient. We need to find a way to get more of them. Eight hours of sleep? James, that's the closest thing we've seen to a healing potion. But yeah, let's see what's in these . . ." Gently, one by one, he crushed the remaining orbs in his fingers.

[+1 Skill Rank : Tae Kwon Do]
[+1 Skill Rank : Repair - Computer]
[+1 Skill Rank : Management - Small Business]

"Anything?" James asked, not really expecting a great answer.

Anesh just shrugged. "Nothing really impressive. A martial art level, though. You got one of those, right? How is it?"

James mirrored the shrug as he helped Anesh to his feet. "It's kind of cool. I move a lot easier now. Like, I just feel like I have a lot more . . . what's the word . . . presence? I'm aware of where my feet are, all the time. It's great. Though I'm also weirdly aware that I'm not strong or fast enough to do all the things I know how to do."

"Mmm. Yeah, I get that," Anesh said as he thought about it.

The two of them, one now more rested than the other but both of them back on their feet, were finally ready to move on. Securing their packs, with James taking special care of the pouch with all the greens, and with both of them opting to keep their coffee canisters on the outside of their bags this time, they got moving.

Moving out of their little clearing, they quickly got back into row after row of towering cubicle walls around them. The overhangs weren't as bad here, though, and the glaring artificial white light beat down on them as they walked. Ganesh would occasionally lift off from his human's shoulder to land on one of the strange wall protrusions and peek around, or just to show them which corner to take at an intersection. They kept marking their turns with sticky notes, refilling the supply from nearby cubicles whenever they started to run low.

This area seemed strangely devoid of anything that was actually trying to kill them. It had been about thirty minutes of walking, at least half a mile, and nothing had jumped them. They'd encountered another shellaxy in one of the cubicles where they'd stopped for a sit and some water, but it wasn't one of the upgrades and had just eyed them warily until they left. And they'd left fairly soon after spotting it.

Neither of them was keen to stick around the mobile computers at this point.

Onward they walked, keeping an eye out for anything dangerous or shiny. As they moved down a particularly long hallway, James caught sight of another flock of bright white printer paper, fluttering by overhead. This one was larger than any they'd seen before. He nudged Anesh and pointed up, and they watched as thousands of sheets of paper, in various folded and crumpled patterns, rippled by in the air. A strange flowing hiss came out of their multitude as they passed.

"I want to catch some of those sometime. I want to see what happens if I use them for origami," he whispered as they watched the streams of flying material go by. Anesh just nodded silently, caught up in the view.

As the flock finally finished passing overhead, they continued down the hall. "Ah, the now-classic 'vending machine and death plant' combo up ahead. What's the play here?" James asked coyly.

Sure enough, the hallway ended in another T intersection. They stopped a few cubicle doors before it to take a minute to stretch and plan. "Well," Anesh said, "we could just smash the plant as a preemptive strike. I don't really want to harvest the whole vending machine when we're this far in, though. I know I pushed for buying those carboys, but we are well over two miles away from the entrance. Also, there's only about an hour left in our time buffer before we need to go back." He gestured at the plant. "You're rested up, right? Here, take this. I'll wait patiently." Anesh finished with a small smile as he handed over his weapon.

James gave him a hammed-up glare. "I feel like you're taking advantage of this situation," he said as he hefted the sledgehammer.

He and Anesh checked the few cubicles beforehand, just to make sure there were no surprises. There were a couple desk lamps that James was almost certain were traps, but they didn't see anything that was planning to come out and kill them if they made a bit of a racket. So he gripped the hammer, took long steps forward, and tried to time it so that he would get the perfect swing on the pot of the giant plastic fern sitting next to the vending machine.

He didn't, though. And he knew about a step and a half ahead of time that he was going to have a bad angle. Still, he stepped in, unwilling to stop now since he was almost sure that he'd seen the fern twitch. As the hammer came down on the ceramic pot, hitting it less than dead-on, the last thing James thought before the nearest frond lashed out at his throat was that this would have been so much easier if the potato gun hadn't exploded.

What followed was brief, rather awkward violence.

The fern stiffened as the pot cracked down the side but didn't break. One of its fronds jutted out toward James like a blade from a fencer, jabbing into his armor padding as he jerked backward just in time. James backpedaled a couple steps, keeping his feet firmly placed as he ducked another high stab aimed at his eyes. It was only because he put some distance between them and managed to keep his eyes open that he saw the second frond coming in from the side. It was just as long as the first but had to bend a bit, so the strike wouldn't have as much force. But it was still razor-sharp, and James wanted nothing to do with that.

He shuffled right, making the plant bend farther to get more than one frond focused on him at once. It wobbled and swayed in a breeze that was not there, artificially green leafy arms weaving back and forth and occasionally flitting out to try to cut into its opponent. James was having no part of it, though, instead keeping his distance, ducking strikes, and getting a feel for how fast it was. His footwork wasn't perfect, and he couldn't seem to safely get into range to land another hammer hit, but he wasn't losing his balance either.

Grinning to himself, he waited for it to move in with two hits at once, and as soon as it did, he hopped backward. The fern overextended, and as its flexible frame snapped it back into place, James took one large stride forward and whipped the hammer around with a single hand on the shaft. The twenty-pound metal head shattered a neat hole in the side of the pot, a spiderweb of cracks radiating out from around it, as James lost his grip on the handle and ducked backward, one of the fronds finally getting past his movements and slicing a thin line on his forehead.

He feinted forward, going for the hammer again, but the plant was there to intercept him. He had hoped that the risky strike would kill it, but now he was left without his main weapon and with no time to draw his axe when he was busy trying to get out of range of this thing. He twisted and dodged another razor-sharp line of leaves, then realized he'd put himself too close to the plant itself. He saw the strike coming and had only a brief moment to process his mistake before it hit.

And then, right before the thing sliced into James's neck, Anesh slipped in and took off the base of one of its fronds with his axe. Ganesh lifted off from his shoulder as he slid by, diving onto the other frond that was turning toward the new threat and stabbing at the base of it repeatedly until it, too, wilted backward with no stem to support it.

James didn't waste time. He yanked the hammer out, planted his feet, and took a swing that would make a professional golfer proud. The tinkling sound of shattering ceramic filled the air with sound. If James had dropped a plate at home, the sound would make his heart sink, but now it filled him with vigor. Kneeling next to the fern, Anesh slammed his gloved hand into the ruined base of the pot and tore out a root system knotted with small fleshy red growths.

As soon as he had done so, the plant just dropped, its fake plastic greenery twisting up on itself, fern fronds drooping and turning a bit brown and withered. James and Anesh both let out a sigh as the golden skill orb manifested above its corpse.

"That was harder than I expected," James said. "Where were you when I missed the first swing?" he demanded of Anesh in a voice that was a bit harsher than he meant.

Anesh stood up, brushing dirt and ceramic dust off himself. "There were a couple of striders. Sorry. Ganesh warned me when you needed help, though. You looked like you were doing really well."

"Yeah, I . . . think I finally found the flow of movement, I guess? Also, striders?"

"Stapler-spiders. They're less like crabs now, and I wanted a better name for them." Anesh held up a couple small skill orbs. "Okay, your choice. The big one from the plant, or these two?"

James picked up the larger orb from the plant. "I feel like I earned this one. Also, I'm going to forget to call them striders constantly," he said as he cracked the skill orb.

"It's fine, I will too," Anesh said, popping his as James felt his thoughts rearranged.

[+2 Skill Ranks : Medical - Bioethics]

James cocked his head. "Well, that's kind of a weird one. Certainly gives a much wider perspective on . . . a lot of legal stuff, actually. Hm. Hey Anesh, have any of your skills mixed with each other? Like, that you know of? I think this one and the government one are sort of linking up."

"No . . ." Anesh said, not really paying attention, as he looked at his own acquired skills.

[+1 Skill Rank : Perception - Pattern Recognition]

[+1 Skill Rank : Anatomy - Weak Points - Human]

James looked over at his friend. "What's up? You've got a weird look."

"James, we kind of assume that all these skills are, in some way, tied to things that people in your office know, right?" Anesh asked slowly.

"Yeah, I mean, the weirder ones are usually explained by the extreme cases of people who have side jobs or hobbies, as far as I know. And a lot of these skills have been business related," James said as they picked back up and kept moving. They had maybe a couple minutes of break, with Anesh getting them a couple juice drinks out of the vending machine, which James was sipping as they walked.

Anesh nodded as his drone sped forward to check the next corner. The tower of blue-and-white tile was visible now, very close by, through the holes in the overhanging walls. They'd be at their destination soon. "Well," he said, "I think someone in your office is either a medical student or a murderer. Maybe both?" he said placatingly, holding up his hands like he was weighing his options as James turned to look at him. "I mean, I got an anatomy skill. Fine. But the subtype of 'weak points, human,' is . . . really specific. And now I know where to hit a guy with a hatchet to make sure he doesn't get back up, and that's really not okay."

"Yeeeesh," James said as they walked on. "That's unsettling. I never really thought about it before, but there probably are a lot of skills that we actively wouldn't want to have, huh? Like, imagine getting a skill for just 'murder.'"

"Exactly," Anesh agreed. "It's not . . . it doesn't make me feel good."

"We need to spend more time figuring out stuff about the orbs," James said. "We know Rufus can . . . process . . . them? I don't know the word, and I don't want to say 'extrude' again. But if you can, I guess, repackage a skill, maybe you could do that? We could use the unsavory ones as power for the little guys and keep the ones that make sense for ourselves. I don't think they use them as skills at all, anyway."

Anesh sighed. "That would be great. Thanks. I just, you know, I don't want to know how to off people." James patted him on the shoulder reassuringly. "That's a good idea, though. We know sod-all about these things." He followed up as they hung another sticky note signpost. "Like, we were talking about testing the greens. We kinda get what they do, they improve places."

"Right, and the orange ones . . . give us stuff?" James kind of trailed off. "Okay, not enough data, right," he said as Anesh made a non-committal noise.

The two of them stopped to go through a cubicle that had a purse sitting out on a desk, just doing a quick check for cash for their adventuring-and-rent fund. "What about the blues?" Anesh asked. "They tell us 'Problem solved,' but . . ."

"But what constitutes a problem, what counts as a solution, what does it mean when it applies solutions to things that aren't problems, what is the relative strength of a given solution, and why the hell did you get precognition from one of them?" James said as he pulled a couple hundred bucks and a pair of sleek sunglasses out of the purse.

Anesh gave a short laugh from his guard post at the door. "I mean, that's the list of questions, yeah."

James came out, and they kept onward. "Well, maybe we can ..." He trailed off as they took a corner, pushing through a cascading curtain of paper and sticky notes. And then, there, in front of them, was the spire. Their goal this day. Blue-and-white tile with clean mortar. It stretched up to the ceiling, cutting off their view of the surrounding false sky. Up close, James could see a thin mist surrounding the lower half of it where it sat in a clearing at the end of this hallway.

Down at the base, recessed into the gleaming bicolored wall, the friends could clearly see two doors. They were a light brown, in stark contrast to the rest of the structure. On each one was a small black-and-white iconographic sign in the middle of the door.

Gents and *Ladies*.

The duo looked at the doors for a while. "It's a ..." Anesh started.

"Nope!" James cried out, throwing his hands in the air and turning on his heel. "Nope! I'm glad we got here, but I'm not doing this today!"

"Wait, hang on!" Anesh said, calling him back. "I know this is stupid, but let's at least take a look inside. We've got ..." He checked his clock. "Okay, we're pretty low on time. Yeah. Ganesh, you can remember the way back here, right?" The little drone did a bobbing nod. "Okay, great. James! Wait up!" He hurried to catch up with his friend.

Neither of them was interested in going into this office's bathroom today. After fighting their way through miles of dungeon, punching out of a spatial trap, experiencing burn wounds and cuts and scrapes, and taking a hike longer than either of them was used to, only to find that the reward at the end of the tunnel was a bathroom door, was kind of demoralizing.

They'd be back, of course. When they had more time and, James thought, had waterproofed their phones. But right now, it seemed like a good idea to head home for the day, taking what they'd earned with them. It was just, at the moment ...

Neither of them wanted to take this shit from the dungeon.

When James said so out loud to Anesh, he'd cringed so hard James was afraid he'd rupture something. "I don't know whether to punch you or kiss you for that pun."

"Please don't punch me," James responded as they backtracked quickly over their trail.

"Hey, before we go, we should actually make use of this coffee," Anesh suggested, ignoring James's quip. "Did you want to try disarming one of the bulbs with it?"

James did. A lot, really. Between his natural gamer attitude and the overlay of skill information on his mind that informed him about rule sets and helped him connect the dots in patterns like this, he was almost certain that there were more orb types. There were too many gaps. If there were only a few orb types, they could have been specified, without a pattern. But there were too many for that, and they had constant functions in the dungeon. The skill orbs themselves were used for the smallest monsters. The green ones were . . . just bigger? James was still working on that. The blue ones were magic items, and the orange ones distorted space. So far, so good.

But the respawning traps? Those hadn't dropped an orb yet. The exploding coffee cups they'd never really disarmed, just triggered. Speaking of which, as he thought of the cups, he poked Anesh. "Hey, remember the coffee mines? I was going to call those 'rocket java,' after the blend, but did you know there's a coffee called 'blast roast'? I'm not sure which one to go with, and you're the names guy. What do you think?"

Anesh peered around the corner they were about to take. "Blast roast. I mean, how can it not be that? Also, what's with you and puns today?" he asked as they hustled back to the door, checking cubicles for any lamps that they could test.

"I've been feeling good today," James said.

He was, too. He just felt a little spark of energy, and not just because of the dungeon. Though a lot of it was that. He was interested to test out the theory that every extension of the dungeon's weirdness, for lack of a better term, had an orb associated with it. He just felt like he was on the right path.

They made it back to the door in about half an hour, deciding not to stop at Anesh's insistence. He wanted to get back and start organizing for their exit, while James could circle the outside again to find a lamp. Though as they unpacked the stuff and James took a drink of the still-kind-of-warm coffee, he pestered Anesh while he finished the drink.

"Burnouts."

"Doesn't really feel right; they don't catch fire," Anesh said, responding to James's idea for a name.

"The glass from them could start a fire. What about . . . I dunno . . . doom . . . bulbs." Anesh stared at him, pausing in his effort to rearrange their bags and note how many things they'd used from their medkits. "Yeah, that one got away from me. Come on! I know you already thought of one, just tell me!"

"Gaslights," Anesh said simply, going back to carefully stripping off his armor. "Because they're . . ."

"Yeah, I get it. Okay, fine. I still like burnouts, but we'll go with yours for now. Anyway, I'm gonna go find and disarm one." His voice started to speed up as the coffee kicked in. Anesh still wasn't sure if this was just how James reacted to caffeine in general, or if the enhancement properties of this drink in particular were what caused it.

Either way, Anesh thought, he couldn't really tell James that they should leave. He, personally, was exhausted. But his friend had essentially gotten a free eight hours of sleep, which was annoying, since Anesh kinda just wanted to leave but also didn't want to begrudge James a few more tries at loot.

The biggest problem with this place, as far as Anesh was concerned, was the time dilation. Eight hours here to three minutes outside. Okay, cool, they could do a lot in here and never be missed outside. But the flip side of that was that every Tuesday his sleep schedule got fucked right up. He came back out expecting it to be midmorning only to find it was still three a.m., and his body was *not* pleased with how this had been going. If they could find and easily identify a lot of those sleep orbs, it would solve this problem. But it was hard enough to get the damn things in the first place.

While he waited for James to come back, he watched Ganesh playing with Rufus. The two of them seemed to be getting along really well, and he smirked to himself as he realized that he sort of thought of Ganesh as half kid, half pet. But watching them made him think of how Rufus could manipulate the orbs, which in turn made him remember his unsavory skill from earlier, and that put him in a bit of a sour mood.

He was interrupted by James jogging back to their fort, still looking fresh and bright-eyed. This almost gave Anesh a spark of angry frustration, but then he felt a sort of peaceful empathy come down on him. James was, for all his faults, his friend, and Anesh wasn't gonna be mad over something as petty as the random drop rate. "How'd it go?" he asked.

In response, James just started laughing madly, holding up a bright red orb in one hand and a lightbulb in the other. "I was right!" he shouted, startling Rufus and Ganesh out of their play-wrestling. The two creatures crawled over to the edge of the desk as James came in. "All I had to do was unscrew the bulb without it seeing me! I am a genius!" he yelled, and Anesh gave him a mock round of applause, noting while he clapped that James's armor had a few dots of cooling glass on it. Clearly, he'd needed a few attempts.

"Well, congrats, friend. Do you want to go get something to eat and crack it at the diner? I know for a fact they're open."

James nodded. "Yeah, it turns out, I'm starving. Eight hours of sleep is great and all, but it's also eight hours sans food," he said. "Oh! I got you a present too!" He dropped a couple smaller skill orbs into Anesh's hand. "Now! Let's go eat! You're buying me a vindication burger!"

Anesh shook his head, smiling. Testing the effects of coffee on James could maybe wait until he had a little less of a headache.

CHAPTER 23

"That guy is a drug dealer," Anesh said, pointing at one of the other patrons of their local somehow-twenty-five-hour diner with his finger close to the table and out of sight of his target.

James looked up from putting ketchup on his victory burger and took great care to not look too suspicious as he stretched his arms and scanned around the establishment. "Really? That guy? How do you figure?" he asked his friend.

Anesh drove his fork into his salad. "Pattern recognition skill. It's . . . honestly kind of weirdly useful. It's not like I'm a detective-serial-level savant, but I'm seeing all these little connections in everything." He munched on a tomato slice. "That guy over there is here every time we come in at this time of night, he's got three different people that he eats with on rotation, and all of them treat him like he's their boss. He always gives them small gift-wrapped boxes like he's some uncle handing out presents, so it's probably a high-impact low-volume drug. He also tips too well, I assume so the staff think he's friendly and don't make the connection on the drug thing. And the weird bit is, I can't be sure about any of those base facts, but my brain just sort of spins them all together and creates a reasonable estimation of a truth from them. Big picture."

"What if, and go with me on this journey, he is just friendly?" James asked, looking with distrust at Anesh's salad.

"I think he just threatened to cut that guy's ear off. This skill is insane, I should be a detective," Anesh said, gesturing with his fork.

"What would you detect?"

Anesh just shrugged. "Crime? I mean, I don't have magic answers, I just sort of notice things now. Like, to a frightening degree. Did you know this city has fewer streetlights in lower-class neighborhoods? I can't tell you if that's cause or effect, but I can tell you it's accurate information, just from the drive over here." He looked around the diner. "I don't feel like I'm a different person or like my mind is working differently, just that I suddenly remember all these little things and see a thousand connections between stuff in the world." He looked up at James, his eyes drooping from exhaustion but still meeting his friend's interrogative stare. "It's kind of cool. *Though*, I can't actually prove any of this. It might actually just be the skill taking all the stuff I already know and slapping it together, and if I'm gonna be honest with myself..."

"You should always be honest with yourself! Also with me, but that's a personal preference."

"I can commit to that." Anesh smiled. "But seriously, I don't know if this is objective information? I'm worried about my own information biases, really."

He and James ate in silence for a couple minutes, with Anesh just making the mechanical motions of putting food inside him while James ravenously tore into his burger. Though he felt like some of the flavor was drained away as he kept throwing glances at the person Anesh had pointed out.

After the third look, Anesh threw his hands up in the air before shout-whispering at James, "Oh, fine, I'll call the police when we leave! But only because of the ear thing."

James gave him a level look. "You were going to do that anyway, weren't you?"

"Yes, but you seemed so upset, I figured I should tell you now just so you'd stop fidgeting. Though it has been making it easy to steal your fries." James looked down at Anesh's words to see a plate about half-empty of its previous fried-potato bounty.

"Hey!" He reached over to steal some of Anesh's food in response and then just stopped. If there was one benefit to ordering a salad at four a.m., it was that it pretty much gave his friend immunity to having food pilfered.

Really, James thought, it felt weird. His friend looked normal—well, as normal as a half-asleep zombie with a few too many obvious burns could look—but he was essentially making logical leaps that seemed . . . out of place, in a way, to James.

"What about the orbs?" he asked. "Any insight into those?"

Anesh swallowed a mouthful of spinach before answering. "Nah. Like I said, this is all just stuff that, *if* we thought about it, we'd notice. We have . . . put significant thought into the orbs. We know they all give skills, we know the general sources for all five of them now, and we sorta know what the dungeon is using them for. I'm not a mind wizard, man, it's just one skill point."

"Yeah," James said, "but you're not using it on purpose." There was a break in the conversation as their waiter came over to ask if they needed anything else and clear their plates away, and Anesh didn't respond while he was there. As soon as the waiter was out of earshot, though, James leaned in again. "You're not, are you? It's a passive. Like me walking like Bruce Lee. You can't turn it off, because it's just part of you now."

Anesh nodded silently. He'd noticed it. Of course he'd noticed it, that was sort of the whole problem. A lot of their skills were active: things that they only really got when they brought them to the forefront of their minds and took action. But some, like this one, weren't. They were passive, like James said, and he was right when he noticed that they were always on. He didn't mind picking up Shakespearean dialogue as a skill, even though he'd never use it; that was fine, since he could just never use it. But he did mind this, because his tired brain didn't have a defense against this level of insight into the world.

He didn't like knowing that their waiter was struggling to make rent for the month, and also that the easiest way to disable him would be to strike for the ankle that he'd sprained last week. He especially didn't like that he couldn't turn that off.

James just leaned back and shook his head. "Well, this sucks. I don't want to have to worry about getting a skill that makes me, I dunno, a complete asshole all the time, without my knowledge."

"I have bad news for you, mate." Anesh said the words before his brain caught up, the joke slipping out a little more hostile than he'd intended with the stress on his mind. He saw James's eyes go wide and felt his own mirror them. "No, wait, hang on . . ." But James interrupted him by bursting out laughing.

It wasn't actually very hard to offend James. Between growing up being bullied and a general amount of anxiety for his own failures, he had settled on a policy of taking as little shit as possible from the people around him. More than once, James had simply exiled someone from their apartment and friend group for crossing a line that they hadn't known they were creeping up on. He had a bit of a temper when it came to cruelty. But here, with Anesh defensively holding up his hands, looking for all the world like a deer in the headlights, James could only find it in him to laugh.

Of course he knew his friend didn't mean him any harm. They'd thrown around worse banter with each other before. Anesh was tired and not thinking straight, and they were both on edge with the knowledge that they might not have full control over their skills, and he didn't blame him for thinking he'd gone too far.

But getting angry over a good dig like that, he just didn't have that in him. Not right now, anyway. James pulled out the orb he'd secured from the trap: a small, fingertip-sized dot of red. He stared at it for a few seconds before looking back at Anesh. How could he be angry when the two of them had done so much tonight? They'd faced death together, looted treasure together. It was a form of companionship that was immediately understandable to the D&D-playing part of James's brain. And it meant, among other things, that Anesh got to call him an asshole whenever he wanted to.

"So," he said when he'd finished laughing and Anesh had calmed down a bit, "you want to see what these things can do?"

James didn't wait for Anesh to answer him. The allure of something new was pretty strong. He'd seen a term recently when going through some game discussion on a forum; someone had mentioned that new games often had trouble getting feedback, especially RPGs, because of what they called "beta tester syndrome." Players just wanted to try out new things, and so they failed to fully delve, explore, and exploit any given mechanic. He felt like that was pretty solidly where he and Anesh were. The skill he'd picked up a while ago subtly pushed him to categorize things like the orbs as "game mechanics," and he understood them pretty well through that lens. He knew that there were probably a lot of little things that they could do that they didn't understand yet; Rufus being able to re-form a skill orb was a huge indicator of that. But while James was certainly interested in filling in the gaps in his understanding over time, he wasn't in the same hurry Anesh was. He didn't feel the need to test green orbs in a variety of locations, and he didn't have any particular desire to scan the small orbs before use, like Anesh wanted to. Well, maybe the blues.

It wasn't that he didn't want to use every orb all the time, though. Really, James just liked the rush. Feeling himself getting . . . better. All that knowledge and improvement packed into a few seconds; he should ask Anesh how it he felt about it, because to James, it was a wild ride that he didn't want to ever get off.

So he didn't hesitate to pop the small red ball between his fingers. A ring of dusty smoke drifted out of it before fading, and James smelled the barest hint of cherries. Though that might have been someone in the kitchen burning pie.

[+1 Emotional Resonance Rank : Melancholy]

He waited for the drifting alien thought to continue, but that was it. "That's it?" he said out loud, and Anesh waved his hand expectantly, motioning for him to spill it. "One rank of melancholy!" he announced.

"Melancholy is a skill?" Anesh sat up a little straighter.

James shook his head. "Melancholy is an 'emotional resonance.' Got one rank of it. I don't . . . know what that means at all. Well, no, I do know what that means, I just don't want to. I already cry at the endings of half the anime I watch; I don't think I need this, too," he muttered.

"To be fair, you mostly watch sad anime," Anesh said. "Now . . ." He pulled out the orange orb that was his winnings from the day and set it on the table. "Thoughts on this?"

"It's gonna give you a motorcycle," James said without hesitation.

Anesh, in his reply, had *plenty* of hesitation. "Why?" he asked, drawing out the word with suspicion.

"Because I want it to, mostly. The last one gave you a driver's license. Seems like the logical progression."

"Your version of logic is a bit buggered, isn't it?" Anesh asked as he picked up and popped the orb.

[Certification Added : Citizenship - Canada]

[+5 Skill Ranks : Appraisal - Furniture - Antique]

"Okay, the orange ones give legal status, it would seem. Also, I'm moving north," he said.

"What, now?" James asked as they stood up. They'd opted to test the greens some other time, being pretty much exhausted right now. These two orbs were their own special treat to themselves.

Anesh shook his head. "Nah, I need to learn new slang first. Start saying 'eh' after every sentence to go with my new Canadian citizenship."

"This feels unfair again for some reason," James griped.

"The world is unfair sometimes, my friend," Anesh told him as he pulled out his newly stuffed wallet. He looked over at their waiter, the guy rushing between eight tables who'd been on shift for well over twelve hours. He'd overheard a few comments between him and the line cook, and from the tone of his voice, Anesh was pretty sure the dude was on the cusp of being evicted. "The world is unfair," he muttered, and James watched out of the corner of his eye as he dropped six hundred dollars on the table tucked under their bill. "But maybe sometimes it can be unfair in a fun way." He looked back up, and James avoided looking at his friend for a second, a tight feeling in his chest. "Ready to go?" Anesh asked like nothing had happened.

"Yeah. Let's go home," James said.

And the two of them walked out into the cool night air.

CHAPTER 24

"No, that's a stupid idea! The noise will get us killed." This was the first thing James heard as he came back into the apartment after his meditation class. The speaker, JP, was one of the cluster of people around his living room table, with Anesh sitting at the head with all his GM notes.

"Hey, guys," James said. "What noise will get you all killed?" he asked as he dropped the multipurpose duffel bag that he felt had taken over his life recently on the floor. A chorus of greetings assaulted him from his friends as he walked over and looked down at their game map.

It was JP who answered first. "Alanna wants to bring a chaingun into this place we found."

"Because it's a great idea!" Alanna burst out from across the table. "I am absolutely sure that I can out-DPS the dungeon mobs! Also I don't actually know if the assault cannon is described in the rulebook as a chaingun. I think it's ... literally a cannon? This book is badly formatted."

"It's a terrible idea," JP nodded and said, speaking to James and ignoring her outburst. "Too much noise attracts more creepy shit, but neither of them wants to go with my plan of being stealthy, since they built combat characters."

A disturbing thought struck James. "Wait, hang on. Dungeon? I thought you guys were playing *Shadowrun*," he asked, looking at notes and character sheets for an unfamiliar system on the table.

"Oh, we are," JP said. "We just found this weird zone outside of normal space in an office building. It's some kind of experiment gone wrong. We've been hired to go in and make it stop warping time and space. Or something. It's not a great job, really."

"I . . . see," James said, staring at Anesh. "So . . . you're coming up with plans for how to do this?"

"Yup!" Dave and Alanna said simultaneously, before alternating back and forth between snippets of sentences. "Figuring out how to get in and out safely." "Figuring out what we can easily loot." "Oh, trying to find stuff that kills the monsters and still counts as weaponry!" "Oh yeah, god, that whole thing with the cable snake was a nightmare!"

James held up his hands, placatingly. "Okay, I made a mistake. I asked people playing an RPG to talk about the RPG. That was my fault, I'm mature enough to admit that." He glanced at Anesh. "You know what you're doing here?" His question was innocent enough to everyone else sitting there, but he was really asking Anesh, *Is this a good idea?* James hated the mental block that kept him from talking about the dungeon with his friends; he'd like nothing more than to get these people in on the whole thing. And while it was super funny for Anesh to use their weekly adventures as RPG fodder, he was honestly worried about what would happen if his friend *did* break that rule.

He cared about Anesh a lot. He didn't want his friend getting hurt by some random brain parasite they'd picked up. Or at all, really.

The dungeon, so far, had made it nearly impossible for them to share information, even by accident. But they both kept pushing that limit, trying to find loopholes and side options. And Anesh seemed to have found something here by phrasing it as a game and changing enough small details. And really, James thought, the biggest thing was that they didn't have the time to *plan*.

He'd noticed this over the course of his day. The dungeon occupied his thoughts nearly constantly, but his mind was exhausted. He wasn't burning out on it or anything, though the actual physical burns weren't great. But he was finding it very hard to generate new ideas. He was just too mentally tired, from everything in his life, to really buckle down and come up with good concrete ideas about how to approach the dungeon.

JP, though? Alanna? Dave? They didn't have to worry about that. They just had a game.

And from their weekly D&D games, James knew at least one of those three people was a mastermind. A clown, sure, but a legitimate genius at getting a group of people to commit to a plan and make that plan *work*. In game, sure, but James had gone to school with JP. Grown up with him. The charm and smarts he played on the table did extend into real life.

It was a real shame JP wasn't trying to take over the world. James thought he'd be able to do it. Even if he wouldn't trust him to actually run things.

"Yeah, I'm good," Anesh said with a smile, answering James's original question. "It's all in good fun. Also, Alanna brings up a good point. Guns are too loud, and you guys are going to get swarmed and murdered. But don't let me stop you! I'm just the GM!"

A round of laughter followed James as he walked down the hall to his room. He shook his head, smiling. That warm feeling that built in his chest at times like this had a bit of a sad edge now. It would have been a ton of fun to get in on the game, but his new schedule just didn't make it work. Even on his off days, he was spending less time here, less time with his friends, and more time improving himself. Meditation sessions, cooking class, and a lot of time at the gym. He could feel himself getting stronger, and he was certainly becoming more adept at moving smoothly. Between his randomly acquired martial art skill and a Krav Maga class, he felt like he took walks now actually *hoping* to get mugged, just to see what he could do.

That was the thing that the dungeon had changed most about him in this short time.

He felt motivated. He felt uncomfortable now relaxing and playing video games, like he was wasting time he could be spending sharpening himself. He felt . . . like a different person. And he wasn't sure he disliked it.

That said, he still slumped into his chair, muscles unknotting as he relaxed. It took him a few minutes of staring at his ceiling before he decided that maybe a couple hours of gaming wasn't *that* bad. Though first, he went over to the little pen where he was keeping Lily to note down the results of the first yellow orb they'd given her and swap it out with another. He and Anesh had tried to get her to scan one of the blues, but the time-to-completion given was upward of a week, and they simply did not have the time for that.

Two hours, six lost roguelike runs, and one hot shower later, James came out of his room to find that the tabletop session had wrapped up. "Oh hey, you're still awake," Anesh said in greeting.

"Well, you're up, and I'm out," JP said from the door. "You missed the other two, and I'm just leaving. Hey, you should get your schedule changed and play with us. This is a pretty cool setting." He threw open the door with bravado, not waiting for James's answer. "Let me know when you get that taken care of!" he called back, throwing his arm over his head as he walked out into the night.

Anesh shook his head. "He's way too energetic."

"I dunno, I'm a fan." James smirked back. "So, get any good ideas from them?" he asked as he threw himself onto the couch, still warm from the people who had occupied it.

Anesh opened up his laptop on the table. "I took some notes. They had a lot of thoughts that I really liked and we should explore. We should look into getting something more geared for actual combat than a five-kilo sledgehammer. Also, real armor. Like, SWAT armor. Turns out you can just buy it, and our friend group knows some really weird facts like that."

"I'm not surprised."

"Yes, well. The other suggestion was getting an actual maul made. Did you know that there are real blacksmiths that have actual websites where you can give them money to make you preposterous weapons?" Anesh said, and James was pretty sure he did so with the clear memory of having exactly that pointed out to him by their friends over the last couple hours. "Anyway, aside from that, when we were playing, JP kept trying to look into things like they were puzzles. You know, like it was an actual RPG-dungeon dungeon. And it got me thinking."

"Why *aren't* there puzzles?" James asked, butting in.

"Why aren't there puzzles," Anesh echoed.

He thought for a second before answering. "I mean, it's not a dungeon, right? That's my first instinct to answer. But it is, isn't it? It has monsters, biomes, loot drops . . . why wouldn't it have puzzles?"

"Why not, indeed," Anesh said, steepling his fingers and leaning back in his chair. "We've been trying really hard to not treat this like a game, but maybe we should go the other way on this bit."

"Okay, but here's my question. Why would it make 'puzzles,' or things that we'd see that way?" James said, thinking out loud. He let himself ramble on a bit, his thoughts starting to click. "We don't even have a framework for what this place is, but it's clearly got rules to it. Maybe puzzles serve a purpose? Hell, do we even know if the monsters do?" He groaned and rubbed at his eyes. "I am too tired for this."

"Yeah, let's just be on the lookout for anything new. Anyway, I've got a short list of gear we should look into. You wanna check this site and tell me if any of these stand out to you?" Anesh swiveled his laptop around to James, who started browsing while Anesh kept talking. "Also, I was reading a while back about how to set up tripwire traps and stuff like that. We should maybe plant a bunch of those around the entrance and just 'harvest' them each week if they catch a stapler or something."

James made a low *ehhhhh* noise at that. "I dunno, man. Like, Rufus is friendly, right? And we've seen a lot of the basic shellaxies not really be that hostile if we don't piss them off. I don't want to just start killing everything because it's convenient for us."

His roommate threw his hands over his head and in a comical mocking voice said, "But how will we be good murder-hobos if we don't?" He cleared his throat theatrically. "Seriously, though. I'm okay with not rigging traps. It would probably be nice to have some back-ups near Fort Door, but I don't want to run into our own traps when we forget where we planted them. Also, like you said, a lot of stuff in there isn't hostile, and I'm not interested in killing what amounts to random wildlife. So I don't mind. Just wanted to bring it up."

The two of them broke off talking for a second while Anesh got up to go make some food, and James kept looking through the literal weapon shop that his partner had found for him. He was pretty interested in getting something that had a little more use than the sledgehammer, but the more he looked at images of spears and battle-axes, the more acutely aware he became of the fact that he had absolutely no real training with these things. He still had a pretty uncomfortable memory of snapping two of his friend's fingers in half with a crowbar, and that was way less damage than he could imagine inflicting with a bad spear swing.

"Okay," Anesh announced on his return from the kitchen with a plate of leftover stir-fry. "What else do we have to go over, while we've got the time and you're awake?"

James let out a sudden "Oh!" and jumped up, rolling over the back of the couch. Anesh watched him run off and then come back a few seconds later holding a piece of paper and a pair of skill orbs. "We've got these two that Lily ID'd for us."

"Weren't there three skorbs?" Anesh asked, confused.

James pointed a stern finger at him. "First of all, I refuse to call them skorbs. We need to work on better nicknames for them. Second of all, yes. And she ate one. It's ... probably fair. Anyway!" He continued on, ignoring Anesh's protests. "We've got two things here, both slightly different. First one is *'Power unit type : Memory. Operational time : 412 hrs/1k. Purity : 44%.'* Not sure what the last bit means. Second one is *'Contained time : 21 hours 9 minutes. Contains traces of : Melody, History.'*"

"Hm. Give me that note so I can actually understand that." Anesh motioned, and James passed over the scrap of paper. "Okay, so, we've seen some of this before. These things are obviously power units for the monsters, we've got that down. What's purity for?"

James shrugged. "Not sure why you're asking me. Hey, where do these come from anyway? Like, does the dungeon just produce power, and this is a side effect of how it manifests? Or is this intentional?"

"I'm not sure..." Anesh started to say.

James finished, "Why I'm asking you, yeah, I know." He repeated his own statement from a second ago. "Well, you've got your spreadsheet up, right? Go ahead and use them and see what you get."

At this point, Anesh wasn't going to turn down an orb. Sure, he'd been burned a bit by the uncomfortable truth about actives versus passives and his own bad luck on one skill, but he felt more or less the same way James did. There was an allure to them, and he didn't want to pass up the opportunity for just a little extra bit of something interesting in his life. He took the two little glowing golden dots from James and cracked them open without looking back.

[+1 Skill Rank : History - Music - Mozart]

[+1 Skill Rank : Tae Bo]

"Well, I know what the music history one is," he remarked dryly.

James looked at him expectantly. "What?"

His friend, with a perfectly straight face, said, "Music history." James turned his expectant look into a scowl before he lost it and started laughing. Anesh didn't bother trying to not join in, and the two of them took a minute to just enjoy the delivery.

"Okay, that's pretty much it," James said. "I don't have anything else I really want to talk about. Except, oh! What's your nickname for the copier enemy?" Anesh gave him a sideways glance. "Come on, you have the best names for everything. And I know you've already named it."

Anesh leaned forward over the table, pressing both his palms to his forehead. Taking a deep breath, he looked up at James. "Of course I haven't named it. It's a copier. It... like, reality did my job for me. It copies things, and it's a copier." James just stared at him expectantly. "No, no! I really don't have one! It's exactly what it says on the tin! It's a fucking copier! No!" He stood up and stormed out of the room. "No!" he yelled from down the hallway. James waited a half minute, and, Anesh stormed back in, grabbed his laptop, pointed at James, and in a quiet and firm tone, repeated one more time, "No." Before leaving for good.

"So are we on for a light run for this Tuesday?" James called down the hallway. Anesh didn't answer. "Guess he's actually not coming back," James muttered to himself. "Damn, I had a great pun about the weapons and us getting all this gear and being maul-ninjas." James sighed. Well, if that was all Anesh wanted to talk about, it was probably time for bed.

He really was looking forward to their next trip. They weren't planning on hitting the bathroom this week, but they still had so many little things to try out. It felt pretty good, really. Like they'd be accomplishing a lot of things, as opposed to just making progress on one big thing. Actually taking the time to "clean out their side quests," as Anesh kept calling it, made James feel like they were doing chores in the best way. And the chores dropped loot and might try to kill him.

Also, it bought them some time for the stuff Anesh wanted to order to actually come in. With their efficient looting pattern last week, they'd managed to collect almost five thousand dollars in cash, so James had no problem giving him control of their funds and seeing what he came up with. Anesh had gotten really into the logistics of the whole thing, and James was pretty much fine just letting him deal with that entirely. It wasn't that James wasn't interested, more that if Anesh hadn't come in and actually started pushing for legitimate upgrades to their kit, James would still be using a crowbar.

And maybe also be dead.

James jolted awake off the couch to the sound of his phone alarm, his improvised nap interrupted by the familiar and jarring tune. It was somewhere around eleven p.m., and he had one last thing to do tonight before he could actually sleep. The dream he'd been having, which he vaguely remembered being about cats in some way, drifted through his mental fingers as he swore and fumbled for the alarm button.

His car was freezing, and he took some time to wait for the heat to come on before driving off. The biting cold had absolutely no effect on the smell of worn faux-leather seats and the lingering aura of fast food. Taking a main road into the center of town, James hummed along with the radio while he headed to his destination.

His destination, at this hour, was something he had mentioned to Anesh after the incident with his boss when they looted the coffee machine. The problem, really, was that there was one entrance that wasn't alarmed and, in general, one person who was both omnipresent and absolutely willing to rat them out.

Frank.

Frank was not a bad guy. He also wasn't really a good guy. At the age of fifty, he was the kind of older person who valued silence. *Gruff* was a good word for him. Gray hair, a goatee that never went out of style, a little more muscle than you'd expect on a wiry old guy frame; he was a good fit for the kind of person who was working a terrible security desk job at four a.m. Again, not a bad dude. But he was the kind of person who felt like anyone trying to get away with anything was doing so at his expense.

It was James's most sincere hope that when he was old, he'd know how to take a joke better than Frank. It was also his hope that Frank was the kind of guy who could let anything slide as long as he thought he was in on the con.

So he'd ended up here, at a bar called Ichabod's, where Frank spent Friday nights like this one drinking. It was recently remodeled and still looked a bit awful anyway. The inside had fancy light fixtures and fresh seats but couldn't shake the perpetual feeling of quiet desperation that kept James far, far away from establishments like this. His target, the old security guard, was drinking by himself at the end of the bar.

The whole place was fairly busy, but James still found an open stool and pulled up next to the man who was working his way through a beer. "Hey, Frank."

Looking over, unsmiling, Frank took a second to recognize him. "Ah, Jim!" he said in a vaguely surprised and totally uninterested tone. His voice was like rough gravel, hardened from a life of cigarettes and cheap beer. "What're you doing here?"

James took a deep breath. This wasn't something he had a lot of experience in, and he was well outside his comfort zone. So he hoped that Frank would be okay with the direct approach. "Well, sir, I'm here to try to bribe you." Frank raised an eyebrow. "A lot, really."

"That's a new one," Frank grumbled. He ordered another beer from the bartender, and James took the chance to get himself a glass of cranberry juice, explaining himself as a driver. "Bribe me for what?"

"Remember the coffee maker?" James asked, and Frank nodded. "Well, there's going to be more things like that. My friend and I bringing stuff in and out, sometimes weird stuff. We'd like you to just not say anything to anyone."

"Weird stuff, eh? Weird like a coffee maker that you didn't steal from anywhere?" Frank set his beer down and pointedly didn't make eye contact with James. "You two playing some kinda practical joke?"

James nodded slowly. "Maybe, though not on you."

"You stealing anything?" Frank asked bluntly, biting off the words like they offended him.

"No, sir," James said, totally honest.

"You hurting anyone?" Frank followed up without pause.

"No, sir," James said, slightly less honest depending on what *anyone* could mean.

"You plan on paying me more than those corporate parasites, Jim?"

James pulled out a thousand dollars in twenties and set it on the bar in front of Frank. "Yes, sir," he said as he saw Frank's eyebrows twitch up just a bit.

Thumbing through the money, Frank turned to really look at him for the first time. "Tell me one last thing, Jim," he said. "This isn't about anything weird and dangerous, is it?"

James couldn't keep himself from smiling a little as he said, "I'm afraid it is, sir."

"Hmph," the gray-haired man grunted, turning back to his drink. "Well. Good luck, kid. And stop calling me sir. I work for a living."

James hurried the hell out of there before he either called him sir again or couldn't tolerate being called Jim anymore. And just like that, one more obstacle was out of their way. And James could finally get home and pass out for real.

It was dark, and bright, all at once. There was a whistling noise that bounced around him like a cat.

James was dreaming.

He realized it and wasn't surprised. He stayed calm as he watched the dream unfold around him, cathedral spires and stone floors pulling themselves together. He walked through the hallways, marveling at the stained-glass windows that showed him faces from his past.

He'd never realized how many friends he'd had in school. How many people he'd stopped talking to over the years.

The cathedral kept going, a kind of temple to James's relationships. He saw Anesh more than once: armed and armored in one, running a game in another, just lounging around watching TV in a bathrobe in the third. He showed up more than anyone else.

And then James started to see Rufus. Not just Rufus, but other dungeon monsters as well. There was the tumblefeed; there was one of the masks. He saw a window that showed a shadowed figure triumphing over a swarm of staplers. And he saw one window that had that stupid copier on it.

God, he hated that thing. Without thinking about it, James realized he had a rock in his hand, and with a slippery mental effort, he hurled it at the copier's colored pane, punching a hole through it with a glimmering sound that bounced around his mind. Behind it, there was simply nothing.

No, not nothing.

There was a glimmering yellow ... something ... out there. With a bit of will, James pushed away the cathedral, the dream, the stained glass, the whole dream. He almost woke up right there, but he hung on to that floating nothing of sleep. And there, in his mind, he could feel something bright and yellow and *alien*. It was a thread, with some small dots along it. He ran out a hand in his mind and followed it, and ran across more bumps and places where it split into other threads. He could feel a connection to them, though.

They were his skills. Sitting here in his dream, and totally outside his influence. James pulled back and saw the whole web of them, a drifting wireframe of shining yellow, with a small splash of red in one part of it. His victories, his growth, laid out before his dreaming eyes.

But there was something else. Something lurking there, behind the darkness, behind everything. Deeper down and farther in. And it had not been invited and wasn't supposed to be here. James could feel it, watching him, pulling on his mind. It thought, but it was not alive. It saw but did not know it was watched.

Here is an experiment: sit with your eyes closed and imagine a ball. Now imagine that the ball is made of interlocking brass rings. Those rings each have a needle running through them that can move in or out, allowing the rings to spin around each other. Now add a core, another ball of rings.

Now imagine that there is a thought inside those spheres that you must keep pinned down. That the slightest slip will allow it out.

That was how James felt, trying to grab that errant part of his mind.

It slipped through his mind's fingers, again and again. It was never in reach; it defied every attempt to contain it. James tried to bring memories of knives and fire, to stab and burn it from its hiding places, but it just ignored them. Pain and death were alien to it, so much so that it could not die. He tried ripping it into pieces, but the dreaming shards drew themselves back together before he'd even finished the thought that cut them up.

On and on, he struggled to destroy the intruder. Like picking at a scab, or trying to ignore the need for breath, he couldn't help himself. But no matter what he tried, it simply. Would. Not. Die.

And then James woke up, alarm screaming, and himself along with it.

It was going to be a long day.

CHAPTER 25

"Okay, so, what are we doing tonight? Do you have a full list?" James asked Anesh as they sat in James's cubicle. He was currently between calls, having just explained to someone that it was reasonably unlikely that their phone was being tapped by the Chinese government. He specifically said "unlikely," because he had a weird gut feeling that on the other side of the world, there was someone at a desk just like his, speaking a different language, explaining to a disgruntled spy over the phone that it was pretty unlikely that the random middle-aged woman he was wiretapping in the United States was actually on to him.

Anesh was standing in the middle of the small desk cluster, of which only one of the chairs was actually occupied. He was staring at the ceiling tiles above James's desk, one of which had been marked by a small Sharpie'd X. "First thing on the list is figuring out why you haven't changed desks if there's a dimensional rift that spits out monsters above this one."

James looked up at the ceiling briefly. "Well, I like this desk," he said before going back to hitting the random button on Wikipedia to kill time.

"There are dozens of empty desks around here. Just pick another one that isn't near the possibly murderous mob spawner," Anesh said, straining his ears to listen for any scratching noises above them. "Wait, actually, why are there so many empty desks? Does your company not employ people? I get that you're not super busy right now, but this floor is huge compared to the two people working here."

"Okay, I get what you're saying," James said as he looked over the Wikipedia page for a Mr. Benjamin Kelsey. "But I don't think it's a dungeon thing. We've just had a lot of people quit, and our corporate overlords have a hiring freeze on because one of their manufacturing facilities is losing them money, and it's . . . it's just a whole *thing*." He tapped at his desk, turning to face Anesh as his friend made a disbelieving snort. "No, really, I mean, it can't be a dungeon thing, right?" A blank stare met his question. "There's no evidence of it! I've seen people just walk out in the middle of the shift, there's no signs of struggle around here unless you count the crippling ennui we all deal with from too much tech support, and if employees really were being eaten by a monolithic entity from outside reality, I'm pretty sure management would *replace them faster*."

"That last one is a good point. Your country has some weird employer policies," Anesh grumbled. James sighed as he took a last call for the night, but Anesh kept talking at him even as the customer did. "But still. We know there's multiple doors now. Or holes? We need a good term for the entrances. We also know literally nothing about where the skill orbs come from, aside from random-ass guesses." James waved frantically at Anesh. "I'm just saying, we aren't really sure about—"

James physically stood up, saying a quick "I'm sorry, ma'am, please hang on." He unclipped his headset, got up, and casually pushed Anesh out of his cubicle area with minimal effort, leaving him standing in the hallway with a short *shh* noise, and ignoring Anesh's ongoing rambling now mixed with giggling. Dropping back into his chair, he unmuted the call. "Now, ma'am, I think I misheard you. I thought you said your phone was hit by a train? . . . I see. Okay, let's look up your warranty."

"How many calls like that do you get?" Anesh asked as they both did some stretches in Fort Door. After one too many instances of burning soreness in their legs after a night of constant running away from things, James had insisted on adding this to their gearing-up routine.

He thought about it for a while. "I mean, probably one in every three is something bizarre. I blame Google, really," he said, limbering up his arms.

"Google?" came the puzzled question.

James nodded. "Yeah, see, as the number of problems that can be solved via Google increases, the density of insane calls to tech support rises as well. If people can fix small stuff, they *usually* don't bother us. So we get more calls from people who are either . . . really dumb . . . or who have fucking weird problems."

"How did her phone get hit by a train?"

"Oh no, *she* got hit by a train and it damaged her phone."

Anesh froze in mimicking James's stretching routine. "And she . . . called you?"

"She was bored in the hospital. Gotta have something to do, I guess." James shrugged as he finished up and started strapping on armor. "Though that does make me wonder how she called me. Borrowed a phone, maybe? Now! Do we have an objective list?"

They did, in fact, have an objective list. James wanted to go pick up those cameras they'd left behind, which had served their purpose quite well but were almost immediately forgotten in the wake of Ganesh being both animate and insanely helpful. It wasn't the most important thing in the world, but those cameras were pretty expensive, and even though they'd probably been in here for a lot of subjective time, he wanted them back if only for his own personal amusement. Anesh's personal goal today was to find one of the vending machines, funnel all the extra four-dollar bills they'd found into it, and fill up those carboys he'd bought with enough novelty beverage to last him through the next year.

More generally, they were looking for another colony of iLipedes. Anesh still refused to touch the things, but he had no problem with James using one to continually litmus-test for magic items. On that note, Anesh had an unofficial and unspoken goal of trying to get

James to call them something other than magic items before the end of the day. James himself also felt like there was never a problem with some casual looting, even though financially, Anesh assured him they were set for a little while. James also encouraged Anesh to put his pattern-recognition skill to use and see if they could find anything remotely approaching a puzzle in this place.

So they worked out their pattern while they strapped on their beat-up armor, and James gave Rufus some much deserved pets. Cameras first, then back off away from the break room. No need to go after another tumblefeed under-armed. Sweep out about a half mile into the cubes and find a vending machine, then trace a path back and get the hand cart with the jugs. Map it out the whole way and also leave signposts. Try to get a general idea for the layout beyond just their instincts.

"Hey, Rufus, you wanna come along with us this time?" James asked the little guy as they were stepping out the door. The strider looked up at his giant friend, and then back down at the paper clip web he was carefully spinning, before holding up two of his pen-legs in an X. "That's weirdly adorable. All right, see ya later, buddy!" James called as he and Anesh, with Ganesh riding his human's shoulder, took off. As they passed by, Rufus raised one leg, and Anesh, seeing it, took a second to high-five the little stapler.

They stalked into the outer ring of cubicles, and Rufus watched them vanish into the beige maze. He appreciated James's offer, but he was never going back in there if he could help it.

"I feel like an idiot," James remarked as they were two turns into the maze. He was taking point, with Ganesh staying low on Anesh's shoulder for now. This part of the office was fairly open, and he could pretty easily poke his head over a wall if needed; no need to advertise their presence by launching a drone up where everyone could see.

Anesh stalked along behind him, casually checking cubicles as the pair moved at a much faster pace than they had before. Neither of them had his weapons out yet, both having realized how fast their grip got tired and their palms got sweaty. "Why, aside from the normal reasons?"

This got a huffing chuckle from James. "I feel like you're abusing the banter license I gave you. But no, it's the stupid armor." He kept twitching his shoulders, trying to get the football padding to settle into a more comfortable position.

"Is it perhaps the giant hole in the back of the armor?" Anesh asked wryly, scanning a cube to their left for anything hostile. It was empty, but there was a suspiciously fresh-looking desk lamp in there, despite this being a cube they'd looted before.

"Exactly!" James said, trying to scratch at his back. "The edges melted weird, and it's poking me, and I hate it. I think I'm just gonna dump it here and go without today. We're not doing anything that should require it, right?"

"That's the logic that gets people who don't wear seat belts killed, James," Anesh said simply as he moved to take the lead. "Keep your stupid armor on. We'll get new stuff next week."

James simply grumbled as they kept moving, leaving the armor on. He wasn't happy about it, though; he didn't like feeling like there was anything motivating him to finish early here, in this place that gave his life so much spice.

They picked up the first two cameras fairly easily and had just gotten to the third when James noticed something. "Hey, this one still has its light on." Anesh looked over from his watch position. "Yeah," James said, "this one isn't dead. The battery is still good. Hang on." He fumbled in his pocket for a second before pulling out his phone, his *actual* phone, not an iLipede, and opening up the camera app. "Check it out." He flashed the screen over at Anesh.

"No way," Anesh replied in disbelief.

On the phone screen was a clear image of the two of them, along with the available controls for the wireless camera, and a battery bar that read 2%. "What the hell? I mean, these things have batteries that are supposed to last for a month or something, but isn't the time dilation too extreme here? Did we ever sort that out?" James asked.

Anesh grabbed his arm and pulled him back a step. "It could be alive now," he muttered. "But yeah, we did the math based on the clocks. Three minutes out, eight hours in. One week out, three years in. This thing shouldn't be functioning, unless we *were* wrong. What about the others?"

"The two we got are dead. Let's see . . ." He tapped his screen a couple times. "Yup, last one's up too, also almost out of juice. The hell?"

Anesh just pulled the camera down off its clipped mount. "Well, there's an easy answer. We're just wrong about the time bollocks," he spat out. "It's been about a month, right? So these bloody things must have only been here for a month, unless the staplers are changing their batteries. And that means there's something we don't know about the entrances."

"You swear funny when you're agitated." James snickered.

"Fuck off." Anesh swatted his shoulder pad. "Let's go get the last one and get moving." He strode off down the hall toward where they'd planted the sixth camera.

James laughed and followed.

Half an hour later, they were prowling back, slipping through the cubicle farm with a level of comfort that they just didn't feel deeper in. "Okay," James said, "drop these off, then go find a vending machine for ya, right?"

"Right," Anesh said. "But first, let's go through these few cubes. I think this is around where you found Lily? I want to see if you can get another one and we can go through a few thousand random things for altered items."

"Magic items," James said, stepping into the cube on the left.

Anesh took the desk on the right. "Nope," he said almost instantly.

James just snickered to himself as he looked through the cube. Pretty quickly, he could see no iLipedes, but he did see a stack of envelopes on the keyboard. "Internal memos?" he muttered to himself, picking one up and turning it over in his hands. "Cubicle number as an address, no name. Hm." He tossed it back down. "I feel like, if there were a dungeon puzzle, this is the part where I've stumbled into the third clue without finding the first, or knowing the goal."

He kept turning through drawers and documents, looking more for anything that stood out to him than something in particular. As he turned to leave, feeling like his cursory tossing of the cubicle was done, he spotted a purse over on a small metal cabinet in the corner that he'd missed the first time. Shrugging, he went over to the thick red leather bag and picked it up to see if it held anything of value.

Well, he tried to pick it up. It didn't work. He tried again, getting a good grip on it and pulling upward, but the purse stayed firmly attached to the two-drawer metal filing cabinet beneath it. James took a step back and looked at the stubborn object with eyebrows comically raised. "Well, ain't that some shit," he muttered. On the other side of the hall, he heard Anesh moving to the next cubicle, already done with his assuredly much more thorough search. James was falling behind his friend, but now he had something to be curious about, and he wasn't too concerned with keeping up.

Circling around to the side of the filing cabinet, James tried to see if there was anything behind it. It didn't look like it was attached to the walls, so he grabbed it by the base and dragged it out a few inches. He looked at it speculatively, pacing circles around the whole thing. James sure as hell wasn't going to stick his hand in the purse at this point, but he was curious as to what this whole setup *was*.

He kicked the cabinet. Nothing. Kneeling down, he gingerly reached out and opened one of the drawers, holding up his other arm in front of his face just in case. Also nothing. He peeked into the drawer. Paper. Which translated to nothing.

Standing back up, he stretched a bit and leaned in, poking at the purse, trying to see inside it.

"What are you doing?" Anesh said from the doorway.

James jumped a little bit. "Oh, just checking this out. You want to get the last cube and I'll catch up with you? I'm trying out this whole 'thinking before I act' thing."

Anesh snorted. "Good luck," he said, ducking back out and going off to keep scouring cubes.

Shaking his head, James looked back at the bag. There wasn't really anything in it, honestly. A few of what looked like lipstick tubes, a handful of business cards, a set of keys that most likely didn't match any existing door. But the damn thing wouldn't let James lift it up, and, again, he had no desire to test it by putting his hand inside if it might literally bite him.

So, in a moment of frustration, he planted his left foot and lashed out with his right, catching the bag with a solid side kick. And the immobile bag slid sideways off the cabinet, thumping into the floor. "Oh, fuck you," James muttered at it as he pulled his leg back from the kick. Leaning down, he went to grab the purse, but when he straightened his back, he found it now firmly attached to the floor itself. "Anesh!" he called over the cubicle wall. "I found something that can only go one way on the *y*-axis!"

There was a moment of silence, and then James heard something brittle cracking, followed by a fleshy tearing, from over the cubicle wall. James waited patiently as he heard something small and vaguely hard *thump* onto the floor over in Anesh's looting territory. "Which way?" he heard Anesh call back, a bit short of breath.

"Down!" he replied, glaring at the bag.

"Break it down into an orb, we can't use that," Anesh said from the door, having come over to look. He wiped some black ichor off his hand as he peered at the purse. "Why'd you drop it?"

"It was an accident," James said, pulling out his hatchet and laying a few hits on the purse. After the fourth one, it dissolved away, leaving behind a clear blue orb, this one larger than the few small ones they'd found before. "Huh. Size two. That makes me wonder if the 'only go down' thing is just really powerful, or if I should have checked for more magic first."

Anesh sighed. "Alterations. And it's probably fine. Here, I got this from the other cube, I think it's well past your turn." He tossed a small yellow to James.

"Thanks!" James said, pocketing the blue and cracking into the yellow.

[+.8 Skill Rank : Art - Painting - Miniatures]

Anesh was already out in the hallway, looking around and getting ready to move on. "Anything good?"

"Only if I'm dumb enough to start playing Warhammer again. Though hey, I got a fractional skill rank for this one. Does that mean that my mini-painting ability was only two-tenths of a skill? I'm . . . either offended or intrigued. How good am I now at highlighting armor plates?"

His friend didn't even look back as they started walking on. "I don't know what that means, but please don't paint my armor."

"No promises," James responded as they walked back toward Fort Door, already considering sticking some kind of space marine logo on his friend's backplate.

James sat on an overturned ceramic plant while Anesh fed four-dollar bill after four-dollar bill into the vending machine next to him. He idly tossed one of the slightly larger skill orbs, pilfered from this particularly vicious ficus, in his hands. "I've been thinking . . ." he said casually.

"Uh-oh," Anesh responded as he started pushing the button for the drink he'd settled on repeatedly. It was a curried fruit drink called, if they read the label right, Water Except It's Red.

"Oh, come on. This is vaguely important." James rolled his eyes as he rebuffed Anesh's quip. "So I've been thinking—shut up, Anesh—that what we're doing here isn't technically illegal. I think?"

Anesh started pulling out bottle after bottle of the drink from the vending machine, setting them in a neat pile next to the carboy he'd set up with a giant funnel for exactly this purpose. "You think?"

"Well," James said, "it's not like there's a law about this. But I think that, from a real estate standpoint, this whole place counts as 'somewhere else,' and not inside the building. So it doesn't 'belong' to anyone in particular." He shrugged, juggling his new skill orb. "I just think this falls under the category of unclaimed resource exploitation. Like if we were to capture an asteroid and mine it. No one gets a cut, because no one 'owned' it."

"Is asteroid mining something we have legal precedent for?" Anesh asked curiously.

"Sorta," James said. "Which is weird, and yes, we're living in the science fiction future, but it's there. I'm just saying, I don't think we need to worry about being arrested if we ever have to tell the police about this place."

"Why would we do that? Seems like a great way to be committed to a mental health institution." Anesh glanced at James. "Or arrested."

James shrugged. "I dunno, if this is secretly part of some apocalypse scenario, I'm passing it off to the guys who have grenade launchers."

"They won't believe you," Anesh said as he filled up his giant jug with soda. "Also, why the flying fuck do your police have grenade launchers? Also! We built a grenade launcher, on a technicality! We are the people you'd want between you and the apocalypse!" he finished excitedly.

"Sure, maybe," James replied. "But I sure don't want to face down an apocalypse myself. Also, that grenade launcher exploded, and I'm iffy on repeating that process. Though, you know, maybe." He looked over at Anesh. "Hey, do you mind if I use this orb? It's really tempting."

"Oh, yeah, go ahead, mate. Like I said, I feel like I've been getting all the good stuff lately. You should have a chance," Anesh said, still funneling his bizarre novelty drink into the giant container.

James thanked him and used the faintly glowing yellow orb in his hand.

[+2 Skill Ranks : Speed Reading]

"Holy shit, this one is actually pretty awesome. Speed reading!" He looked over at Anesh. "Probably just going to get more reading done. But hey, that's awesome. Do you know how much fun stuff there is to read on the internet?"

"I've heard it's 'some,'" Anesh replied. James laughed, and the duo lapsed back into comfortable silence, with James keeping watch while

Anesh went through the tedious process of filling up each of the three big jugs he'd brought with a choice drink for them to take home.

James just took the time to look around at his surroundings. Really look, that is. There were a few things posted on the outside of the cubicles around here, little comics or memos. Some of them looked like real-world newspaper comics, but with the word bubbles scrambled or left blank. The memos were all different phrasings of the same thing. "Someone's birthday today, looks like," he tossed over his shoulder at Anesh. "There's cake in either the conference room, the manager's office, or the overhead ventilation ducts, depending on which of these is accurate."

He glanced up and saw no overhead. They were maybe a mile, mile and a half in. They'd had to go through the break room to get here, but fortunately they didn't stumble across a tumblefeed on the way. They'd also been very careful and avoided all the rocket java on the way in, rather than risk making too much noise. Even still, there wasn't a ceiling here, just very tall cube walls. Visibility was pretty hard to achieve when the walls around you were ten feet tall, and the corridors were, while spacious for an office environment, still an office environment. But overhead, he could see distant white ceiling panels and fluorescent lights, unchanging and uninterrupted in their pattern.

And also something else.

"Hey, there's something moving up there," he muttered to Anesh. "Anesh! Hey!" His friend looked up.

Anesh peered at the ceiling as he dumped one of the last bottles into his final jug. "I don't see . . . Oh, there it is. Huh. Moving kinda fast. What is it?"

"I think . . . it's a paper airplane?" James squinted. "Yeah, it's far away, but it sure seems like it. Shit, that's cool. Maybe it's like the hawk predator to the pigeons that are the loose paper?"

"Maybe," Anesh said. "Just make sure it doesn't get too close. I don't want to get stabbed in the eye today." James gave him a mocking salute and went back to keeping watch. It was only a few more minutes until Anesh finished up. "All right," he said, "let's get out of here. We can check the time at the door and then go from there, yeah?"

James agreed and helped Anesh load the carboys onto the hand truck, tying them down with bungee cord. "I honestly am not sure how you expect our friends to react to this stuff."

"Well, I expect at least one of them to hate it, and that'll be funny, and at least one of them to like it, which will just be cool. And I'll tell them it's from England so no one questions it." Anesh shrugged. "Seems like the easy way to get around the mental coercion is to just tell really stupid lies. You have to try to be convincing, but that doesn't mean you can't make the lie itself obvious and dumb," he said, slapping one of the labels from Water Except It's Red onto the associated jug.

Shaking his head and chuckling, James led the way as they started heading back. He was all for Anesh trying to bait people into asking direct questions about the dungeon, really. It was just worrying that this level of mental control was happening to them. He thought back to his dream and the familiar feeling that the monster in his mind gave off. He was almost certain he recognized it, but he couldn't get a good look, or a good grip, on the intruder. Anesh still wasn't convinced that what James had seen was real, exactly, but James knew. And it was only a matter of time before he could strengthen his mind, just like he was doing with his body, to the point that even this level of coercion wouldn't stop him.

But for now, there was soda to swipe and monsters to watch for. And if they were lucky, before the end of the day, a few more orbs to crack.

"That's five yellows and an accidental blue," James said, tracking their gains. "We really need to go deeper in if we're going to find an iLipede today. Do you know why Ganesh stayed back at the fort?"

"No idea," Anesh said, peering around a corner. "Wait, hang on." He held up a hand. "Something weird there. Look."

He stepped aside to let James move up and look, and James peeked out around the tan fuzzy wall to see the hallway that led back to their home base. Normally, the halls here were more or less empty, with the occasional vending machine, water cooler, and oversized hostile plastic-potted plant sitting in the frequent intersections. But here, there was a waist-high metal pushcart sitting in the middle of the aisle, with tied bundles of paper sticking out of the sides of small slots and boxes. "Is that a mail cart? How'd it get here?" James asked.

Before Anesh could answer, James felt a dropping feeling in his stomach. His hand reached to his belt, and he unclipped his axe to grip tightly. Anesh mirrored his actions, the hair on both their arms standing up. "What the hell?" Anesh muttered.

James pulled back from around the corner. "Something's wrong here. Move back."

Anesh felt the creeping chill, but he wasn't as convinced. "Why? What did you see?" he asked, but James was already pushing him in the other direction.

James caught at his friend and turned him around in front of him. "Come on. It's one of the empty people you saw." He kept his voice at a sharp whisper as he shoved Anesh back the way they'd come. Behind them, he knew, that thing was stepping back to its mail cart and would be moving at any time. He didn't want to be there if it came toward them.

Bracing his feet, Anesh stopped James from shoving him along. "Hold on, just one? Calm down, man!" He broke James's grip and shoved his hands back a bit. "We can take just one!" he whispered rapidly, looking at James's too-serious expression.

"It looks like someone who used to work here!" James barked out in a low tone. "It looks like Jerome! It's just . . . absolutely not, and it's creepy! So that makes two things we've been horrifyingly wrong about in about an hour, and I'd like to get the fuck out right now before it gets worse!" he said.

"Okay, okay!" Anesh said calmly. He held up a hand. "I'm going to go check on it first. This matters, and you need to calm down. This is the first time we've seen one this far out in the ring; we need to see what it's doing."

James took a couple deep breaths. His friend was right. This place had been spooky since day one, and it wasn't like this changed that. Nor did it actually prove anything, though he had a gut feeling that told him that he knew exactly what this proved. "All right, fine. But it's moving around. I think these things pay a little more attention than the tumblefeeds."

They crept back to the corner, trying as hard as possible to move silently in the dead office air while wearing their light armor and heavy boots. This time, James went first, making a quick scan of the hallway before ducking back.

What he saw was . . . weirdly normal, while being utterly horrifying. The Thing That Was Not Jerome was, as Anesh had told him, shaped exactly like a person. It was wearing a blue polo shirt, it had one of those phone watches on, it had a cup of coffee on its cart. It moved like a human did, but not quite. The thing just didn't quite make the proper fluid movements, looking not exactly like it was jerking around, but more that it was just mistiming its own steps. The hollow person was pulling a stack of paper off the cart—letters and memos, from the look of it—and turned to take it into the next set of cubicles. James watched cautiously as it would go in, toss some mail down, then move on. It didn't seem at all concerned that these cubicles had been looted of anything of value, but then, maybe it didn't see value the same way he did.

He turned to whisper to Anesh that they should switch, but as soon as he did, he saw something behind his friend that made his heart rate spike. Pointing, wide-eyed, he watched Anesh spin around and see the same thing he did. A tumblefeed, the giant ball of tangled cables moving with shocking stealth; this one looked like it was made up mostly of power cords and phone chargers, and it was already only about ten cube lengths away, maybe a hundred and fifty feet tops.

James didn't have time to make an informed decision. He just knew they needed to get out of there. So he grabbed Anesh's arm again and pulled him around the corner, toward the inhuman human thing. Anesh started to protest, but there wasn't time to really worry about it or debate. James had a plan, even if it was a stupid one.

He strode down the hallway, and when the hollow man stepped out of the cubicle it was delivering mail to, James just gave it a wide smile and a wave and said, "Evening!" in a cheerful tone, walking on past.

Anesh glimpsed the face of the thing as they went by. Dark skin and white teeth turned up in a smile that would have been quite pleasant if it were on an actual person. Then that same face suddenly transformed into a sharp frown, and Anesh felt his skin go cold.

"Weapons are not allowed on company property. This is in the employee handbook." The flat voice from behind them was both monotone and strangely oscillating at the same time, with the emphasis on the wrong syllable in half its words. James turned to give a snarky answer, still walking backward, only to see the hollow employee holding up a brilliant purple orb.

He stopped walking for a second, curiosity and a bit of greed getting the better of him. Anesh stopped too and started to say, "Oh, we'll just..." But before he could finish, the creature... used... the orb.

The thing didn't break it like they did. Instead, it did something else that James couldn't quite process. He could tell that it did something, that action was impressed upon the orb in its hand, but not exactly what happened, because there was no physical motion. Even still, the orb split apart, and thin smoke and a few small points of light spun out of it, hurling down the hall toward them.

James threw out an arm and pushed Anesh behind himself. A heartbeat later, the glittering dust hit him, and he could sense more than feel it burrowing into his mind, not his body.

There was a *thunk* as his hand axe hit the ground. He hadn't told his hand to let go, but then, there were no weapons allowed on company property, so of course he wouldn't carry it. "Well, fuck," he said out loud. "We need to go. Now. Run. Go!"

The hollow thing was there, though, right in their face. James lashed out with a fist in a short, hard punch, but it ducked under it. The thing grabbed for his head, but James twisted out of the way, aiming a kick for its knee, which connected with an unsatisfying *whump*.

Anesh, seeing his chance, swept down and grabbed the discarded axe and arced both axes toward the not-a-man as it tried to grab James's neck. It dodged one of them, seeming to rotate its spine in a way that would kill a human. The other one hit its shoulder, and a burst of dust and shredded paper poured out of the wound.

Howling, it twisted around, contorting itself to launch forward at Anesh. He yelped and tried to step back, but he stumbled, and the creature caught one of his arms in its grip.

There was a slow, ugly snapping. Like a wet stick being broken over too many seconds by a bored high schooler. And that was the exact way the creature looked, too. Anesh screamed as his arm was folded in half, casually, by the monster that had caught him. James saw this and howled his own battle cry, aiming the hardest kick he could muster at the creature's wounded shoulder.

The arm simply flopped off, its grip on Anesh disappearing as soon as it was no longer connected to the main body of the empty man-shaped horror. Anesh fell onto his ass, pulling himself backward with one good arm and scrambling legs. James hauled him to his feet by his good shoulder and pointed, getting him moving. He waited a half second before following, starting out with a backward jog to keep an eye on the hollow man, now staring at its own flat arm on the ground but turning into a full-on run when the tumblefeed breached over a cubicle wall into the hallway.

His heart pounded in his chest and his fingernails dug into his palms as he ran behind Anesh, just barely keeping up. Behind him he heard an unearthly wail and assumed that the sound had to be coming from the not-person.

He didn't bother to look. He couldn't waste the energy.

The two of them flew down the halls, taking turns as fast as they could while wearing padding and running at full tilt. Both of them knew they couldn't fight the tumblefeed. But if they could lose it, then maybe, just maybe, they could take the employee of the month back there. James heard another hissing scream behind them, one of frustration and annoyance, sounding more like the tumblefeed than the alien sounds of the employee. They'd lost at least one of their pursuers, it seemed. But the damage from the noise was already done. He could hear clicking, the familiar skittering of a hundred tiny legs.

There was a swarm coming, and he was too mad to deal with this right now.

"Anesh! Split up! I'll lead them, you get back to the fort. Make sure Rufus and Ganesh are safe, then send him out for me later!" James panted out at his friend as they came up on an intersection.

Anesh thought this was the stupidest idea ever, but there was no time to argue, and no clear thought through the pain. He veered right, taking his cue from their sticky note signpost, while James paused for a minute. He waited until the hollow man came around the back corner, a carpet of stapler-crabs (striders, James reminded himself) flowing around his feet.

As soon as James was sure the "employee" had seen him, he took a deep breath, flipped it off, and bolted down the left path.

He ran and ran and ran, until he wasn't sure where he was anymore. He took turn after turn in the maze of indistinguishable halls and walls, well past where he and Anesh had mapped out. On several occasions, a strider would dive at him from a wall as he passed, and James took one hit to his neck before he realized that he was being attacked. After that, every one that tried got slapped out of the air once he was paying attention.

No weapons, after all, didn't mean he'd just give up.

James took another corner and decided he'd gone far enough. He could hear the distant hiss of hundreds of striders chasing after him, and the occasional "shout" from the employee, but he was out of breath, out of stamina, and, more importantly, out of hallway. For the first time he'd hit a dead end, and he hoped that it wouldn't be the last.

Slumping into a large padded chair, he stared at the door to the cubicle, trying to breathe as quietly as possible. Five minutes passed, then ten, and James just sat and rested. His legs ached, the puncture wound in his neck itched, and his hand hurt from where he'd slapped a strider into a wall at the wrong angle. But he was alive, and if it had worked, so was Anesh. All he had to do was sit tight until the little drone came to get him.

In the meantime, he started fiddling with the computer here. After checking that the tower wasn't going to bite his legs off, he turned on the monitor and got a username/password prompt. Well, he wasn't going anywhere, so he had some time. It took him about two minutes to find the sticky note on the inside of the desk drawer that had the password, and another ten minutes of trying permutations of usernames based on the name tag left on the desk to get the right combo.

His reward for his persistence was... nothing. The desktop had a bunch of random text documents on it, one of which appeared to just be a recipe for a green bean casserole, but nothing usable. The documents folder contained a few things that James initially thought might have been statistics on the dungeon itself, judging by the titles, but quickly turned out to appear to just be random numbers. The one thing he found that sparked his interest was the single file icon in the "music" folder.

It was a song, from AC/DC. And he'd never heard it before.

As he sat there, listening to what was clearly Brian Johnson singing about the fall of the second Cuban utopia, he had a thousand conflicting thoughts. Where did this come from? Was it just generated like an advanced Markov chain? Or did the dungeon pluck this from an alternate reality where both Cuba had a utopian society and AC/DC was a political commentary band? Or was this just some random chance thing, a few stray thoughts smashed together into something that was, at some point, picked up by whatever the hell this place was, who knew how many years and miles away?

He wished he'd brought a flash drive. This was twice now. But he wasn't going to delete this one. He'd come back to it later. Or maybe not. But it was a piece of art, either way, and he'd be damned if he'd let his desire to collect more blue orbs turn him into the kind of person who destroyed art. Especially something that might literally be one of a kind.

James was jarred from his thoughts by a strider slamming into his head, his helmet having been set to the side while he clicked through menus. He bit his tongue, tasting blood, and had to snarl to resist the urge to start yelling at the little nightmare. Its pen-legs drew scratches on his scalp as it tried to find purchase, but it only took James a second to reach up, grab it, and slam it down onto the floor. His boot came down on the upturned creature a second later, snapping legs off and bowing the chitinous underbelly inward with a *pop* and a small splatter of black goo off to the side.

Sighing to himself, he collected and cracked the skill orb that spawned above the corpse.

[+1 Skill Rank : Botany - Greenhouse]

Neat, he thought, as he sat back in the chair, rubbing his head.

James sighed with relief as he heard the buzzing of a quadcopter drone overhead. It had been a long and productive day, even with this whole problem. He just hoped that one of these blues would fix Anesh before they had to go to the hospital again.

He stood up and dusted himself off, noticing for the first time that there was blood dripping from a cut on his leg. "Goddammit, the ER is going to ask us all kinds of dumb questions about this," he muttered, looking at the staple embedded in his calf.

CHAPTER 26

"Aw, fuck," James gasped out as he jogged through the entrance of Fort Door. Before him, Anesh had apparently made it back and then passed out. Probably from the pain of having a snapped arm, though James could only speculate. Rufus was waiting just above the entrance and gave James a friendly hiss as he came in, Ganesh riding on his shoulder. "Okay, this is a problem. Um . . . wake up?" he said expectantly.

Anesh did not wake up.

"Oh hell, come on, man. I cannot carry you out of here." James leaned down and patted Anesh's cheek, trying to get him conscious. "Come on, I have a blue here for you, but it's probably gonna do your laundry and we're going to need to get to a hospital. Also I cannot carry you, or your soda, I am so tired, please get up." He shook his friend, careful not to jostle his arm too much. Still sitting uncomfortably on his shoulder, Ganesh let out a small wailing cry.

Anesh stirred a bit, cracking his eyes open. "My arm hurts . . ." he murmured.

"No shit!" James let out an explosive huff of breath. "Okay, get up. Or, wait, no. Use this." He pulled the size-two blue out of his pocket and handed it to Anesh, who winced a bit as he tried to use his broken arm before remembering.

"Why did I get a broken bone again?" he whined softly as he took the orb.

James quickly stripped off his armor, tossing his medkit onto the table and swiftly opening it. "No idea, maybe you should have *fucking run when I told you to,*" he snapped out as he applied disinfectant and hemostatic powder to Anesh's neck before covering the area with a large bandage. James was aware of the historic hypocrisy of his statement; he, after all, had not run when Anesh had told him to before, and he'd had a *far* stupider reason.

Anesh looked like he couldn't tell if he was furious or passing out again. "I sa . . . saved your ass," he muttered back, pain leaving an edge of real anger in his voice.

"Crack your damn orb," James replied, annoyance tinting his words as he repeated the process with the blood dripping from his leg.

His friend just glared at him for a second before a spike of pain burned through his arm and made him wince. Anesh let out a soft sob, dropping the blue orb to roll along the floor. James was there in an instant, worry on his face. "Come on, come on, it's fine, I'm not actually mad. Here, take these." He pressed a pair of high-strength painkillers to Anesh's lips, followed by a water bottle. "Where'd the orb . . . ah. Thanks, Rufus."

The strider gave a small nodding bow as it held the orb up to James before stepping back a bit. Rufus stepped back and forth in worry as James pressed the orb into Anesh's hand. "Here. Use it," he said, holding the orb down in his friend's palm.

Anesh, on the verge of blacking out, applied minor pressure to the orb in his hand. James felt an eerie crawling sensation on his palm as the orb popped, and a vibrating energy flowed away from him, down into Anesh.

[Problem Solved : Acquired Shipment]

[+2 Skill Ranks : Cooking - Indian]

"Didn't . . . work," he murmured, dropping his hand away from James's.

Around them, both Rufus and Ganesh had gone stock-still. Then, in a flurry of motion, Rufus rushed the front wall and started scaling his web. Ganesh shoved off from James's shoulder with a blast of his rotors, pushing into the air and over the wall in a hurry. James cocked his head as the two seemed to suddenly flee, but then he heard it. Footsteps, running, from somewhere nearby. And then a voice. "Trespassing is *forbidden* on *company* property!"

"Nooooo." Anesh tried to get to his fee, but couldn't find the strength to stand. "Don't wanna. Gotta get out." He leaned toward the door from his slumped position at the base of one of their desks.

James ran over to the door and pushed at it to prop it open for his friend, but for the first time ever he found it locked. He checked his watch; they had plenty of time, it just wasn't opening right now. Feeling the edge of terror in his mind, he ran back over to Anesh, and knelt down.

"Not an option anymore," James said softly, with a calm that surprised even himself. He was already going through Anesh's pockets, looking for, and finding, the other two small blues that he had held on to since they'd first realized it was an option. With a bit of concealed panic, he stuffed one of them into Anesh's hand. "Crack it. Now."

Anesh gave him a look, rolling his head to make eye contact with James. "Why? Just . . . drag me out. I can survive to the hop . . . hopsital."

James wrapped Anesh's hand in his own and pushed it down around the blue. "It's not opening right now! Also, do you want to try to rehome Rufus and Ganesh out in the real world? Or just leave them to die here? I don't think either option gets us a lot of good karma! Now crack the fucking blue!" James stood up before waiting for a response.

The dark, warbling voice came through the air again. "Hello? *How* are *you* today?" it asked, distant but closer to the fort than before.

James sighed, rolling his shoulders. "I'm doing fine, you son of a bitch," he muttered under his breath. Unzipping the backpack on the table, he pulled out a thermos of coffee. "Anesh. Get under the desk. It's gotta be that guy holding the door shut somehow. So if this doesn't go well, wait for him to leave, then slip out." He heard Anesh protest weakly behind him, but there wasn't time to go over this now.

And then he walked out to the front of their home base, standing in the open in the no-man's-land. Rufus chittered nervously from the paper clip webs above him. Off to the left, he saw Ganesh out of the corner of his eye, flying low to the ground, come out from the cubicle maze and head back toward James, perching on the wall behind him. He looked up. "Tried to draw it off?" Ganesh nodded. "Didn't work?" Ganesh shook his head. "Of course. Well, you tried," he said, nodding at the drone.

Across from James, turning a corner at the end of a hall, walking quickly but not running, a hollow thing-that-was-not-human came into view. It wore dark skin and a pale blue shirt, and it slowed when it saw him standing there. About a half dozen striders skittered around at its feet. Taking a deep breath, James unscrewed the lid to the thermos and chugged down the coffee, tossing the metal bottle back behind him.

"Okay," he said, as the employee came closer, walking at a steady but slow pace. It paused as he started talking, tilting its head. "I like this place. A lot," James said. "I also like my friend, quite a lot," he continued. "You jeopardized one and hurt the other. So I'm going to fuck you up, okay?"

"*Threats* of violence *are reported* to huuuman *resources*," it droned out in that strange voice, like a dial tone speaking to him. Accusingly, it lifted a finger to point at James. "Violation of *company* policy," it said, as if it expected him to care. James, feeling the coffee start to take effect, slipped into a fighting stance, shuffling one foot forward and raising his fists. The hollow man, though, wasn't done. It pulled its hand back to its face, and *pulled*.

James watched in startled horror as the thing's face ripped away from itself, leaving only an empty, featureless plane of skin on the body where a face should be. The removed face itself, he saw as soon as it was detached, was simply a paper mask, composed of folded sheets of paper, with sticky notes trailing behind it to form a wreath of dark purple hair. "Ah" was all he had time to say before the thing flung its now detached face at him.

And then James's view of the world narrowed significantly.

The mask flew toward him, screaming, little bone spikes extended around its edges. James saw it coming, with the employee's thudding steps right behind it, striders dancing around his feet. He planted his feet and prepared to grab the mask, but before it got to him, there was a rapidly rising hum, and then Ganesh slammed into it from the side, dragging the mask out of James's vision.

James blinked, shocked. He would have watched the aerial duel between the mask and the drone, but the employee was on him then, and there was no time. It came in, arm extended like it wanted to shake his hand. But the blank face and the force of its movement told James the gesture was anything but friendly. He stepped forward, feeling the coffee kicking in. James's arm blurred out, his fist slamming into the wrist of the offered hand. The speed of his strike bent the arm where he hit it, the wrist folding around his hand like there was no bone inside at all.

But as soon as he pulled back, the thing's arm was back to normal, and it swept up at James in an attempt to grab his face.

James whipped himself backward, arms stuck outward to keep his balance. He jerked back up as the hollow employee overextended on a swipe and brought his knee into its rib cage. His enemy almost folded in half from the force of the blow, and James didn't relent, taking advantage of the opportunity. He rained punches down on its chest and neck as it tried to right itself. The speed from the coffee made it hard for him to keep track of his own motions as he sent strike after strike into his opponent, aiming to crush vital bits or break bones, neither of which it actually seemed to *have*.

Then the striders made it to where the pair were trading blows. James noticed the first one when it lunged for his ankle, and he twisted his foot out of the way, throwing his shoulder into the non-human to drive it back while he regained his footing. Part of regaining his footing was bringing his boot down as hard as possible onto the little stapler monster, and it let out a squeal as he smashed its chitin plates into its internals. The second one he just booted away, because there was no time, and his boxing partner was up and coming at him again.

It was fast. Faster than anything should be. And he knew that if it caught him, he was dead. He'd seen how it had snapped Anesh's arm like it was a piece of rotten wood; he couldn't afford a single slipup like that here. As it leapt toward him over the half dozen or so staplers still moving in, he snapped out a kick that took it in its midsection and sent it crashing to the ground. It might be fast, but the coffee made him faster. His brain was catching up with his enhanced speed now, and he was starting to feel more in sync with what he could actually do.

Taking a deep breath, wishing he had something to hit this fucker with, he steadied himself and got ready to keep fighting. He almost lost his mind giggling when the mask flew past his field of vision, Ganesh and Rufus tearing it apart midflight as it screamed, "Merrrr-gerrrrr!"

There was no time to laugh, though, and the thought of giving ground to this thing sobered him up right away. James punted another strider away as it lunged for him, then shuffled in a ninety-degree arc around the not-a-person, moving fast to keep out of biting range of the strider pack while he fought. It was back on its feet now, a couple of gashes in the space where its face should have been and its throat leaking bits of dust and shredded paper confetti. "All right, creepsman. Come on." He held up his fists in a guard position.

The enemy moved like a wolf, catching James off-guard. It dropped back to all fours, leg and arm joints shifting to allow for the different form of movement, and it exploded forward in motion, slamming into James's right leg, even as he pivoted to dodge. The force of the hit spun him around, and he fell backward, catching himself with one arm as the creature continued moving, taking a sloping turn to come back around for another pass. James yelled out a cry of pain and defiance as one of the staplers sank metal teeth into the back of his palm, and he grabbed the thing and hurled it at the incoming employee. The heavy improvised projectile left an open gash on its face but didn't slow it down. James dropped, rolling right, as it sped by, one of its shoes clipping him in the side and cracking one of his ribs with a burst of pain that left him coughing.

To his left, he saw three more striders moving in rapidly, staple fangs out, going straight for his face. He was still moving faster than a human should be able to, and he grabbed the lead one and flung it *away*, not bothering to check the trajectory. But he was getting tired, he was getting hurt, and the creature was coming back. These little things were painful and possibly lethal distractions from his main foe.

Which was why he was relieved and surprised in equal measure when Rufus slammed into one of them, tumbling end over end and removing it from his frame of vision. The other strider paused for a second, as if deciding whether it should go for James's exposed eyes or help its friend, but it took too long to think, and before it could move, Ganesh was on it like a hawk. Literally, like a hawk. James barely had time to register that the drone was coming in before it had grabbed the unsuspecting stapler and dragged it off into the air.

James didn't waste his respite. He rolled over and pulled himself back to his feet in a small hop. Staying in a crouch in case he got hit again, he scanned around, looking for the employee. The hollow man wasn't hard to spot; it had stood up again and was currently brushing itself off, as if all this were just a gentlemanly distraction. But as soon as he made it to his feet and made "eye" contact with it, the thing tilted its head in confusion.

"Yeah, I'm not dead," James muttered. "Come on, come get me. Come on!" he yelled, fists clenched, not really sure what he was yelling or why, just that he felt like he should say *something*. The thing just shrugged in a jerky, exaggerated way and rushed him. It wasn't trying to grab him anymore, resorting to strikes and kicks in patterns that felt oddly like clunky replications of what James was using. Its fist came in, and James swept an arm up to catch it, but he forgot that even though he could see its movements clearly, the physics of his body didn't keep up with his increased reaction.

The fist hit the arm guard and shattered it. Hard plastic snapped in half, and the straps on his arm went loose, as the pieces of the armor that were still attached to them didn't have anything to support themselves. The impact of the hit also knocked James back and shoved his arm out of position, with a sharp soreness that he *knew* meant he'd be dealing with a bruise for a month after this. James staggered back, barely getting his arm back up to sweep the second punch away, deflecting the force instead of taking it this time.

He lashed back, planting his fist in the gash on the thing's face, and felt a moment of panic as his fist ripped it wider and slipped into the monster. Jerking back before it could grab him, he took a handful of shredded paper and dust with him, and it staggered away from him as he shook his fist off.

"What the fucking hell are you?" James muttered, casually shuffling his foot to the side to brush away one of the striders that got too close. It didn't answer, of course. Instead, it reached into its coat and pulled out an ornate-looking pen, which it clicked open forcefully. "Oh, come on." James sighed, wishing not for the first time that he had his axe. His hand searched his pockets for anything he could use, and he felt the round smooth shape of the blue orb that he had taken from Anesh. Figuring there was no time like now to solve a problem, he cracked it quickly before pulling his hand back out to a guard position.

[Problem Solved : Apologized]

[+1 Skill Rank : Jeet Kune Do]

"Okay." James grinned. He felt a bit silly now, not using this one earlier. But just as he was starting to feel the coffee wearing off, this could be what he needed to finish his opponent off. He tightened up his stance and centered himself with a deep breath. He was ready for this, he lied to himself.

The paper-filled skin thing lunged in, pen whistling by his ear as he dodged. James shot a hand up and grabbed its arm, then pivoted and *slammed* it into the ground. The pen went skidding away toward Fort Door, leaving smoking wounds on the floor where the tip touched. "Oh, fuck that." James said his thought out loud, before jerking back, applying as much force as he could and ripping the thing's arm off again. It made a sound like construction paper tearing and leaked strips of loose paper that looked like it had been run through a shredder out of the shoulder. The arm in James's hands went limp and hollow, and as soon as it wasn't connected anymore, he could see and feel that it was nothing more than elaborately folded heavy paper.

Almost casually, he threw the arm away from himself. "Maybe this time it'll stick," he said, standing back up as fast as his shaking legs could work, trying to put some distance between himself and the paper man.

It rolled over, popping back to its feet, and James started to lose hope. He'd done so much damage to it, and it wasn't even slowing down. This now-faceless nightmare thing wasn't going to stop, and all he had was his fists to deal with it. It jerked forward, too fast for him to follow; he realized too late that he'd overextended and that his coffee buff wasn't working at full capacity. Its hand closed around his throat before he could even move, and he felt, rather than heard, a voice telling him that security would escort him from the premises.

James clawed at the fingers and wrist that pinned his neck as it started to lift him off the ground. He couldn't breathe, and he felt his strength draining away rapidly. *Well,* he thought as he lost control of his arms, *at least I went down swinging.*

And then James was on his back on the ground, looking up at the blank face of his enemy, sliced open by his blows from the fight, yes, but also with a flat black metal blade punched through right where the right eye would be.

And then Anesh ripped the boar spear out vertically, splitting its head in half. He held the spear braced under his good arm and flipped it to the palm of his hand, bringing it down into the monster's back, burying it up to the crossguard and kicking it to shove it upward, leaving a gash the length of its spine.

James stumbled to his feet, wincing as he felt his ribs protest. He made eye contact with Anesh as his friend pulled the spear out again, and the two of them stood in silence for a minute. He glanced down and noticed that his roommate's arm was in a cast.

"Ah. The blue worked, then?" he asked hesitantly.

Anesh stared at James in disbelief. "Most people would open this conversation with 'Thank you for saving my life,'" he said. "But no, you go with that. Well, whatever, you're welcome."

"Um . . . where'd the spear come from?" James asked, massaging his forehead as he tried to get his bearings. "Oh, also, thank you. Fuck, man, good timing."

"It was the first blue. Sped up the delivery time on the Amazon order, I think. Which . . . um . . . reminds me. We need to actually order exactly what this is when we get home."

James made a strangled noise in his throat. "Um, *what*? No. Please don't break causality."

"Breaking causality saved your life *twice* now. So it's fine. Probably. But I'm leaving it here just in case," Anesh said. He looked around at the open area, littered with scraps of paper, some of James's blood, and the wrecked husks of about twenty striders. Rufus scuttled over, bumping into James's boot with Ganesh riding his back, and as soon as they got close enough, the drone lifted off to alight on Anesh's shoulder. "Looks like you had it mostly under control," Anesh said, smiling.

"Oh, hell no. Let's not do this again. Rufus, none of them got away, right?" James asked, and the red-and-black stapler shook its head. "So our entrance is still more or less open. Okay, grab the orbs, let's get out of here," he said.

Anesh nodded. "Yeah, I'm ready to go home. The 'medical attention' problem solver apparently gave me painkillers too, but this still hurts like hell, and I feel like I could sleep for a week. Oh, make sure to leave some of the yellows for Rufus and Ganesh. Unless . . . they want to come with us?" He looked at the drone on his shoulder and raised an eyebrow.

Rufus, having scuttled up onto the wall of Fort Door, shook his head when James looked up at him and tapped one of his legs forward on the wall. "I think he's claimed this place as his castle," James said. "What about Ganesh?"

"I think he's gonna stay here too," Anesh said, gently setting the drone onto one of the desks with his good hand. "You two be good, okay? Don't fuck with the employees if one of them shows up."

James and Anesh went about methodically grabbing up the small yellows from all the striders. Rufus brought over one of the larger ones from the mask, but James just pushed it back to him. He never would have had a chance if he'd had to deal with that thing simultaneously, so he figured Rufus had earned it as a trophy.

The thing that caught both their eyes, though, was the orb that spawned out of the paper employee. "Not a purple, that's disappointing," Anesh said, looking at it.

"Yeah, sure." James snorted. "But it's the size of a bowling ball. And... does this one look like it has different swirls of tone in it? It's really cool. Maybe I could use it as a lava lamp, replace the one I have."

"You... wait, you mean you've just been keeping that size-two orb in your room as a night-light?" Anesh asked with an incredulous tone, holding his hand out in disbelief. "Why?"

"It's a nice reminder that this is all real, when I'm not wounded," James said. "Anyway, let's pack this up and get out of here. Oh! And this pen!" He held up the fancy gold-and-blue metal pen from where it had fallen. "Do. Not. Use. This," he emphasized to Anesh. "We could break it down, but..." He dropped the pen on the floor.

Anesh quirked his head. "Why'd you do that?"

James just sighed. "I contextualized it as a weapon, and I can't carry weapons." He punched himself in the side of the head. "This is getting really stupid," he muttered.

They finished packing up, saying their goodbyes to the little critters that shared their home base. James watched warily as Anesh leaned the boar spear up against one of the walls. That thing made him nervous, since it technically came from the future. At Anesh's insistence, James actually wheeled out the hand cart with all the soda he'd collected. He thought it was a bit silly at this point, but hell, they'd both worked for what they got, so who was he to complain about his friend's choice in loot? He still chuckled a bit as he shouldered the bag weighed down with the massive skill orb.

It was like this—bruised and scraped and cut and shattered, in pain and exhausted, overburdened with the spoils of their victory—that James and Anesh stepped out the door and back into reality.

CHAPTER 27

"What's the difference between a spaceship and a missile?" James asked as he sat with Anesh in the ER waiting room. He was rolling one of the green orbs in the fingers of his left hand, looking at it and not even glancing up at Anesh as he talked.

Anesh blinked himself out of the dozing nap he was taking, rolling his neck to stare at the ceiling. "Whether it's David Bowie's 'Space Oddity' or David Bowie's 'The Man Who Sold the World' that plays when it launches?"

Around them, a dozen other people with various problems sat in padded chairs that were still somehow uncomfortable. The scent of disinfectant hung in the air, drowning out everything else with an overwhelmingly, unnaturally clean feeling. Lights that reminded James too much of the dungeon, or worse, work, hung overhead, lighting the whole place with bright white light that lit up tiny details. A parent tried to comfort a screaming child, a nurse took someone back to the triage room, and somewhere in the distance, an angry man uselessly argued with the front desk that he deserved to go first.

They'd dropped in after getting some real coffee and real pancakes. James had pushed for it, saying that they really needed to make sure Anesh's arm was fine and that they couldn't idly trust that the cast the orb had materialized on his arm was perfect. Personally, Anesh thought that they could trust the mysterious system that had set and plastered his broken bone for him while also providing intimate knowledge on the care and feeding of Labrador retrievers. But that had been shot down when James pointed out that Anesh was both high on painkillers and also just generally more suspicious of the dungeon.

"That's remarkably specific for someone who just woke up," James said.

This earned James a protest of "You woke me up!" from Anesh.

James nodded. "I did, yes. So anyway. The thing I was saying before you interrupted. The difference between a spaceship and a missile is the use case. In addition to the soundtrack, spaceships carry people and tools and stuff. We think of them as being totally opposite things, but really, a shuttle is just a missile with seats instead of a warhead."

"Is this going somewhere or can I go back to sleep?" Anesh asked, giving his friend a hyperbolic glare.

"Yes, it's going somewhere," James said. "What is this?" He held up a green orb.

Anesh jerked forward, sitting up. "It's not something you should have out here, and it's also part of our test material," he said quietly.

"Sure, but look," James went on. "What does it do for us? Well, when we use it? It improves the place around us. But the dungeon? What does it use it for? It's not just stronger enemies, obviously; the stuffed shirt just had more yellow, and it was the most powerful thing we've seen. So, what does this do? What's its missile to our spaceship?"

There was a period of silence, broken only by the crying kid in the background. Eventually, Anesh spoke. "You get really weird when you're tired." He shook his head a bit. "I don't know. I'm not the dungeon, I can't tell you the difference. Maybe it's because we just haven't seen enough of them to really get that BBC nature documentary angle going on. Or maybe it's because the painkillers are wearing off and I cannot think straight," he finished irritably.

They both went quiet as a group went by, a couple nurses wheeling a gurney with someone on it. At this hour, most of the people who were here were already half-asleep, and the kid on the bed seemed like he was already there himself.

James sighed a bit. "Yeah, on that note, want to do our first test here? I'll make the notes if you don't want to, but I brought an extra green. Seems like a hospital is a pretty decent target for improvement." He reached into his pocket and handed another one of the orbs over to Anesh.

"The bonus to this is that we can then reasonably tell Alanna that we're not actually the bad guys in this whole scenario," Anesh muttered as he popped the emerald sphere in his free hand.

[Local Area Shift : Average crime rate, −18%]

[+4 Skill Ranks : Program Use - Excel]

He relayed what he'd gotten to James, who noted it down in his phone. "Lower crime rate is interesting, but so far, still 'good.' Also, you seriously think we're the bad guys here?"

Anesh snorted. "We're wandering into a resource-rich territory, killing the natives, taking whatever we want, and generally making a mess of things. We're proper imperialists, my friend." He shook his head as he saw James looking worried. "But no, we're not the bad guys. You go out of your way to be nice to the peaceful things, and I don't think it counts as being conquistadors when the place isn't . . . you know . . . reality."

"Well, that's a relief," James said. "Still nervous about it now, though. I just don't want to be the asshole in this scenario, you know? I'm still in this for the orbs and the thrill of adventure, but if it comes at the cost of being a Saturday morning cartoon villain, I think I'll pass," he decided as he cracked into his own green orb.

[Local Area Shift : Increased Value, $22,825]

[+4 Skill Ranks : Camping]

Anesh shifted around in his chair a bit as James nodded and made a note of his own gains as well. "Hey, what did you . . . Is this a different chair?" he asked, a bit startled.

"Apparently, I bought the hospital slightly better furniture," James said, his brain starting to register what had happened. While he'd been focused on the skill gain, the vaguely uncomfortable and half-padded seat beneath him had shifted into something different. It was still a chair, but it felt newer. More comfortable, a little less worn, and a totally different color than previously. A quick glance around showed that pretty much every chair in the ER waiting area had changed, along with the tables, the tile floor, and one of the drinking fountains. "I hope no one noticed that too much," he muttered.

At that point, a nurse called Anesh's name, and the two of them got up, leaving the newly improved area to the rest of the people here.

"That was impressively awkward," James said, stretching his arms as they walked back to his car.

They'd been in the hospital for about three hours, and the sun was starting to come up. It was just light enough out for everything to be tinted an anemic blue; the sunrise itself hadn't started yet. The whole process should have been simple, but Anesh had slipped up from either pain or exhaustion and revealed that he didn't remember getting the cast on. There was no record of him actually getting any medical care in their system, so there were a few X-rays to do and some other tests to run.

And all of that took forever. And it didn't help when Anesh was asked how his arm had broken in the first place, and he'd muttered something about tripping over a curb. James had been asked to leave the room so the doctor could talk to Anesh alone, and it was this that Anesh was busy complaining about as they drove home.

"He thought we were dating!" he half yelled, his tone incredulous.

James held in laughter with a wide grin, trying to focus on driving without bursting out at his friend's words. "I mean, we could be dating," he offhandedly replied, trying to make the statement as casual as possible so as not to spike his own heart rate.

This statement was ignored in the wake of Anesh's indignation. "It's not about that!" he said, waving his good arm around. "He assumed you were the cause of this!" He punctuated his words by tapping his cast.

"I mean, technically—" James started, but Anesh cut him off.

"It doesn't matter. I have a bunch of Vicodin now, I don't have to answer any awkward questions when I get the cast off next month, and I don't have to explain that you're not repeatedly physically abusing me," Anesh said, sighing.

James repressed a snicker and tactfully changed the subject. "So hey. Here's a thought. Ganesh and Rufus actually probably literally saved my life in that fight. Can you talk to Neil and maybe get us a few more drones?"

"Why?" Anesh held up a hand as James started to answer. "To clarify. Why don't *you* do it, and also why do you assume they'll animate like Ganesh did?"

"Because Ganesh did?" James said slowly.

Anesh leaned back into his seat, pinching his nose as he answered. "But only Ganesh did. Not the armor, bags, cameras, the stopwatch, the weapons, or the food."

"That last one is probably for the best," James said, and Anesh grunted in agreement.

"Sure," Anesh said, "but the important part is that Ganesh seems like an aberration in the system, not a rule. I mean, I'm fine testing it, but I don't think the dream in your head of having an air force is going to happen naturally."

James rolled his eyes. "Still want to try. Although that does make me think of something. Is Ganesh . . . how to phrase this . . . is he a digital life form? Like, is he the 'programming' of the drone? Because if so, maybe before we test the animation thing, we should get an upgraded drone and see if he can transfer over to it."

There was a pause where the only noise was the faint radio music and the wheels on the road, as Anesh thought over that. "I have no idea," he finally said. "But we should ask. I keep forgetting to mention it, but isn't it kind of weird that those two guys both seem to understand us and are smart?"

"Of course it's weird," James said as they pulled into the apartment parking lot, his car cooling quickly in the crisp morning air when he killed the engine. "Everything about this is weird. There's a hundred and fifty pounds of assorted drinks that have never once been sold on Earth in my back seat so that we can try to trick our way past the *brain parasites* in our minds. I have a bowling ball that looks like a lava lamp and is probably going to teach me how to fly a fighter jet if I touch it the right way. And we're not broke anymore. This whole thing is messed up," he monologued as they trudged up the steps to their door.

"Okay, just so we're on the same page there," Anesh said as they went in, kicking his shoes off. "Now. Before I go to sleep, and to make up for the fact that I'm not getting any dungeon fun for the next month, do you want to use another two of the greens here? You know, for science."

James stared at his friend, a hint of a smile on his face. He knew how Anesh felt, honestly. There was a glee that came with opening up an orb, and it had been really hard for him to avoid the temptation to just crush every single one he found in his hand without thinking about it. The fact that they'd both been playing it cool and resisting the urge long enough to bring the orbs home, divide them up, and wait on using them until they'd let Lily scan some of them was really honestly impressive.

And now Anesh wasn't going to be able to come with him for a while. Hell, James himself might not go back in every week if he wasn't going to have backup. It was a problem, and it hurt to think about. Especially now, when he was so tired it left a scratching anxiety at the back of his eyes that made him feel one step away from total panic.

So he got it. He really did. They had some orbs, and they were pretty sure the green ones were safe now; they might as well have some fun. Carefully setting his bag down on the kitchen table, he pulled out a couple of the emerald spheres, each one the size of his fist and seeming to glitter a bit.

"All right," he said to Anesh, "I bet you half my share of the cash that at least one of these actively makes our apartment a little less . . . convenient, I guess is the word."

"Deal," Anesh said as the two of them closed their fingers around their prize, with James going first.

[Local Area Shift : Ambient temperature adjustment, +/- 2°C toward 21°C]

[+3 Skill Ranks : Cryptography - Encryption]

And right on his heels, Anesh followed.

[Local Area Shift : Rent change, -$255/month]

[+3 Skill Ranks : Bureaucracy - Insurance]

"Well, shit," Anesh said. "What did you get? Because I just lowered our rent, which, while useful, is sort of boring."

"Yeah, I think I win?" James said with a confused tone. "Um... hey, here's a question. Is twenty-one degrees good, or bad, in Celsius? I'm a little too American to understand this one perfectly."

CHAPTER 28

"I," James announced, "am bored."

Anesh looked up sharply from the table, over to where James had been meditating on the couch. A small hint of frustration mixed with mild worry was going through his head. He'd been sitting there working on homework while James had sat cross-legged on the couch, enjoying the mild social presence of another human while he quietly worked through the cold tyranny of number problems. While he'd noticed James grimace a few times, his friend hadn't said anything, and Anesh was content to enjoy his day off just silently sharing the room.

But now, James had opened his eyes, an annoyed expression on his face. "So bored," he said.

"How bored are you?" Anesh asked casually, setting down his pen and looking over at James, sticking his elbows on the table and folding his hands to make a spot for his chin to rest.

"I am unbelievably bored," James said, rolling back onto the couch, breaking the illusion of himself as a Zen master. "Not just a skateboard, but a longboard. If it were colder, I could be a snowboard."

"More bored than the Chunnel?" Anesh chimed in with laughter in his voice.

James lurched forward, rolling off the couch and under the table. From below the wooden surface, Anesh heard him keep rambling. "I'm the chairman of the board! This is my boardroom!"

At this point, Anesh didn't even bother trying to hide that he was laughing. "Board up the windows!" he managed to say between fits of giggling. Beneath the table, James also broke down into a fit of roaring laughter.

Eventually, the two of them calmed down, and James crawled out from under the table back up to his spot on the couch. Settling down, he looked over at Anesh. "When did you get here? I wasn't really paying attention. And why is it so warm in here? It's still technically winter."

"It's perfectly normal for the end of February to still be a cold and blighted hellscape," Anesh said, turning up his English accent to eleven for effect. He chuckled a bit at his own words, then shook his head a little. "Anyway, I got here about an hour ago. You were really into your meditation. I must say, it's a bit weird to see you actively getting better at doing nothing. I thought you'd perfected that a long time ago."

James lobbed a pillow at Anesh. "I'll have you know, I'm the master of nothing! Wait, no." He paused for a bit to let Anesh stop laughing. "Okay, but really. I'm getting better at isolating the outsider thoughts in my mind. Working up to trying to kill the smaller one, which is the thing keeping me from using weapons."

"Killing?" Anesh asked curiously.

"Yeah, I don't think it's just a curse or an enchantment or whatever. It moves around, it pokes other thoughts and . . . areas? . . . of my brain. It also feels less like a set of words or anything solid, and more like a fish thing." James reached up, stretching and draping himself over the back of the couch. "Hey, you've got a fire going!" he said as he saw the fireplace, upside down in his vision, with a roaring blaze in it. "That's why it's so . . ." He trailed off as he watched the flames.

Anesh nodded, shutting his textbook and shuffling his stack of finished work together. "It was cold. Turns out, two degrees closer to comfortable is still bloody cold around here." He poked James with a pen, leaning over to jab at his friend. "Hey! Get back up here and tell me about your fish thoughts!"

"Anesh," James said with growing concern. "Are you burning that infinite magazine you found?"

"Unimportant. Fish thoughts."

"Very important! Why are you torching it? That was a work of art!" James protested.

Anesh just sighed. "Because I'm bored too, I guess? It's weird now to have a Monday where I know I'm not doing anything exciting later tonight." He walked over behind the couch and prodded at the fire with the cast-iron poker. "Also, because entropy can sod off. Also, like hell it's art!"

Still staring at the dancing flames, James responded sadly, "I actually think that the dungeon might make legitimate art. I don't think it can just randomly generate music that sounds like music, but I found a file on a computer that really did sound like an actual song."

"Weird," Anesh said, sitting down on the floor. "I'm still not convinced that a magazine about horses counts, though."

James stuck out his tongue at his roommate. "Whatever. You're still burning something with apparently infinite mass, and I'm not super happy about that."

"Aren't you supposed to be at work?" Anesh tried to deflect James away from the fire.

"Aren't you supposed to be . . . at school? Do you have class today?" James retorted.

"Normally yes, but I took the day off." Anesh was tired of classes. The effort of carrying around a backpack with one arm in a cast was exhausting. Not to mention that it felt like every day, someone new wanted to know how he'd broken his arm. He hadn't even tried to come up with something convincing, instead going with blatant lies every time someone inquired. Bear attack, fought off a bank robber, lost a bet, got beaten up trying to rob a bank, anything that was clearly nonsense. It kept people from pressing, got a laugh, and made him feel like he had an aura of mystery.

James nodded. "Yeah, I do actually have work in an hour or so, but . . . I just . . . don't care. I know I need to keep the job so we have access to the dungeon, but, like, we're set for almost a year on rent. I'm not panicking about money. And if I'm not going to get to actually do the one amazing and exciting and magical thing in my life, then what's the fucking point?" he said bitterly.

Both of them sat there for a bit, staring at the fire. Anesh nodded minutely at James's words, because they both understood. The way James felt wasn't something he tried to hide; the setback that was keeping them out of the dungeon for another month while Anesh's arm healed had him pretty obviously down in the dumps. James just felt like every ounce of motivation he'd had was cut away from him, suddenly and without warning.

James had never been great at dealing with setbacks. When he got on a roll with something, personal or professional, he'd feel unstoppable. But as soon as something interrupted it, the emotional whiplash could keep him feeling useless and pinned down for weeks. And right now, Anesh could not just understand, but also feel a bit of that too. Not much to make you feel like you weren't going to be doing anything fun for a while like a broken arm, after all.

And right now, it'd already been two missed doorways since they'd been in last. Three or four weeks, and it was back to another Monday evening. The myriad little cuts, scrapes, bruises, and burns had taken a while to mostly heal, but at this point the two of them were looking more or less in fighting shape. With one exception. James had gone back in alone the first week, just to check on Rufus and Ganesh, but ducked out without exploring. He was still feeling too injured at the time to feel safe delving alone.

Both of them were restless. Waiting. Like a coiled spring. Anesh had been joining James at the gym, the two of them sparring together awkwardly to get used to fighting things shaped like humans. James had been spending every waking hour trying to improve himself in some useful way, while Anesh had been putting a distressing amount of time into seeing if he could make thermite grenades one-handed. He could, but it took forever and felt precarious.

They were at the point where they were ready to do something reckless and stupid and amazing and glorious.

But Anesh was still out of commission, and his pain management pills kept him that way mentally as well as physically. So they were both a bit annoyed, though not at each other.

"I get that," Anesh said, after a lot of thought. "You want to ignore our responsibilities today and get ice cream instead?"

He didn't have time to finish the sentence before James was saying "Yes!," snapping back to an energetic mood as the opportunity presented itself. "Wait, hang on," James continued, feeling a bit less lethargic than thinking about work had left him. "You're still burning the damn magazine! We need to deal with that!"

"Oh, relax. I got a bucket of sand right here. I already tested this," Anesh said with a roll of his eyes. "It does really seem to be infinite, which is kinda cool. I think it would be possible to automate the creation of an artificial star with this." James just stared at him, mouth slightly open. "Okay, with the help of a government with a space agency. But we could do it. Like I said: entropy can sod off."

"Anesh," James flatly stated as he threw on his coat. "Put out the magic fire."

In the end, James decided to go to work. Buoyed by the overly sweet bounty that was ice cream, and not making any progress on honing his meditation, it seemed like he might as well show up. There was a certain wall in his mind that he'd crossed over at some point today; all the stress shut off behind him, and he just moved forward with a casual smile. Sure, he had to take some calls, but the knowledge that he *could* quit if he wanted to made it so much easier to tolerate it. None of these people held his fate in their hands.

So he sat in his cubicle, still unmoved from his spot under the haunted ventilation unit, and fiddled with a paper clip while he read through the brick of an essay that Anesh had texted him about the changes to their apartment.

He was intermittently looking up at the ceiling and considering waiting until no one was around to try to crawl back up into the black-and-white-speckled tiles again. No particular reason, just to see if there was some kind of hive being built up there, or maybe if the striders were spying on him personally. The thought that he could maybe get his hands on an orb, free of the guilt of running ahead of Anesh, also played a part in his daydream.

But there were just too many people on the floor tonight. It was pretty nice, since a lot of them were new and were getting the larger number of calls for training purposes. So he had plenty of time to read about how Anesh was trying to measure where the temperature shift exactly ended, and what his findings were.

"Inconclusive" was a polite term for what James would have phrased as "doesn't make any damn sense." But then, the orbs just didn't seem inclined toward sense. They didn't have a unified system in the sense that they covered all aspects of reality in an ordered method; they just . . . did what they did. They were internally consistent and followed patterns, but those patterns were quite literally surreal.

He started texting back some of his thoughts on the orbs. Anesh had probably already covered this in his own head, but it helped to say it out loud, or via phone in this case. The yellows were the easiest, because they had the most experience with them. They just improved a person's ability. That was almost, *almost* normal. So close to normal, right on the edge of it, really. But James had a dozen problems with how they did it. They didn't change your body to match the time that exercising it would take to learn how to throw a proper punch. They didn't link up new knowledge as if you'd actually internalized it. They didn't make it clear whether they were something that became part of you or just sat in the back of your head, or why there was a difference. They just . . . didn't do a lot of things that would make sense.

They had a pattern, and it was incomplete and annoying. Or maybe he only thought that because if he were designing this game, he would have done it differently.

The blues were infuriatingly worse, since they didn't have a reasonable sample size, so he ignored them. The oranges were the same, though they seemed fine. Even the red, he could sort of understand. It was the greens that bothered him. Again: imperfect patterns. They changed an area, but what counted as "local" to them? If they altered a building, what happened when the building was demolished, or even just changed function? And, most importantly, why did the outside thoughts that informed them of the effects of the orbs give him measurements in Celsius?

It all bothered him, and he tried to explain as many of his concerns to Anesh as possible while still using the phrase *but this doesn't mean we aren't using more, obviously* at least three times. The line of conversation went on for about twenty minutes, and James didn't even notice that he'd just flat-out ignored an incoming call on his monitor.

"James!" The cheerful voice startled him almost out of his chair, sending his heart racing and breaking his focus on Anesh's concerns about their impact on the local economy going forward into the future. The paper clip he was twirling in his fingers spun out onto his desk with a light pattering as he turned to face his boss.

Theodora looked like she'd seen better days. An angry black-and-purple splotch of a bruise marred the skin of her cheek, and he could see another one peeking out from the shirtsleeve on her forearm. Her hair, normally kept short at a precise length, had been shaved off on one side, giving her a real punk look.

"Yes!" James responded with a little more of a squawk to his voice than he intended. "Whoa, what happened to you?" he said before she could start talking, this time in an earnestly concerned tone.

"Sports stuff. Don't worry about it," she said quickly, waving a hand as if to dismiss any notion that it was important. "So, bad news, you're stuck on the night shift and still have to work Saturdays. Good news, though. You're not fired! So you can work nights and Saturdays for as long as you want!"

James felt like his head was going to spin from the back-and-forth of Theo's words. "Um . . . do I get a choice?"

"No!" she announced with a cheerful smile.

"What if I quit or mysteriously vanish?" James asked ominously.

Theodora just waggled a finger at him, not letting her mysterious good mood falter. "That's not a very positive professional attitude for the one person who shows up to work every day and is getting a five-hundred-dollar bonus," she said.

"I . . . Wait, what?" James felt the onset of an actual headache trying to figure out what was going on. "Why? Actually, how? The business doesn't do bonuses. They replaced those with the secondary education thing."

She nodded sagely. "Ah, but this one is more of a personal favor, from me. And it's less of a bonus and more of a bribe. I came into some cash recently, and I'd like you to cover for me while I take a weeklong vacation. But alas! Cruel fate! I have no vacation hours!" She smiled at him, grinning with teeth that he would swear she sharpened with a file. "Ah, but look, what fortune!" She shifted her voice pitch to a low tone. "A convenient workaround presents himself."

"So . . ." James sighed and rubbed his forehead with his palms. "I clock you in, answer all the emails, and pretend to be you on the phone, and in return, you basically pay me your wage for the week?"

"Yes."

He thought about it for a second. One second, because that was exactly how long it took him to think, *She's absolutely going into the dungeon, she knows everything, that's where the money came from and why she's injured and happy.* Unfortunately, actually thinking that, knowing that in his heart, still didn't shake the alien claim on his words that would let him tell her that he was on to what she was doing.

It was starting to drive him insane. To feel like he didn't have a hold on his mind. And more importantly, to feel like he knew something special and to be forced to stay silent about it.

Internally shaking his head, James simply said, "Sold. Have fun on your 'vacation.'" He mimed quotation marks around the word *vacation*.

Theo laughed and slapped him on the shoulder hard enough that it felt like it rattled his bones. This short, compact woman had muscles like a fucking truck, and it just further drove home to James how likely it was that she'd been doing what he was doing this whole time.

Not helping was the fact that he couldn't even make a bad joke about it. Maybe he hadn't been making progress with his meditation and his attempted self-exorcism, but he was sure as hell going to try when he got home.

Rufus was happy to see his friend when he came through the door. The little creature understood that there was an element of timing to exactly when James would show up, so he wasn't upset anymore when long stretches passed with just himself, with the enemy and Ganesh for company. He understood this because, last week, James had explained it to him. If he'd been a more perceptive stapler-crab-spider-thing at the time, he might have noticed that James didn't really explain it directly and was more just aimlessly rambling to himself while he rested here in Fort Door.

But he wasn't. So he didn't actually know that James hadn't fully come to know how smart Rufus actually could be. This didn't bother Rufus, though. He was a patient and kind stapler-crab-spider-thing, and he would let his human friend take as long as he needed to learn. Everyone required time to learn things; he certainly had when James had first found him.

"So the time looks like eight hours to three minutes, going by that clock on the wall. But this stopwatch, which you took care to protect—thank you, Rufus"—Rufus purred a bit at the praise; he was a dutiful stapler-crab-spider-thing—"this one shows that a week went by. So, what the hell?"

Rufus didn't have an answer for his friend. At least, not one he could really explain. Of course the door wasn't always open, that was how doors worked. But he figured James knew that, so he wouldn't waste time trying to convey that. Rufus needed to learn to speak, he decided to himself. James and Anesh did it, and it made things a lot more exciting and expedient.

"Eh, it's probably something Anesh can do math at. Or, at least, it means that the time dilation stuff isn't as certainly dangerous as we thought. That's probably good, right?" he asked offhandedly. Of course it was, Rufus wanted to say. If it weren't, he'd have gotten bored waiting and left.

James hung around for a little while longer, and Rufus stuck around in the fort with him as he rearranged all their piles of stuff. He bagged up his old, partially laser-melted armor to take out and toss, while also making a point to carefully set Anesh's oversized Amazon order off to the side. Untouched. Until they actually got the delivery receipt for that order, he wasn't taking any chances with causality.

For his part, Rufus had no such qualms and had already checked out the insides of the box. It was full of good nesting material, and he hoped they'd let him have it once they were done taking out the inconvenient hard bits.

He continued following James around as he did some "chores," for lack of a better term, nodding empathically as James complained about foolish clients at work, helping him find all the candy wrappers that cluttered up the floor to add to his garbage removal, and giving a hopeful squeak when James mentioned Anesh's and his recovery.

Rufus was a big fan of Anesh, mostly because his own partner was as well. Ganesh had a personality that didn't exactly mirror but rather complemented the other delver's. Creative, energetic, and yet stoic. Rufus cared a lot for Ganesh, and the drone cared for Anesh. And so, Rufus had decided, he would as well.

The garbage removal, incidentally, was something Rufus was happy for. The place was a mess, and even Rufus, who used a shredded backpack as a hammock and nest, was not a fan of having loose candy wrappers and splashes of blood around his home. He had piled some of them up in a corner but hadn't really had time this week to go through every nook and cranny and collect the trash that James and Anesh had left behind. So seeing James actually wipe down the desk and chair where he'd done quick first aid on himself was nice. Rufus didn't know if James had noticed it, but there was a smell in the air that came from blood, and it became less pleasant over time.

Maybe humans didn't have a great sense of smell. That would make sense, Rufus thought.

"What in the hell . . ." James muttered, looking under one of the desks. Rufus had to scramble over the surface to try to distract him, but it was a little too late. "Rufus, I have a concern." He turned to face the stapler that was now at eye level with him. "Is this," James asked, holding up a golf-ball-sized chunk of staples, pressed together with the spiky bits pointing outward, "an egg? Or did you just crap in this drawer?" Rufus reached out and carefully took the ball from him before setting it back in the small side drawer pocket it had been in. He then reached out a single pen-leg and tapped James on the nose.

"Okay," James replied. "I shall leave that alone for now," he said with a raised eyebrow. He made a mental note to talk to Anesh about this, but even if it was inexplicably an egg, it didn't actually cause any problems. They could totally afford to have a baby Rufus running around the fort.

"Well," James said, looking around the cleaned-up base camp. "That's about all I can think to do today. I . . . really want to go poking around a bit, but that seems really stupid." Rufus was proud that James was learning things. "Also, Anesh would be annoyed." James sighed, dropping to his knees so he could give Rufus scratches on the back part of his main joint, which Rufus had learned was the best place ever to receive scratches. "You know, buddy, you've got it pretty easy. There's a whole lot of other life in here that you can share this place with. I know a lot of it's hostile, but hey, I made friends with you, and Ganesh is . . . nice for some reason. You can always make more friends and peers here. But Anesh and I are the only humans who get to know about it, and boy, is it just the goddamned worst." James stood up and reached his arms over his head, twisting his spine around to try to loosen up his back after a night of sitting at work. "We have a bunch of . . . well, we have a couple friends I'd love to share this with. You'd probably get along *great* with JP. He does that thing you do where he stares at someone and looks stupidly cute until they feel guilty for saying stupid stuff!"

Rufus tilted his head to look at James questioningly, his main eye blinking in slow, smooth strokes.

"Yeah, that thing!" James said with a laugh as Rufus bumped into his hand. "All right. Well, I guess when Ganesh gets back, tell him I said hi. Ask him if he's a program, if that's a concept you can accurately transfer," he said over his shoulder as he walked out, in a tone that made it pretty clear he didn't really expect Rufus to understand or share that information.

Rufus liked James. James was the one who'd given him a chance at something different, and it had paid off for both of them so far. James was also friendly and gave great scratches. James had brought him Ganesh, who was now Rufus's second-best friend. And it really made Rufus feel bad that James was so torn up about not being able to share this home with any of his own friends. Everyone should have a good friend, Rufus thought, as he climbed his webbing to watch for Ganesh's return.

And so it was, as James walked back out into the other world, that Rufus couldn't help but feel just a bit guilty.

CHAPTER 29

"The fuck happened to your arm?" Alanna asked as she gently pushed her way past a surprised Anesh and into the warm air of the apartment.

James silently opened his eyes from his claimed spot on the couch. It was one of those pleasant evenings when Anesh was back from class, and James didn't have work, and the two of them were just hanging out and watching old episodes of *Sliders* in their living room. Mostly just as background noise, while they planned out next week's delve.

Anesh was getting his cast off in a few days, the doctor erring on the side of caution since he had no medical record of ever *getting* the cast, and they were both eager to get back into the swing of things.

In the meantime, they'd had to go with some pretty flagrantly bad lies to their friends about exactly what had happened to put that arm in a cast in the first place, as well as deflecting a few questions about the various burns, scrapes, and scabs that kept appearing on each of them. Most of their group had just kind of accepted that the reason was secretly embarrassing but not overly damaging and let it drop.

Alanna, though, was the outlier who made it *most* and not *all*.

She'd noticed, as everyone else had, that Anesh was injured when they all met up for their weekly game night about a month and a half ago. And had, as everyone else had, asked what the fuck had happened to his arm. Anesh had applied his now-familiar tactic of telling her that he was injured in a tragic zeppelin accident, and everyone else had laughed, and Alanna had narrowed her eyes and said, "Like hell you were."

It hadn't been dropped since then. Every time she came over, which was a bit more frequently these days, she'd asked again. James suspected she was not-so-subtly checking up on his friend, making sure he was okay. Which was cool, really. They both liked Alanna, and James himself was pretty fond of Anesh, so he didn't mind at all that someone else cared enough to keep an eye on him and make sure the injury wasn't ruining his life. But it also meant that they both had to try to answer questions that they literally could not answer.

Anesh closed the door behind her, shutting out the evening chill. It was March now, and James felt like it should be close enough to spring for the weather to stop being so damn hostile, but it was still a biting cold out every night. "Welcome, welcome. Do come in," Anesh said, rolling his eyes. "Good to see you too, of course. Why yes, I'm doing fine, thank you."

From the couch, James spoke up and answered Alanna's question in Anesh's place as she strode in and stole his friend's seat. "Oh, I broke his arm. We're in a mutually abusive romantic relationship now."

Alanna lashed out with a foot from her draped position on the chair, catching James in the shoulder with a light thud. "No, you aren't, there are popes more abusive than you."

"Not a high bar you're setting there," James shot back.

With a series of incoherent grumbles, Anesh stalked around the table and threw himself onto the other end of the couch. "Took my damn seat," he muttered. "Also, yeah, he's talking about how at the hospital, the doctor thought we were dating and had him leave the room to ask me if he broke my arm." Anesh threw his working arm in the air. "It's silly!"

Alanna grinned madly at the two. "Nah, I can see it," she said with a shrewd tone. "Anyway, how'd you break your arm? Tell meeeeeee."

"Why are you here, anyway?" James asked, trying to redirect the conversation. "I mean, not that you're not welcome, but were you here for anything specific?"

"Yeah!" she said directly. "I'm trying to demand answers before you go in to have your cast off and everyone forgets about it!" There was a brief pause. "Also, I'm bored. Not much to do around here tonight."

It took a lot of effort for James to not break down laughing at that. He was originally going to, but then a small thought popped into his head that doing so might reveal something, and then the beast in his mind locked him out of it. He'd figured out over the last couple of weeks, by pushing at the boundaries of what he could and couldn't post on the internet, the limits and terrifying power of the mental coercion that he and Anesh were under.

Any time he thought something might reveal . . . well, anything, really . . . his own mind would rebel and stop him. If he thought he should tell someone, he'd invent reasons not to. If he could conceive of a way to get around that, then as soon as he knew it would work, he also knew enough to *know* that he shouldn't do it. Even accidents weren't working anymore, ever since Anesh had hinted at them being possible. He was on guard now, vigilant for any information leak, and actively finding ways to patch it.

And James *hated* it. His own intelligence was being turned against him by an entity that was equal parts mysterious, invasive, and frustrating.

He let his eyes refocus. He'd zoned out a bit, and while he was silently screaming at his invisible rider, Anesh and Alanna had gotten into a bit of a back-and-forth. ". . . good reason, then just fucking *tell me!*" He paid attention in time to hear Alanna's voice escalate to a yell.

"Fine!" Anesh snapped back, seeming on the edge of legitimate anger against their friend. "I got my arm snapped in half by a paper doll from the uncanny valley that we got in a fight with in the extradimensional dungeon zone that James found in the back stairs at his office!"

There was a moment of silence, and Alanna opened her mouth with a glare on her face, as if to tell Anesh to stop making up increasingly elaborate bullshit. But before she could say anything, James cut her off.

"What?" he said, staring at Anesh. His friend looked back at him with wide eyes as James snapped up his arm to point a dramatically accusing finger at Anesh. "What?"

"Guys, if you don't want to tell me—"

James cut Alanna off, not even paying attention. And good thing he wasn't, or he might have shut himself down. He could feel the coercion on himself still going strong. "How the hell did you say that?" he asked Anesh, confusion salting his words.

"I have no idea!" his friend said. Anesh then turned back to Alanna, wanting to make sure this wasn't a fluke. "We've been looting randomly generated desks for money. There are monsters that drop skill orbs. I have a pet drone that looks like a praying mantis and that I named after a god because I'm very sarcastic. James has almost gotten us killed six times now!" He whipped his head back to James. "It's gone! I can say whatever I want!"

"I . . . can't," James said, gritting his teeth. "In fact, I just had a very uncomfortable thought about the nature of information leaks. Hey, Alanna."

"Yeah?" she asked with rapt attention.

James had to force the words out of his mouth. "If I were to, say, murder Anesh. You'd probably want to investigate that, yes?"

"Fuck, what kind of question is that? Of course!" she yelled at him.

"Great. So that would be a terrible way of keeping information from spreading. Gotcha." He sighed, a very horrifying mental compulsion crumbling away as he became convinced that it wouldn't actually stop information from being distributed. "Okay, I'm going to leave the room, because I need to be literally anywhere else right now. It would help a lot if you could promise me, Anesh, that you *absolutely won't* tell Alanna anything else. Because I trust you."

Anesh got it. He understood how bad the mind control could have been, though he hadn't been pushing it exactly as far as James was. And he knew, from what James asked, that it would have been more than capable of forcing his friend to extreme violence if Anesh kept talking without thinking. So he agreed. "Yeah, of course. Won't tell her anything."

"Hey!" Alanna started to say, but Anesh shushed her.

"It'll be fine," he said calmly. "I don't think I need to share any more at all."

James just nodded, trying not to focus on that, even as his mind raced. "Welp. I'm going out. You guys have fun, explicitly keeping secrets." He stiffly stood up and walked over to the door, throwing a coat on and shoving his feet into shoes. "Don't cause too many problems. Don't tell people Anesh and I are dating, Alanna." She opened her mouth as if to argue, but he stopped her with a hand held up. "We've been friends for a long time, I know you were going to. Don't argue. Yes, I'm reading your mind." Her face twisted into an amused snarl. "Yes, I'm a jerk. Okay, bye!" The door slammed behind him, perhaps a bit louder than he meant, as he left.

Alanna turned back to Anesh. "What the fuck was that about?" she asked. "You're really not going to tell me?"

He smiled, knowing what James was doing. "Of course I am. He just can't be here when I do." Anesh went over to the bookshelf and pulled up the file folder full of documents that he used for their RPGs. "Here," he said, pulling out the second set of papers, the maps and notes and things that were a little bit more important than the ones for their current game. "That game I'm running for you guys? That's based off reality."

"Bullshit," Alanna said simply.

"No, really." He spread out the maps, the sketches and battle plans for some of the larger life forms, the printouts of Amazon and eBay orders for combat equipment. "He found it, did a few dives inside before inviting me. At some point, both of us got hit with some kind of nightmarish mind control. For the last . . . two months? Three? Neither of us has been able to talk to you, or anyone, about what we've been doing every week." The last thing he added to the table was his phone, opening up his image folder to show Alanna a picture he'd taken of James, holding Rufus in the palm of his hand and giving the strider a mock high five.

She looked at the pile of notes and the image. "I'm almost sure you two are fucking with me somehow, here. This is a long way to go for a joke, but you guys are bored enough to do it."

"Okay," Anesh said. "Come with me."

He stood up and maneuvered around their living room furniture to walk down the hall to James's bedroom. Alanna watched as he opened the door and disappeared from her sight. A second later, she jumped up and followed. In her head, it hadn't really clicked yet that this might even possibly be real. James and Anesh were her friends, but she was fairly sure that they could pull off bullshit of this caliber. It wasn't beyond the time they'd faked James's death on Halloween, though it was significantly more fantasy than that one.

So it came as a bit of a shock to her when she walked in to see Anesh uncovering a small cat pen in the corner of his roommate's bedroom. "I didn't know you guys got a pet!" she said excitedly. "Is it a kitten?" Anesh just shook his head and motioned her closer.

"Look," he said, pointing.

She peered in, excited to see their new pet. But what Anesh had presented was anything but cuddly. Nestled in a ring of blankets sat a yellow ball the size of a human head. It glowed slightly, and differing shades of yellows, tones dark to bright, shifted under its surface. That, on its own, was kind of weird. But the thing that sat atop it took the cake.

It looked like an iPhone, and for a second, she thought that was exactly what it was. But then it moved, a fluid organic twitch that showed off a segmented body and a myriad of tiny copper legs that made it look like a computer chip and a centipede had some kind of nightmare offspring. Alanna recoiled, letting out what she would have called a roar and Anesh would have called a scream, if he felt like getting punched. "What the fuck is *that?*"

"Well, that's Lily," Anesh said, backing away. "It . . . she . . . is an iLipede that James brought home, because he's a wanker."

"The fuck's a nilipede?" Alanna crawled up onto the bed to get a better view of it, while still staying safely out of range of . . . anything it might do, really.

"No, no. An iLipede. Millipede, but without the *M*. And a lowercase *i*, because . . . you don't care. Okay." Anesh smiled a bit as he draped the blanket back over the pen. "It's an iPhone, but a millipede.

So far, we've come up with good wordplay names for just about everything, because . . . well, James and me, right?"

"Right . . ." Alanna said, still kneeling on the bed.

"Anyway. Yes, it's real. No, it's not a joke. We were originally planning on telling more people so we could get more exploration done, and also share it with everyone we actually like. But then, as mentioned, mind control." He led Alanna back out into the hallway, hitting the light and closing the door after they left the room.

They wandered back to the living room, Alanna still trying to process the whole thing. "Okay, okay, wait," she said. "Just hang the fuck on." She paused for a minute to collect her thoughts, staring at the table now covered in notes and maps. After a long minute, and a deep breath, she finally spoke. "What's in there?"

"Quite a lot," Anesh said. "Cubicles, mostly. Endless cubicles. The horizon is far away and beige. There's stuff, too. We've been paying rent from the contents of the wallets we find in there. Oh, and all that candy that I told you guys was from England comes from there, too."

Alanna slapped the table with a resounding crack. "I fucking knew that Baby Things weren't a real candy!"

"Well, they are a *real* candy, just not one that's available to the public," Anesh countered. "Like how JP is JP's real name, even if no one knows what his parents call him."

"Dave knows. I think." She wasn't impressed with that answer. "What else? What else is in there?"

"Monsters." Anesh spoke softly. "Dangerous things. Twisted images of office supplies turned into life forms, or things like life. Exploding coffee cups. Balls of hostile Cat 5 cable." He rubbed the cast on his arm, the thing that had started this conversation. "Things that could kill you if you're not careful."

The gesture didn't go unnoticed. "That's why you're hurt." It wasn't a question. "Why go in there at all, then? Why not just tell someone, sell the information, and leave it alone. Or, I dunno, call the government? Do they have a division for this?"

"Probably!" Anesh said with a sudden cheerful turn. "But this one isn't theirs. It's ours. Well, it probably technically belongs to the company James works at, but that's not the point. That big basketball thing that Lily is sleeping on? That's a skill orb."

"Wat," came the squawked interruption.

Anesh cleared his throat. "I'm trying to explain, come on. Give me some word space." He pushed her two thin sheaves of paper, each one labeled with a name. "James found it first, when he killed one of the staplers. They use these things as power sources, we think. But when we use them, crack them open, it adds things to our minds. We think. Again, this is mostly experimentation at this point."

He pointed to the lists of skills that he and James had acquired, and the notes next to each of them. They'd done more than a little testing on that front, Alanna saw. There were notes on which ones tied into others, what was "active" or "passive." What the jump in ability actually felt like. Anesh had a thing for written organization of data, and the pile that he'd handed her went pretty deep on it.

"You learned how to fence?" she asked, looking up and raising her eyebrows.

A shrug in response. "I learned how to use a rapier. It's different, somehow. Not . . . quite sure yet."

Alanna leaned back, now with serious consideration written across her face. This was a look Anesh knew pretty well; anyone who spent time around Alanna eventually saw it. It meant she had an idea. A big one. One of those "change the world" ideas.

"What are you guys using this for?" she asked quietly.

"Self improvement, mostly," Anesh said. "Also dragging ourselves out of poverty. Also, I think James might literally be addicted to the adrenaline rush of combat. But that's . . . not much of a problem, I think?" Anesh sighed, turning sideways on the couch to stare at the ceiling. He never understood how James made this seem comfortable. "We've shared some of the money, quietly. Helped a few people make rent. Used a couple of the green orbs in a hospital. Oh, those improve locations somehow." He sighed. "Look, I know you're probably disappointed, but ... we can't find the exploit, if that makes sense. If there's a way to use this place to do more to help the world, I'm not seeing it."

Alanna nodded silently. "I don't know. I'd have to see it, I guess. From what you say, you're right. I'm not going to judge you two for not doing enough, but it does seem kind of ... small?"

"'Small' is a good word for it," Anesh said, feeling a strange and unnecessary guilt. "We don't have a plan to fix everything, just ourselves."

"Anesh, you know you're part of everything, right?" Alanna said in an amused tone. "I know I yell about the utopia fallacy a lot, and I know that James and Dave think I'm some kind of blind idealist, but I'm not *mad at you* for this." She stood up, reaching her arms over her head to stretch, her height making her look like a titan in the small apartment. "Improving yourselves is part of improving the world. You've got a line on that sheet that's got a million underlines and circles around it, and looks like it let you skip six months of math classes that I can't understand, right?"

"Right ..." he said hesitantly.

"Great. Use that. Don't waste it. Push the collective knowledge of humanity forward a bit." She walked into the kitchen to get some water, calling back, "It's not evil to seize power, only to squander it!"

Anesh wasn't sure he fully agreed with that. But then, he had a totally different cultural background. There was a certain dichotomy that came from growing up in England with an Indian bloodline, and so he could probably name any number of reasons why seizing power wasn't a great idea. But he also knew that just because history showed empires being evil didn't mean that those mistakes had to be repeated. In a large way, he envied Alanna's view of the world as something to improve, as opposed to how he and James treated it as something to be *survived*.

She walked back into the room, fairly casually for someone who'd just learned about the existence of literal magic, Anesh thought. "Look, here's my offer," she said. "I'll keep this secret, like you guys were *before* the creepy mind control thing." She pointed an accusatory finger at Anesh. "But I want in. Because of course I do. But, well, it's like you just said. You're improving yourselves. Don't think I haven't noticed how fucking happy James has been lately. Or that he's put on muscle."

"Yeah, it's kind of impressive," Anesh said slyly.

"Oh, and don't think I haven't noticed you noticing either. The only reason I'm not telling people you guys are dating is because I'm waiting for you to do it." She ignored Anesh's flushed face and stammered attempt at a comeback and just rolled on with what she was saying. "The point is, the government, or the company, or whatever mysterious bullshit organization handles this sort of thing? They're not going to use it right, and we all obviously know it. So I want to get in while there's an opening. I want to be better, I want to learn random crap like this. Because if any of it's useful, well . . ."

Anesh composed himself as she was talking and tapped the table as she trailed off. "If any of it's useful, then you're more useful, and you can do more."

"Right," she said.

"When you run for president, I'll vote for you," he said with a grin.

Alanna laughed, a loud booming chuckle that carried through the whole apartment. "Wait, you're not a citizen! That's a hollow promise!"

"I'll make James do it, then!" Anesh said with a laugh of his own, feeling the tension draining from the room and the guilt he'd been worried about with telling Alanna leave him as well. "Okay. The door opens every Tuesday at 3:44 a.m. As in, stay up late on Monday."

"Got it. Are you guys going in next week?" she asked.

Anesh slapped his cast with his good hand. "This comes off a day earlier. Then we're going delving again. And yes, you're welcome to come along. We can carpool, to make it easier."

"Wait, they just let you in?"

He shrugged. "The staff were fine with it at first, and then I think James bribed the security guard after he got in trouble for us taking a coffee maker. Oh! Magic coffee! I forgot!"

"I'm going to need to take some time to catch up on this, aren't I?" Alanna asked as she cracked her knuckles.

"Probably," Anesh said. "I still don't know how James is going to react to it, or if he *can* react to it. This might be weird. Er. Weirder. I still don't know how long I can talk about it for, honestly. I want to tell JP, but he's on vacation with his family. I do *not* really want to tell Dave. This is very important. James and I discussed it, and neither of us trusts him to not be a jackass."

"Agreed" was the all-too-fast response of someone who knew exactly what kind of friend Dave was.

"Aside from that... Well. This might be a little odd, but want to look at melee weapons on Amazon before James gets back?" Anesh asked.

Alanna laughed again; this time it had a sort of bitter tint to it. "Buddy, I'm super glad you're telling me about this and eager to let me come with you, but at this point, I don't think you need to keep saying that stuff is odd. I mean, let's be honest. I haven't seen anything this *effed* since episode six of *Sesame Street*."

He just sighed. "Yeah, it's hard to keep that in perspective sometimes."

It felt good, though. For Anesh, it was puzzled relief that his mind was his own again. For Alanna, it was excitement at what her friend had trusted her with. And even for James, still walking his detoured path back from the burger joint he'd visited, there was a sweetness in the air.

Because James knew he could trust Anesh, and he implicitly trusted him to share with Alanna. But at this point, the knowledge was already out there; there was no reeling it back in. The creature in his mind had railed against him as he'd walked down the sidewalk, trying to push him to ideas on how to stem the information bleeding. But he just kept walking and kept pushing back. Softly at first, then with more confidence. He'd hummed as he'd casually put one foot in front of the other, letting his mental momentum build up with his physical stride.

It was losing the fight. It was weakening. It still held a grip on his mind; James knew he wouldn't be able to just turn to the guy passing him and tell him about this one time when he got to launch a fire grenade into a walking computer that shot lasers. But he cordoned off the part of his mind that it had assaulted when Anesh had started sharing. And he was fairly sure that he could talk to Alanna about it now.

Still, though, it would be nice to know exactly why this was happening. Or what the strange fish-shaped thought-thing was. The mind control had never been a high point, and now that it felt like he was gaining ground on the monster in his head, well ...

James had a strange idea then, on the nighttime walk home.

Maybe he should just ask it.

CHAPTER 30

"Is it like this every day?" Alanna asked in a quiet, disbelieving voice.

"I'm afraid so," Anesh said in the same tone.

The two of them stood side by side, unable to look away. It was like watching a train wreck. There wasn't anything they could do to stop it, just stare in horror as the inevitable tense nightmare came to its logical conclusion. Most people probably would; what they were witnessing was no less than the end of a human soul. Stripped away, layer by layer; all defenses torn apart and left shattered, only for the soft core to be crushed to nothing.

They were, of course, standing outside James's cubicle.

"No, sir," he was saying in a calm but strained voice, his teeth gritted together so hard his jaw hurt. "I *promise* you that I will not be fired for *following protocol*. Now, there is no higher level available at this hour, but if you call back tomorrow at . . . nine a.m. your time, you can get a supervisor to look at the extensive list of charges on your account for the rather impressive amount of pornography you purchased." There was a pause. "Yes, sir, you have made me aware that you will get me fired. Is there anything else I can help you with today?"

Alanna and Anesh just watched as James's face went through a series of tortured twitches. "I can't tell if he's planning to kill someone or actually having an aneurysm," Alanna whispered out of the corner of her mouth.

"Both?" he suggested with a look of concern on his face.

"Neither," James said, slapping his headset onto the desk, hard enough to make a satisfying *thwap* but expertly placed to do no damage to the hardware—the maneuver of someone who'd had a few calls like this before, and probably a few mistakes as well. "Oh, don't get me wrong," he said, noting their disbelieving looks. "I'm still furious. But, like, the dude tried to tell me he 'accidentally' bought four grand worth of porn. That's objectively hilarious." James took a deep breath. "But yeah, I'm not too worried. I can't get fired, I don't think. And also, it's Tuesday now, which is great."

Tuesday. Technically Tuesday. It was what Alanna had started calling it: that time when it was the early morning of a day, but the "day" hadn't really ended for some people yet, so it still felt like Monday night. But to James and Anesh, it felt like a lightning bolt of excitement. The thrill of adventure hanging in the air, heavy on their minds and pulling at their spirits.

Alanna wasn't really that into it, but she smiled to herself as she saw the two guys' eyes light up while they talked a bit. Unlike Anesh on his first night, she didn't have any thought that this was a practical joke. Lily on her . . . its? . . . own was enough to convince her it was real. It wasn't that it hadn't sunk in yet either; she got it, honestly. The temptation of what these two casually offered was huge to someone who wanted to be a power player in the world. It just felt like she had more of a nervous feeling from being in someone else's workplace than from being about to go delving, as those two called it.

But their enthusiasm was infectious, no matter how much she wanted to play it cool. It had been one thing to stay calm over the last few days as they'd gone over maps with her to drill escape routes in, or taken a walk out to an open field so she could get a handle on exactly how much force it took to smash something with a sledgehammer. But now that they were here, and both her friends were putting off an attitude that she'd never really felt from them before, it was getting harder and harder to pretend this wasn't just the coolest thing ever.

"Yo! You awake?" The words from James startled her out of her thoughts, though she made no outward sign of it.

Straightening her back from where she'd been leaning on the cubicle wall, Alanna let out a small yawn before answering. "Yeah, still alive. Your work is awful. Are you the only one here or something?" Alanna looked around the nearly empty floor.

James just shrugged, repeating the motion a few times to loosen his shoulders, which were still stiff from sitting all night. "Kinda? I'm currently filling in for my boss, and a lot of the newbies that we hired to fill in the empty spots quit. Again. So there's a couple other techs who just got here, and that's good, because I'm so done with this job tonight."

"So you could get away with anything?" Alanna asked slyly, wiggling her eyebrows at James.

"No," he said with a flat laugh. "Because there are cameras, and Frank, who I did not bribe enough to let me get away with burning the building down."

"You bribed Frank?" Anesh cut in as James shoved his personal effects into his pockets.

"Of course I bribed Frank. Why do you think he helped us load carboys full of mystery drinks into the trunk of my car? And didn't comment on how we went in totally fine, and you came out six minutes later with your arm in a fucking cast?" James rubbed his hand on his forehead. "He went from reporting us for taking a coffee maker to actively supporting us!"

Anesh cleared his throat. "I . . . did not notice that. But in my defense, I was a bit, you know . . ."

"Demolished?" James asked as their group walked down the hall.

Alanna slapped him on the back of the head, while Anesh let out a "Hey!" James just laughed, while Anesh kept walking in front of them. "It's not like I got killed or anything. And I saved your life at the end!" he said, spinning around to point at James accusingly, walking backward for a few steps while he talked.

"I know, I know," James said, "I'm just pointing out that whatever painkillers you were on may have muddled your mind a bit."

The three of them talked a bit more while they made their way through the strangely mazelike halls of the building James worked in.

Alanna was actually kind of impressed that Anesh had navigated to James's desk so easily, even though he'd been here many times before. Even if she'd known which of the seven floors of this building to even go to, Alanna figured she would have been lost and somehow two floors down from where she started before realizing that she had no way to find her friend at all.

When she asked, James just shrugged and said, "Yeah, it's like that. They've remodeled a few times, so some of the hallways are sorta 'extra.' It gets confusing sometimes."

She'd asked him if that seemed a little suspicious, given the nature of the extradimensional nightmare-space that the building housed the doorway to, but James just shrugged. It was just one of those things, to him, that corporations did. When there were too many people in charge of things, he figured, then there were always going to be small greebles in the plans. Things got misplaced, doors got stuck in weird spots, no one corrected the contractors because they didn't know if the orders came from their own boss. It was like how, sometimes, the company planned for layoffs even when they were hiring to replace lost employees.

Just corporate nonsense at its finest.

Before Alanna could complain to James that this was probably something worth looking into, they'd arrived at the door.

"Just in time," Anesh said. "We've got about thirty seconds."

"You ready?" James asked Alanna, a smile on his face.

Alanna nodded. Of course she was ready. What a silly thing to ask.

James and Anesh leaned forward, each of them placing a hand on one of the door handles. Together, they pushed down, and pulled the heavy metal doors outward. Sweeping their other arms down with a slight bow, they presented the scene to Alanna.

Stairs.

"What the fuck?" Alanna barked out.

James jerked upward, confusion on his face. He leaned around the door and looked in. "What the fuck?" he stuttered, looking in.

Anesh, unable to stop himself any longer, laughed. Loudly. James and Alanna both whipped their heads around to glare at him. He shut his side of the door, still laughing, even as both of them silently scowled. "So is this all one really impressive practical joke on *me?*" Alanna asked, "or is this Anesh being a dick to both of us, but in a much smaller way?"

"That second one," James said with a roll of his eyes, letting his side of the door pull shut. "He thinks he's funny sometimes."

Still giggling a bit, Anesh responded, "Hey, I'm hilarious." He couldn't quite get through the whole sentence without snorting with laughter as he saw the exasperated look on Alanna's face, though.

"Okay, so, for real this time, and with a bit less gravitas," James said, checking his phone's clock to make sure that it was actually 3:44 a.m. this time. "I wanted this to be kind of a moment, but *someone*"—Anesh broke into another fit of giggles as James glared at him—"couldn't let us have nice things."

He opened the door, and this time Alanna saw something different.

There was something strange about the dungeon, Alanna decided.

Well, apart from the obvious.

It was that it had an outside wall. While James and Anesh fell into what had become a ritual for them—greeting Rufus and Ganesh, and then Anesh checking gear while James just sort of soaked in the beauty of the horizon—Alanna couldn't stop staring at the wall behind them.

She'd met Rufus. He seemed ... interesting. Alanna got a strange vibe off the little guy, who was in the process of rolling what looked like a ball of staples around when the trio had come through. It felt like he was a lot bigger than his form looked. Rufus hadn't really acknowledged her outwardly, but she got the impression that he was upset; it reminded her a lot of how her mother would act whenever Alanna had come home from school with new bruises and scrapes. Not angry, certainly not going to say anything, but somehow, the atmosphere of the house had been disappointed.

She hadn't said hi to the thing that Anesh referred to as Ganesh. She had asked why he'd named it something just one letter off from his own name, and he'd thrown up his hands and said something about how it was a clever reference before deliberately walking over to the other side of the little fort and busying himself pulling sets of body armor out.

Of course, Alanna had been curious about a lot of things. She'd just wanted personal experience before rapid-fire asking Anesh things that would probably be obvious when she could see in person.

But now, after getting a good view of the interior, she had questions. The cubicles seemed to go on forever, sure, but that wasn't as weird as the fact that she could see them starting to curve toward the ceiling in the distance. It reminded her of what a ringworld would look like, though not nearly to the same massive degree. Of course, the higher walls cut off vision before it was really noticeable, but Alanna wouldn't have been surprised to learn that there really were hundreds or even thousands of miles of dungeon out there.

And the dungeon itself was huge and terrifying in its scope, sure, but . . . it had this outer wall.

That was what she kept staring at as the guys discussed the plan for the night's delve and what things they wanted to show her to ease her into the operation. The wall.

"Anesh," she said, interrupting their conversation. "Why is there a wall?"

"Because buildings have walls," James responded as Anesh furrowed his brow and put a hand to his chin. Then, a second later, James continued, "No, wait . . ." and unconsciously mimicked the motion Anesh had made. "Because there has to be a boundary?"

"But the door on the other side just leads to stairs when it doesn't lead here. So where does this door, here, lead, when it doesn't lead back to the little lobby area outside the elevator?" Alanna asked.

James and Anesh looked at the door, then around at the rest of the wall. "I don't like that thought at all," James said quietly.

"It's fine, it's fine," Anesh said. "We've gone fairly far down both directions. The wall curves a bit, but we haven't found a place where it terminates, and no other doors. And we are *never* here when this door doesn't lead back out, so we never have to know what's on the other side." He sighed a bit. "I don't think that's a perfect answer, but it's what we've got."

"Oooookay..." Alanna drawled out. "I'll take it, but I'm not happy with it."

There was a silent, awkward moment as she continued to stare at the wall, her eyes drifting over the clock, the large whiteboard a few meters down, and the endless gray monolith that was the rest of the outer boundary of the dungeon.

James broke the quiet first. "So! We've been thinking. Yes, we're okay, don't worry, we survived the experience." He cut off Alanna's joke before she could make it. "Anyway. Anesh wants to do some experiments here by the door, double-check all our time dilation calculations. Also do a little scouting farther along the widdershins wall."

"The fucking what?" Alanna asked incredulously.

"Um . . . that way." James pointed. "Counterclockwise. Right. Anyway. He's basically staying in the safe zone, which is good, because we only have two sets of the security armor, and I want to try going deeper in. So do you want to come along with me, and I can show off some of the more interesting stuff to you?"

Alanna cracked her knuckles dramatically, rolling her shoulders. "Yeah! I'm getting into this now. This place looks so much weirder than I imagined. And I want to see how the wildlife stacks up to what you said about the endless series of murderbots you described."

"They're not really robots . . ." Anesh started to say before Alanna waved him off. "All right, all right. Well, hey, let's get you two suited up. You're about our size, so this armor should fit you. It's class one, so it's gender neutral, which is good. This isn't full SWAT armor, so it isn't fitted or too bulky."

They took about twenty minutes to get both Alanna and James geared up. Thick gray armor, padded cloth around a layer of Kevlar. Plates of arm and leg guards that slotted into each other and strapped tight, giving the impression of a person truly prepared to take damage. For James, his trusty axe in its sheath was strapped to the clip on the hip of the main portion of the armor before he threw on a backpack with one of their first-aid kits and a thermos of coffee that Anesh had brought. Alanna got a similar backpack, at Anesh's insistence, and had the small sledgehammer that they'd brought back in. Both of them slid radios into the outside chest pockets of the armor. James was really into all the little pockets and clips that made the armor look like it had a complex combat webbing on it. He'd wanted to throw his Maglite and all that rope he'd brought in so long ago on there as well, until Anesh pointed out that they'd never found anywhere dark, and the rope was absolutely more of a liability than anything else. He'd relented, but only begrudgingly.

Finally, they were ready. James asked Anesh a few more times if he really wanted to stay behind today, and Anesh had to really reassure his friend that yes, this was actually what he wanted. Even if he didn't have some ideas to test out, he had also just gotten his cast off. His arm felt fine enough, but he didn't want to push it too far today getting into fights with bone-snapping monsters. Again.

Anesh did send Ganesh with them. The little drone perched on James's helmet, still tossing glances at Alanna every now and then. She didn't seem to have noticed that the small creature wasn't warm toward her, but Anesh hoped this would be a good chance for them to become friends. Alanna was, at heart, a nice person, no matter how many times she swore in casual conversation, and Ganesh would learn to care for her the same way Anesh did. Also, on a more personal note, he wanted to be able to check through Ganesh's camera just to keep an eye on things, and stay up to date on any new discoveries.

"All right, so, the first thing to remember is that we need to be pretty quiet when we're in there," James was saying as he led Alanna across the open space toward the first row of cubicles.

Anesh nodded to himself. They'd be okay together. In his heart, he wanted his friends to be safe, but he didn't worry too much about them as he watched them take a corner, James showing Alanna how to do the quick one-two check-and-move-up pattern that a duo of delvers needed to perfect to stay safe.

Then he was alone. Well, almost alone.

"Rufus," he said quietly, inclining his head toward the stapler, who was carrying another of his little staple balls across the top of the desk. The little stapler-crab stopped briefly and looked up at Anesh, who pulled a chair up and sat in it, turning to fully face Rufus. His tone dropped, becoming stern, but not angry. "I think it's about time we had a talk."

CHAPTER 31

There was a muffled roar, and a *thump*. James checked down the hall to his left and right before turning to look inside the cubicle that he'd had his back to. He'd been keeping watch while Alanna checked out the interiors of some of the cubes, giving small hints where needed on how to quickly scour the small rooms for money and targeted high-value items. Honestly, he'd kind of forgotten that most people didn't instinctively have looting patterns and search tactics burned into their minds.

Probably a result of spending too much time with Anesh in here, and not enough time in reality *not* trying to maximize the value of his haul.

But here, these were important things to internalize. Grab small stuff and cash every time; if it's easy to carry and worth it, don't skip it. But know that on the way out, it's easy to fill your bag with extra stuff. Random pens, notebooks, computer hardware, digital clocks, desk toys, whatever. These things weren't usually worth anything, but sometimes they might have a blue orb in them or have incremental value just because every now and then, you wanted a pen or a Newton's cradle for your desk.

So James tried to give Alanna space to learn without being overbearing. He knew how easy it was to get angry when a teacher spent too much time telling you that you were wrong.

Now, though, he heard her yelling and things breaking, so he moved to assist.

What he saw through the door was her scattering papers and a keyboard onto the floor as she reached across the desk to grab at the handle of her sledgehammer, which she'd left leaning against some drawers on the far side. Looking down at the source of the *thump* he'd heard, James saw a single strider, upside down on the floor, legs twitching like a panicked turtle unable to right itself.

Alanna, though, looked more than a little flustered. Her helmet was tilted a bit, and James put together a quick chain of events in his head. It had dive-bombed her, probably from the taller stack of cubbies on the desk, and she'd panicked and flung it. Simple, but then the office chair and its perilous wheeled form had tripped her up as she went for a weapon. James nodded as he watched her scramble to right herself. Good response time, really.

"Are you okay?" he casually asked as he slammed his heel down on the stapler-crab, snapping half its legs off and splintering the more brittle chitin of its underbelly.

Alanna looked up, panting a bit, hammer in her hands, just in time to see James reach down and snap up the yellow orb that had dropped from the corpse. "What the fuck?" she demanded.

"It's a stapler-crab. Well, they're more like stapler-spiders, really. Striders, for short. Though we waffle a bit on that name." James pocketed the orb for later, just in case Rufus or Ganesh needed one. "Wait, hang on. You met Rufus, you've seen these before!"

"It wasn't trying to kill me!" she snapped back.

James nodded, taking the smile off his face. "Yeah. I understand. It's not easy to get used to at first. Are you hurt?"

She checked herself for injuries. "My head stings from where it hit, but no, it didn't bite me."

"All right, good. Let's finish up here and move on," he said, turning back to the door. "I'm gonna make sure that the noise didn't call a horde, so try to be a little quieter. You would have been fine without me, remember that." He stepped back outside and slightly to the left, keeping the door clear and also putting himself out of her line of sight.

James sighed. He was really trying to not just tell Alanna things that she already knew. He knew she was a fast learner, and she paid attention in a weird active way that caused her to catch stuff that James would have missed unless it was spelled out. She'd probably already figured out that keeping her weapon closer at hand and more stable was smart. She probably was already learning to move in the bulkier armor sets they weore, which James was still working on himself. And she'd probably already figured out that yelling wasn't helpful.

But maybe not? He didn't know. He just didn't want to piss off his teammate this early into the delve, especially not when they'd just gotten back in. He'd talk to her about it later if it came up again, though he suspected it wouldn't.

"Ready," Alanna said, stepping out and putting her backpack on again. She looked like she'd taken a deep breath to compose herself, and James nodded approvingly.

"All right. So we haven't been down this particular aisle before, so most of the cubes should be untouched. But if we go a little deeper, we can try to find one of the water cooler spaces and pick a fight with a plant, or see if we can find another iLipede nest so we can hunt down enchanted items. Your call, really," he said, offering up a couple of options from his own mental quest log.

Alanna took another breath, closing her eyes briefly. Letting out a hum, she looked down the length of the corridor, the cubicle walls rapidly gaining height here and giving the appearance of a very thin staircase. "I kind of want to just keep exploring, see what happens. Though if you see any monsters, please let me know so I can actually hit them before they see me."

"Can do!" James saluted with a grin. His expression drooped a bit as Alanna just rolled her eyes and started moving down the hall. James gave a soft sigh and muttered to Ganesh, "I think I liked doing this with your human more. He appreciated banter. Appreciates. Appreciates banter, he's not dead." James corrected himself when Ganesh tapped on his helmet.

He followed after Alanna, moving as quietly as he could and trying to get used to the bulkier padding that Anesh had bought for them. It certainly felt protective, but James couldn't shake the feeling that he was one awkward step away from knocking furniture over by accident.

The one thing that Alanna did do well, which James took a second to appreciate, was the actual teamwork part of this. Since they weren't really looting specifically, it was mostly just moving and keeping an eye out, but she took to their simple system of shoulder taps and leapfrog movements easily. James started to get comfortable with her as they quietly pressed on, marking the few turns they took and occasionally poking into a cubicle to look through coat pockets.

It was shortly after Alanna happily pocketed a twenty-dollar bill from one of those stops that James started to get suspicious.

"There aren't enough hostiles around here," he murmured as they came to an intersection. And there hadn't been, at all. Aside from that first strider, there hadn't been anything in this section of the dungeon.

Alanna scanned the area, her eyes moving deliberately and methodically, mostly checking the tops of cubicle walls. "Doesn't look like anything is following us or watching," she said. "Do we keep going, or turn back?"

It was a good question, and James took a second to consider the options. There was really no good reason to turn back, aside from it feeling a little weirder than normal. But going forward was risky, and a little extra weirdness might just be the end of them. Still, his sense of adventure called. In some ways, the possible risk stirred something in his chest that drew him forward. "We keep going," he said confidently. "We've only taken three turns; you know the way back if we need to run, right?"

"Right." Alanna nodded.

James took the lead, moving toward the upcoming intersection. They were approaching from the side this time, and he could see only the black monolith of the vending machine from this angle, a small garbage can sitting next to it. He tapped his helmet. "Ganesh, go see if there's a plant on the other side. Just crawl over the top; don't risk getting caught."

He set the drone on the floor from the palm of his hand, and it scurried forward. The more Alanna saw the thing walk, the more it reminded her of a praying mantis, using folded forearms to guide its walking and somehow climbing the side of the vending machine as if it were a lizard. "How are we supposed to know if there is one?" she asked James. "The drone can't talk."

"He's smart, he can nod or shake his head," James quietly responded. "If there is a plant, then I'll go in and distract it; you'll just need to land a good hit on the base with the hammer, then break the big red thing in there."

Alanna snorted. "The plants have weak spots?"

"The plants have hearts. They're in the pots, because . . . I mean . . . that's where I'd put a plant heart, I guess. Kinda fleshy, too, so don't kick it unless you have to." Alanna nodded. Weak spots were a video game concept; organs were real. This was something that she could deal with.

They both watched Ganesh approach and look over the edge of the vending machine. James waited for him to turn around and give a signal, but their insectile companion instead jerked back, rotors flaring to life with a low buzz. Not fast enough, though, as the edge of a large leaf came up over the edge and just scooped Ganesh up, rolling him in greenery before dragging him back over the other side.

James was already moving, heart suddenly racing. Ganesh wasn't really his friend or anything, not the same way Anesh or even Alanna was, but he was a reliable ally, and he really seemed to care about Anesh, if not James himself. James couldn't imagine letting the little guy get hurt, and he didn't even think before he had his axe in hand and was rushing forward, closing the thirty or so feet to the vending machine, moving fast enough that he had the momentum to slide around it and lash out blindly at where he assumed the plant would be.

He wasn't wrong. But this plant was bigger than anything they'd seen before. It looked like a cross between an agave and an areca palm, all thick and spiky leaves, with a couple of massive fronds sprouting out its sides. The fern branches that split off from its main trunk were dozens of thin strips of green, each one looking razor-sharp, and it was one of those that James caught with his surprise attack. The axe cut deep into the main branch, and he couldn't tell from the feel if he'd hit wood or plastic, but either way he'd pinned one of the offshoots and snipped it clean off.

It wasn't enough, though, and the other branches and the spiky leaves at the base all turned to him as soon as the plant recovered from its shock. James was already rolling to his feet, taking another swing. He'd pulled back a bit too hard and so his hand axe was slightly too far out of position for the follow-up strike to be perfect, but he slammed it forward with enthusiasm and managed to smash another of the razor fern branches before it could lash out at him.

Then one of the succulent leaves near the base exploded into motion. It must have been hiding quite a bit in the root system of the large ceramic pot, because while each of the leaves only looked maybe a foot long, it was about six feet of solid, waxy green that slammed into James's chest, lifting him up just a bit off his feet and almost casually *flicking* him down the intersecting hall. He barely had time to register that it had hit him before he was flat on his back.

Coughing wetly, dragging air back into his lungs after the breath was knocked out of him, James staggered back up. He wasn't done, not by a long shot. He couldn't let this thing just take Ganesh like an afternoon snack. He rushed back forward, seeing that the plant was ready for him. It had pulled the frond containing Ganesh around to the front, a hostage to keep James from attacking too viciously, but that wasn't what he was going for this time. To his right, up against the front of the vending machine, Alanna stood with the heavy hammer raised up in a two-handed grip, waiting. So James ran in, and at the last second he skidded to a near stop. When the plant lashed out at him, he wrapped one of his arms around the tendril that now had far less force behind its strike than expected. Throwing himself backward, James pinned the plant, keeping it stretched out and pulling him upright to avoid tipping over itself.

Alanna took advantage of the situation. There wasn't much space to maneuver between the huge soda dispenser and the plant's pot base, but she made it work. She stomped down, using a heavy step to pin the tendril attacking James and tip the plant forward. The plant, now off balance, gave Alanna an opening to bring the hammer down across its left side. Ferns and branches snapped off, the unfolded leaf ripped down the side, and one of the succulent tendrils at the bottom sprayed a juicy pulp across the floor as the hammer crashed to a stop on it. But despite damaging it, she'd ignored James's advice to go for the heart, and it wasn't nearly dead.

Lurching back upright, the plant shot a half dozen razor fern branches outward with surprising speed, the first one catching Alanna right in the face. She howled in pain, dropping the hammer and bringing her hands up to protect her head as she staggered backward, but the distance wasn't enough. The ferns seemed to get longer and longer as she backpedaled, harassing her with their bladed edges, though no more of them landed hits as she kept her guard up.

Through this, Ganesh wasn't idle. He'd struggled to reorient, trapped in the plant's overly large frond. But as soon as he got some stability, he started stabbing with the spike that made up his main eye. Small cuts started cleaving their way through the leaf, and soon he turned one of the small holes into a large rift, bursting free and firing his rotors to turn a fall into a takeoff. James, he saw, was on the ground now, keeping about half of the plant's actual firepower tied up, shouting at Alanna to kill the damn thing. But Alanna was having some trouble, though not a threatening amount. Ganesh made a decision and swooped to assist James. As he did so, though, one of the razor ferns diverted from its attack, bending in midair in a disturbing angular motion and flying toward Ganesh.

The drone was tough, but his chitin and plastic plating was not enough to withstand many of the high-speed and absurdly sharp hits that an enemy like this could dish out. Still disoriented, he was focused on getting to James and didn't see the strike coming.

Alanna did, though.

Dropping half her guard and stopping her retreat, Alanna lunged forward, a hand in a thick glove lashing out and clamping down on the branch. Another of the ferns quivered and rushed forward to her unprotected eyes, but with a snarl, she ducked it and *yanked* on the branch in hand, snapping it off and peeling a good strip of bark away from the main trunk as she did so. Without the time to get a good grip, she whipped the branch back at the other attackers and was surprised to see many of the little strips of fern go flying away as they cut themselves to shreds. Now with forward momentum, Alanna was able to get a hand on the dropped sledgehammer before pulling backward, keeping her head down.

Out of the corner of her eye, she saw James hacking away at the vine he was holding, trying to separate it from the main body. She also saw Ganesh, a blur of motion, dive on and snip off one of the smaller razor fern twigs with his front claws as it had rushed to catch her blind spot. With no time to think, Alanna plowed forward into the plant, taking a solid hit from one of the thicker vine leaves on her shoulder, before she could bring the hammer down in a golfer's swing and crack open the side of the pot, leaving a neat ceramic spiderweb around the hole her hit made.

Ganesh was already there as she pulled back. With an angry hum, he flitted down through the damaged plant's branches before crawling into the exposed hole. Alanna would have watched with fascination, but the tendril that had hit her shoulder earlier came around on the backswing and slammed into the side of her head as she tried to catch her breath, knocking her sideways to trip over the vine that James was hacking at. She kicked backward and felt her foot hit something, but before she could worry about whether it was going to make another attack, the whole plant went limp.

James sighed in relief as it withered and died, as much as a plastic plant could. "Okay, that could have gone better," he said with a groan as he stood up. "You okay?"

Alanna was not okay. Actual combat did not agree with her, it seemed, and she slumped forward on the ground where she'd landed, trembling as the adrenaline wore off. It took an effort of will not to throw up.

After a couple minutes or so, she raised her head to see that James had already plopped his backpack on the floor, pulled out the medkit, and begun unwrapping small bandages. It took her a second to realize that they were for her own face.

"Why the hell do you do this?" she asked him as he dabbed blood from a cut just under her eye. "That was fucking insane. Ten seconds decided if we lived or died!"

"But we lived," he said. "I know how you feel. Really. It's part of why I do this, I guess." James looked a little sheepish as he admitted to it. "Honestly, I like testing myself this way. Feeling like I'm really being challenged. But no, the big reason is that." He pointed to where Ganesh had crawled out of the damaged pot, pushing a size-two skill orb in front of him. "That."

Alanna looked down as best she could without flinching while James stuck a bandage on her cheek. "It can't be worth it. This hurts so bad." Her voice cracked a bit as the stinging pain from a half dozen cuts crept in.

James nodded. "This was a pretty bad one, I admit. But here, you tell me. Is this worth it?" He plucked the orb up and held it out in one hand to her. She looked at it suspiciously before taking it in her own still-gloved hand.

"Do I need to do anything special?" Alanna asked as she peered into the slightly luminescent orb. "Like, is skin contact required? Any magic words or thoughts?"

"Nope," James replied, packing back up. "Just crack it. I think you could technically step on it? Maybe the intent is required, since I *must* have stepped on one before. Doesn't make sense that it's only the hand, though. That's . . . not really the point." He trailed off. "You can just squeeze it. Go ahead. See if this is enough to make you want to come back."

Alanna applied light pressure, giving the orb a firm press with her hand. A second later, it popped with a violent outburst that made her blink but somehow had no pressure to it. And then, for the first time, she had an obviously alien, politely intrusive thought echo through her head.

[+2 Skill Ranks : Snowboarding - Jumps]

James raised his eyebrows at her, apprehensive but also curious.

There was a very long pause, the only noise the sound of Ganesh's claws clinking against metal as he climbed back onto James's helmet.

"Okay." Alanna broke the quiet. "Let's go find another plant."

A grin spread across James's face to match the one his friend now wore.

CHAPTER 32

"You're smarter than you look," Anesh said to the stapler-spider on the desk in front of him. It wasn't a question. He said it with a steeled voice, his brown arms crossed in front of him as he leaned back in the office chair.

Rufus had frozen, legs coming to a halt midstep. He was carrying one of his little balls of staples, all the teeth pointing like a really nasty bur. Anesh had waited for a while after James and Alanna left, just casually sitting and watching Ganesh's point of view through his phone. Rufus had carried on with what he was doing, pulling about a half dozen of the spiky things out from various drawers and collecting them on one of the desks. Anesh had waited until he was sure they'd have some time to talk before he'd started in on talking to the friendly strider.

Anesh waited for a second, and Rufus didn't make any indication of responding, so he said a bit more. "I mean, I'm not accusing you of anything. I'm just observing. You're smarter than a little stapler thing looks." Rufus set down the staple ball that he was holding and crossed his front pen-legs together in front of him in an X. From his chair, Anesh raised an eyebrow. "You're not?" Rufus shook his head and tapped a single leg on the table in front of him. "Ah, you're exactly as smart as you look, I'm just looking at it wrong."

Rufus nodded.

"Okay, well, that's neat and all, but I've been thinking. And I don't want you to think I'm mad at you, but I have some questions. Concerns, really," the human said.

Rufus started to back away, his single main eye flicking back and forth. This wasn't a conversation he really wanted to have.

That didn't stop Anesh, though. "See, here's the thing. James didn't have any problem talking to me about this place when he first decided to share. It wasn't until right after he brought me in that he had trouble. And I knew about it for about a week beforehand, and I didn't have a problem thinking about telling our other friends. I didn't, sure, but I could have." He looked at Rufus and leaned forward a bit. "So it couldn't have been using the orbs, see?"

Rufus saw. He nodded a bit, bobbing his front up and down. He also took a couple steps back, which Anesh absolutely noticed.

"And of course, there's this last month. When I haven't been here, but James has. So the effect must need to be refreshed. Perhaps by this place itself, but, well, how long did it need to make that happen? James was only here briefly. Specifically, he was only in *here*. Do you see where this is going?"

Rufus turned and bolted for the wall.

He didn't get far. Anesh jerked forward and brought his hand down on Rufus's body. "So tell me, small friend. Do you happen to know anything about that?" he asked calmly as he lifted the scrambling, panicked creature up to eye level.

Rufus froze, then slumped a bit. He lifted one of his front legs up to eye level. "Yes?" Anesh asked, and Rufus repeated the motion. "Okay, that's yes. So I'm going to set you down, and we're going to talk like rational adults, yes?" This got another yes, though a slower one. Anesh nodded and set the strider down on the desk.

He'd been thinking about this for a little while. There was just no sign that the dungeon itself was alive. Well, that wasn't quite true; there was no sign that it *gave a shit* about Anesh and James. There was no coordinated response to James being here, and nothing changed when he brought Anesh in. There was only one consistent factor in each of their dives, and that was the presence of Rufus. Ganesh as well, but he came later. The fort and their modifications to the environment came later. Every different type of orb came later. It was only Rufus who had been here from the start.

In truth, Anesh hadn't even been sure if there was anything to be suspicious of. But it hadn't taken very much prompting before Rufus bolted, and that was that. Not exactly proof of guilt, but it was enough.

"Oh, Rufus," Anesh muttered. "What did you do to us?"

The spider thing hissed back. Not angry, but insistent. His eye focused on Anesh and stopped flicking around, and Anesh couldn't see anything like guilt there.

He was already frustrated trying to talk to something that couldn't speak. "You didn't do it?" Anesh asked. Rufus hesitated for a minute, then shakily raised his front legs in another X. "You did do it, then?" This got a *yes* reply. "Okay, just checking. So ... this might be a bit of a trick to answer, but ... why?"

It was a trick to answer. But Rufus tried. He mimed out walking in with his front two legs, and Anesh nodded, following so far. Then, he did the same thing, twice in quick succession.

"First James, then me?" This got him an affirmative, and he nodded. "With you so far."

Rufus took a second to puzzle out how to "say" this. It didn't help that he didn't actually know a language. He could understand the concepts and intents of what James and Anesh said, and he could "read" their notes, in a way, but he was incapable of speaking or writing back. This left only the most awkward game of charades ever as a way to share with Anesh. Tapping around his eye a couple times, he swept his leg around at the ceiling. Then mimed out more and more people walking in, and followed it up with a much more frantic eye tapping.

Anesh rubbed his chin as he watched. "It was getting too crowded for you?" he muttered. "No, that's not right," he said, before Rufus could correct him, "it was getting too crowded, though. Yes? Yes."

Rufus kept tapping his eye, and then frantically waving his legs around at ... nothing in particular? It took Anesh a second to get it. "Ah. The dungeon. It watches? No, it *could* be watching. You were afraid we'd attract attention, yes?"

The little stapler slumped down, guilty, and shakily raised a single leg. *Yes.*

"James was fine, because he was just one person. But as soon as he brought me in, you realized that he had other friends, and you didn't want too many of us." Anesh started talking to himself now, as much as Rufus, standing up and pacing. "You're worried that the dungeon will see us? Or at least, something in the dungeon. Does that mean you're hiding out here from something in particular?" Rufus X'd that idea. "Just in general, then?" No response, so Anesh shrugged. "Either way, you didn't want more people, so, you . . . cursed us."

Rufus shook violently at that, shaking like a dog trying to get water off. Anesh almost laughed at the display, before remembering he was supposed to be angry. "I have no idea what that one means," he said. "Probably that I'm wrong. You didn't curse us? Or it's not a curse?" Rufus quickly made *yes* and *no* gestures in succession. "Okay, it's complicated?" *Yes.*

For a few seconds there was silence, and then Anesh sighed as he palmed his forehead. "This is really quite frustrating," he murmured. "So you did something to us so we couldn't share, and you must have been refreshing it every now and then, because it's still sort of on James, but it wore off on me. Right? Right. Okay."

He thought it through. There was one thing that was still bugging him. Well, a few things. James, through his skill pickup and actual real-world classes, was starting to get a handle on his own mind. And he described the mental coercion as something that felt mobile, almost alive. Fish-shaped thoughts. That, on its own, was worrying. Did that mean that it was alive, and if so, did that mean that the one in his own head had left a fish-thought-shaped corpse somewhere in a corner of his mind that he couldn't perceive?

Also nagging at him: how did Rufus even do this in the first place? They'd seen the paper pusher use a purple orb on James, which had added a second little geas to his friend, but they still hadn't figured out where the purple orbs *came* from. Had Rufus had one? Did he have more? How had he gotten it in the first place?

Actually, that led Anesh back to something else. "Hey, Rufus. James walked out of here armed, even though he wasn't supposed to be able to. I asked him how he was doing it, but he didn't actually respond. Is this also your fault?"

Rufus X'd his legs again, and this time he tilted his head a bit in confusion. After a moment of consideration, he threw up his front legs and scampered over to the desk where Anesh's gear was laid out. Clamping his mouth down on Anesh's hand axe, he dragged it over to the side of the desk. Then he alternated between tapping it and stabbing one leg out to point at the boar spear that Anesh had leaning up against their staging area.

"Weapons? Like, collective weapons?" Anesh felt like screaming in annoyance, but he kept calm. Rufus was trying, and that was saying a lot for something that Anesh hadn't really been sure was sapient up until a few minutes ago when he'd accused the little guy of treason. So Anesh thumped his head back against the wall and ran through options in his brain as he watched Rufus struggle to get the message across. "Sharp things. Dangerous things? Sorta dangerous things, okay. Um . . . oh. Oh! The spear is a bigger weapon?" Rufus signaled he was correct, and Anesh felt tension uncoil as the puzzle clicked together in his mind.

The spear was a larger weapon. It was bigger, it was more dangerous, it was . . . "The other mind-control thing, it wasn't as big as yours, was it?"

Rufus reared up and pumped both his front legs in the air, a symbol of triumph and power. If it had been for anything else, Anesh would have smiled, but here . . .

"It's a predator, is that what it is? They *are* alive, and the one that keeps James from talking fucking ate the other one. You weren't refreshing it at all, it was always going to wear off, it's just that his had another food source."

As soon as he said it, the pieces fell into place. That was why James hadn't even acknowledged his question; the part of his thought space that kept him from holding a weapon had been absorbed—eaten?—by the part that locked out their ability to share information. There was no grand plan, no evil entity at the heart of this place keeping them mute and chained.

There was just a scared kid and a dumb mistake.

Anesh reached out, hesitantly at first, his hand pausing in motion. But then, with a bit more conviction, he brought it down on Rufus's back. The strider jerked a bit, but then stilled as Anesh lightly stroked down his spine. He repeated the motion a few more times, settling back into the chair as Rufus crawled over, into Anesh's lap, accepting his pets.

"I get it," he told the strider. "I'm not mad. Don't worry. I'm not mad at you." He was reassuring himself as much as Rufus. He wasn't mad, though. He wasn't sure what he was. Worried, at least, though for whom he couldn't say.

Composing himself, he pulled out his phone and started typing. It was time to make a plan, time to find a way to solve some problems. And, Anesh had a feeling, the answers weren't going to be out here on the edges of the dungeon, where reality was still more or less stable. They were going to need to go deeper, which they'd always planned on, but not under the condition of duress.

Item one, find a way to kill a thoughtform. Corollary to item one, think of a clever name for a life form that lived in a human mind. Item two, they needed to learn more about how this place worked. Not just the doors but the whole system. They didn't have enough data; they'd only seen a few imbued items, a few types of entities, and only a handful of instances of most of the orb colors.

They just needed more data. And yeah, maybe that meant more people: more eyes and minds.

But Anesh was hesitant about that. It wasn't that he thought Rufus was in the right. The small strider, now curled up in his lap like a slightly pointier cat, had still done something pretty awful to both himself and James that had caused them no end of stress and was still making problems for Anesh's friend and roommate. But from what he gathered, Rufus had acted out of fear. Fear of what, Anesh didn't and probably couldn't know just from guessing. But fear of something.

And while it might not take much to make a creature the size of an office tool afraid, Anesh felt like discretion might be the best course of action for now. After all, they'd just brought Alanna in. They might as well take time to get her up to speed before worrying about whether or not to up their party size.

Still, there were some things they could do with just the three of them. And the part that made Anesh's blood sing in his veins was also the easiest part: more orbs. More data points for the spreadsheet meant they'd just have to acquire and use more and more of those mysterious balls of light and flavor.

What a sacrifice they'd be making for science, Anesh thought with humorous sarcasm.

No matter what, though, they had limited time in here every week. If they were going to be exploring farther and farther, they needed to be making more efficient paths. He and James had talked before about bringing a couple bikes in here and clearing straight lines through the cubicles in some of the outer areas, and judging by the fact that the cubicles they'd already moved didn't respawn or reset, Anesh thought that would probably work fine. Just getting to the bathrooms last time had taken them almost two hours of careful walking, and then a half hour light jog back, and that wasn't even counting the time spent trapped in a spatial warp.

If they could cut that time down, they could spend a lot more time actually pressing forward. Hell, just having better maps would be helpful. Anesh added a line to his to-do list: make some larger posters of the maps they had to hang up around Fort Door.

Oh, there was another thing to check: what was behind the door. Maybe Anesh could talk to James about lining up some time off from their respective responsibilities and camping here for a week together. That might be reckless, though, without knowing in advance what was there. Still, it would only be a week, since apparently the time dilation was flexible over the course of the day.

And of course, there was still the matter of the money.

It turned out, money was useful. For Anesh, being able to bank enough to pay for his school without needing to worry about whether he could get enough loans next year was immense. He didn't come from a rich background, and even getting to this part of the States was an exercise in scraping money together. He'd thought before about the process of strip-mining this place for material and wealth, but now he wondered if the rewards deeper in would be large enough for some very specific goals. Could they get enough together to buy the building James worked in? Or at least lease out the single floor that the portal was on?

Did the building even lease floor to floor, or was it owned by the same company? Another note for things to figure out.

Regardless, he couldn't rule out the idea that there might be a briefcase with a million pounds in it somewhere deeper in. Or an orange orb that gave them the deed to the property. Was that something they could do? They'd given legal statuses so far; was ownership a legal status? His list of questions was getting too long, and he was starting to get a headache. James had originally said that he wanted Anesh in on this whole thing because he was more analytical, but this wasn't exactly the kind of information processing Anesh was good at. He liked math and physics. He worked with numbers, hard data, taking it apart and putting it back together. His strong suit wasn't in asking lateral-thinking questions.

Really, that was Alanna's thing. It was how she ended up throwing every D&D game they played into turmoil. Just a simple recontextualization of a situation that Anesh didn't catch when he'd planned it out. Maybe he'd offload his notes onto her and just let her take care of it so he could focus more on tag-teaming laser-squid-computers with James.

Hell, this place led to weird sentences in his thoughts.

He sighed as he stood up and cracked his fingers, sending Rufus skittering onto the floor. "Okay," he said aloud. "Time for some light exercise. Come on, Rufus. We're gonna go see if we can disarm a couple burnouts, and you're my backup." The stapler looked at Anesh with an expression that he would almost describe as apprehension, letting out a small whine. "Oh, come on. It'll be fun. I'll give you half of any orbs we find, and I really don't want to go out alone. We'll just go along the wall, okay? No going deeper in," he said, cajoling the strider.

Rufus shuddered a bit, then conceded and gave a small nodding bob. Even after finding him out, Anesh was still being friendly. If he was angry, he wasn't showing it to Rufus, and the stapler didn't know how to feel about it. He'd never wanted to hurt the two, especially not James, but he acknowledged that his actions weren't the actions of a good friend. But Anesh, it seemed, had already forgiven him, or was at least willing to set it aside. So he would be a good friend now.

It also didn't hurt that he'd possibly earn a few more orbs for his backup cache. Rufus wasn't the best long-term planner, but he understood the concept of value. And he had what he felt was a small fortune saved up and hidden around the area. This would be a safer way to add to it than how he'd gotten some of them to begin with.

Skittering over to where Anesh was strapping on his old football pads, Rufus carried up the last thermos of coffee and plonked it down on the desk. Anesh smiled a bit. "Thanks, friend," he said as he clipped one of the radios to his belt loop and picked up the remaining axe.

The words sparked off a warm feeling in Rufus. Friend. Yes. He could do that. He could be that. He'd been hiding here for too long. If his humans, no, his friends, were going to keep going back in, well, it was the least that Rufus could do to go with them.

So it was that he and Anesh set off, Rufus racing ahead of the lanky human. Even though he was the shortest of the three, Anesh still towered over the stapler, so Rufus had to put some effort into moving to stay ahead of him. But Rufus had a lot of experience in skittering at high speeds from place to place, and he was a bit too awkwardly shaped to perch on Anesh's shoulder like Ganesh could do with grace.

So he ran, and he kept watch, and he and Anesh explored. Rufus had never explored this place before, even though he was born here and expected to die here. He'd only ever survived. Never seen it with wondering eyes the way Anesh did. But he tried now. And even though it might not have worked perfectly, it made him feel something every time his friend made an excited noise or asked what something was in that way that meant that he didn't expect an answer from anyone but himself.

And when the two of them began heading back an hour later, Rufus shared the feeling of triumph that Anesh had in his chest. The coffee was gone, the axe had a chip in it, Anesh had an angry red mark on his arm where a bit of molten glass had briefly landed, and Rufus had lost the bottom half of one of his legs. But they carried with them three red orbs, six yellows, one blue they'd accidentally gotten, a set of earbuds that Anesh was thrilled to discover could not tangle, and the thing that Rufus himself had found.

A pair of sunglasses. He'd poked at them while Anesh had been trying to do something with the computer in that cubicle. When Rufus had bent down to look through one of the lenses, he'd seen the world in a blur of colors that he'd never experienced before. After getting over the headache that instantly gave him and almost falling off the desk, he'd brought them over to Anesh, who had quickly made the connection. The glasses saw the world in infrared. But unlike a heat map, they didn't translate it into reds and blues; they actually expanded his range of vision.

Anesh joined Rufus in his headache. But this was something important, something that could be not just useful but life-altering. They'd gone into the bag, and Anesh had promised Rufus an extra orb for his discovery.

So the two of them walked back with confidence. A couple minor crises battled together, a skirmish fought, traps disarmed, and loot pilfered. Rufus felt like the king of the world, and Anesh smiled as he watched the injured strider move with a bit of swagger in front of him as he strolled back toward Fort Door.

It had been a good day so far.

Anesh just hoped James and Alanna were doing as well.

CHAPTER 33

Twenty minutes later, James and Alanna, along with Ganesh, got back to the fort to link back up with Anesh. The two of them came in a bit stiffly, the hits from their fight with the plant starting to develop into bruises. But that didn't stop them from wearing triumphant looks on their faces and walking with their heads held high.

"You two look like you had fun," Anesh commented with a smile, holding out a hand for Ganesh to land in as the drone launched itself off James's head. He was sitting at the desk with Rufus, idly reading from a stack of papers in a manila folder. None of them said anything useful, as far as he could tell, but he'd had just enough time to grab *something* to do before they got back, and he wanted to present an impressive image.

Dropping his bag onto a clear part of the desk, James threw himself into a chair. Alanna similarly deposited her gear but opted to simply sit down rather than vigorously fling herself onto the seat. It was interesting to Anesh how two people could make the simple action of sitting down so different: one with gusto, as if he were excited to get back up again, and the other with something halfway between caution and poise, as if good graces would protect against the dangers here. Their formed hard plastic and thick-layered cloth armor made movement just tricky enough that all of their motions were a bit more deliberate.

James started to say something but was cut off by Alanna. "I wouldn't call it fun," she said. "A lot of things. Crazy. Adventure.

Awesome, in a way that high schoolers don't use the word *awesome*. But not fun. How the fuck did you let James talk you into this?" she asked Anesh.

"It was mostly the promise of money, food, and power," he replied smoothly. "Also he's my friend, so keeping him alive was a factor, even if he is a wanker."

"He is!" Alanna enthusiastically replied.

Off to the side of their conversation, James took a second away from worriedly fussing with Rufus's injured leg to let out a "Hey!," which was more or less ignored.

"Still, though. It's grown on me," Anesh said. "I wasn't sure if I wanted to keep coming back at first. A big part of me was going over arguments for how I could convince James to back off on it, or at least excuse myself from it. But, well . . ." He paused as he collected his thoughts, and Alanna gave him space to think. "This whole thing is so far from normal. I don't think I could ever live with myself if I gave up the opportunity to just be here and experience it. Candy or not, it's got an uncanny-valley kind of beauty to it."

Alanna nodded. "The cubicles look dumb and mundane on their own, but when you can't see the end, it gets trippy. Also, things like Ganesh, who is . . . kinda cool, yeah."

The little drone hummed from Anesh's shoulder. He'd been warming up to Alanna since he'd seen her preemptively act to save his life. Not enough to use her as a perch, especially since he was legitimately afraid of getting tangled in her hair, but enough to not be aloof.

"Ganesh is cool," Anesh said. "So is the giant tile spire that is the bathroom here."

"Oh, that reminds me. Is there an actual bathroom here? I don't need it now, I'm just curious if it's going to be a problem."

Anesh shook his head. "We haven't found a real one. It hasn't been a problem, but then, we don't spend too long in here. If you do need to go, we can just leave. Though if you're good, I think we'd like to go farther in tonight, as a group."

"Farther in? How far did we go that time?" Alanna looked up at James, who took notice and wandered over.

He set Rufus down on the desk behind Anesh and then leaned on it himself. "Not very far. Maybe two hundred cubes?" He sighed. "We need a map."

"I'm working on it," Anesh said. "I spent some time with Ganesh taking wide-shot images of the place around here. I'll turn them into something we can print out and stick on the wall here this week."

"I can help with that," James said, excited. "I can finally put that AutoCAD skill to use."

Alanna interrupted them, waving a hand to catch their attention. "Sorry, you said you wanted to go farther in? Isn't that really stupid? James almost died. *I* almost died!"

The other two shared a quick look. How do you explain to someone that combat gets less scary over time? That the call of exploration and adventure starts to overpower the fear of death? Especially to Alanna, who still had some of her own dried blood on the side of her face.

"I mean, I'm sorry you almost died?" James said, and Anesh wanted to strangle his friend. That was quite possibly the direct opposite of tact. "But look, there's just a feeling to it," he continued, passion building in his voice. "We get hurt sometimes, sure, but we've always survived. And that feeling is amazing: knowing that we're good enough for this, or at least not stupid enough to die. And there's still so much to see."

Alanna shook her head. "I still don't want to get sliced up again."

James shrugged. "I can't promise that won't happen. All I can say is that it didn't kill you. And I won't let anything kill you if I can help it. But there's more to see, and I want to see it. I want to be there." He finished with a calm, powerful tone, a hint of melancholy in his words.

It surprised Anesh to see that James's points hit home for Alanna. If there was one thing that he always forgot, it was that tact wasn't useful with someone who preferred the direct approach.

Standing up, Anesh paced away, not sure what to say to break the thick silence that had fallen on them. He didn't feel like it was time for a joke, and nothing he was going to say was going to tip Alanna any further. So he just quietly left, a little awkwardly, while she made her decision, and started double-checking their gear for if they did decide to go deeper in today.

The coffee was still available, and still hot. James had discovered over the last week that it had to be hot if they wanted to get the buff, but right now it wasn't a problem, and they had three thermoses full of the still-steaming drink. There were a couple more small yellow orbs in James's bag that the two of them must have found and been saving. Anesh tossed them into one of the desk drawers with the reds he'd gotten, thinking that he needed to bring in some kind of bowl to store these things in. Maybe a fruit bowl; make it look like a batch of weird-colored grapes. That made him laugh in his head.

They hadn't used any of the gear really, except the medkit. So Anesh mostly took the time to make sure everything was still there and split up some things among three packs. Mostly, it was just food and water and medical supplies. They each had one small bundle of rope apiece, as well. Just in case. Not too much of it; that stuff was heavy as all hell. But it might come in handy, just like the duct tape.

Into one of the drawers, the one that currently only held a very dangerous pen, he placed the sunglasses he and Rufus had found. Those might be incredibly useful in the future, but he didn't want to take them out without both a strap for them and a little more practice to make sure the headache wouldn't kill him.

Just as he was zipping up the bags, Alanna came over. "Anesh. Are you thinking of going in with James?"

"I am. I want to see farther inside as much as he does. And I don't think either of us wants to tackle the bathroom today. So as far in as we can go in two hours."

"Two?"

"It gives us a safety net to get out," he said.

Alanna nodded. Despite really wanting to go, Anesh wasn't going to push her on it. If she didn't want to come along, she could stay here or just head out of the dungeon. But he did think they'd get a lot more done with three people, and just having someone else there . . .

"Okay, let's go." Alanna's words jolted Anesh out of his contemplation, and he snapped his head around from deliberately staring at the gear to look at her.

"Are you quite sure?" he asked.

James came over before Alanna could answer, casually tossing Ganesh into the air, only for the drone to recover midthrow and glide down to alight on Anesh's shoulder. "I bribed her," James explained with a smile. "Those last two yellows we got, plus the pen. A steep price, but hey, there's always more, right?" he said with an exaggeratedly dramatic swoon. Anesh casually opened the drawers and tossed the orbs to Alanna. He handed the pen over with a little more caution but no hesitation.

She almost asked if *they* were sure about giving this up, but the ease with which they parted with the loot had a strange reassurance about it. They weren't the kind of people who would let greed get in the way of friendship, or of function. And it was with that thought that she answered, "I'm quite sure, yes," as she cracked the two orbs.

[+1 Skill Rank : Etiquette - Corporate - Tech Firms]

[+1 Skill Rank : Singing]

Smiling through closed eyes so she could better see the thoughts in her head, Alanna felt her spirit soar. "Feels good, doesn't it?" She opened her eyes to see James and Anesh both looking at her, grinning as well. From anyone else, it might have felt malicious, but she quashed the part of her heart that yelled that at her. These two were on her side; more than that, they were friends.

"It does. Really fucking good," she said, rolling her shoulders. Alanna casually reached down a muscled arm to hoist the hammer she'd leaned against the wall, rising up to her full height as she shouldered her backpack. "Okay. I'm ready." Ignoring the bandages on her face, not feeling the bruises on her arms, all fatigue falling away, she stepped up to the door. "Are you two coming or not?"

James looked over at Anesh, hoping to get someone to appreciate his eye roll, but his friend was already moving after Alanna, out the door and across the open area toward their planned path, spear in hand, drone on shoulder, and straightening the old football pads he was wearing. Looking down at Rufus, James said, "You appreciate my sarcasm, right?"

Rufus thought for a second, then held up his front legs in an X. James just sighed as he went to pick up the bag Rufus was sitting on. "Okay, I need this now. I'll be back later, though, and I'll bring you an orb or two." But Rufus didn't get off, instead just latching on with his legs. James started to let out an "um . . . ," but Rufus just pointed a single leg after their friends, now gaining a significant lead. "Okay, so you're coming? Even hurt?" Rufus rolled his single eye, a gesture he'd learned from James. "Right, fine. I get it." Shouldering the bag, careful not to dislodge the strider, James headed out as well, jogging slightly to catch up. "No one appreciates my sarcasm," he muttered.

They'd been moving for about half an hour, and it was going well. Alanna was getting used to the level of caution and quiet that they employed, and James and Anesh were both becoming more comfortable with a third person involved. Ganesh was still relaxing on Anesh's shoulder, dug into the football pad armor there, and Rufus was presumably taking a nap in James's backpack. In total, they had probably gotten about a mile or more into the dungeon, mostly because they weren't taking the time to loot every single cube they walked by. And they were walking by a *lot* of cubicles.

This side path, just a few aisles to the right of their normal entry point and a few turns farther away from their usual path, still had the same environment of thousands and thousands of cubicles, with the walls getting gradually taller and taller as they went in. To James, it felt like descending into a cave, while Alanna and Anesh both felt like they were walking into a dense forest.

Whatever it felt like, they'd all decided that pillaging the outer shell of the dungeon was something that they could basically do at any time. So they just pressed through it. Forging past all the potential loot made James a bit twitchy, and every time he moved past the door to a cubicle and saw a coat on a chair, or glimpsed a briefcase on a desk over a wall, he would wince a bit. Still, he wasn't going to slow them down grabbing up cash that they could get when they needed it. A bulging wallet was satisfying, but it wasn't really what they were here for, exactly. Not today.

Up ahead, Anesh checked the cube on the right, while Alanna checked left, and then they both signaled James forward. He moved up, checking the right himself, while Anesh moved to the left, then they repeated the process. On and on, keeping up the pattern, moving deeper and deeper. They saw more than a few striders on their path, especially as they started moving into the area of the dungeon where paper hung like vines and staples made webs across the doors and hallways. But none of them made any hostile moves, instead content to watch the trio as they walked.

Maybe it was because they weren't invading the cubicles, James thought; as long as they didn't violate the homes or territory of the staplers, they wouldn't lash out. Or maybe it was just because there were three of them now, five with Rufus and Ganesh, and the striders weren't that violently suicidal.

Either way, they weren't having much trouble.

That lasted about two minutes after James had that thought.

They took a corner, one of the simple bends, not an intersection. And James saw in front of them another hallway. Standard, so far, though he could see ahead small clusters of cubicles where the walls were only at about waist height. These groups of two-by-two desks gave the impression of open spaces; even when the walls of other cubes arched up overhead, they still created gaps of open air that made the gloomy space feel a bit less claustrophobic.

The other thing James noticed was that the carpet here switched from the flat gray with some dots on it to a series of large green-and-black squares, with a smaller overlapping circle of purple every few squares of the pattern. It wasn't anything impressive, but it was the first time they'd seen the carpet change except for the break room.

"What the hell is that?" Alanna had come up beside James and was pointing down toward one of the low-walled clusters. There was something in the middle of it that James had initially thought was a support beam, but now that he looked at it more, it was twisted and there was something hanging off it on the other side.

"No idea," he replied. "Anesh! We've got something up here!" James motioned their friend up from where he was keeping watch on the hallway they'd come down, suspiciously eyeing one of the cubes they'd seen a strider nesting in. Anesh turned at James's low-pitched call and headed up to peer over the shoulders of his companions.

Looking down the hallway, he nodded. "Yeah, that's a suspicious floor."

"What?" James said, confused. "No, the pillar thing over there." He and Alanna both pointed.

Anesh shook his head, a concerned frown on his face. "That thing's probably also going to try to kill us. But I don't like the floor. Too... Indiana Jones."

"You've seen Indiana Jones?" Alanna asked.

James and Anesh both gave her a stunned look. James spoke first, while Anesh just had his mouth hanging open. "He lives with *me*." And Anesh just nodded, pointing at James in agreement. "Anyway. If you guys are actually worried about the carpet, I'll go first and be careful, okay?"

He stepped forward, probing the carpet tiles ahead of himself with one foot. Nothing happened. He put more weight on his outstretched foot, and still nothing. Shifting forward, he tapped the green square to his right and found a similar result of "nothing at all." Finally, he took a few cautious steps farther in and reached out to thump the toe of his boot onto one of the purple circles.

James had to admit, he was holding his breath. He didn't fully agree with what Anesh meant about the carpet being suspicious until he actually stepped out onto it, and now he was worried that the smallest motion would open up some kind of pit trap. Probably with sharpened desk rulers at the bottom.

Still nothing happening, though.

Breathing out a sigh, James straightened up. "Okay. Nothing to worry about!" he called back to the others. "Let's go check that thing out." Alanna and Anesh moved up, side by side, to catch up with James. He turned back and started leading the way toward the low-walled cubicles and the strange pillar.

As soon as he stepped onto one of the thin lines where the different carpet swaths met on the floor, two dozen small holes opened up in the tall wall to his right. Alanna saw it first and yelled a warning at James, shouting "*Down*" at him as fast as she could. He reacted to her warning with almost absolute trust, starting to duck and throwing his arms up over his head. He wasn't quite fast enough, though.

In a volley from ceiling to floor, rows of bright yellow, needle-pointed number-two pencils launched out. The noise of their firing screamed through the air with the heavy buzz of an electric pencil sharpener. Each row of three pencils spat out before the one below it, and they cut into the far wall so deeply that they hung there without falling back out.

James had maybe two seconds from when Alanna yelled to when the pencils started hitting. He'd begun kneeling down and starting to roll forward, but it wasn't enough to fully get him out of the line of fire. Of the eight rows of office-supply spears that scythed through the air, the top four missed him entirely. The next two were at the level of his head, but he'd leaned forward enough that one of them stabbed into his backpack, but the rest flew past.

The rest of them, though, started hitting *him*. Several deflected off the shaped hard plastic that he was wearing. He felt impacts on his shoulder and elbow that just redirected into the floor, and a few more that cut into the thicker padding of the armor but didn't reach him. Two of the overly sharpened pencils, though, cut through the armor: one into his upper arm, and the other one at a weird angle, right across his ass, cutting a thin line through the back of his slacks and leaving a similar red line on his flesh where it scored him.

And then it was over. The buzzing cut off abruptly, and James finished throwing himself onto his face. The holes in the wall closed off, and all that was left by way of evidence was about twenty yellow wooden shafts stabbed into the far wall and scattered on the floor. And in James.

"Okay, ow," he said from the floor, standing up carefully to avoid jostling the pencil jammed into his arm. It wasn't in deep, but it hurt like hell, and he was worried about pulling it out right away.

Anesh ran over, yanking out a medkit, while Alanna moved ahead of him and bent down to grab James under the arms and drag him away from the trap, back to the bend of the corner. "Shit, shit, shit," Anesh intoned as he pulled out a packet of hemostatic powder and a roll of medical tape.

"That's my line," James said calmly. "Whoo. This looks a lot more painful than it feels." He wiggled his arm to make the pencil bob a bit. After unstrapping the armor pad there and carefully pulling it over the pencil, Anesh wrapped his hand around the shaft, yanking it out in a smooth motion. Blood started to flow immediately, and so did James's swearing. "Okay! Okay, now it hurts!" he cried out as his friend dumped powder on it to clot the blood and then quickly laid down a gauze pad and taped it down. As he wrapped it up, Rufus crawled his way out of the backpack, pushing the zipper apart to poke his snout out and chitter at the pencil now impaling his improvised nest.

Anesh was about halfway done with the bandage when Alanna gave out a warning. "Staplers! A bunch of them!" James almost choked on the mouthful of water he was using to swallow a painkiller, and he and Anesh looked up to see Alanna standing just a few feet away, brandishing her hammer. On the walls down the hall from where they came, every other cubicle had a strider or two sitting on its lip. A couple more hung from staple webs strung across the low ceiling where walls bent together. And still a few more were just moving forward across the floor.

Apparently, the creatures were just restrained enough to wait until it looked like the group was injured to attack.

James cupped his hand over Anesh's where his friend was frantically fumbling with the bandage. "Go," he said. "I got this, I'll be right there."

Taking hold of the tape, he started undoing it from where Anesh had twisted and made it too tight, working calmly but as fast as he could.

Dropping his spear, Anesh unclipped his compact hand axe and stepped up with Alanna, keeping a pace back and far to the left. Ganesh, on his shoulder, took flight with a hum. "Deep breath," he said to Alanna, who was noticeably freaking out at the high number of approaching hostiles. "They're still just staplers. We've got this," he said, half believing his own words.

Alanna started to say something, probably something pessimistic, but from behind them, they both heard James shout, "Fuck 'em up!," and Alanna let out a snort of laughter before taking an aggressive step forward, roaring. Whipping the sledgehammer forward with both hands, she spiked a strider that had been running along the wall of the cubicle to their right, hitting hard enough that it punched through the plywood and cloth of the cubicle. The strider didn't come out of the hole that was left as she wrenched the hammer back.

And then the rest of them charged forward, and it turned a bit chaotic. Anesh stomped down on one of the striders on the floor, pinning it in place while he used his hand axe to one-two slap a pair off the edge of the wall to his left before they got in lunging range. Kneeling down, he started lashing out to chop at the bodies and legs of any that got too close. At one point, he had to frantically blink ichor out of his right eye as Alanna smashed one with perfect accuracy to his right, splattering the liquid across the aisle.

When one of them lunged for Anesh, he tried to slap it away and missed. But all it could do was ineffectively try to cut its teeth on the chest of his armor. It might just be sports gear, but staplers still weren't getting through it. Still, he grabbed it in a free hand and pitched it back down the hallway before it could climb up to his exposed arms or face. To his right, he saw Alanna miss with one of her overpowered hammer strikes, leaving an indent in the floor and probably jarring the bones of her arms hard enough to hurt.

Alanna did indeed feel the sting from that one. But she lashed out with a foot and kicked the oncoming strider away, buying time to lug the hammer back up and take another shot. What she didn't see was the one that was crawling through the staple webs above her, and she didn't see it about to drop down, aiming to concuss her and take her out of the fight. She also didn't see Ganesh whip through the chains of paper clips and cut the legs out from under it, leaving a tumbling strider to crash into the ground about two feet farther down the hallway than it intended.

James saw it, though. And he grabbed it while it was still stunned, careful to keep his fingers away from the mouth as he pinned it down and took it apart with his axe. He then turned to deal with the one that Rufus was wrestling off the wall behind him, a straggler that had been going for the presumably defenseless James.

The fight would have gone on longer, but the remainder of the striders, perhaps seeing that there weren't any downed individuals at all, pulled back, quietly slipping away with a light skittering sound of dry pens and unsharpened pencils.

James walked up to Anesh and Alanna, who were both panting heavily. About a dozen crushed, cut, and mangled strider bodies were scattered around, glowing points of yellow drifting in the air above them for a half minute before dropping back to the ground. "Well, that went well!" he said, his smile turning into a wince as he pulled at the bandages he'd applied to the cut on his rear end.

"I'm ... going to ... hit you with this," Alanna gasped out, leaning on her hammer. She was in good shape, she was strong, but making targeted hits with something that weighed over twenty pounds over and over again, while things tried to kill her, was enough to leave her out of breath and sweating.

"I'll help," Anesh said, miming strangling James.

James just laughed, though. They were kidding, and he wasn't trying to be too much of a dick. "All right, all right," he said, smiling and placating them. "I'll grab up the yellows. You guys just relax for a minute."

The total haul, after he found the one that Alanna had put through a wall and gave up on the one he'd seen Ganesh dive-bomb into the horizon, was thirteen orbs. Coming back to the others, he asked, "Do we want to use these now? Or wait until we get back, then divide up everything?"

"Wait," Anesh said.

At the same time, Alanna perked up and said, "Use 'em!"

"Okay, that's unhelpful." James sighed. "As tiebreaker, I'm going with Anesh. We still need to make sure we have extras for Ganesh and Lily, and then we'll have a weird number to divide up here." Alanna groaned and made puppy-dog eyes at James. "That's not going to work . . . very well. Anesh, help." James looked over at his friend pleadingly.

"Hey, Alanna," Anesh said by way of distraction. "Didn't you want to go check out the pillar thing?"

She jabbed a finger into his padded side. "Don't try to distract me! But yes."

James shook his head as he turned away, amused. Still, he wanted to get moving forward again. Cautiously, he moved up to the line that had triggered the pencil dart trap the first time. It was one of the tiny, almost invisible points where two sections of carpet were joined together. He poked it, from as far away as he could manage. Nothing happened, though. He tapped around it, putting different amounts of pressure down. Still nothing. Finally, he took a deep breath and cautiously stepped over it, careful not to touch the line itself.

Nothing! No darts. He moved forward a few cubes before approaching the four-way intersection, made a lot more open by the presence of low-walled cubicles ahead. He was careful to watch for more lines on the carpet, but it seemed like the patches of carpet were pretty large. Still, it would be something to watch for going forward. Maybe get himself a riot shield.

And then, after checking around the intersection to make sure that there was nothing moving, he took a closer look at the pillar in the middle of the four open cubicles. Eyes widening, James quickly motioned to the other two. When that didn't work, he said, "Come on, guys. Stop fighting and get up here. Don't step on that line," pointing behind himself at the mark on the floor.

Anesh moved up first. "We're not fighting, just disagreeing passionately."

"What happened to your pants?" Alanna asked as she joined them.

"Not important, either of you. Look at this. Just . . . look at this thing," he said, staring.

This thing was what they'd noticed from a distance and hadn't really been able to make out. Up close, though, it became more clear what it was. A trunk, really, was the only way to describe it. It had a thick, black plastic outer layer. It was actually two parts, not just one: two massive cables, coiled around an actual support pillar. Small bits of white paint peeked through the massive cords wrapped around it. A handful of smaller cables coursed up around the outside, occasionally splitting off to form small branches or coiling together to make knots and bulges.

But the fact that there was a plant made out of cabling wasn't the part that was making James stare. It was the fact that the cables coiled together, up above the ceiling around them, through the open space where the walls fell away and left a courtyard of clear air. James had thought it was strange that it wasn't much brighter around here, despite there being fewer ceiling pieces to block out the fluorescent lights above. And now they could all see why.

Shapes of dim glowing plastic came out of the coils at the peak of the plant where they spread out. It was like a tree, with shapes of petals and leaves growing like lotus blossoms. They were computer monitors. Folded, warped, nowhere near the standard golden-ratio rectangles that sat on desks across the world. But still recognizable as a staple of the personal computer.

And they covered the sky above them, blooming off the cables where they grew out from the main trunk, blocking out the view of the lights above and casting a strange glow down into the twilight they left below. Screen savers of dancing color lit many of them, neon blues and oranges moving across panels of glass.

The three of them moved forward, stepping up to the low cubes and staring upward.

James had never seen anything like this. Alanna let out a laugh like a series of bells. Anesh said something awestruck. But James didn't look down; he just kept gazing up at the marvel above them. He didn't look away, out of fear that it might disappear before he could turn back, their own personal dungeon mirage. But it was real. James stepped up as close as he could to the center of the cubes, reaching out to place a hand on the corded black roots, feeling even through his glove the sturdy nature of this creation.

The branches moved in an unfelt breeze; there was a chiming sound like a handful of password prompts singing together, and above them, colored shapes and star fields danced. For just a moment, everything felt brighter and new.

On Anesh's shoulder, an artificial life form looked upward and saw beauty for the first time. From out of James's backpack, a creature gazed up at a part of its home that it had never seen before.

Overhead, small six-legged things ran across the branches, poking their heads out through the glowing segments to look down at the guests at their home's base before turning back to bathe in the light from above and around them. They called at each other with chirps and dings, and they wore slivers of monitor across their bodies as scales.

"And then there's stuff like this," James said, answering Alanna's earlier question. "There is magic in this world, waiting to be found." His soft voice echoed through the almost silent office. He felt tears in his eyes as he saw something truly beautiful and unique for the first time in this hostile place.

It would have been the perfect moment for anything to ambush them.

But the office stayed quiet. And they watched with wondering eyes, uninterrupted for a time.

CHAPTER 34

The trio sat in office chairs they'd pulled up into a triangle, leaning back and staring up at the tree. They'd taken about fifteen minutes just relaxing, watching the colors dance. It was also a good chance to rest, sip water, and munch on one of the slightly smushed sandwiches Anesh had packed.

"We should probably consider getting up," James said, cracking his knuckles.

Anesh and Alanna groaned as they stretched out sore muscles, nodding. Sitting forward, Alanna rolled on the balls of her feet and stood up. "Okay, where to now, guys?" She raised her arms and did a few jumps, flexing stiff legs. "Do we go—"

She cut off as Anesh started making a distressed series of "Um!" noises. James looked up from where he was zipping up his bag, and Alanna glanced down from her check of the hall to see him wildly jabbing a finger up at the tree they'd been sitting under.

The monitors were glowing, but as they watched, an increasing number of them dropped the screen saver, replacing the dancing colors with text on a black background. *Out*, the first one James saw said.

"Well, that's kinda rude," he started to say, before more and more monitors flickered to text.

Farther and *Wait*, the two other big screens said. Then smaller ones started shifting, and James had to squint a bit to see them. *Use resources. Damage tree. Rest. Scout. Infighting.* And then smaller and smaller words on other blooms that James could no longer read.

James and Alanna looked at each other as Anesh fell backward out of his chair. James helped him up while Ganesh buzzed around their heads, hauling his friend back to his feet while trying not to laugh.

"Okay, calm down," Alanna said. "Is this thing reading our minds?"

"I was considering all of those things," Anesh said. "I was going to ask you guys if you wanted to go farther or back to the entrance. I was also thinking of eating one of the candy bars—shut up, don't judge me." James closed his mouth and put his hand down. "So maybe it's reading our minds? Is that . . . a problem? Is it going to kill us?"

"You were considering infighting?" James asked, and in answer, Anesh lightly whapped him on the head with a desk ruler.

Looking up at the tree, Alanna reached over and rapped her knuckles on the trunk that spread down to the cubicle they were all in. It felt like just thick rubber, and the organism itself didn't react at all. "Well, what do we do about it?" she said.

The monitors started changing. *Investigate. Leave. Unnecessary violence.*

"Oh!" James said, as Alanna narrowed her eyes at the tree and looked around for her hammer. "Wait! No need for unnecessary violence!" He reached out to hold her back as she stepped forward and started looking for somewhere to stand on the desk. "It's a decision tree!"

Alanna let out a pained groan, while Anesh clenched his fists and simply asked, "What the hell are you talking about, and why do you have to hurt words like that?"

"It's showing us options!" James said, making a logical leap to the idea. "We asked what we should do, and it's showing us what our choices could be! Watch, and I hope this works or I look like an idiot: which of us should get the next skill orb?" he asked the tree.

Alanna. James. Anesh. And then the smaller screens started spelling out more options: *The one most hurt. Nobody. Rufus.*

"Why is Ganesh not up there? That hardly seems fair," Anesh said, and Ganesh buzzed agreement on his shoulder. "Wait, hang the fuck on, does that say *The survivor?* That's not okay! I don't like this tree anymore!" he loudly grumbled.

James snapped his fingers. "Okay, I'm calling dibs on naming this one. It's a decision tree, I'm hilarious, and let's get out of here before we find out it's actually mind-controlling us."

"Agreed!" Alanna and Anesh echoed together.

"I really don't understand why this is here," Alanna grumbled, eyeing the plant with suspicion.

James shrugged. "Why is anything in the dungeon here?"

"That's kind of a worrying attitude to take," she replied, still looking up at the twisted trunk of rubber and screens. "I mean, you guys had a theory that this place is a kind of ecosystem, yeah? Well, if that's the case, and this thing fills the slot of plant life, what exactly is it feeding off? How does it grow? Why did it evolve that way?"

"Oh, no way anything here evolved this way," Anesh said smoothly.

James made a *pfft* noise, dismissing Anesh's comment before answering Alanna. "I mean, it has those little things crawling on it. Maybe it's a symbiotic thing? Wait, no. Rufus and Ganesh both eat the skill orbs, they need them to keep going. Maybe the tree . . . produces them? That can't be right . . ." He trailed off, lost in thought.

"Yeah, see, it's *weird.*" Alanna threw up both her hands to gesture to the tree. "We have no idea what it does, but we're sitting here staring at it! What if it's eating *us?*"

"It's not, though. It's just waiting for us to decide if we're leaving or not. Maybe that's what it eats?" Anesh suggested.

"What, decisions? Like, we make the decision, and it eats it, and we just stay here?" James narrowed his eyes. "If that's the case, I'm considering going back to the unnecessary-violence plan."

Anesh laughed and shook his head. "No, like, it eats . . . what the decision means? Also, if it ate it and we were still here, we would have decided to stay here, which is . . ."

"Nope!" Alanna cut in. "Got a headache now! Thanks! Let's just get out of here before it actually decides it's sick of us and sends the lizards down to eat us."

They finished packing up quickly, and Rufus and Ganesh didn't stop keeping an eye on the tree until the humans shouldered their bags and turned to go.

As they walked out, Anesh looked back briefly to see one of the small six-legged things moving down the trunk, walking almost vertically. Its exterior appeared to be scales of flashing color, just like the monitors blooming overhead. As he watched, it shifted to a darker gray, blending in a bit with the cord trunk that it walked on.

"I'm calling those monitor lizards," he said, pointing. "And both of you can shut it. If James gets to make puns, I get to make puns. Those are the rules," he said with satisfaction as he took the lead and began walking ahead of the other two.

Alanna leaned down to mutter to James, "If you stop making puns, we can end this now, and I won't even need to punch anyone."

"No deal," he responded, shaking his head sadly. "I'm already addicted."

"What the hell was that?" James asked himself. Or maybe Rufus.

The duo were scouting in a slightly different direction from Anesh and Alanna. They'd come to a three-way intersection and had decided it was a good chance to safely split up. They'd dropped their bags there and headed down the different corridors, with the agreement to come back in fifteen minutes or as soon as they had to take more than one turn.

They'd taken one turn so far, and down the exceptionally long aisle that he'd found in front of him, James could see the tile floor and uncomfortable plastic chairs of a break room. It was far away, but having seen one before, he could recognize what it was.

What he couldn't recognize, though, was the thing moving past the door, out of his line of sight. It was too far away for him to hear anything, and it didn't look messy enough to be a tumblefeed. But something about it set his hair on end. Maybe it was the fact that it was a monster he didn't recognize in some kind of magical kill-office. Or maybe he was just being paranoid.

Either way, he radioed Anesh and Alanna to let them know what was up, and that he was turning around. The response he got was that they were checking out something in a cubicle, and they'd be back shortly. James kind of wanted to go join them, but he also didn't want to turn his back on what might be a hostile right now.

He thought for a moment, then knelt down to tap Rufus on the head. "Hey. Can you keep watch down here for a minute? I'm going to see if there's anything worth grabbing in that cube." Rufus raised one of his legs in a mock salute, and James smiled. "Thanks, friend." He stood back up and moved over to the cubicle, trying to sneak in as best he could in the thick armor.

The armor had so far probably saved him at least a pint of blood and half an elbow. But no matter how durable it was or how invincible it made him feel, that didn't make it any easier to move in. The incident with the pencil trap, however, had made him feel a little more realistic about how much this thing improved his survival chances—which was to say a bit, but not an infinite amount.

Probably the worst thing that could happen to any of them was if they started believing they were invincible.

Maybe James would see if he could convince Anesh to buy some chain mail to cover the areas that weren't hard plastic. Functional, *and* he'd get to look like a riot control officer took levels in cleric.

Shrugging off that line of thinking, he stepped into the cubicle. A quick check showed no obvious desk lamps or coffee cups. A quick mental check showed that, yeah, that was kind of an odd sentence for James to have to run through. He stepped up to the desk and started poking through things. This one was messy, something they didn't see very often.

At this point, James and Anesh had plundering down to almost a science, at least when they were just doing a quick search like he was to kill some time. Money, valuables, food, in that order. Purses or wallets? Check them. Are there coats or dry cleaning? Check them. Then start going through the drawers, don't go too fast, can't rule out traps at this point. Or just iLipedes waiting to ambush. They hadn't seen them be hostile yet, but anything was possible.

After finding sixty bucks in ones and fives tucked in various places around the desk, James was a bit frustrated. That was offset a bit by the fact that he was sixty bucks richer, but this was the first time he'd had to pull a dollar bill out from where it was wedged behind a shelf against the cube wall, and it was a lot less convenient than having it all piled up neatly in a wallet for him. The computer he'd confirmed as not-alive, but also not-useful, as it wasn't logged in, and he'd be damned if he was going to go password hunting in this mess.

The one thing he found that instantly caught his attention was when he accidentally knocked a cup of pens and pencils onto the floor, and one pencil just . . . didn't fall. It spilled out of the cup, sure, but it sat there, about four feet off the ground, unmoving. James tried moving it and found that, unlike the stupid handbag from several weeks ago, it was quite easy to move around. It even felt like it had weight in his hand. It just . . . didn't . . . fall.

So sixty bucks and a magic item. He knew that Anesh and now Alanna were trying to think up some kind of cool term for these things that wasn't *magic*, but James knew the truth. If there was magic in the world, it was, in part, imbued into this pencil, and he was going to call it that no matter what. Still a pretty good haul for a quick stop.

He stepped back out with a grin to see Rufus about to get eaten.

The strider was standing exactly where James had left him, keeping watch down the hall. Like, actually exactly. His single frontal eye was still focused down the path where James had asked him to keep watch while he did a bit of looting. And rearing up above him, perhaps the size of an adult dog, was a snake, about to strike.

James instantly classified it as a snake, but it also reminded him of a tumblefeed if it were woven together. A main body, sinuous and thick, made of cables that flexed like muscles and bulged as it rippled forward. Its spine was lined with red LEDs, and James hoped to hell they weren't what it used for eyes. The mouth at its front sat open, raised above Rufus and about to come crashing down, with what looked like a dozen needle-sharp quill pens for teeth.

What really made his skin crawl, though, was that instead of anything resembling a face, the creature had its head cables wrapped around the boxy shape of a security camera. It was an older model, not one of the sleek new ones you could find in a shopping mall or grocery store, but the kind of gray metal that he still saw in his own office. The thick lens pushing out down the creature's snout was fixated on Rufus, twisting in and out of focus.

James let out a terrified yell of "No!" Lunging forward, he whipped a fist toward the thing, just hoping to put it off balance long enough to arm himself and kill it. He assumed it had poisoned Rufus already, because the strider wasn't moving, and James could only hope his little friend wasn't dead.

The snake bobbed its head around to look at him as James moved in. And as soon as that camera lens locked onto his face, he froze, midlunge. The yell died in his throat, his fist refused to move forward, and it was lucky his feet were planted with good form or he would have toppled over. Screaming in his head, James found he couldn't move, at all. None of his muscles responded; he couldn't even blink. The snake, the *basilisk*, closed in on him, slithering up and pulling itself to full height so that it was only about a head shorter than James's eye level. It tilted its head back and forth, as if examining him, before letting out a pleased hiss and opening its mouth wide. James watched in horror as teeth the size of his fingers got ready to rip into him, and he was sure the armor wasn't rated for this kind of hit.

Rufus stapled the snake's tail.

The strider, no longer being watched, had exploded into motion as soon as James distracted the snake. He was going to run, but seeing James now frozen like he was, he turned back and moved straight for the end of the corded serpent. Slamming his metal teeth down, he left three staples buried in the monster before it started thrashing and slapped him away with a movement of its tail.

It turned, hiss-screaming at Rufus as he got its attention, freezing Rufus midescape. And as soon as it did, James jerked forward, no longer held paralyzed. He recovered as fast as he could and brought a knee up into the snake's mouth from where it was trying to threaten Rufus away. One of the teeth caught above the knee guard of the armor and slipped in, cutting through cloth like nothing at just the wrong angle. But it didn't cut James, just sat there, reminding him of how stupid that was. Another tooth snapped off, and the snake's head whipped back up as he put a lot of force behind the blow.

Of course, now it was looking at him again, and he again found he couldn't move as his hand tried desperately to pull his axe. Rufus again charged it, but this time he got hit away casually, and the basilisk didn't tilt its security camera head away from James.

"Well, shit," he tried to say, but he couldn't move his mouth. He watched Rufus scale the far wall of the hallway as the snake approached him more carefully, not wanting to get hit again. James started forming a plan for when it looked away, mentally tensing himself to move since he couldn't physically get ready. And when Rufus launched himself, chittering fiercely, and the snake turned its head around like an owl to stop him in midair and send him crashing to the ground, James lurched forward.

He clamped one hand around the base of the snake's neck, and the other one grabbed onto the base of the camera. "Rufus! Go get the others!" he shouted as the snake rolled backward and slammed him into the ground.

He wrestled with the basilisk while the strider rushed off. Rolling over, he felt a brief burst of paralysis as his hand slipped in front of the lens. Then he slammed his weight down on top of it, hoping to break something. But it just lashed its tail and body around, coiling around one of James's legs, yanking him off balance.

He felt his grip starting to slip, his fingers screaming in protest at the force of it, but he refused to let go. James knew what would happen if he let go. So he did what he'd seen alligator wranglers do and kept pressure on its head and neck, not letting it twist, not letting it get its fangs around to his neck or into his hands.

He also kept knee-dropping into it whenever their turning took him the right way. The one advantage that Team Human had in this match was knees, and he planned to abuse the hell out of it, he thought as he drove down on one of the LEDs hard enough that something popped.

It couldn't last, though. James was getting tired, and the basilisk wasn't. It was going to get free in just a minute, and he had to hope Rufus had been fast enough.

"James!" It was the most glorious shout he'd ever heard, as Anesh and Alanna came around the corner, moving fast enough that he had trouble tracking them visually.

James pinned the snake's head to the floor with one last burst of effort. "Help! Stab it! Don't let it look at you!" he tried to gasp out as it bucked him off.

Anesh was there, lunging forward with his boar spear but then simply halting in the middle of his thrust as the writhing cableform creature got its head up and stared him down. Was this what he'd looked like, James wondered, when he got frozen? It was a strange effect. All forward momentum just gone, even though he was moving fast enough to blur; that probably broke at least one physical law.

With Anesh suddenly not moving, Alanna almost ran into him as she stepped to the side to bring her hammer down. The snake twisted, finding its own inner reserve of strength, and threw James back with a whip of its length, his head crashing into the wall behind them. The basilisk snapped its gaze between Alanna and Anesh, making sure neither of them could advance as it tried to move back. It was on the retreat now, and they could have just safely let it run.

But James was pissed now. It had tried to eat Rufus. It had tried to kill his friend. Unacceptable. He wasn't the vengeful type, but that was behavior that couldn't be allowed.

Unclipping his axe, he sat forward. He didn't have time to stand up or get a good angle before it would be past him, so he just put as much momentum as possible into one long chop, keeping his arm straight and his aim as good as he could manage. The snake didn't see it coming, which was good for two reasons. His blade buried itself at the base of its neck, and it started thrashing wildly. Anesh and Alanna found themselves with a lot more freedom of movement as James hauled himself forward by the handle, grabbed at the camera, and pulled it up to view the ceiling.

A few seconds later, Anesh plunged the spear into its chest, stripping cables and fraying wires as he cut down the middle. Alanna moved around to the side, bringing the hammer down on its back, a little closer than to James than he was comfortable with, but still more or less well aimed. LEDs broke, but the snake kept thrashing.

"The camera!" James gasped, still with the wind knocked out of him from the hit. "Gonna let go, hit it!" He signaled Alanna, who nodded and got ready.

James pulled the camera toward him, forcing the snake to look at him and not the other two. As soon as too much of him was in its vision, he locked up again, and it easily slipped through his fingers. It started to let out a hiss as it lunged forward for his throat. But then, looking like the most amazing baseball player James had ever seen, Alanna brought the sledgehammer in a huge swing right through the snake's camera eye, knocking the whole assembly out of its head with a tearing of wires and a cracking of glass.

And that was that. It died silently, and James sighed in relief as he lay back on the floor, half the heavy weight of its cables still on his legs.

Then there were some words exchanged around him that he didn't quite catch, and a few loud thuds and slamming noises that made him look up. Anesh and Alanna were cleaning up a couple of striders that had come in to look for an easy scavenge, perhaps. James dropped his head back down; he was too tired to move, and his arms felt like noodles. He'd help later, when they needed him to do something fun, like use whatever skill orb this thing dropped.

He rolled his head over to see it: shining emerald green, and a size two at that. A small smile danced on his lips. That had been worth it, he thought as he closed his eyes.

They hadn't let him rest for very long. They were getting short enough on time that it was time to head back, and Alanna complained that this place needed bathrooms. So he'd grudgingly gotten up and followed along with them.

"How'd you like the coffee?" he asked Alanna as they set a brisk walking pace back through the office, tracing over their signposted route, following Ganesh as he buzzed ahead to scout. It was mostly clear, but no sense taking chances. They'd already almost run into a shellaxy, which had gotten angry about their intrusion into its patch of hallway and tried to eat Anesh's legs.

"It was good but now I'm having trouble using pauses in my sentences and does this wear off quickly it's starting to give me a headache," Alanna answered rapidly, her foot tapping the floor in a staccato beat.

Anesh laughed from ahead of them. "It's not just you! I assumed that was just what caffeine did to you, but it looks like this coffee has that effect on some people."

"Yeah, it wears off." James smiled. "So, what did you guys find before I interrupted you?"

"Oh, that!" Anesh started. "Well, we . . ."

"We found a briefcase and it was locked and it wouldn't break and there was a work order on it and we were trying to figure out where to deliver it and if it was something worth looking into and then I found a laser pointer and we found a bunch of iPhones eating an Android and then . . ." Alanna breathlessly and excitedly explained with a fiery gleam in her eyes.

"Okay, calm down there, sparky." Anesh made a lowering motion with his hand, quieting her down, while James broke down silently laughing at Alanna's sudden and enthusiastic energy. "But yeah, we ran across a couple things. None of them basilisks. What the hell was that, anyway?"

"A basilisk," James said coyly as they moved up to check a corner before moving on with their journey back.

Anesh lightly slapped James in the back of the head once they were clear. "I mean, what purpose does it serve? Alanna has me thinking about that now, and I hate it."

"Oh," James thought. "Security camera, so, sentry? Actually, I'm more concerned with why it dropped a green orb. I thought those were for the really huge monsters that actively try to kill us."

"It did—" Anesh started to say.

James shook his head. "No, I mean, really try to kill us. This thing was just hunting, it felt like. It was going for Rufus, not patrolling the area or anything like that."

"So you think the greens are for hostiles?" Anesh asked.

"Have been so far," James replied grimly.

Alanna poked her head between them. "Hey, Anesh, what are you calling the basilisk?"

"What?" they asked in unison, cut out of their train of thought on dungeon ecology.

"The basilisk," Alanna said, coming down from her caffeine high. "You've got a name for it, I know you do. What are you calling it? I won't pretend I'm mad about the pun, either," she said as they passed by the cubes that held the decision tree and headed back into the relatively safe part of the office, carefully stepping over the carpet break line that triggered the pencil dart trap.

"There's a weird EM hum here," Anesh muttered to the other two. "I thought it was just another monitor or something, but I think it's actually the trap trigger." He leaned down to press his ear near the ground. "Yup. Okay, that's something to look out for." He stood back up and started moving on. "As for the snake, no, I don't have a name for it. Not everything here actually has a good pun for a name."

"What?" Alanna asked, confused. "That can't be right. You guys have had weird names for all this stuff so far; I thought it was endemic to the dungeon."

"No, no," James explained, "this place just happens to have opportunities for names like that because it's all normal stuff. If these were actual monsters and not repurposed office supplies, it wouldn't be an issue. It just feels weird because all the names fit, but they only fit because we make them fit, because it's real-world stuff." He stumbled over his point at the end there. "Did that make sense?"

"James, we're in another dimension that's shaped like an office and has cable snakes in it, none of this makes sense. Oh! Cable snake!" She snapped her fingers. "That's the name!"

"Sure, works well enough, though it's a little on the nose," James said as they hustled their way through now-familiar territory.

Alanna just scowled and shook her fist. "Don't ruin this for me. You both got one, it's my turn. It doesn't have to be good, I just want to name something. Maybe I'll go research puns when I get home, don't think I won't."

"I know you will, that's what worries me," James said as they walked on, their laughter and the humming of a drone's rotors the only noise until they got back to the door.

CHAPTER 35

James looked down at the desk, the sting of excitement running through his blood. It felt like Christmas morning as a kid all over again, before age and increasingly harsh depression had dulled Christmas from something magical to something dreaded. But this wasn't socially significant gifts or a stressful dinner with family he'd grown apart from; this was magic that he'd fought for and earned.

Next to him, Alanna let out a low whistle as Anesh added the contents of the drawer to the pile of loot on the table. First, there was a pile of assorted cash, food, miscellaneous things, eighteen small yellow orbs, a single medium yellow orb, and one small green orb next to them. All of this they had amassed on their way out and back. The spoils of their trials. Anesh put in three more yellows, six small reds, and his own pile of money and candy bars.

"Did you intentionally go for every Baby Things you could find?" James asked with a smirk.

Alanna unwrapped one and shoved half of it into her mouth. "Is it Baby Thing, or Baby's Things?" she asked around the mouthful of chocolate.

"Baby Things, singular and plural. And yes, I did. I like them, so stop eating my candy," Anesh remarked dryly as he finished by laying out a pair of sunglasses on the desk.

"This has come full circle," James said with a small huff.

Anesh set the shades down separated from the more random loot, along with a few other things. The sunglasses, of course. But with them, a pencil, a laser pointer, a deliberately tangled Newton's cradle, and a pad of sticky notes. He handled all of these with tender care, to which James mostly rolled his eyes; they weren't ancient artifacts, and no one was worried Anesh was going to drop the Holy Grail. They were just mildly magical stuff.

Well, he assumed. He hadn't actually seen what most of them did.

"Okay, first things first," Anesh said. "How are we dividing this up?"

"We pay Rufus and Ganesh first, I think," James replied, and Alanna nodded along. James had known for a while the massive value those two had in both exploration and battle, and now Alanna too was well aware of it. "We also need to keep one for Lily, so she has something to eat that isn't the giant one."

Alanna pointed a finger at James across her chest. "Yeah, hey, what about that one? Can I have it?"

"No." "No." The replies were swift and simultaneous.

"I get it." "James gets it." The follow-up comments were equally overlapping.

James started a bit. "Wait, what? Why do I get it? I was kidding."

"You did something bloody stupid and heroic," Anesh said as he folded his arms. "Now shut up and enjoy the reward for your sodding altruism."

James just nodded, trying not to let any emotion onto his face. He didn't really know how to respond to that, what to think or feel here. So he tried for outward neutrality. What he got was probably closer to outward confusion, but hey, he wasn't an actor. It was probably a better image than weeping with joy or kissing Anesh thank-you.

"Soooo . . ." Alanna said, cutting into his thoughts. "Two each for Rufus and Ganesh, right? And one for Lily. That leaves us seventeen of the skill balls, one of them large. So five for each of us, and rock-paper-scissors for who gets the large one and the leftover?"

"Actually, there's something I've been thinking about," James said. "We've mostly been holding off on experimenting with these things because we've never really had enough, and it's always more fun to use them than test stuff. But as long as we have an extra anyway, I kind of want to see what happens if we use it on an inanimate thing."

"How so?" Anesh asked, slowly and suspiciously.

James shrugged. "I don't really know. But we know there's a way to re-form the orbs once we've used them, we just haven't figured it out. We talked about use cases, remember, Anesh? And we know that, somehow, blue and red orbs get used for magic items and traps."

"Xenotech," Anesh said, correcting him.

"*Magic. Items*," James continued. "And traps. So why not try to put a yellow orb into something and see if we can make our own magic?"

"Because yellow orbs make living creatures?" Alanna said in a way that made it clear it wasn't so much a question as a statement. The unspoken part was *James, stop being an idiot*.

"Hm. We could make another ally, maybe," James mused. "Maybe something that would be an effective sentry for the fort. If we built our own computer, do you think that would get us a friendly shellaxy?"

Anesh split the orbs into four piles and held up a hand. "I'm going with Alanna's idea. Rock-paper-scissors, winner gets the big one, runner-up gets the extra. I have no desire to test this theory today."

"Bah! Fine, I'll do it later, with my own reserves," James said, throwing up his arms. "You lack vision!" James put his own fist out for the game, and Alanna quickly mimicked the motion.

"I lack the desire to start a petting zoo of office supplies," Anesh responded, starting the arm movements and counting off. "One, two, *throw*."

Anesh was glad that he got James off that track for the moment, but he was a bit less smug when he promptly lost and got to watch Alanna and James face off over the course of fifteen ties for the actual prize.

"I feel like they're not taking this seriously," he muttered to Ganesh. The drone made a motion like a shrug, something he'd learned from Rufus, and hovered down to grab his own payment, helping Rufus carry off the orbs that they'd earned themselves over the day.

"Hmph." Anesh let out an indignant noise. "Okay, well, when you guys have finished that up, let me know," he said to the still-competing pair on the other side of the desk as he started sorting and tallying the cash.

When they finished, Alanna had won, but both of them were happy enough, and Anesh couldn't help but smile as James dramatically played up his loss.

"All right, before we crack these," James said, as they all collected their individual treasures, "I have one thing I want to try. No, *not* making more friends; calm down, Anesh, I see you getting ready to complain." He quickly cut off his friend. "Okay, so, we know the big orb has a few different shades of color in it, and these little ones have slight variations too. We should actually be making a log of the color as well as the skills when we crack them, just so we can try to find a pattern. Maybe some basic identification before using."

"That . . . All right, that's smart," Alanna conceded. "Why weren't you doing that before?"

"We're easily distracted. Also usually injured by the time we get to this point," Anesh said without humor.

James nodded enthusiastically. "Not much of an excuse, though!" he said with a smile. "I'm injured now, and I thought of it! I think this place is making me wise beyond my years."

It took a little while for them to wait for Anesh to get some paper and record all the different shades of yellow. They quickly realized that even if James was right, they didn't actually have something that could accurately give them perfect color information. So they were left with a sliding scale of dark to bright and a hope that it might be enough to at least get started.

While Anesh was going through that process, James broke the Newton's cradle. The little office toy, which he hadn't asked about before fiddling with it, he'd untangled and started swinging. It had almost immediately started making a screeching noise in his head, like rough metal grinding on glass. Neither Alanna nor Anesh seemed to notice, but they'd both looked up when he'd chopped down with a flat hand hard enough to snap the desk toy in half and calmly add a blue orb to their pile. As dignified as he could, he dusted himself off and cleared his throat, turning to look away as if nothing had happened.

"Fine. Didn't want that thing anyway," Anesh muttered. "All it did was mild telepathy, nothing there that we could exploit for the betterment of the world and our own wallets." He finished writing out the list and numbering the orbs with a Sharpie they'd found. "Okay, done. Now, one at a time!"

"Wait, first, what about the . . . xenotech . . . ?" James asked, conceding to Anesh for time purposes. "What are we keeping, what are we cracking?"

"The pencil abuses physics; I think we should save it for now. The sticky notes don't seem to do anything except show the emotions of people they're stuck on, so we can probably lose those. A fun novelty, but I'd rather have a potential lifesaver," Anesh said.

"Agreed," Alanna chimed in.

"You also already broke the cradle, which . . . fine. And the shades, I think we should all get used to so we can use them going forward. They would seriously improve our ability to spot stuff." Anesh held up the sunglasses.

James reached out questioningly. "Can I try?"

"Sure, just be—" James put them on and almost instantly ripped them off, screaming. "—careful. Bloody hell!" Anesh watched as James dropped to his knees, holding his hands tightly over his eyes. "That was not how bad my reaction was. Alanna, do you want to—"

"Nooooooope. Sure don't."

"Right . . . well, I'll hold on to these then," Anesh said quietly. "Um . . . sorry. Again." James just held out a thumbs-up. He wasn't seriously hurt; his brain just couldn't process the effect and turned it into a sensation that he could only assume was pain. The fact that Anesh only got a mild headache from it, apparently, both shocked and impressed him.

Alanna reached over and picked up the last object. "So, the laser pointer, can I claim this one? It makes maps."

"Can I see?" James asked from the floor.

She nodded, pointing it at the front of Fort Door. The pointer started out as a dot, then quickly expanded to a series of lines and shapes as Alanna held it still.

"What's that?" James asked, pointing at a big rectangular blob of red light. "I get that the empty area here before the next lines is the no-man's-land, and this is the fort, but what's this in the fort?"

Alanna raised her arm, and it vanished; she brought her arm back down, and it showed up again. "Desk, I think. As far as we could tell, it takes a horizontal slice of the world and projects that. I'm not sure if it's useful, because it's very short range, but it's still cool."

"I bet you everything from next week that it's useful." James didn't hesitate to make another wager.

Alanna was equally unhesitant in her reply. "No."

"Well, then. Two more blue orbs, we'll keep those here with Rufus for safekeeping. No one wants the reds right now, they're weird. So if that's all cleared up, skill orbs, one by one?" Anesh asked hopefully.

The three friends were battered, tired, and wounded; some of them still were covered with their own dried blood, making their skin itch. They were hungry for an actual meal and, in one case, really wanting to hurry this along and get to a bathroom. But still, they smiled as they gathered around and, one by one, popped their prizes.

Naturally, the first one James burst in his fingers made him grimace.

[+1 Skill Rank : Sex - Fellatio]

"Well, that sucks," he said, the joke coming out before he could stop it, unappreciated by his companions.

"What?" Anesh asked, pen at the ready. "That was number four, right? What did you get so I can write it down?"

James just gave Anesh a pained look. "Can I tell you later when Alanna isn't here to say ... anything, really?" Anesh shrugged, Alanna punched him in the shoulder, and James sighed internally in relief. He then moved on to the rest of his orbs.

[+1 Skill Rank : Riding - Horse]

[+1 Skill Rank : Marketing]
[+1 Skill Rank : Firearms - Sidearms]

"And that's it for me." He finished explaining his upgrades. "Maybe this is what finally pushes me into bringing my gun in. I mean, we make a ton of noise sometimes, and we haven't hit another horde. We should probably try to figure out the conditions those occur under, but I don't ... really ... want to *test* that ... Anyway. I'm going to save the last two for experiments, or maybe just Lily, since she's almost done with the big one."

Alanna went next, gleefully finding new ways to crack the orbs. First smushing them against the desk, then learning that if she hit them hard enough it still worked, and serving the rest of them like a tennis ball with her palm.

[+1 Skill Rank : Cooking - Recipe - Pan-Seared Salmon]
[+1 Skill Rank : Anthropology - South America]
[+1 Skill Rank : Anxiety Management]
[+1 Skill Rank : Etiquette - Military - US]
[+1 Skill Rank : History - French - Political]
[+2 Skill Ranks : Negotiation - Contract]

"Hey, I actually have one of those already!" James said, surprised. "Anesh! Add that to the list of suspicious things to look into that we really have no way to accurately test!"

"No." They did not have that list, and Anesh wasn't going to humor James's thought that they were ever fully blocked from researching further into the nature of the dungeon. They had a proper list, with questions that simply didn't have answers yet.

"Great!" James exclaimed, before pulling out his own phone and making the note anyway. "But really. You're not going to save any of these?" he asked Alanna.

"I'm saving nothing!" she proudly declared. "I shall take them all! Self-actualization for the win!" James and Anesh gave her small claps for her impromptu call to personal betterment, and she half bowed. "Great. Now, Anesh, do yours and let's go. Self-actualization doesn't mean I don't have to piss like a racehorse."

"Classy," James quipped.

Alanna punched him again. "I'm charismatic, I don't have to be classy."

While James desperately tried to find the words to reply to that, or even process it, Anesh ignored them both. Finishing up his notes on Alanna's skills, he turned to his own and, taking inspiration from James for once, decided to hold back one of his. He did it quietly, mostly just thinking that, now that he could freely talk about this place, it would be useful to introduce someone else to the dungeon's allure.

[+1 Skill Rank : Inventory Management - Arrangement]
[+1 Skill Rank : Makeup Application]
[+1 Skill Rank : Craft - Papier-Mâché]
[+1 Skill Rank : Meteorology]

"All right, that's me done," he said, sharing with the others so it wouldn't feel unfair. "Now. Let's get out of here. I need to get some sleep now that we've ruined our internal clocks."

"Oh man, this place does that, doesn't it!" Alanna slapped her own forehead. "Why didn't you warn me?" she demanded.

James blocked her playful punch this time, casually swatting her slow-moving fist aside. "I literally *could not* have told you about it. And I bet it was one of the first things Anesh let you know when he listed off the dangers."

"You can't prove that."

"Anesh is *right there*. I can just ask him." James waved over at Anesh, who had their take-out bag set up, everything else already packed. "Also, come on. You can complain later, let's get out of here. You remember reality? It's terrible, but it has usable toilets and they're right outside that door."

Alanna considered it briefly. "I accept your terms," she said solemnly.

"Great. Let's go, because Anesh already left. Good night, Rufus, Ganesh! We'll see you guys next week! Stay safe, kids!"

"Kids?"

"They're basically just especially useful kids."

"Agreed."

For James and Anesh, this part was getting pretty familiar, and though it had lost that electric charge of something totally new, it was still fantastic. But for Alanna, standing there on the threshold of the door, she couldn't help but look back. Rufus waved a single pen-leg at her, and Ganesh tried to mimic the gesture with one of his rotor-legs. Beyond them, the office beckoned her back, thousands and thousands of chances to be something *more*.

It was probably a good thing that she now desperately needed to use the bathroom in James's actual office building, or she might have turned around right there.

CHAPTER 36

The road lazily rolled on ahead of him. James walked, not alone, along the molten asphalt. Waves of heat fluttered in the air like birds, making the dry grass and barbed-wire fences on either side of the road seem more like mirages than they really were.

One foot down. Then the other.

The sun beat down. All of the suns beat down. The six dancing stars in the sky above played a staccato drumroll down on the world around James and his walking partner. The landscape burned without fire, but still, he kept walking.

One foot down. Then the other.

In the fields to their left, a lone scarecrow stood. It had been there for over ten thousand years, and it had stood a solitary and noble watch over these fields. It had seen the grain, perfectly ripened, sit untouched for centuries. It had heard the endless roll of cicadas herald the summer for millennia. It was eternal. It never tired of the beautiful world around it, or of seeing the passing travelers that sometimes came by, following that river of a road.

One foot down. Then the other.

James wiped his forehead and looked around. Fields, forever. The road, forever. "I'm dreaming," he muttered out loud, realizing it but holding himself in that sleeping state. The realization was almost startling, but he kept moving, stopping only for a minute to pick a rock out of his shoe. It had been bothering him for decades. He leaned on the fencepost for a second, feeling the old wood, understanding how many children had gotten splinters off it over the years. Then he grunted and kept going.

One foot down. Then the other.

James said he was dreaming, and it wasn't a question. But three miles later, the answer came anyway. "**Yes.**" The person walking with him spoke without moving its mouth. James hadn't realized it was there, or that it could speak. If it had been the waking hours of his life, his heart would have exploded out of his chest, but it wasn't. Here, in the dreamlands, James reacted with a purity of purpose, his response untouched by fear or nerves. He just kept walking.

One foot down. Then the other.

He didn't turn to look at his walking partner. "Who are you?" he asked. He knew what was there. It was shaped like a human, but it was not. It was just wearing a shell, here in the dream. The thing was something else. But it wasn't just a thing anymore, James felt that. It was a person. It was a who. So he asked. And then, looking around, he felt the atmosphere of this countryside and decided to add a bit of politeness to his question. "I'm James. What's your name?"

One foot down. Then the other.

It had been a month of walking since he introduced himself. Time didn't mean much there. It was just another way to mark the road, the dust, the occasional rusted signpost, and the eternal wheat. The air smelled like the thought of powdered ivory when the creature trying to be a person spoke again. "**I am someone,**" it said, uncertain. James nodded, understanding. This thing is new to being a person. They continued their stroll.

One foot down. Then the other.

It was a hundred miles and two speed limit signs later that James shot a glance at his new friend. It was him, sort of. His face, his long brown hair up in his ponytail, his Powerman 5000 T-shirt soaked in his sweat. A mirror. But not quite. There was something off about it, something that reminded him of salt and iron, something that didn't belong there, or as part of him. "Have we met before?" James asked as they both stopped to watch a flock of crows soar overhead in a dancing spiral.

The other nodded slightly, then gave a strangely sincere smile, as though it was proud of the gesture. **"We spoke once."**

Taking this as a good enough answer, James smiled back at him as the last crow fell through the end of their dance and vanished into the sky. They stood there for a minute to rest muscles that weren't real before taking the next step on the road that was not there.

One foot down. Then the other.

"You're the other one, aren't you?" James asked, without hostility.

"I am an interdiction," it responded.

"Fish thoughts," James muttered as they passed an old rusted ruin of a tractor. The skeleton of metal stood in stark contrast to the grain around it, a dark brown spot of lifelessness in the otherwise perfect sea of gold. "We made some kind of deal, didn't we? I don't remember."

"Secrets." It nodded. James nodded back, not understanding, but accepting. They walked on together, comfortable in each other's company. The heat felt like a bonfire on the back of their necks. Both of them wished they had a hat. Everyone who walks the road does.

One foot down. Then the other.

They came to an intersection. A beat-up old stop sign that the local kids used for target practice sat on the corner in a patch of dry brambles. It was a four-way intersection, the kind that's slightly imperfect on the angle, so it's not quite ninety degrees. These used to drive James crazy. Now, though, it was just another part of the road. The two of them stopped and sat together on an old log off on the side. There were no cars to watch; there never had been and there never would be. But they watched for them anyway.

"Can you tell me what our deal was?" James asked directly.

The other James nodded, again smug that it had done so. **"Your secret. My meal. I keep. I stay here."**

"Here?" He looked up at the everlasting sky. It was a shade of blue that made his bones hurt. Like the air itself was painted to look like a perfect sky.

"Here." It leaned over and tapped James on the forehead. It wasn't really his head, but he got the point. It was living in his mind, making a nest of his thoughts.

"Why?" James asked, askance. He wasn't mad, for the same reason he wasn't afraid. There wasn't room for that in this sleeping world.

It stood up, dusted itself off. A very human gesture that felt stiff and unpracticed, but like the thing meant it. "**I am becoming happy.**"

James stood as well, swatting away a horsefly that buzzed around his head. "Well, you have to chase your dreams, I guess," he said. The thing that wore his face tried to smile, but it didn't have much effort behind it. Maybe it was still working on the sense of humor. James didn't mind, though. It was good company. He ignored both other options on the intersection and crossed over, continuing down the eternal black ribbon that was the road ahead.

One foot down. Then the other.

James woke up to the smell of pizza and the sound of small things clattering on wood. He briefly considered keeping his eyes closed and letting sleep take him again. Despite the fact that his bedside clock told him it was four p.m., he wasn't in any hurry to get out of bed.

But the call of food and the laughter and conversation from his living room were enough to convince him that maybe it was worth it to get up.

Ten minutes and a few failed attempts to find a pair of pants later, he felt a bit more alert and ready to go see what was going on in his apartment. Before leaving his room, he took a second to check on Lily. It—though James really did think of her as a *she*, the iLipede was fundamentally genderless—it was still sitting atop the giant orb they'd brought home. Lily looked pretty comfortable, occasionally twitching a leg or antenna in a way that reminded James of a cat lazing in the sun. The screen that made up her back was still displaying a progress bar, as it had been for some time now.

"Ninety-two percent done, eh?" he said quietly, not wanting to startle or wake up the small mobile device. "Well, keep at it," James said in a kind tone. "We'll make sure you get all the orbs you can eat when you're through, okay?"

Standing up from his crouch over the small pen, he wandered out of his room and down the hall. The living room had a lively feel to it; a cluster of people sat around the table, chatting. Alanna gave him a joking salute as he walked in, and James spotted Dave out on their back porch, probably having a smoke.

It was getting on toward spring. Still cold, though not as bad; crisp instead of biting. The weather hadn't warmed up much, but it was staying light later and later, and it made for some great sunsets. James always loved how the light through their big glass porch doors looked when there was a cold sunset. He took a second to appreciate it before JP bounced a d8 off his chest.

"Ow," James said without pain. "Also why."

"I asked you something and you just stared out the window," JP responded. "We're wondering why you're not at work." The others at the table nodded, especially Anesh.

"Yeah," Anesh said, "I think we agreed that you getting fired was a bad idea?"

James rolled his eyes. "I am aware that a sudden case of joblessness would be a problem, yes. I have the day off. We actually get most holidays off." Blank looks from everyone. "It . . . it's Easter?" James said tentatively.

"Easter is a holiday?" Alanna asked with a bit of sharp confusion.

JP looked over at her. "Okay, I know that I forgot about Easter, but at least I know that it's a holiday. What's your excuse? Wait, hang on, I've met your mom. I've *been to your house*. She has more crucifixes than most churches."

"I know what Easter is, you fuck." Alanna flicked a chip at JP, who ducked it, sputtering. "I didn't realize that people actually got it off. I thought it was one of those things that isn't important to anyone but nutjobs like my mother."

Clearing his throat, James cut off their impending argument. "Um . . . it's not. I mean, it's not normally a day off. My company actually gives us a surprising amount of days off. It's one of those weird things that make up for working in a corporate office hellscape. Anyway, the point is, I'm here tonight. What're you guys playing?"

"Still on the weird dungeon delve thing," JP said.

James raised an eyebrow and looked over at Anesh, who just shrugged. "Isn't this . . . um . . ." He pinched the bridge of his nose and thought for a second, eyes closed. "Okay, I don't know how to phrase this, so, why are you guys doing this?" he asked.

"I have no idea what you're talking about," Alanna said with a wolfish grin.

"Yeah, what's wrong with a novel and obviously unreal game scenario, James?" Anesh asked.

JP just gave him a shrug. "I mean, I think it's fun; I don't know why it bothers you. I normally just play whatever Anesh wants to run though."

"No, JP, you're excluded from this disdain," James said, turning his attention back to the other two. "You guys know damn well why. Is there a reason, or are you just screwing with me?"

"That second one," Alanna said before Anesh could answer and keep the joke going. Anesh cut himself off, mouth still open, sitting forward, before getting a dejected look on his face and leaning back in his chair.

James took a long sigh. "JP, the reason this is dumb is because this isn't fictional. We found an office dungeon. Well, *I* found an office dungeon. It's real, this is mostly real, because I don't know what creative liberties Anesh took, and the original reason for the game was to farm you guys for ideas." JP started to say something, and James jumped in. "Yes, really. Yes, we have proof; Anesh saved some of the skill orbs for exactly this purpose. Yes, skill orbs. No, I'm not kidding. No, I'm not psychic, I'm just getting good at this conversation. Any other questions?"

There was a long pause. "Why tell me?"

"Because we're not main characters. Having a larger team increases our odds of survival, our applicable skill pool, and how far in we can go. I would also say our supply of ideas, but Anesh actually solved that problem."

"Why tell me *now*, not earlier, since it seems like this has been going on a while?" JP clarified.

"Oh! Mind control. We took care of it. It was a misunderstanding," James told him, clarifying very little.

"I'm... not sure what to make of this. Do I get a choice?" JP asked.

Anesh slapped Alanna on the arm as she started to give a quick and snarky answer. "Obviously, yes. We aren't going to drag you in against your will. That would be stupid. We do ask you to keep it secret, though. I actually prepared a short set of guidelines that I'd like everyone to go over and sign off on. Sort of a charter thing, but that can wait. I also was hoping that Dave would be here when James came in and saw this."

"What about me?" Dave said as he walked back in through the sliding glass door. "Oh, hey. You're awake! Don't you have work?"

James rubbed at his eyes. "Okay, I'm not repeating this. You guys have fun. The door is on Tuesday around three a.m., I'm going to get food, I'll be back later. Don't scare Dave off." He threw open the door and took a deep breath of the cool evening air. "Oh, and someone keep an eye on Lily. The thing's almost done," he called back as the door swung shut behind him.

Without a moment's hesitation, Anesh and Alanna both cried out, "Not it!" A half second later, Dave joined them; he didn't know what he was un-volunteering for, but a lifetime around James had taught him that it was better to get in early with this sort of thing.

JP shrugged, figuring it wasn't that bad to have to go do a quick check on... "Wait, who's Lily?" he asked. "Guys?" JP started to get a small sense of worry when Dave just shrugged and neither Alanna nor Anesh would meet his eyes. "Dammit, guys, come on..."

James strolled down the sidewalk. It felt good to stretch his legs, and the delightful feeling of not going to his job tonight really helped bolster his spirits. He felt good today in general, really. It was a rare effect on him to not just feel like he was surviving, but thriving in life. And a lot of small things came together today to make that happen for him.

His friends were assembling into an RPG party, which was cool. He had the night off. The weather was pleasant, and as a proud resident of a state with weather all over the board, he got to be smug about not "needing" to wear a jacket. And also, the booster shot to his finances that was the dungeon made it possible for him to go down to the barbecue place near his apartment and ask them to put as much brisket on a piece of bread as they were legally allowed to serve him.

It was there, in that restaurant, sitting in a little booth in the back corner, that James pulled out the blue orb he'd been holding on to.

It was the size of the tip of his index finger. It didn't quite glow in the low light of the restaurant, but it had a feeling to it that went beyond just the shine of the color. Like it was lit up in James's mind, if not in physicality.

He'd been holding on to this one since he'd accidentally torn one of the filing folders on a desk and the orb had popped out. It had sat forgotten in his pocket for a while. And while he hadn't intentionally kept it out of the loot pile, he did decide that he wanted to try something with it before offering it to Alanna. He would offer it to Anesh, but he figured that his buddy had already had his fill of problem-solving.

Okay, that was flimsy justification. But still, he had an idea he wanted to try, and he was worried that Anesh would shoot down his rationale on the grounds that they needed to save these kinds of resources for emergencies. And really, he could understand that. Anesh had taken some serious punishment in the dungeon, and wanting to be able to mitigate and *survive* that was reasonable. More than that, it was just smart.

But James had an idea.

He and Anesh had talked before, partly while his friend was under the influence of painkillers and exhaustion, and then partly later when he was a normal human, about the idea of different uses for the orbs. Simply put, they could be used in different ways. "Cracking" them, as they tended to do, was one way. The dungeon clearly used them in a different way, creating monsters and traps and warped areas of space. It sort of looked like Rufus and Ganesh did a third thing: consuming the orbs as a power source. But James had a suspicion that it was just an extension of the dungeon's use: infusing an orb into something to give it properties.

The thing was, while James had never seen Rufus eat a blue one, he was pretty sure he could. It would just change him, or perhaps more accurately, power him, in a different way. And while he had never seen the stapler-crab crack orbs, he was almost sure he could. And yes, obviously, a human wasn't a stapler-crab, but he didn't see any particular rule that said that he couldn't absorb orbs the same way Rufus did.

James was realizing as he thought this out that it was a pretty long list of assumptions.

But he had a feeling in his gut. Like he'd started to form a pattern map of how the orbs worked. This really should have been Anesh's thing, given the skill he'd gotten. Hell, maybe he had already sorted this out. Or maybe James was making illogical leaps and hoping they worked.

His food arrived, and he thanked the guy who brought it over. Had a burst of small talk about the weather and how the day was going. And then he was left alone, with about a sandwich's worth of time to decide if this was a bad idea or not.

Well, he figured, with his mouth full of tangy barbecue sauce and beef, the worst-case scenario if it didn't work at all would be that he'd have wasted a blue. The worst-case scenario if it worked *badly* was that he'd die, he guessed.

He didn't wait to finish his sandwich. He picked up the orb in one hand, after wiping off barbecue sauce on his paper napkin, and pressed it against his forearm.

It didn't break. He didn't want it to, this time. He had a different goal in mind here. He didn't fully expect it to work, but he wanted to see. So he kept pressing, applying a little more pressure. Still nothing happened, though. But he was pushing down well past the point when the orbs normally popped.

Taking a short breath, he set the orb to the side. His fingers were sweating a bit, and he didn't really have a plan beyond "see if this would work." But he didn't feel like he'd gotten a solid line on what he felt was the way forward.

So he took a couple more bites of food and thought while he chewed. The orbs, so far, had all been about will. If you wanted to use it, you used it. It barely required any physical contact at all, as Alanna had discovered when she'd started spiking them into nothingness. The only real exception was the first couple they ever picked up, where simple curiosity had done the job. Well, curiosity and a bit of pressure.

James rolled the orb around on the table with one finger. He was almost sure this was possible, he just needed to figure out the trick to it.

Cracking an orb was a human action. He knew this. Curiosity or will or just plain old luck. Those things got you a skill point, or a problem solved, or a Canadian citizenship. But the dungeon wasn't human.

Okay, point of order. The dungeon probably wasn't even alive. But the things *in* the dungeon weren't human. They worked differently. What were the orbs to them?

James picked up the orb again and tried to think of it in different ways as he pushed it in his fingertips. He stared into the blue and thought of it as a battery, taking a minute or so of gazing at its surface to change how he considered it. That didn't do anything, though. So he switched over to food. It was pretty easy to think of it as food while he was eating, he found. So he took some time to consider it as a dessert, and still nothing.

James sighed. This wasn't working. What was the difference, really? Cracking the orbs still felt like they were, well, absorbing them, for lack of a better term. They internalized the skills, they really just took the contents of the orb into themselves. Maybe it was about whether it was intact?

Trying these few thoughts on didn't yield any results either.

The whole thing was a bit demoralizing. James figured he'd hand off the orb when he got back, and got ready to leave. His lunch had been delicious, but being tainted by the sting of failure wasn't a great seasoning. With one last puff of breath, he went to stand up and had a single final thought.

"Hey, Secret," he muttered, projecting the thought at the creature living in his brain. "Give me a hand here, will ya?"

He squeezed down on the orb and felt something from his subconscious reach out and *twist* how he saw it. It couldn't be as simple as a human looking at something from a different human perspective, of course. The trait it took to internalize an orb was something wholly alien from a human. But of course, James wasn't just a human; there were two different things living in his mind.

The orb slipped into the palm of his hand.

James grinned madly, wanting to punch the air and scream in triumph. Then a wave of pain unlike anything he'd ever felt hit him. It felt like his blood was shattering and his eyes had turned to glass. The nightmare lasted for a second before the world went white and he lost consciousness.

James awoke to an EMT leaning over him, shining a flashlight in his eyes. He tried to bat it away but found he was strapped down to a gurney. The world around him rocked, and it took a second to realize that it was because he was in an ambulance and not just completely off balance.

"I'm fine, I'm fine," he tried to tell the EMT, but all that came out was a mumble. Clearing his throat, he tried again and got out a bit more. The medic backed up and started asking him questions about what he remembered, and James tried to answer as best as he could.

But it was a bit difficult when the first thing that flashed through his head when he'd come back was an intruding thought. It felt like it had been waiting politely for him to wake up, and it also sounded quieter somehow. Could an external alien thought feel guilt? James wasn't sure, but it definitely felt like it. Either that, or it would really appreciate it if he didn't do that again.

He focused on what it told him, instead of what the EMT was telling him, and it passed off the information before leaving.

[+14 Activations - Sublimate Rubber]

"Oh. Super," he muttered out loud, thumping his head back on the thin pillow and trying to not let the thought of having to sit in the ER for six hours ruin his night.

Things had been going so well.

CHAPTER 37

"Frank!" James said with a cheerful smile as he threw open the double doors at the base of his office building. The glass doors and brass fittings were intentionally just a bit too heavy, or spring-loaded, so that furious employees couldn't slam them against the walls when they stormed into their monotonous jobs. But they weren't so weighed down that James couldn't make a semidramatic entrance when he was in a good mood.

Frank looked up from his paper. The older man, with his short and rough goatee and his graying hair, did a perfect impression of someone who'd just popped in from twenty years ago for a visit. He had an old, chipped ceramic mug of black coffee and a big cake doughnut on the security desk in front of him, he was doing a crossword on a hard-copy newspaper, and even his shirt looked like it was just a little bit different from the modern style.

James was pretty sure that Frank did this on purpose, to throw people off. Because James was absolutely sure that Frank had a laptop under the desk and snuck in games of online poker when no one was around. It was a long-term disguise: the cultivated image of an old man, someone who was just sort of a fixture and not to be worried about.

And now, he was an impromptu ally in sneaking stuff in and out of the building.

"Jim." The old man spoke in a deep, throaty voice, thick from a lifetime of smoking. "Is it Monday already?" he asked with a huff that James had come to associate with his version of laughter.

The fact that Frank had caught on to the pattern of James's happiness enough to realize that Monday nights were the special times was kind of worrying. Then again, he'd so far helped them move several jugs of fictional soda and at least one unconscious and injured person into a car. So maybe it would have been stranger if he hadn't noticed.

In response to his question, James just nodded. "Yup. Say, I wanted to thank you for your help over the last month."

"Don't mention it," Frank said, in a tone that indicated that he was more interested in discretion than avoiding praise. "Don't mention it to anyone, really. I don't."

"Well, I appreciate it. And I know my friend appreciates it." James cleared his throat, leaning on the desk. "Speaking of which, I have a couple other friends coming through tonight, if that's okay?" Frank folded his paper deliberately and leaned on the desk in front of him, raising a single eyebrow at James. That technique was impressive, James thought; he tried, but the most he could ever get was one eyebrow slightly above the other. Frank had the full-on Leonard Nimoy thing going on. "Ahem. Anyway, I just wanted to make sure you knew." James casually set the stack of folded bills he'd been holding in his pocket onto the desk, under the small overhang where the sign-in sheet was.

"A'ight," Frank muttered through his mustache. "Thanks for the warning. Good talk." He looked back down at his crossword, the money already having vanished into a pocket somewhere. James hadn't even seen him reach for it.

Walking toward the stairs, James mumbled to himself quietly, "I'm putting 'vampire street magician' on the list of potential backstories for that guy."

"No, I'm sorry, ma'am, but we can't send a technician out to find your remote." James had his head on the desk, his back folded at a sharp angle to let him more fully attempt to merge his forehead with the treated wood. "Yes, I understand how annoying it would be to have your TV stuck on the same loop of the intro menu to *The Sound of Music*. That sounds awful. But it's not a problem that a technician can really solve." James thumped his head into the desk. Hard. "Have you tried unplugging your television? That would at least be a temporary fix until . . . Why not? . . . Ma'am, the contract with the cable company is not dependent on leaving the device plugged in. You have my personal promise on that . . . Yes . . . Yes, you're welcome. Have a good night."

James hung up the call, making the case notes without bothering to look at the screen. He'd done this so many times, he knew exactly how many times he had to hit the tab button to get to the bits where he had to find a way to explain that someone just wasted a half hour of the company's time because they lost their remote.

"Is it always like this?" A quiet voice caught James off-guard.

He yelped, a bit louder than he was comfortable with, and twisted sideways to try to see who was talking. As he did so, his chair rolled a bit on the hard carpet floor, which his ass hit a second later as he fell, sprawling on his back.

Turning his head slightly to the side, he saw a row of people staring at him over the low wall of the cubicle that surrounded the desk segment where James sat. Anesh was shaking his head in mock pity; JP was just watching and trying not to laugh. James couldn't see Alanna over the wall, but turning a bit more at a noise made it clear that she wasn't holding back at all and was instead visible through the gap in the cubicle wall, doubled over and roaring with laughter.

"I'm afraid so," Anesh said. "Every time we come here, this is happening. At this point, I'm willing to believe his job is secretly some form of torture."

"Hey, guys," James grumbled. "How's it going?" He rolled himself over, dragging his chair back to its normal position and hauling his slightly bruised form up into it.

He got a "good" from Anesh, and an "I'm all right, you?" from JP. Alanna was a little bit more energetic. "It is *Monday!*" she excitedly let out.

"It is Monday," James agreed. "Where's Dave? Did he decide not to come?"

Anesh shrugged. "Wanker grumbled about it a lot, but I think he was mostly just mad we didn't invite him first. He said he'd be here."

"I'm here!" The weaselly voice of their friend hit them as he ran around the corner, panting and out of breath. "The old guy gave me bad directions."

"That's weird. He gave me very efficient directions. Did you take a wrong turn somewhere?" JP asked in a pointedly neutral voice. Then, in a more concerned tone, he asked, "Why do you smell like a wet dog?"

"I had to wash a dog," Dave said. "Okay, okay, I didn't have to. But I was bored and nervous, so I washed my dog while I was waiting." He looked around at them as they all stared at him. "What? Don't you guys do things to calm down before stressful situations?"

JP shook his head. "I took a nap, but I'm also not feeling that nervous. Although I'm also not sure this isn't a big old practical joke yet."

"We hear that a lot. Also, I mostly just read the news while I wait," Anesh said. "Alanna? Any pregame rituals you want to share?"

"I'm more concerned with the fact that Dave apparently thinks that giving a dog a bath is a way to calm down. That's not normal," Alanna quipped.

James raised a hand. "I do my job?" he asked with a mix of confusion and coyness.

"Not as far as I can see." A deeper female voice sounded from the other side of the crowd of people around James's cubicle. James's own enjoyment of seeing his friends jump a bit as they were snuck up on fled quickly as his boss moved through the crowd and walked up to his desk. "James. I'm glad you're making friends, but why are they here?"

"Emotional support?" he ventured, feeling quite small in front of the short, dark-skinned woman in front of him. "Actually, I don't know why they're all here. Can you do that thing where you scare people away?" he asked, in a quieter voice.

"Go wait in the break room! I assume you know where it is!" Theo commanded, not bothering to turn around. James watched, hiding a grin, as his friends scampered away to wait for him in uncomfortable chairs. "Now, James, my favorite employee! How have you been?" She leaned on the back of his chair, a little too close for comfort.

James leaned away, trying to put some distance between his grinning supervisor and his vulnerable neck. "Oh, all right. You know. Spent another week pretending to be you. Got good at forging your signature. Forgot you were coming back tonight. The usual."

"Right," she said. "And all your friends there?"

"Mostly just here to harass me before I clock off."

"Oh reeeeeally?" she drawled out, leaning in toward James a bit more. The proximity made him quite uncomfortable, and he was having trouble coming up with convincing lies while under pressure.

James was pretty convinced Theo was a delver. Ever since Anesh had brought it up, James had been unable to believe his own explanations for her odd behavior. Sure, his boss played sports, but showing up with weird injuries was the sort of thing that *he* did. And yeah, she'd just taken a second weeklong under-the-table vacation, which was exactly the sort of thing James would pull if he could get away with it. But it was also the sort of thing that James would pull if he was taking a weeklong excursion into the dungeon. All that, mixed with her pointed questions that she asked him sometimes, made James feel like she was absolutely mixed up in all of this nonsense.

Which was what made it a really hard decision to outright lie to her.

They'd had a group discussion over the course of the week, in a private chat room that Anesh had set up for them. And at some point, JP and Alanna had both asked James exactly what it was his company *did*. Several Google searches later, it turned out that they did a whole hell of a lot. And they were diversified enough that it didn't take much imagination to think that they could absolutely be exploiting a dungeon, should it be discovered. So they'd taken a vote and collectively agreed that it was too much of a risk to outright invite Theodora to join them. Or even let on that they knew.

She would have been a great asset. James knew she had the sense of humor to get along with him and Anesh, at least; they both loved that kind of snarky banter. She would absolutely love the dungeon; James had no doubt of that. But she was management. Even if it was only low-level, she was too much of a risk to their operation. And none of them were willing to give up what they had just yet. Maybe if she ever got fired or quit, James would extend an invitation.

That was quite likely. This office had a turnover rate that rivaled the trenches of World War I.

For now, though, he just had to lie, and keep lying. He hated it. He was fundamentally an honest person. But in the pursuit of wealth and power? He'd do it.

"Really, boss-lady. Mostly just getting away with hanging out while on the clock, since no one was around to tell me otherwise," James said, rolling his chair back and causing Theo to take a half step forward before gracefully catching her balance. "Which I assumed was fine, since we're just ignoring company policy now."

Theo nodded sagely. She took a small hop and planted her short frame up on the edge of James's desk, kicking her legs out while she talked. "Hoo boy, yeah, it's a mess. I'm still waiting on info from the higher-ups on whether I'm promoted or fired."

"How long have you been waiting?" James asked, concerned.

"Since the last floor supervisor quit one night and I stole this position," Theo responded.

He thought for a second. "Wait, do you actually . . . Does the company *know* you're doing this job? Or is it just total anarchy around here?"

"Yes!" she responded with too much energy, hopping off the desk. "Now get back to work! As your elder and superior, I command it!"

"You're three years older than me," James muttered as he hit the button to rejoin the call queue. "Good evening, sir, can I get your account number for—" James cut off at the torrent of profanity. Muting his mic, he called out after his retreating boss, "I'm taking your job forever! You probably can't stop me!"

"All right, so, here's the deal tonight." James addressed the group as they filed through the breach and into Fort Door. "This is kind of short notice, so we didn't have time to get you guys any useful gear. I note with some trepidation that JP has shown up with a sword." Anesh and Alanna both winced at that comment. "So we drew straws, and Anesh has the unfortunate duty of showing you guys the ropes. Make sure you know the basics without dying."

Anesh tapped James on the shoulder. "They're not listening, mate."

They were not listening. Both JP and Dave had taken a few steps in and frozen. They were transfixed, JP by the expanse of gray and beige that he could see through the main door, and Dave by the fact that Rufus and Ganesh had both come out to greet their companions.

Rufus hesitated. There were new people, and while Ganesh had made him aware that Alanna was generally okay, he wasn't sure about the two new people. Ganesh, though, didn't hesitate. He just launched into the air with alacrity, homing in on Anesh's shoulder and his rightful perch. Unfortunately, this sudden burst of motion startled the hell out of Dave, who let out a high-pitched screech and tried to hammer Ganesh out of the air, his shoulder bag falling to the floor as he lashed out with a half-formed fist.

James pivoted, ducking under Ganesh's flight path and casually catching Dave's strike on his forearm, lowering his guard back down and taking the other man's fist down with it. "All right, ow. Calm down there, punchy," he said, mimicking Alanna's nickname for him. "I refuse to believe that no one told you about Ganesh. Relax."

"It tried to kill me!" Dave said.

"No, you wanker," Anesh said, giving Ganesh a small pet as the drone landed on his open palm, "if he wanted to kill you, he could probably take you. Relax."

James cleared his throat. Loudly. "JP, you alive?" His friend turned away from the door, where he was gaping out at the landscape. "Okay, you and Dave, over here with me." He waited for the two to assemble. "All right, here's the plan. Anesh is going to show you guys some of the low-risk areas. Alanna and I are going to go scout out what we think are the bathrooms."

He gestured around, at a loss for words to sum up their survival and loot strategy. "I . . . don't really know how to teach you guys this stuff. Um . . . any questions?" James asked the two newbies of the team.

Dave raised a hand. "You never really said how big the monsters get."

Before James could answer, JP cut in with his own question. "What's wrong with my sword? A sledgehammer isn't even a real weapon."

The two kept trading questions. "Why is there a paper airplane out there that doesn't seem to come down?"

"Is that pencil hovering?"

"Can I try one of the orbs if you have any here?"

"Are there respawns?"

"Do you have skateboards in here?"

"Do you have a map or something?"

"Bathrooms?"

James crossed his arms in an X in front of him, mimicking something he'd seen Rufus do. "Okay, okay, stop! In order, pretty big, though most of them are small. Your sword isn't going to cut it in here, pun intended. Don't ask about the blackhawk. Yes. No. Probably not. That's a good idea, but no. And yeah, we actually do have maps now. Anesh is putting them up over there." He gestured to the walls where Anesh was pinning up a bunch of posters they'd brought in.

He and his roommate had taken a lot of time and some meticulous notes and turned them into some fairly accurate maps of the areas they had knowledge of. The FedEx employee who'd helped them get poster-sized versions printed out hadn't even asked about it, which was convenient, and had left James wondering how soul-destroying that job must be. Now, the work had paid off, and they had large maps they could study, use to plan routes, and mark off looted or dangerous areas on. It felt satisfying, and also like they were putting more effort into their strategy, which James was happy with. He was reckless sometimes, but he knew the value of planning ahead.

Those maps were now tacked up on the wall next to a ton of color swatches in various tones of yellow and a poster that Alanna had brought back from somewhere in the dungeon that proudly encouraged the viewer to BE SEIZED BY OPPORTUNITY.

James agreed with Alanna. He loved that poster. Anesh hated it; he said it felt too real.

"Oh," he finished, "and the bathrooms are some kind of hundred-meter spire of tile, buried in an overgrown region of the dungeon. We think they're the bathrooms, anyway. This place is weird sometimes."

"You don't say," JP said casually, buffing his fingernails. "Well, I admit, we probably need to get our feet beneath us here. So we'll watch you guys and try to learn all the stupid things not to do. It's . . . We're interns, aren't we? James, did you make us interns?"

"No, you get paid," James said, as he started buckling the hard plastic shells of his armor on.

"Do we get armor?" JP asked with a smile.

"No, you're interns," James responded, getting a boisterous laugh from his friend. There was a reason that James liked JP. In addition to him just being a nice guy, with a soothing tone of voice and a habit for disarming awkward social situations, he was also really good at lobbing jokes low and over the plate.

Dave cut in abruptly, ending their joke spree. "Hey, what's that thing doing?"

"Rufus?" James asked, looking over at the stapler. "Oh, he's got a little garden going on over there. We're . . . not sure what he planted. Don't disturb it; it's the part of the desk marked out by pencils and filled with staples, kind of hard to miss."

"This place is weird, James," Dave said. James stared at him, wide eyes mocking, before slowly nodding. "No, I mean, really weird," he said in a rather miserable tone.

"Well, you volunteered for this, and you're our intern now," James flippantly told him as he finished securing his armor, turning himself into a black-shelled extra from a sci-fi dystopia. "But really," he followed up more sincerely, "if it makes you nervous, it's totally okay to just hang back here. We won't force you in, obviously. Just . . . take it at your own pace, okay?"

Dave nodded, grateful for the lifeline. He'd feel a lot more comfortable going exploring in this spooky place if he knew that he didn't actually have to. "Thanks, man," he said, letting out a long sigh.

"All right," James said. "If that's all the easy questions that we forgot to answer over the last couple days, I'm gonna get geared up and head out. Talk to Anesh about our general battle plans for the wildlife we tend to see around here, okay?" They both nodded, and James stretched his arms, loosening up. "All right. Have fun, try not to get hurt. I'll see you both later, okay?"

JP saluted him. "Aye, aye, mon capitan," he said with cheer. "Anesh! Tell me your secrets!" he said, jaunting off and dragging Dave along behind him.

James shook his head, making a grumbling noise in his throat. He didn't want to feel like the grumpy adult in this situation, but somehow, he was drifting into it. Even after a couple months of doing this, the sense of wonder and excitement was nowhere near fading. But it was now tempered by a healthy dose of caution, from having almost died more than once. He didn't want his friends making the same mistakes, but he sort of instinctively knew that they were going to anyway, no matter what advice they got.

"Oh, goddammit," he said aloud. "This is how my dad feels, all the fucking time."

"Feels how?" Alanna said, catching him off-guard as she walked up, already armored and holding her hammer.

James clipped his hand axe to his belt, eyeing the spear on the wall, but he ultimately decided to leave it for Anesh today. "Oh, constantly disappointed," he told her.

"That's . . . kinda sad. You, um, feeling okay?" Alanna asked with a bit of trepidation.

He shrugged in response. "I dunno. I'm having an off day. An off week. Everything feels like shit, even though I know I should be loving this. Like, I almost just yelled at JP for asking questions that I totally asked myself when I first got here. I'm just . . . trying not to take out my own shitty mood on everyone else."

"I get ya," Alanna said, resting a hand on his plated shoulder. "I can't do much to help, but do you want to go kill some stuff and level up a bit? Would that help?"

James took a deep breath. "It probably won't hurt. I'll try not to drag my feet."

Alanna squeezed his shoulder. There was a moment there when both of them considered giving the other a hug, but a mix of their own awkwardness with physical contact and the bulky padding of the armor killed that idea. They shared a smile, amused at the situation. "All right," Alanna said, "let's get out of here before Anesh goes full professor mode on those two."

"Why, what's he doing now?" James asked, still feeling a bit of that personal comfort in his chest.

Alanna pointed over to where Anesh was lecturing the two. "If you see a stapler," Anesh was saying, "do not pick it up. It might be a monster and will try to kill you. Do not touch any coffee cups; they are a trap and will kill you. Do not approach desk lamps unprotected; they are a trap and will kill you. Do not step on the joining lines of carpet sections; they are a trap and will kill you. Do not make too much noise; it will attract . . ."

"Yeah, okay," James said, tuning out his friend. "Let's go find the bathroom. I don't need a reminder of how many things in here are trying to murder me."

He and Alanna slipped out quietly, not wanting to disturb Anesh's teaching plan.

CHAPTER 38

"I want a shield," Alanna said as they ducked under a rope of braided paper hanging at about head level.

James was swinging his pack around to pull the bolt cutters out, having spotted a series of clip webs up ahead, blocking the way forward. "Why? You have a two-handed weapon."

She shrugged, setting the hammer down and taking off the thick gloves to wipe her hands while James went to work on the webs. "I could get a smaller hammer. Anesh keeps sending me links to mauls."

"Ah. Shopping mauls," James said, almost reflexively, and Alanna whapped him lightly on the back of the head.

She snorted. "Honestly, this week kind of flew by. I thought you guys would have put more work into the equipment."

"Normally we do," James responded, wincing. "We've been trying to reinvest our funds into better stuff, find new ways to fight things in here, you know. But this week Anesh had a bunch of tests, and I just felt more like crawling in a hole than doing work." He grunted as he snapped a chain of strangely durable paper clips in half. "We do have a list of stuff we want, though. Or at least, I have a list."

"Yeah? What's on it? Aside from my shield now."

"Lots of stuff, really. We need to get actual workshop equipment, and a workspace somewhere, so that Anesh doesn't have to rely on a strangely oblivious chemistry department to make us thermite . . ."

"What?"

"We need to rebuild the potato gun, or maybe just buy a black-market grenade launcher. I want to buy some bikes or, as I was just reminded, skateboards, and then clear some easy paths through the cubes to points of interest. A fast travel system, basically." James ignored her interruption.

"No, go back to the thermite." Alanna had an alarmed look on her face.

"I also want to get us some flare guns, so we can signal each other at range. Might be a little awkward, but I think it's important. More wireless cameras, though that'd be kinda awkward to actually cover enough ground. But we could use them to form small hunting grounds; those things are really expensive."

"James. Thermite," Alanna demanded.

James had set the clippers aside and was now just counting off on his gloved fingers. "A bunch of USB drives, extra backpacks to replace the ones that keep getting fucked up or turned into critter nests, backup sets of armor. Oh man, the armor is going to be so expensive, this stuff is not cheap."

"James!" She couldn't tell whether it would be better to just laugh and let him have his fun or punch the answer out of him.

Seeing the violent glint in his teammate's eye, James capitulated. "All right, all right!" He laughed, trying to smother it so he didn't make too much noise but unable to keep himself from letting out a sharp snort of laughter. He took a second to calm down, red-faced from embarrassment at the weird noise he'd made, and then answered her. "I could have sworn we told you about this. Anesh was making thermite grenades so we could kill the first tumblefeed, and then we adapted them to a big old potato gun, which . . . um . . . exploded."

She gave him a dry glare. "From the thermite?" Alanna half asked, half stated.

"No, from the lasers," James answered. "I'm positive we told you about the 2.0s, yes?" he asked tentatively.

"Oh, yeah, those things. Okay." Alanna grudgingly nodded. "So, what else did you want to buy? I mean, we can take some time on the way there to loot, if you think that's a good idea?"

James's eyes lit up. "Yes! I've actually been annoyed that we didn't get much chance for that last week, what with the stabbings and the time limit. Like, don't get me wrong, I love exploring, but I also want to make rent and eat Thai food every day."

"I hear ya. Fucking retail does not pay enough to support my ambitions," Alanna said.

James scoffed a bit as he pushed the bolt cutters back into the backpack loop. "Your ambitions are, if I recall correctly, 'ruling the world with an iron fist'?"

"You can be my henchman," Alanna said with a straight face.

"Deal," James said with a weak smile. He was having ups and downs of energy, and while Alanna was doing a good job keeping him engaged, it still didn't make it easy when it felt like he didn't have the willpower to lift his own arms.

She nodded, rapping her knuckles on James's helmet. "Excellent. Now, I'm not gonna tell you to cheer up, because that's fucking stupid, but let's go see if we can find one of those briefcases and smash it open."

"Also deal," James said, his smile strengthening into a more solid grin. The two of them swept aside the remains of the paper clip netting that was strung across the hallway and moved on, deeper into the dungeon. He kept talking as they moved on, but in a softer voice so as not to alert anything sleeping nearby. "Oh, I also wanted to buy guns for everyone."

"Guns?"

"Yeah, I think at this point, with five or more of us, the amount of firepower we could deploy probably offsets the danger of the noise," James rationalized as Alanna went cube to cube, quickly grabbing wallets. "I mean, I haven't brought my gun because Anesh and I have had to run from swarms before when we were too loud, and I thought that—"

Alanna cut him off. "You own a gun?" she demanded. "Fucking you? You hate guns!"

"I have viewpoints on guns as an element of society. That's different than hating guns," James retorted. He checked the cubicle door on the opposite side of the aisle from Alanna's looting spree. The first one had a stapler on the desk, and another lurking on top of a set of drawers. Maybe the dungeon had spawned the cube of—he checked the nameplate—Martha Willard to belong to someone who just really loved staplers. Maybe she frequently lost them and kept a spare. Maybe she had to staple so much during the day, at such a fast pace, that she needed a second stapler to keep up the flow while the first one was reloaded.

Or, maybe, James was going to save his energy and skip this one.

While he dug through the dry cleaning hanging in the stapler-free zone, Alanna hollered over at him, "You are on record as saying, and I am quoting you here, 'no one should be allowed to own a gun, ever, you can quote me on this.' Is that or is that not true?"

James stepped out into the hallway, sixty-three dollars richer. Sixty-nine if you counted six-dollar bills, which he did not. "I said that, sure. I don't think I should be exempt, either. I'm just hypocritical. Or maybe I'm outside society, since I'm spending a good five percent of my life in another dimension? Either way, the gun is for here, not out there. Which, yes, shut up, is not a good excuse." He rolled over Alanna's protest as she came out of the last cube on her side, tossing a wallet back into it while pulling out folded bills.

"Your political views need some touch-ups. Also, hey, I keep finding loyalty cards for coffee shops that don't exist. What's up with that? Like, the money is for a country that's real, presumably. Why not the gift cards and stuff?"

James thought for a minute. "Maybe it's . . . No, that's stupid." He started counting off on his fingers. "If it's random what it duplicates, then the money doesn't make sense. If it's not random, then the cards don't make sense. If they're both random, then we've just gotten lucky?"

"Wait." Alanna held up a hand. "How does the nonreal money factor in? Like, the three-dollar bills?"

"Fuck, this place confuses me so much," James grumbled. "Everything here comes across like the GM is just leaning on a bunch of d100 tables, except..."

"Except there's holes in that," Alanna muttered, sharing a look with James, as if prompting him to provide an answer.

James idly rapped his knuckles on the wall next to him a couple of times as he considered it. Alanna looked at him expectantly, waiting to see if he had any better ideas than she did. Alanna was the sort of person who knew her capabilities pretty well, and also knew about the point where she lost any ability to contribute. James and Anesh were sci-fi and fantasy people; Alanna just wasn't, not to the same degree. She played D&D with them for the role-playing, much like how JP played for the characterization and social element. She just wasn't there to be part of a high-fantasy experience.

But James? James was. Anesh certainly was. They built worlds, they had brains full of tropes and magic systems. They made narrative connections. If Alanna was going to trust anyone to figure this place out, it was them. She was here as muscle and for the free education; James could be the one to unravel the mysteries.

"I got nothing," he said, looking up from his examination of the carpet.

Alanna snapped out of her reverie and almost choked on her own laughter, covering her mouth and turning it into a cough so as not to make James think she was mocking him.

And it was like that, with Alanna half laughing and half hacking up a lung, that the first stapler threw itself off the top of the cubicle behind James and slammed pointy bit first into Alanna's back.

The armor, thick padding and hard plastic that made them look like extras from a bad dystopia movie, stopped the staple from going into the flesh of her back. Hell, the armor was probably thicker than a staple was anyway, regardless of the fact that it was pretty hard to puncture. But it was still one of those bulky staplers, the kind that looked like a brick and weighed roughly as much.

Alanna stumbled forward, not staggered or winded, but caught off-guard and shocked. She flailed her arms and caught her balance on the nearest felt wall. James snapped out a warning, but she wasn't listening, instead trying to grab the stapler still dangling from her armor. The staple held it in place like a cat's claws caught in drapes, and right in that spot where human arms can't reach. She was just righting herself and stretching her arms around to grab it when the second one hit her in the face.

This one didn't bite; instead the strider itself was caught off-guard by her sudden change in position and just slammed into her cheek. Alanna jerked backward, a few drops of blood splattering the floor as her face was gashed open. But the cut was small; the real damage was the spike of pain through her jaw and the feeling like one of her teeth was loose.

There was a crack from nearby. James had snagged a third strider, thrown it to the ground in its open state, and just stomped on it until whatever it had that passed for a spine cracked in half. Alanna did the same thing, sort of: bringing a heel down to pin the one that had hit her on the floor, bending a few of its pen-legs and keeping it in place while she got the other one off her back.

"These fucking things—" She was interrupted by a crash as, from the door of the cube behind James, a shellaxy bulldozed its way through. It hit the wall a bit on the way out, knocking it out of alignment with the rest of the hall. Perched on its back, just above the flaring blue LED eye of the computer below it, was a single strider. It looked noble, almost, atop its mount; fancier pens with gold clips and cursive script made up its legs, giving it a regal appearance. Below it, the shellaxy was a mess of power cables, spreading out like a mobile thornbush to haul its body forward. The two CD drives on its front were open, showing off multiple rows of circuit-board teeth.

James effortlessly slid into a fighting stance, toes pointed in the same direction, feet spaced apart with one forward and one back, keeping his center of balance perfect.

Then he hit that strider with a snap kick that sent it soaring down the hallway, tumbling end over end in a dazed pile of executive pens and dripping a few spots of ichor. Bringing the kick around, he planted his foot on the other side of the shellaxy and shuffled his other leg around to place himself behind the angry, but unwieldy, beast.

Alanna took the strider she'd managed to grab off her back and chucked it at the face of the beast. It made a satisfying metal crunch as it hit, which made her grin, even as James winced at the assault on his ears. The strider righted itself quickly and equally quickly got trampled by the shellaxy as it charged Alanna. Those teeth were inset, and hard to actually clamp down on a person, but James had let her know that the shellaxies could pop open unseen hinges to really get into someone's arm or leg, and Alanna was less than one hundred percent confident in the armor's ability to stop a rampaging PC.

She backpedaled, keeping an eye on it but also looking at James as he rushed down the hallway, building up speed in the short space he had. As she stepped backward, Alanna snagged up the sledgehammer from where she'd left it leaning against one of the cube doors during their little looting stop, pulling it into a batting stance as the shellaxy closed the gap between them.

Then James caught up to it and lunged forward, slamming both knees into its side. The creature tried to keep itself upright, and its thick tangle base of cables did a good job of doing that, but as James let himself fall forward, putting more and more weight down, it inevitably toppled.

It also tried to bite his arm as he caught himself on the ground. Those hidden hinges popped part of its mouth open, and it struggled forward to sink its teeth into his wrist and forearm. But he jerked his arm upward before it could shred the armor, using the momentum to roll himself sideways off the shellaxy. He left behind a few scraps of cloth on its teeth, but he got away mostly clean.

And then there was a heavy crunching thud as Alanna slammed the hammer down onto its side. The metal case dented inward, and the shellaxy started flailing even harder to drag itself back upright. But before it could make too much progress, she brought the sledgehammer around in another arc and hit it again, pushing it back down. And again, and again. The metal warped under repeated strikes, until screws were popping out and its innards were exposed. And then there was enough room to swing the hammer through the gap and into its insides, and there was a pop and a spray of bluish-gray liquid that smelled strangely like coolant to James, and it went still.

James nodded up at Alanna from his spot on the floor as she swung her weapon back over a shoulder and stood there, framed against the fluorescent lights of the ceiling, grinning down at him. "Okay, I'm gonna take a nap down here," James said. "Good job. You go on withouuu—owwww!" He screamed as the forgotten stapler sank metal into the thinner part of one of his gloves, the feeling of a needle going into the webbing between two of his finger joints both painful and nauseating.

He grabbed it, feeling the staple pop out and a rush of warm fluid start drenching his glove. It wasn't hard for him, at this point, to just snap these things open. But there was always the risk of dropping them when he did, as they struggled constantly. This time, though, it wasn't getting away. A short rush of pained enthusiasm filled James as he tore the protective cover back and smashed the stapler down on the floor, sending staples and ichor flying in equal parts.

"Okay!" he said with a snarl. "I'm super angry these things are mostly metal, because I would *eat* that fucker if I could!"

Alanna was half frozen between bringing the hammer around and not wanting to hit James. After he disposed of the enemy, though, she dropped it and quickly started looking for her first-aid kit. "Yeah, well, maybe we'll find something farther in you can snack on. Oh! Coffee elemental?"

"Don't jinx us. We don't talk about possible monsters. It's bad form," he responded as she rubbed blood off his hand.

She just whapped him on the helmet. "You two have been here maybe four times more than I have. You cannot possibly have superstitions yet."

James tapped his temple as he stood up and pulled his glove back on. "Oh, you'll see," he said. "I know how this works. You'll believe me soon enough.

"Stop it! I don't want to believe your weird nontraditions!" Alanna laughed as she collected the yellow orbs. "So, want to crack these now?"

"Sure. I'll take two of the smalls; you take the big one and the other small. Seems fair, since you did most of the work," James offered.

"I'd argue with you, but whatever, I ain't gonna turn down free . . . free what? EXP?" Alanna trailed off. "What do we call the output of the orbs?"

James stared at her for a couple seconds. "Skills. 'Cause it says skills," he said flatly, maintaining direct eye contact and an intentionally comedic incredulous look while he raised his hand and cracked the two orbs in his fist.

[+1 Skill Rank : Cooking - Baking]

[+1 Skill Rank : Judo]

"I'm getting really lucky lately with these martial arts ones," he said.

Alanna threw a mock punch at him, and he ducked it and started strolling off. "Heh. Yeah, I can see how that's helping you," she muttered as she cracked her own orbs. "I'm gonna need a new hobby if you get good enough at dodging."

[+1 Skill Rank : Geology - Rock Identification - Igneous]

[+2 Skill Ranks : Repair - Smoke Alarm]

"Jaaaaaames!" she called after him as he stepped out of the next cube down, which he'd been looting. "I hate these things now!"

"I hear that a lot." James nodded sagely. "Hey, so, I think we should probably be keeping a bit quieter. And moving away from here. We made a ton of noise on that guy, and . . . I dunno, but did it feel like we disturbed a nest or something to you?"

Alanna cut the joking tone. "Yeah, I got that feeling," she said. "Like, they were a unit, not random monsters."

James agreed with her. "Maybe it's 'cause we're deeper in. Well, regardless. Update the map, I'm going to go check that corner. We'll just have to be more careful. Oh, and . . . I totally forgot, we were supposed to be checking the colors on these things." Alanna slapped her forehead as he reminded her. "Yeah, so, maybe we don't tell Anesh about this part? He's ... really into the record keeping."

"All right. I'm with you there. He's scary sometimes when he's disappointed," Alanna replied.

The two of them moved on, deeper into the dungeon. They were a bit richer, and a bit more tired, and now they had a tiny bit more of an edge against the world. It felt good, and for James, it was even enough to make him raise his chin up, stand a little straighter, and put some vigor into his movement. For a while, at least.

"What the fuck is that ..." Alanna whispered.

She and James were crouched at a T intersection, peeking around the corner. At the far end, the cubicles opened up a bit, spreading out on either side, and had lower walls. Not waist high, like the clusters of desks where the decision tree grew, but still low enough that Alanna could see over it on her toes. James could too, if he got Alanna to give him a lift up, which he was not prepared to sacrifice his dignity doing.

At the end of the intersection, there was a window. Natural light poured in, mixing with the sharp white of the fluorescents, creating a kind of sickly-feeling atmosphere. James stared at it, trying to make out what was on the other side but seeing nothing but a pale white blob beyond the pane of glass set into the wall.

"It's a window," he said. And promptly got smacked on the back of his helmet by Alanna, who was perched over him. One of the downsides to peeking around corners Scooby-Doo style was that he didn't have much of a chance to dodge the fallout of his snide comments.

"It can't be a window, you chungus," Alanna told him. "We're not in ... a ... building?" She trailed off again. "Are we in a building?" she asked. "Did you guys ever establish where the hell we are? Like, is this actually just a dimension that ends at the walls, or is this ... in ... a ... place?"

James rolled his head up to look at his teammate. "You forgot how English works, huh? But really, we don't know. We never knocked out the walls to check if there's an endless Minecraft void out there. You're the one with the hammer, want to try later?"

"No."

"Your loss, I guess?" James snarked. "But hey, if you want, we can go check the window out, we can see if there's an outside. That might have some, let's say, consequences." That was putting it lightly. As far as James was concerned, a single office as a subdimension? That was okay. But a whole world?

A world couldn't be contained as easily as keeping an eye on one door for three minutes a week. A world implied a lot of horrible shit, especially since things got objectively worse and worse the farther from the door they got. There were a lot of things that a world could contain that went far and away beyond the scope of an office. Things that James knew, beyond any doubt, that he and Anesh couldn't handle. No matter how many friends they brought in.

Alanna agreed, and the two of them crept forward, keeping quiet and checking the cubes around them. They actually did have to crouch-walk; the ceilings in the corridor they'd come down weren't that low, but there were a lot of jutting features that stuck down from them, beige spikes of wall material that made maneuvering awkward. They'd kept low after a sudden iLipede had leapt onto James's head from one of the stalactites, freaking him out and trying to claw through his helmet.

So they waddled along, low to the ground and down far enough that they had a range of vision in the dark tunnels, using the flashlights that James had kept since the start to spot any potential ambushers. The whole thing had netted them four more small yellow orbs and a healthy hatred for low ceilings. It opened up ahead, and they were both looking forward to standing up again.

Of course, the walls couldn't just go back to normal. And the area around the window actually ended in the wall that the window was set into. James could see it, but not how high it reached, since there was actual ceiling here. Foam tiles and all. There was an aisle along the wall, too, so James knew they could follow it down the rows, and maybe find a quicker shortcut through to the bathrooms. Scouting was the point of this trip, no matter what distractions he and Alanna got up to.

"Hold up," Alanna said. "You hear that?"

"No, what?" James froze. He strained his ears but didn't hear anything except for the hum of monitors and lights around them. "I don't hear anything."

She held up a hand and tilted her head. "It's the same as... There!" Alanna pointed at the floor, and it took James a second to realize that she was pointing at the carpet. Specifically, the split in the carpet.

"Fuck, pencil trap?" James asked, and Alanna shrugged, nodding. "Yeah, that's an issue. Hang on." He took the flashlight, clicked it off, and lobbed it forward. There was enough light here that he didn't need it in hand at the moment, and Maglites were built like tanks, so he wasn't worried it was going to break.

It hit the tripline, and nothing happened.

"Huh," Alanna said. "Did you miss?" She rolled her own flashlight along the floor, a rattling metal tube meant to trip the trap and clear their way. And again, nothing happened.

James actually *growled* at the trap trigger. "Don't tell me this is one of those bullshit traps that only trigger with a live human?"

"Oh, an iPhone screen, but as a trap," Alanna suggested.

"I hate that I believe that." He stood up. "Okay, I got this. Hang on." James shuffled forward, bit by bit, toward the line. "Get ready to run, I guess?" he said, and then pushed his toe the last inch and hit it.

There was an electric snap, static discharging, and then a soft grinding. James looked around but didn't spot where the trap was. Then the pencil darts started pouring past. On his right side, from *behind them*. From the back of the hall, at the corner they'd just turned. The first volley was on the far left of the path as he turned to see it. Then another line of shots hit a little closer, a bit farther to the right. But he could see those telltale holes opened up all across the wall.

The next line fired, and James jerked into action before it was too late. He stepped forward and grabbed Alanna under the shoulder.

The next line fired, and one of the pencils glanced off his elbow plate, leaving a scar in the plastic from the razor tip. He hauled with all his might and rolled his friend across the floor, from the right side where she was crouched to the left, as another row fired.

James pivoted, trying to get himself clear of the next row as well. He'd crossed Alanna over the line of fire, and now he needed to do the same himself. He almost made it before another line fired, and he felt pressure on his chest. Then he and Alanna were against the far wall, and the darts finished firing, hitting nothing but air and the wall around the window downrange.

The whole thing took maybe six seconds.

"Whoof." James let out a gasp. "You've, uh, got a dart in your hair." He reached up and plucked the yellow number-two writing tool out of Alanna's ponytail, a strangely intimate gesture, as the two of them sat there half leaning against each other, coming down from the adrenaline rush as they came to terms with how close death had been.

She shook herself a bit, swallowing heavily. "Thanks. You've, uh . . ." She reached down and pulled, and James felt another bit of pressure. He looked down and saw a pencil buried in the front of his armor suit. If he'd been a half second slower, it wouldn't have cut into the side of his torso padding, it would have embedded itself in the side of his *torso*.

"Well. Well!" he said, with a shaky voice. "Let's get the fuck out of here before that sets back up again."

The two of them crossed the line and took a couple of chairs into one of the cubes near the window. They sat for a bit, slightly more comfortable than being on the floor. James trying to stop shaking as Alanna made a note on their map about the trap here.

"Hey," he said, "add a ten-foot pole to that list of things we need to buy."

The D&D reference wasn't lost on her, but Alanna just responded, "I didn't write that down! I'm keeping the map, you keep the shopping list."

James scowled as he went to pull out his phone before realizing it was in pockets now covered by armor pads. "I'll do that before we leave, sure." He started poking around while Alanna marked lines and made notes on their progress. Usually, he'd loot while she did this, and they'd both come out happy with their work.

This time, he fired up the laptop first. Password protected: score. James had come to two conclusions over their delves about the pattern of computers. First of all, if they had a password, then they had blue-orb-laced files on them. These were essentially digital treasure chests. He didn't know what to think of that, really. It implied that they were intentionally placed there to be opened, which was uncomfortable at best. Second, he'd realized that the dungeon had a strangely functional sense of social engineering as a method of breaking passwords.

People in reality often wrote passwords down. If not, then they used passwords that were birthdays or pet names or phrases they liked. In the real world, websites were getting wise to this and requiring numbers or capital letters, and ruining the ability for sneaky bastards the world over to trick passwords out of people. But the dungeon hadn't caught up to modern security yet, it seemed.

It took James six tries to hit on the answer. It was the name of the dog in one of the photographs on the desk. The dog photos never actually stopped freaking him out; something about the eyes wasn't quite right. But the name tag on the dog, *Harvock*, got him into the system.

He poked around for a bit before stumbling onto an .mp3 file, just as Alanna was clicking her pen away and folding up the map back into the file folder in her backpack. "All right, done," she said. "Ready to go?"

"Hang on, I want to see what this is." James turned in the chair and pointed. "I found an audio file. It's the only thing on here, and usually these things are weird. Want to check it out?"

Alanna leaned over and swiftly snatched the mouse from him and double-clicked it. "Yes!" she said enthusiastically.

"I don't want you to go," said the voice on the computer. It was a young girl, maybe ten to twelve. "You need to quit!" The words had all the conviction of a child who knew they were correct, no questions asked.

The voice that responded was male. Older, maybe early forties. "Sorry, little shark. But it's important. People count on me. You wouldn't want me to let everyone down, would you?"

"But . . . but . . ." the child responded.

"Hey, you wouldn't like it if I let you down, right?" the adult, probably her father, said.

There was a sniffle, the kind you got from kids trying and failing to hold back tears. "You'll come back?" she asked in a tiny, quiet voice.

"I'll—" The thirty-second audio file ended there.

James sat back in the chair. "Huh. That's weird. Do you have any idea what—" He turned to Alanna and saw her standing against the far wall, jaw clenched, one of her arms held over her eyes. "Hey, what's up? Are you okay?" James trailed off, knowing how useless that question sounded.

Alanna sniffed in a wet breath of air. It reminded James for all the world like that little girl from the recording. He stood up and went over to check on her, and as he approached, Alanna dropped her arm to show a tear-stained face. "That was . . . that was my dad," she gasped out. "I remember that night. That was my dad," she repeated.

"Hey, talk to me. What's going on?" James said, confused.

Alanna took a breath and wiped away her eyes with gloved hands. "When I was eleven, my dad went out on an assignment. That was me, talking to him, the night he left." She waved a hand loosely at the laptop. "I don't know why, but that was it. Exactly what I remember him saying, exactly what I said. Like they recorded the whole thing, over a decade ago."

He nodded, listening, but then stopped, as a thought occurred to him. "Wait, why do you remember it?"

"It was the last time I saw him," Alanna said. "He was . . ." Her words caught in her throat. "He was a cop. He died. That's all. That was the last thing he said to me." She shook silently, trying and failing to hold back tears.

James stepped forward. Normally, he was awkward comforting people, but this time, something pushed him forward. He put his hands on Alanna's shoulders, holding her steady. "Hey," he said. "It's okay. It's not . . . okay. But I'm here for you, if you need anything." She fell forward into him, and he found himself trying to comfort and hug someone while both of them were wearing full body armor.

After a few minutes, she straightened up, wiping the fresh tears away and catching her breath. "Thanks," she said with a small smile. "For everything."

"Anytime." James smiled back. He didn't know what *everything* she was talking about, but he knew what it meant to be in grief, to fall apart like that. He also knew when it was important to change the mood. "Hey, want to delete that file? I can't promise it'll give a blue orb, but maybe it'll be satisfying for you?"

"No!" Alanna said quickly. "No, please. I'd like to . . . save it, if that's okay."

"Sure," James said, pulling a USB drive out of one of the armor pockets. "We can do that."

She looked at him weirdly, her tone turning from shaky to wry in a heartbeat. "You're just carrying that?"

"Yeah, duh," he said, sitting back at the laptop. "What if we find a file that we like?" Alanna stared at him, unbelieving. "Like, for example, this one!" he said, turning back to the computer.

As he reached for the mouse, though, he accidentally clicked again, fumbling with his gloved hand. And in doing so, he hit the play button again, and the file started playing.

"I'm not gonna tell him." A male voice came through the speakers. Alanna and James both looked at each other, eyebrows raised. The voice sounded vaguely familiar to James, but he couldn't quite place it.

"Just do it!" a young woman's voice came back. It was cheerful and bright, and James could almost feel the room lighting up as she spoke. "What's the worst that could happen? It's a great idea, trust me, I know everything!"

"Eeehhhh. I dunno." There was a long pause. "What if it turns out he doesn't feel the same way? Can you imagine how awkward that would be? We'd have to deal with . . ."

The file ended again.

"James, what the shit was that?"

He looked up at her, panic in his eyes. "I don't know! I hit play again, and it was something else!"

"That was you, talking, wasn't it?" she said. "When was that?"

"That's what I sound like?" he asked, surprised. "Wait, no, that couldn't have been me. I don't remember that conversation."

Alanna bopped him on the helmet again. "You can forget conversations. Maybe it was one of the less important ones."

"No, I mean, I don't recognize who the other person speaking is," he said. "It doesn't sound like anyone I know. And the tone of the conversation seems pretty serious, not something I'd talk to a stranger about. So . . . if that's me, who am I talking to?"

"Fucking weird," Alanna said grimly. "Okay, save that file. Let's go check out the window and then get a move on. We've got an hour and a half left to get there and turn around."

James did so, careful not to play it again. "Are we going to worry about this at all?" he asked as he pocketed the USB drive. "It seems like another weird dungeon thing that I'm going to hate."

"Oh, absolutely," Alanna said. "But right now? Fuck it. I'm angry about things outside my control again, so let's go find something I can smash the fuck out of."

He patted her on the shoulder as they walked back to the hallway. "Your method of anger management needs work. But I'm here to help, so, hey. Want to break a window?"

"Absolutely," she replied, and the two of them shared a smile before turning to investigate the glowing square.

They moved forward, trying to push their moods away from the sudden burst of darkness that had been dredged up. James didn't really know exactly how Alanna was feeling, but *recklessly violent* would be his first guess. So he moved at double time checking the low-walled cubicles for monster nests as they approached the window. They all seemed clear, but there were a couple coffee cups on desks that he let Alanna know about. James also had to push aside a lot of paper curtains to check everything.

And then they were at the window. Well, almost. They paused at the intersection with the aisle along the wall and waited for a flock of paper to fly by overhead. James kept an eye on the makeshift birds, wondering if another paper airplane would show up. But none did, and once the rustling noise passed, he and Alanna moved forward.

The window was semi-opaque, the kind of frosted glass that you saw in hospitals, usually. Alanna moved to press her face against it, but James had a weird feeling and held her back. "Hang on, something isn't right."

"Of course something isn't right. This isn't the exterior wall," Alanna told him. "I looked at the map. This wall cannot be the outside of the dungeon. So do you want to just open it with smashing?" She hoisted the hammer. James looked around, trying to figure out what it was that had set him on edge. While he did so, not responding, Alanna shrugged and moved up. "I see a splash of green down there," she said, looking through the window. "A tree, maybe? Can't tell if there's cars." She looked up, trying to peer around the edges. "No sun or anything. Maybe 'cause it's almost four a.m. But then why's it bright?"

"I think we should get out of here, actually," James said, with a little more urgency. He'd realized what it was that was bothering him.

Alanna glanced at him, turning away from the window. "Why?"

"Because," James said, pointing at the window with one hand while he unclipped his axe with the other. "There are shadows moving on the other side of that thing, and you just looked down. So that means that we're not at ground level, and those are . . ."

There was a hollow, echoing *thunk* from the windowpane.

"Birds," James said.

Another *thunk*, louder this time. The sheet of glass, set into an otherwise featureless wall, cracked slightly down the middle.

There were more shadow shapes moving on the other side. A lot more. Alanna took a step backward as the ambient light from the window was blotted out by the moving, fluttering shapes on its other side. There was another hit, and another. The glass held for a few more, but then the crack widened.

"Jaaaaames," she said, unsure what to do and looking for guidance.

James looked at the window, then looked around. He wanted to say *Run* and call it good, but it was too late for that. They were too deep in the dungeon. They could not, *absolutely could not* get lost now. They had to stay on the mapped path. He looked, and thought, and got an answer.

"Run!" he shouted. "This way!" And he turned and ran back the way they came.

Alanna turned to follow, and the window shattered behind them.

The window itself didn't break. It . . . shifted. Something hit it, and it shattered outward, and the shards of glass, instead of spraying onto the floor, layered themselves onto the form that came through. It had no body; it wasn't a body at all. It was just the window itself, breaking inward, the vaguely bird-shaped thing that flew through looking half like it was built out of broken glass on the fly, and half like it was diving through a pool and leaving an afterimage. Instead of a dangerous patch of ground to walk on, there was only a single large long-necked bird, like a crane. Except for the additional set of wings offset ninety degrees from the more normal pair, and the fact that its entire body was split open along the middle, a molten red core showing through. A crucible, fed by hundreds of grinding glass teeth.

Alanna barely glimpsed the thing before turning and sprinting with James. James himself saw none of this, and didn't want to. He had a plan, and if it worked, maybe they'd live.

He let go of Alanna's hand, the two of them running full tilt, her right on his heels. And then he hit the line in the carpet. He had to stagger a step to do it right, because he was aiming for it. He hugged the right side, and Alanna mimicked him.

There was the feeling of static discharging. And the darts started flying.

James wanted to roar a challenge to the trap, to dare it to hit him as he ran full-bore down its sights. The holes at the end of the hallway were already starting to fire on the left side, sweeping across the open space with row after row of needle-point pencil darts. But he couldn't spare the breath. Behind him, Alanna found the energy to let out a furious yell as the incoming fire got closer and closer to their left flank.

Just a few more steps, James thought. Another row of darts whipped past; these were close enough to touch. One more step; another row, these right next to him.

He grabbed the corner of the cubicles and swung himself around, converting momentum so fast he almost fell. But he couldn't fall, and he couldn't pay any attention to the pain in his fingers. He reached back, grabbed Alanna by an outstretched wrist, and *hauled*, bringing her around the corner just as the darts started firing their last three rows. The rows that would have killed them.

But they didn't.

Two seconds later, there was a sound like a waiter dropped a tray of dishes, and the impaled form of a glass bird skidded to a stop at the end of the hallway, right at James's feet.

Panting, Alanna stood up, slipped her grip on the sledgehammer down from near the head where she'd held it during their run, and brought it down on the creature made up of milky-white shards.

It practically exploded under the impact; glass sprayed out across the floor, some of it molten. Alanna swore as a few droplets hit her legs, cooling quickly but still red-hot beads of melted glass.

There was silence again.

James rolled over and pushed himself up to his feet. Alanna stooped down to grab the small green orb floating above the body.

"Let's find a different way around," they both said at the same time.

CHAPTER 39

"It wasn't like this last time." Alanna winced. She was sitting in one of the chairs, this one devoid of both wheels and comfort. James was currently applying a bandage to her left hand, affixing the adhesive to the bits not currently slathered in disinfectant or blood.

They'd backtracked and taken a different turn about a quarter mile back from the window, and when that path had hit a dead end, they'd gone back and done it again. Along the way, though, as they poked through oddly shaped desks and coats with the wrong number of sleeves, they encountered resistance. An escalating amount of resistance, really.

The disturbing part wasn't that there was more life, all of it hostile. It wasn't even that there were new things trying to kill them. Neither of those was the case. It was that the things that were trying to kill them were getting smarter. Or maybe just luckier. Either way, the handful of striders that were currently causing problems for them were not making it easy for the pair to fight back.

Every time they stopped to loot, every time they tried to take a water break, every rest or pause for conversation. Every. Single. One. They were there. Six striders, moving as a unit. They came in fast, took one or two hits at the pair of humans, and then they were gone. Back over walls or up into the arches that made up the low-hanging false ceiling above them. The damn things would pop up, harass, and flee.

It was very frustrating to James, who had gotten used to surviving fights and being rewarded with skill orbs. It was even more frustrating to Alanna, who was getting stabbed a lot more than she wanted to.

"Yeah, I'm not a fan either," James told her as he finished applying the bandage, and she slipped her glove back on carefully. "This isn't something I've seen either."

Alanna flexed her fingers. "We should get out of here," she said. "I'm getting the impression that this place is kind of shit."

James shoved stuff back into the medkit as fast as he could, ignoring organization in favor of getting moving faster. "Agreed. When we get back, we can mark this hallway as unusable. What the fuck is going on with these guys, anyway? It's like fighting Stapler Team Six over here."

"Maybe they're elites. Do you think they drop better orbs?" Alanna asked as they started backtracking once again. The two of them moved with their backs to each other, watching the walls around them with sharp eyes. They both had their weapons in hand and were in no mood to fuck around anymore. A dozen small attacks had made them wary, and a handful of bruises and puncture wounds had made them angry.

Which was why it was extra bonus frustrating that they hadn't been able to land a single hit on their assailants.

"I doubt it," James said. "Because that would be cool, and so far, no part of this is cool to me." He was a little bitter. James wasn't like Anesh, who could calmly plan out a way to counter bullshit like this; he was a fan of the stand-up fight, the contest of skill and might. And, yeah, he was fine *applying* bullshit tactics to things in here; it just stung to be on the other end of it.

They moved on as quickly as they could, cutting back through the hallways. James almost had a heart attack when they passed a water cooler and Alanna bumped into it, making it move just enough that he thought it was alive. She didn't even take the time to mock him for slamming his hatchet into it; she just took a second to assess the situation, made sure the tank was actually not trying to kill them, and then motioned him onward.

Pulses raced and palms sweated as they kept moving. They didn't dare stay still, not here. Nothing physically had changed; they were still moving through slightly warped cubicles, with the occasional feature like a water cooler or potted plant, either of which might try to kill them. There were banners and vines of paper and sticky notes, there were posters and nonsense regulation sheets tacked-up. It all looked more or less like what they'd come to expect as normal from the area. The only difference was in the shift in tone.

For the first time, James felt like he was being hunted.

"Fuck," he heard Alanna mutter, and James spun quickly before she caught him and pushed him back. "No, stay there!" she snapped, the tension getting to her. "I just saw one of them, two cubes back. It's just watching, I think it's trying to be a decoy." James really, really wanted to look. The desire was an almost physical pressure at the back of his head, but he resisted it for now.

"Shit," James said, and followed that up quickly with "No, don't look. I heard something from one cube up. Might be a shell."

"Might be the rest of them," she muttered back in a low voice.

James's eyes darted around the walls around them. There was only one hallway out of here, unless they got desperate and punched deeper into the territory of these shockingly vicious striders. They had to go this way if they wanted to get out and stay in their own mapped zone of the dungeon. But now, with Alanna spotting their enemy's scout, and James hearing small noises from up ahead, it was feeling more and more like this was a trap of some kind.

"Okay," James said quietly, "we can probably assume this is a trap. Do you think they'll actually be able to stop us if we just run?"

"No," Alanna said with confidence.

James nodded and reached behind himself to tap her on the shoulder. "Great. Run." He said it flatly, but with determination, making it clear that he meant it.

Alanna hesitated for a second, tensing up. Then she flexed her muscles and kicked into sudden and powerful motion, long strides eating up the distance to the end of this hall and the possibility of safety. James was right on her heels, the thud of his heavier boots mixing with the dull impact of Alanna's running shoes as they gave up on trying to deal with this menace and just hoofed it.

The still air whipped by James's head as they built up speed, whistling across his helmet. Alanna almost stumbled as she slammed weight down on her bruised leg, but she recovered and kept going. Both of them were already tired; they hadn't had a chance to really rest, they were both battered, and they had a few extra stabs in them. But all of that wasn't enough to make either of them not put their whole heart into this run.

The hallway was long. Too long. There were a few tiny gaps between some of the cubicle rows, but they weren't really intersections. And Alanna had heard from Anesh and James just how awful it was to get pinned down in one of those tiny crevices. So they were left with a mostly straight line of about sixty cubes to run down and hope that they could put enough distance between them and the threat.

They hit their stride, blazing past one of the cubicle doors every second, closing the gap. Both of them felt their breath running short, but the end was in sight. James started to slow a bit to prepare for the right angle of a turn, making sure that he was far enough to Alanna's right that he was in no danger of running over her if she stopped suddenly.

Alanna stopped suddenly.

James skidded to a halt beside her.

He doubled over, gasping for breath, before coming back up with a groan. The reason Alanna had slammed on the brakes was that there was a strider in front of them, standing in the hallway in plain sight. It was holding up a single leg to them, and Alanna had chosen to stop rather than just power through.

"Why..." James started to ask, breathless. Alanna cut him off, just pointing up a bit. And there, on the arch over the hallway, formed by the wall of the cubicle on the left side bending backward like an ancient tree, stood four more striders. Two pairs of them, each pair holding between them, with delicate stability, a single not-Starbucks cardboard coffee cup. "Well. Shit," James said. A spike of fear went through him, and his legs tensed up as he prepared to lunge away from the oncoming explosion.

But it didn't come, and James started to feel a bit of confusion. Alanna, next to him, tapped her fingers down the handle of her hammer, deliberately not hefting it or making threats. "Are they going to kill us, or . . ." she muttered out of the side of her mouth.

She shut up as the strider on the ground in front of them stepped forward. This was very clearly one of the group that had been harassing them with the constant attacks. It was bright green, one of the variants they'd seen around with a pair of eyes, one on the top of its head, and the other right on the front. James had to repress a snicker, since it also had what looked like a dead strider drawn in marker on its side.

"It has a tiny tattoo!" he whispered to Alanna, who just punched him lightly on the arm to shut him up.

The strider stepped forward and rolled a single tiny yellow orb out onto the floor. James was confused, though for an odd reason. While Alanna was trying to figure out what it was doing, he was more curious where the hell the thing had been storing the orb. After placing the yellow bead on the floor, the strider tapped its foreleg down on the ground next to it a few times and then made a sweeping motion toward James and Alanna.

Alanna looked over at him. "What?"

"Oh, we're being robbed!" James said with a surprising amount of relief. "They want our skill orbs!" He sighed deeply. "Yeah, this is totally fine. You okay if I go into my pack to get them out?" he asked the striders in front of him before moving. James was more or less okay with trading a few orbs for his life, or at least to avoid serious burns, and so he planned on being careful to avoid provoking any sudden attacks.

But his partner had other ideas. "Hell no, I'm not giving up my loot!" Alanna said. "We worked hard for those!" It was impressive that she could be indignant even when on the wrong end of explosives.

"Yeah, but they have bombs. Look, they got us this time. And, hey"—James turned his words to the strider—"you're gonna let us go after this, right? Like, no backstabbing? We both walk away?" It nodded, then made the sweeping gesture again. "See? It's fine. We just give them all the orbs we have."

He reached into the outer pouch, pulled out four small yellows and one that was slightly less small, along with a single red orb, and knelt down to place them gently on the ground next to the one the strider had used to prompt the mugging. The stapler bandit moved over, poked at them, and then with a twitch of its leg shoved the red one back toward James.

"You guys don't care for these either, eh?" he said. "Yeah, I'm not a fan myself." The strider let out a chirping hiss, and another two stapler-crabs darted out from the cubicles to the sides, collecting the orbs and scurrying away. "So no hard feelings for trying to hit you with a hatchet? We can go now?" James asked.

It was almost magic how quickly the staplers vanished. They were gone in a heartbeat, back into hiding spots or up into the ceiling, leaving James and Alanna alone with only a pair of coffee cups balanced gently on the arch above them.

Alanna shoved James forward. "Let's get out of here before those fall. I'm not going to get fucked up by coffee if I can't sue a company for damages over it. Especially not since you gave away our damned loot."

"It's less giving, more surrendering," James said. "I mean, I don't like it, but I like the part where we get to leave without more injuries." They collected themselves, made sure they still had everything, and then jogged down the rest of the hall, taking a few more turns to get back to the intersection that had offered them this option in the first place. "Oh, also," James said, panting as he caught his breath, "I think he was totally fine with what he got, and didn't mind that we kept a good two-thirds of our loot. Nice guy, really."

Alanna let out a snort of laughter while she tried to steady her breathing.

The duo found an empty cubicle and pulled up a couple chairs, taking the time away from the territory of the strider gang to sit and actually rest. They went through what was becoming a routine ritual of checking each other for missed damage: wounds that didn't hurt enough to be noticed during a crisis but should be treated.

"You're all good," Alanna said as they finished up. She stood and twisted her torso around, trying to work out the muscles in her back. "I know they're kind of animal-level intelligence, but I can't believe you bluffed that thing. That was so stupid."

"You were mad at me for giving up the orbs, now you're mad at me for saving them! I don't get any respect!" James said indignantly, sprawled over a chair. "Anyway, it worked, and that's what counts. Also, we're now running low on time. We should head back, we'll have to actually map this out some other day. I'm honestly kind of surprised that Anesh and I stumbled onto the right path the first time, if this is how fucking hard to navigate this place is."

Alanna poked through the cubicle as James talked. Flipping open folders and looking through pages of gibberish reports and numbers, she replied, "Yeah, well, you stumbled on this in the first place, so you're a bit of a lucksack, aren't you?"

Giving an appreciative nod, James hummed. "I am. Anyway. See if you can find anything good, I'm gonna radio Anesh and the others and let them know we're on the way back." Alanna went back to looking through drawers with gusto while James unclipped his radio and thumbed the button. "Hey, Anesh, you there? Over."

There was a crackle of static from the handset. A second later, after a warped hiss, James caught what sounded like the end of the sentence. "—ay inside," he heard in between the interference.

"Come again? Over." He clicked the radio's transmitter button, narrowing his eyes as he tried to focus on the words. His hearing was, he admitted, not that great when he couldn't also see the person speaking.

This time around, he got Anesh's voice more or less clearly. "I'm here. What's up?" Then a brief pause. "Over, you ass."

James chuckled to himself and heard Alanna huff out an amused breath behind him. He smiled as he hit the button again; that joke was probably worn through now, he should stop giving Anesh a hard time about it. "We're just on the way back. Wanted to check in first, let you know. Over." He looked up to see Alanna with a beaming, openmouthed smile on her face. The wild grin was apparently her reaction to having found a Nerf gun in the desk drawer. "Yeah, we've found a few of those," James told her, his voice quiet so he could hear Anesh's response. "Don't get your hopes up, they're always normal."

"All right," Anesh replied over the radio. "We're back at the fort waiting. Dave went and got hurt, so JP and I are working on adding some more to the fortification while we wait. See you when you get back, yell if you need support. Over."

James couldn't help smile as he heard Anesh's short report. "Thanks, but we should be good on the way—*fuck a shit what the fuck was that?*" His words turned into a scream as an inferno of heat and light roared over the top of his head from behind where he was sitting. The orb of death hit the far wall of the cubicle and didn't even slow down. In an eyeblink, it had tunneled through at least two dozen walls and was out of sight.

Turning slowly in the chair, James looked up disapprovingly at Alanna's face. She sheepishly avoided eye contact, casually and cautiously holding out the Nerf gun to him by its barrel. One of the six darts in its cylinder was suspiciously absent.

"So you *told* me . . ." Alanna started to say.

James just cut her off with a wave of his hand. "I know, yes, I know. That was my fault. Naturally, something was going to go wrong. The stuff spawned in the dungeon is, of course, stuff spawned in the dungeon."

"That's tautological," she quipped.

"Also correct, and you know exactly what it means." He gingerly took the weapon and popped it open to start pulling out each of the darts. "Here. You hold the ammo, I'll hold the gun. That way, there's a lot less of a chance that we plasmaficate one of . . . us."

Alanna raised her eyebrows in shock. "You want to bring this with . . . Yeah, I just thought about it. Of course you want the fucking fireball gun. Duh." She opened up one of the side pouches of her backpack and tucked the remaining five darts in.

"James? James! Are you there?" The radio crackled from the floor. With a slight wince, James bent down and snatched it up. "Yeah, sorry. Still alive. Just a small accident. Nothing to worry about, over."

Another burst of static, with James barely able to make out a few words in the mess of noise. *"ave . . . skkkxxx . . . ever . . ."*

"You'll have to repeat that, friend," he said down the line. "I'm having a hell of a time hearing. Think we're too far away for these things. Over."

"I said, are you sure? Over." The last word was added hastily, and even through the low fidelity of the walkie-talkie, James could hear worry in Anesh's voice.

He nodded before stopping and realizing that Anesh could not in fact *see* him. "Yup. We're good. Really. We'll see you when we get back. Over." He looked up at Alanna. "All right, if you're through trying to burn down the dungeon, let's get going."

The two of them zipped up their bags, Alanna shoving a folded-up jacket into hers to pad out the extra space. James gave her a look as she took the article of clothing from the coat hook in the cubicle they were occupying. "What?" she said. "I didn't find a wallet in here, and I figure this can go for twenty bucks on Craigslist."

"Isn't that a bit desperate?" he asked as they made their way back into the safer territory near the main door and started encountering familiar signposts.

Alanna almost snapped back. "You were literally talking earlier about how your rent went up again and you'd welcome the extra cash."

"Yeah, but not, like . . ." James thought about it. "I guess that's a good point, really. I've been actually kind of confused, since our bills went up, and I don't actually know why? Like, we actually got a green that lowered our rent at one point."

"Wait, you got a *what?*" Alanna said. "I remember Anesh telling me the green orbs influenced places, but he kind of neglected to mention they could do *that*."

"Oh, man, yeah, the greens are weird," James told her as they took a corner, checking beforehand to make sure there weren't any surprises. "You know the local diner that we always end up at, despite how their food is too greasy and makes half of us sick?"

"Yes . . ."

"It's open twenty-five hours a day now."

Alanna frowned at him, eyes wide. "Thaaaaat's not even a little okay. Remember how I told you guys that I was okay with how you were using this place? I'm changing my mind."

In defense of his position, James told her, "We also lowered the crime rate at a hospital! And got them new chairs!"

There was a pause as she processed that information. "Okay, I'm sorry, was that . . . from the skorbs? Or just in general? I'm losing track."

"From the green orbs. Please don't let Anesh convince you that it's okay to call them skorbs. He speaks only in lies and terrible name ideas."

"He named the tumblefeed."

James nodded, then held up a hand as he checked the inside of one of the cubicles they were passing. They snuck by in silence, doing their best to not wake the shellaxy sleeping in there. Without talking about it, they'd both sort of decided that they were done hunting for the day and that getting out without any more fights was the best plan of action. After they'd cleared a few more rows, and James was pretty sure there wasn't anything left to challenge them, he finally let himself relax.

"And there's the door. You ready to go home?"

Alanna let out a gasping sigh. "Oh, hell yes. This armor is itchy as hell, and I want a shower. Hey, how do you guys handle the fact that this place ruins your sleep schedule?"

"Badly," James told her flatly.

The two of them were laughing as they crossed the open area that he and Anesh had carved out to make Fort Door. Their little base was a bit exposed, what with all the missing cubicles around it, but James still got the feeling of a fort in a jungle when he saw it on his way back. It was amazing how, even though it was pretty big, and getting bigger, judging by how Anesh and JP were locking another wall into place, James never saw it from a distance. There was always that moment of taking one last turn and seeing "home." That bit where he knew he was going to make it out safe and that it was time to sit down, relax, divide up the loot, and reminisce about what they'd seen.

He smiled as he walked forward. He wondered if Anesh had any good stories from today. Maybe he'd bet a few skill orbs on finding the weirdest stuff.

James felt his luck, like his spirits, riding pretty high.

CHAPTER 40

"Turn around!" was not the first thing James was expecting to hear Anesh shout at him as he and Alanna took long, casual steps down their hallway toward Fort Door. But it was what was being yelled at him, and that was just something he was going to have to deal with.

"No!" he replied in a cheerful and upbeat tone, putting just enough emphasis on the word to make it pop without sounding like he was actually mad at Anesh. This got a snort of laughter from Alanna next to him. At the end of the aisle, Anesh just crossed his arms and gave James a disappointed look. "Oh, come on," James said. "Is this the part where we find out that you're betraying us and leaving us to fend for ourselves in the dungeon, like some kind of Saturday morning cartoon villain?"

Anesh pinched the bridge of his nose in frustration before responding. "No, James, this is the part where I just wanted to test something. Calm down."

"Oh." James was almost disappointed. "I'm almost disappointed, really," he told Alanna.

She gave him a look out of the side of her eye, just barely tilting her head. "Are you looking forward to that for some reason?" Alanna asked him with dark curiosity.

"Nah, not really. But, I mean, it would be kind of a good excuse to . . ." James started to answer, but a brief pause was the perfect opportunity to be cut off.

Both Anesh and Alanna, simultaneously, let out a sharp "No." For both of them, it perfectly summed up their opinions on being trapped in the dungeon for the one week to three years that they estimated the door was closed for on this side. No. They didn't want it. Maybe James would be happy leaving behind his whole life to become the most enthusiastic wandering dungeon dweller, but the others actually had life goals, and they were not at all keen on giving them up.

Burying those dark thoughts for a second, Anesh raised a hand in front of them. "Okay, but really, can you blokes just walk back down this hall for a minute? You can come back, obviously, just need to see something."

Alanna shrugged and turned around, and James followed shortly after. They moved fast, having already scouted through most of these cubicles, and also knowing they were in a relatively safe area of the office. With nothing on his mind to talk about, James just counted steps. After about twenty paces, they heard Anesh call out to them from back down the hall and turned around. "Can we come back now?" James asked flatly, and got a beckoning wave from Anesh in response.

Giving a frustrated sigh, he started back, ignoring Alanna's grin. He let his mind wander, running through what their debriefing was going to be like, and also wondering if everyone would be okay with doing it at a diner so that he could get some real food inside him. James was, it turned out, *starving*, and dungeon candy wasn't going to cut it for nutrition. He wanted something with actual vegetables.

Before he knew it, they were back in front of Anesh. "So?" their friend prompted.

"So what?" James said.

"Did you notice?" Anesh asked again, a bit eager.

Alanna, James suddenly noticed, was scowling again. "Hang on a fucking second . . ." she said. Motioning James to stay put, she walked back down the hall, counting off out loud. Ten steps down, she stopped, and turned around. Fifteen steps later, she was back in front of them.

"Wait, what the hell?" James asked, startled. "What did you do?"

Anesh gestured energetically at the hallway. "I knew it! Hah! It's longer in one direction!"

"Does that . . . Is this a problem?" James asked, looking between Alanna's annoyed glare and Anesh's excited smile. "Is this good? Look, I'll be honest, I might have a concussion, and it's kind of hard to think about if this is something that I should think about."

Alanna opened her mouth to say something rude about the hallway, but Anesh just rolled over the conversation. "It's amazing! The chance to observe non-Euclidean space in person is always amazing! You're physically traversing space that is only present in a specific vector!"

"This is like the Möbius hallway, isn't it? You're just really jazzed that the dungeon is breaking space." James sighed. "Okay, so, where is it?" he asked.

"Where's what?" Anesh replied with a question of his own.

James waved a hand around. "There's gotta be an orange orb here somewhere. Personally, I think that might be a bit more useful than a hallway that takes longer to get through. Also, wait, hang on. What did it look like from your perspective when we were walking back?"

"Like you were walking back," Anesh said quizzically. "I don't know if I understand the question. Also, I . . . guess we can find the orb, sure. Knowing this hall is here is useful; it means there's probably a lot more small twists out there, probably that we just didn't notice." Anesh was the kind of person who would really like to poke at those refractions and warps in the fabric of space, no matter how strong the human instinct that they were potentially lethal.

The trio walked back into the fort, now quite a bit expanded from when James and Alanna had left it. "No," James said, "what I mean is, how does it look when we take steps on the floor that you literally cannot see from that angle. Are we just walking in place?"

"Oh." Anesh thought about it, glancing up at the ceiling. "I . . . hm. Bloody hell, I don't know if I can answer that. You saw Alanna come back, right? It didn't look like anything, but it clearly looked like something. So . . . that."

James had a headache from this. "Anesh, you are my friend, but if I find any broken physics around here, I'm ripping the orbs out and worrying about the frontiers of science later, okay?"

"Yeah, that's fair," Anesh conceded. "Anyway. How was your expedition?"

"Hungry," James told him. "I was actually gonna ask. Do you guys want to split up the orbs we all got here, and then go get dinner and talk about—"

"Yes!" "Yes please." "Hell yes, there's no food in here." The barrage of responses from the people around him caught him off-guard.

James just nodded. "Okay, great. Glad we settled that." He unstrapped and started dropping chunks of armor plate onto one of the chairs in the main section of the fort. Alanna joined him, and a couple minutes later, the two of them had lost about sixty pounds of bulky protection.

"Um . . . James, why is there a pencil in the back of your armor?" Dave asked, coming out from one of the side rooms. "Wait, why are there holes in this armor at all? This is supposed to be armor!"

"There's holes in the armor because there aren't holes in me," James said. "Ergo, the armor works. Calm down." He and Alanna emptied the orbs out of their bags onto the table, adding them to the smaller pile Anesh and the others had already made. "Also, Anesh, do you have a list of things we need to buy? I have one now, but I just want you to know that 'some kind of bowl' should go on it," James said as he scrambled to stop a couple small yellows from rolling away.

Anesh nodded. "We should compare lists later. Anyway. How do we want to mark this up? You two obviously brought back more. Do we . . . hm. We didn't think this through at all. How *do* we divide up loot? Especially the orbs."

There was spike of fear in James's chest. He'd kind of known this might be a problem, but he'd hoped that, somehow, it would all sort itself out without any kind of issue. No one would have to actually talk about their relative contributions, or complain that they weren't getting enough. It looked like Anesh and Alanna didn't have any easy answers either, though he couldn't see the same level of social anxiety on their faces that he had.

To his surprise, it was actually JP who came to their rescue. "Hey, okay, this is actually something that's not too hard to manage. It's just loot shares, right? I was reading about this the other day. We do it like old pirates used to."

"Why were you reading about pirates?" James let his amused curiosity override his concerns.

JP pointed a finger at him and proudly declared, "If no one makes you learn, then learning counts as fun. Calvin and Hobbes taught me that. Also, pirates are cooler than you, so shut up. Anyway, it's easy. We put them all in a pile and divide up by shares. One share a person, do something awesome and you get another share. Do something *useful* and you also get another share. So Anesh and James probably have two by default, just for being the guys who manage everything and the guys who get us in, right?"

Alanna raised a hand. "I have a concern." JP nodded at her to go on. "What happens when, like tonight, James and I bring back more? I totally don't mind sharing, especially since you derps are new here, but how do you balance that?"

Giving off a winning smile, JP answered, "It's not always even. That's a personal call, right? If someone is never pulling their weight, that's bad. But there's always going to be imbalances, and if we're all here, it'll even out over time. I don't know about you, but I don't think we need some kind of crazy achievement system to decide who gets what. Though we could keep anything that's especially cool out of the pool, as a reward to someone who really earned it."

James let out a slow breath. "That's . . . surprisingly fair. And yeah, I totally am okay with you guys splitting some of our loot. It seems like a good system. Thank you for . . . Wait, were you reading about pirates and their systems because of the dungeon? Did you actually plan for this?"

JP just smiled in reply. "All right," he said, "if everyone is okay with it?" There were nods. "Then roll to see who picks first, and we'll go around the table."

"You have dice on you! You son of a bitch!" Alanna exclaimed. "You *were* planning for this!" She barked out a laugh.

A tap on James's torso from the desk he was leaning on reminded him of something. "Oh, right. Before we split, we do need to take a couple out to feed Rufus and Ganesh. That's just general policy." Everyone nodded at this. Well, everyone except Dave. He still wasn't on board with the exceptionally spiky spider that Rufus reminded him of, but he also wasn't prepared to argue too much. "Okay then!" James said. "Let's get this divided up and go get dinner."

In the end, there was plenty for everyone. Or at least, enough that everyone got something. Alanna got one of the blues, and Anesh took the other one. And after carefully, meticulously marking down the exact HTML color codes for each of the yellow orbs, the group burned through them together.

For James, the results were a mix of impressive and amusing.

[+1 Skill Rank : Driving - Pickup Truck]
[+1 Skill Rank : Communication - Active Listening]
[+1 Skill Rank : Templating - Phone Book - New York]
[+1 Skill Rank : Criminology - Statistics]
[+2 Skill Ranks : Bookbinding]

"Hey, I got the same skill again!" he exclaimed. "That's never happened to me before!" He set his mind down the path of thinking about phone books. He could instantly recall, with near perfect clarity, the proper procedure for adding advertising images and special case fonts. "Oh," he muttered out loud. "Kinda wish it'd happened to something better. What did you get, Anesh?"

Anesh had gotten the following:

[+1 Skill Rank : Writing - Advertising Copy]
[+1 Skill Rank : Aerobics]
[+1 Skill Rank : Climbing - Rappelling]
[+2 Skill Ranks : Acting - Improvisation]
[+2 Skill Ranks : Disguise - Camouflage - Prop Use]

"Well," he said. "I can now safely start my career as a stage performer." There was a moment of quiet as everyone looked at him expectantly. "No, no," Anesh said, shaking his head, "it's not like the one that put half a Shakespearean playbook into my head. I'm not gonna start quoting lines." Everyone looked disappointed, and before James or Dave could bug him further on it, Anesh deflected their attention. "Alanna, anything good?"

Alanna considered her gains.

[+1 Skill Rank : Falconry]
[+1 Skill Rank : Stealth]
[+1.8 Skill Ranks : Etiquette - Local Government - US - Northwest]
[+1 Skill Rank : Arms - Jitte]

"Yessss," she said, carefully. "Yes. I've decided I want a bird. And a sword. JP, what happened to your sword?" Alanna looked over at him, only to see a look of sorrow and loss on her friend's face. "Ah. Um. Dave! What did you get! Quick, change the topic!"

Despite his thoughts on the quality of the segue, JP had scored a couple interesting skills himself.

[+1 Skill Rank : City Planning]
[+1 Skill Rank : Lockpicking]

"I think I'm either a criminal or a civil servant?" he said.

"Fuck, that was my thing!" Alanna exclaimed from the side.

Dave let out a confused noise. "Which one? Also, it's not like he stole it from you."

JP put a reassuring hand on Dave's shoulder. "She's just kidding, dude. Anyway, I want to know what you got."

Dave had gotten something less interesting. Dave also had taken the only red orb, not noticing that everyone else had pointedly avoided it when picking shares.

[+1 Emotional Resonance Rank : Liberty]
[+2 Skill Ranks : Animals - Horse]

"I got . . . horse?" Dave cried out bitterly. "Why horse? That's such a weird feeling, and all I get out of it is horse?"

"It could be worse," James told him reassuringly.

Dave glared over at him, half snarling before taking a small breath to calm down. "How?"

James put on a knowing expression and nodded sagely. He knew Dave had some small anger problems, and he didn't want him to think that he'd been cheated. "Trust me. It's better than having a phone book memorized."

"I . . . yeah," Dave conceded. "Yeah, I can see that. But now I can't stop thinking about horses. This is not my fetish."

Anesh facepalmed from where he was packing up their gear, while Alanna and JP just started laughing boisterously. "Dammit, Dave," Anesh muttered, holding back a smile.

"All right!" James shouldered his backpack, giving Rufus a few pets goodbye before leaving. "Enough about how much Dave is or isn't into horses. Food! Now!"

It was with a bright mood that everyone left, waved off by Rufus and Ganesh. They'd taken a risk, bringing in more people, but James felt like this opened up a lot of new possibilities to them. He had a little more direction now: plans with Alanna for a shopping trip, and plans with the group for direct exploration of the zone that he and Anesh assumed were the bathrooms. All in all, James felt like he was being picked up to ride this success through the next week. Just a little extra nudge in the right direction for him.

They filed out of the heavy metal security door. When they were on the other side and the door swung shut, it felt reassuring in its bulk. Like it could hold the entire dungeon with no problem at all.

James filed that thought away under *I sure hope so, at least*.

"Owd oo urt yerhelf?" James tried to speak around a mouthful of pasta and chicken.

They were sitting in a booth at their local diner, Parlour Street. It was the same place that James and Anesh had accidentally bent time around, and the effects of that tampering were currently entirely unnoticed. If anything had changed over the last month, they couldn't spot it right away.

They'd all driven here mostly separately and had, by mutual agreement, refrained from talking too much about their actions this evening to avoid having to repeat things. Now, they'd settled in, gotten some food and a mostly clear part of the diner, and were prepared for their after-action reports.

Around them, the place had a handful of customers sitting in the comfortable padded booths, the kind of people who were out at four in the morning: people who had to wake up too early, or college kids who went to bed way too late. No crowds of younger kids at this hour, since school was back in session, but James wouldn't be surprised if a few dumb children had decided to stay up until five a.m. with their friends, blowing their money from part-time jobs at the only place in town open past their bedtimes.

After all, that was what he'd done when he was younger.

Across the table, Dave looked up from his pie. "Sorry, what?"

Taking a large swallow of his food, James repeated himself in a slightly more understandable voice. "Ahem. I said, how did you hurt yourself? Anesh said you got injured and that's why you guys turned back, but you seem fine."

"I didn't hurt *myself*," Dave countered indignantly. "I was attacked by one of the monsters that I was not at all warned about."

"A shellaxy tackled him," Anesh clarified, sipping a drink that he insisted was coffee but that James thought had more the consistency of road tar. "He sprained his ankle. It's very ignoble."

Next to him, JP nodded, talking over Dave's protesting cry. "That was also the thing that ate my sword."

"Oh yeah! How'd that happen? Story time!" Alanna demanded.

JP just shrugged casually, a fluid motion that felt strangely practiced. "Well, it wasn't a very *good* sword, mind you. So I tried stabbing it in the... mouth... bits... and it just ate it. Chomped it right in half. James, didn't you say one of those bit you once?" he asked, to which James nodded, already chewing more food.

"They're nasty buggers, aren't they?" Anesh chimed in. "Anyway, James! Alanna! How'd your scouting go? Did you get us a clear path back?"

"Nnnnooo. No, we did not," James admitted. "We had some problems. We did check out four potential paths, all of which are no-gos if we want an actual safe run, though Alanna has a map that we can expand and use to plan if we do want to go with one of the riskier areas in the future. Found a few more traps, had to deal with more organized creatures, and also ran into a window."

"A window?" Anesh asked, raising an eyebrow.

JP leaned forward a bit. "Isn't the dungeon in another dimension? Does it have an outside? Did you *find* the outside?"

"A window. We don't know that for sure. And no, we didn't find the outside. Though if it does have an outside, it's not friendly. A bird came through the window. Kind of. Look, I don't know how to explain it, the long and short is that it tried to kill us and probably could have." James ran out of breath at the end of his frantic series of answers. "The point is, we have two options left on intersections that go back toward where the bathrooms should be. We can check those next week, maybe as a group so that if one of them pans out, we can all be there. Alanna, am I forgetting anything?"

Alanna looked up from her phone, caught in the middle of a bite of her sandwich. "Nah, not really. Oh, we found a . . . file. On one of the computers. James thinks the dungeon uses password-protected PCs as treasure chests, so we should try checking those more, if only to prove him wrong."

"Thanks . . ." James muttered. He'd caught that Alanna didn't really want to describe what they'd found in detail, though, so he let it drop.

"Aside from that," she continued, "Anesh, I wanted to ask you. Do you have any idea why that place has money that's clearly U.S. currency, but gift cards for places that don't exist?"

Anesh started answering right away. "Yeah, that's because it's . . . um. Huh. Wait, hang on, you're right, that doesn't make any sense, does it?"

"Why not?" Dave asked. "The rest of it doesn't make sense either."

Anesh shook his head at that. "No, see, the money is random, right? And sometimes it has weird denominations, but it's always in the style and format of America Bucks. But the gift cards don't do that. They're clearly gift cards, but to companies that don't exist. If it followed the same pattern, they should be Starbucks cards with pictures of eyeballs or something creepy, and random amounts on them. This is like if we were finding money from the Republic of Chad."

"That's a real place," JP commented over his drink.

"I . . . forgot about that. Fine, money from the . . . Empire of Wank, I don't know." Anesh fluttered a hand in the air, dismissing that line of thinking. "The point is, Alanna's right. It is weird. Though Dave is also right."

"I am?" Dave exclaimed, excited.

"He is?" James asked, amusement tinting his voice as he faked disbelieving.

"It's the dungeon," Anesh said. "Sometimes, I think, we're going to have to accept that the place is just . . . a bit . . . weird."

Everyone nodded. Even JP and Dave, with only a few hours of experience in there, could see it. It wasn't always going to make sense, and they were just going to have to roll with it sometimes.

James leaned back, full of food and enjoying the company. This felt, to him, like exactly what he'd always actually wanted out of life. He was part of an adventuring party, a real one. He fought things for a living now. Well, he also took tech support calls for a living, but that wasn't important. He was an explorer, he'd seen things no other human had, and it felt . . . magical.

He was doing it: making his dreams come true. Anesh wanted his math degree and to expand the fields of human understanding; Alanna wanted to be in charge of either a city, a nation, or an entire species; JP was going into showbiz or something, and Dave . . . probably had realistic ambitions. But for James, this was it. This was the height of his desires. Or at least, the basis of them. He wasn't trying to use the dungeon to pull himself up to something greater. The dungeon *was* the something greater that he aspired to.

It held treasures beyond what humanity had access to on Earth. It concealed secrets that would baffle the most ardent seeker. It had threats that challenged beyond anything James had ever seen.

And it had life in it: not just monsters, and there was a very good reason that James and Anesh refrained from calling them monsters too often. Such life that would make David Attenborough drool with wonder. It certainly caught James's imagination. Not to mention that he now had a very real friend in Rufus, much as Anesh did in Ganesh. While it was mostly clear to him that the life in the dungeon wasn't exactly human-level in terms of intelligence, they were obviously individuals, and smart enough to be friendly with. James couldn't really imagine going a week without stopping in to say hi to his stapler buddy, and if the time ever came to leave the dungeon forever, well.

He'd bring Rufus out to see the wider world. And figure out a way forward from there, consequences be damned.

Someone talking brought him back to reality. Alanna had just asked him a question, and everyone was looking at him. "What?" he said, blinking. "Sorry, repeat that?"

"Heh. You spaced out there," Alanna said. "I asked you what you think we should add to the equipment list you've got if we plan on intentionally fighting a swarm of striders."

"Oh. Um . . . running shoes?" James made a stab at a joke. "Really, I dunno. Seems like a terrible idea. Let's not."

"Fiiiiiine," Anesh groaned from the other side of the table. "We should find some way to harvest a whole bunch of orbs, though!" he said. "Also, I just realized how tired I am. It's . . . morning. And I always forget that the time dilation makes me be awake for too bloody long. James! Fetch the check!"

"You get really weird when you're tired." James chuckled.

One by one, the group paid, said their good nights, and filtered out. Dave and JP both promised to keep in touch over the next week, and the group committed to getting some kind of way to message each other for planning and prep work. Anesh told James that he'd see him at home and took off too, leaving only James and Alanna in the booth.

Stifling a yawn, James reached into his pocket and pulled out the USB stick, setting it on the table.

"I don't know if it'll play back the same thing again," he told her, "but you should keep this. It seemed ... important to you."

Alanna nodded before speaking softly. "He was my dad, you know?"

"I know," James said in an equally quiet voice. "Anyway. I need to go sleep. Let me know if it turns out that thing is eating our memories or something."

"Sure thing, punchy. Sleep well," Alanna called after him as he left.

The cool late-night air felt good on James's skin as he walked to his car. Above him, stars shone through the clear night sky. He smiled as he settled into the driver's seat. He was happy to have done something kind for his friend and already excited, daydreaming for next week.

CHAPTER 41

James fell through stained glass, glittering shards of color vanishing out of the corner of his eye. He could see the floor below him flying toward his face, but he kept hitting window after window of intricately crafted glass art, his falling form destroying artifact after artifact of great creators before him. He tried to stop himself but couldn't gain control. He was spiraling downward, toward a silver blade and the shade of a green tree and a scarf on a small grave marker and . . .

He stood atop a hill, overlooking a town. There was no detail to the buildings, just washed-out blocks of gray, motionless in the distance. Beside him stood a person who was not human but wore his face.

"What is this?" James asked, strangely aware of the state of the dream he was in.

Secret stared out over the town. "You were panicking. I am trying to help."

A moment passed. James took a seat on the grass beneath him, finding it more like the texture of scratchy carpet than any plant. "What is this place?" he asked Secret. "I've never . . . felt . . . a city like this before."

"This is what I imagine a city to be," the thought-thing that was Secret replied. "I have only so many bits of dream and memory; many of them go toward my Self." James could somehow hear the focus and important weight of *Self*, despite the monotone that Secret talked in.

He looked at his dream companion for a long moment before Secret filled in the silent air with "I am finding that I enjoy creating ideas."

James shrugged. Or thought about shrugging. He didn't have fine control in his dream. "It's good to have a hobby."

"Yes." The thing wearing his face nodded. "I understand that, I believe. I also believe. This is a new experience." His double turned to face him. "But that is not why I brought you here."

There was a moment where James felt a rush of worry flood through his mind. The silent air was punctuated by the sound of an aircraft going overhead, and a massive shadow passing by them on the ground, though when he looked, there was neither sun nor a plane to shade it. He looked back down to the city of gray blocks and unclear streets. "Why *did* you bring me here?" he asked hesitantly.

He could almost hear the thing's nervous laugh. It was a warm and comforting feeling, one that felt like it was pulled from James's memories of his uncle's house when he was three years old. Most likely, he thought, it was.

"I have no ill will toward you," Secret said. "Your mind is an interesting home. You do not fill all of it out, and there are places within yourself that you are not. When you come here to visit, there are many more places. I have been making sure they do not become troublesome for you. You would want to know, I think, that someone is at your home." He moved fluidly, for the first time James had experienced him doing so, and pushed a hand against James's forehead. "Wake up, please," Secret said, and shoved him backward onto the grass.

James jolted awake, the sensation of falling backward without moving leaving an unpleasant warm feeling spreading down his neck. The memories of his dream rippled away until he was left with just the reminder of a city that was never alive, and the fact that apparently Secret was keeping an eye on his surroundings while he slept.

File that thought away under *potentially useful, certainly worrying*.

More disturbing was the soft knock that came from his bedroom door a second after he'd snapped back into wakefulness.

James felt a spike of fear, and the combat reflexes he'd been developing over the last couple months kicked in as he rolled off his mattress to land in a crouch on the floor, leaving his blankets in a tangled pile. His hand dipped under the bed and gripped at the reassuringly solid chunk of metal that was his crowbar. It wasn't until he started standing up that his brain, still groggy and waking up, made the connection that if someone was quietly knocking, then they *probably* weren't here to try to kill him.

He checked his bedside clock. 4:14 a.m. He'd really fallen asleep early tonight. The dungeon run yesterday had thrown his sleep schedule for a loop, and he was left struggling through work, almost dozing off on the drive home, and flopping into bed as soon as he got back. And now, someone was ruining it for him.

Staggering over, reasserting his balance as he moved, James cracked the door open a bit. "What," he mumbled out of a dry mouth. To his surprise, it wasn't Anesh bugging him for input on the shopping list he'd handed off, but Alanna. She stood there in the hallway, looking a bit awkward waiting in the dim light of the streetlights outside. "Alanna?" James looked up at her. "Why're you here?" He opened the door a bit more. "Actually, how are you here? How'd you get in my house?"

"You guys gave me a key, like, a year ago," she said. "Can I talk to you . . . ?" she asked apprehensively.

"Yeah, sure. What's up?" James asked softly, hearing the concern in her voice. He opened his door and turned back into his room, turning on his computer and the lights. "Are you doing okay?"

Alanna stepped in after him, hands shoved in her pockets. "I was . . . um . . . cute underwear," she said, a small smile forming on her face, a hint of laughter in her voice.

James looked down. "Dammit." He grabbed the comforter off his bed and wrapped himself up in it. "Sorry. Or, well, sorry that you're going to comment on that for the rest of my life, I guess."

"It's fine, I woke you up," she said, not pressing him. That fact alone, that Alanna didn't follow up on a chance to poke fun at him, set James to worrying. Alanna was many things, but restrained was not one of them, not when it came to chances to throw banter and jokes around. James perched himself on the edge of his bed, tapping at the floor around Lily's small pen with his foot, while Alanna took a deep breath and pulled a USB stick out of her pocket. "So . . ."

James glanced over. "Oh, hey. Is that the one from yesterday? Did it work?"

She sat down in his computer chair, the PC now open to his desktop. "Yeah, it . . . worked. We just didn't get what it *did*." Alanna leaned down and plugged the USB drive in, clicking open the folder on James's computer.

"There are any number of ways you could have told me about this that weren't 'coming into my house at four a.m. and using my computer without asking,'" James said, without much malice. He rolled himself over to the other side of the bed where his desk and computer sat, coming up to a sitting position with his back against the wall, so he could face Alanna as she sat in his chair. "A text message. A phone call. Waiting until dawn. Any or all of these would have been normal human modes of communication. What's so important that you couldn't wait?"

Alanna looked at him, concern in her eyes. "This," she said, and hit the play button on the audio file that they'd pulled out of the dungeon.

"Doing anything this weekend?" The voice was a guy, either a teenager or early twenties. It was a cocky voice. James hated him already.

"No, and go fuck yourself." James instantly recognized the voice as Alanna, though the fact that the words sounded angry instead of flatly delivered made him think this was a younger version of her.

There was a long gap where the only noise was the sound of a shitty teenager getting rejected, a chunk of *uhs* and *buhs* that made James almost giggle, before the reply of "Fine, fuck you, you stupid wh—"

"Who the hell was that asshole?" James asked idly.

Alanna turned in the chair to look at him. "*That* was Scott Ogden. He was a douche I knew in high school, in that he kept hitting on me and I ended up getting suspended for punching him. Repeatedly."

James cocked his head, tapping his chin. "Oh yeah! I remember that! Though I can't remember if you mean 'suspended multiple times' or 'punched him multiple times,' but I can take a guess."

"For multiple punchings, yes. That one. Anyway." Alanna made a chopping motion with her hand. "This is a different conversation. I've listened to about two dozen awkward moments from my past in the last day. Every time I hit play, it's a different one." She pointed at the screen. "Always thirty seconds, always two people, always my voice, even if it was when I was a kid."

"So?" James asked.

"So, remember when you played it?" Alanna asked, with a voice that indicated that she clearly knew the answer and was leading James down the right path.

He nodded slightly, then stopped himself. "Look, I'm kinda tired. What's the point?"

Alanna just hit the play button again, listened for a half second, and then restarted the file. She did this a few times, motioning for James to wait for a second while she hunted for something specific. James threw himself back on his bed, leaning over the other edge to hold out a hand to the iLipede that was now awake and active and moving around her pen. He scooped Lily up and started petting her, which in this case meant fiddling with the touch screen and some of the more mundane apps. Lily seemed to like that, so he went with it. He also opened up the identification app and checked the progress bar. 99%. Almost done. But he could be a bit more patient; they'd learned early on that they couldn't put the iLipede to work 24/7. Lily actually needed breaks.

After about two minutes, James started to ask, "Is there a *point* to—" just in time for Alanna to shush him harshly.

"Wanna get something to eat?" It was a girl's voice, bright and bubbly. James felt a pull in his chest as he heard it, the feeling that he just wanted to smile a little.

It was, of course, Alanna who answered. "Sure, I guess. Um . . . what do you like?"

"Oh, I'll eat anything! I just figured that if you're gonna be over more often now, I should get to know you a bit better!"

On the recording, Alanna chuckled a bit. "What a direct approach to life. Does that—"

"Okay, so?" James asked. "Alanna, please, just tell me. I'm really tired, and the six extra hours of not-sleep from the delve did not help. What's the *point*?" He felt some frustration creep into his voice, and he instantly regretted it. The last thing James ever wanted was to be pissed off at his friends, and he knew how easy it was to slip into an anger spiral if he let his exhaustion control his emotions. "Sorry, sorry, I . . ."

"It's fine. The point?" Alanna leaned over and grabbed his shoulders through the heavy blanket. "That was the same person from your conversation."

There was a beat, and James felt like the floor had just vanished beneath him. "Oh." He knew the answer already, but he still couldn't stop himself from asking the question. "Who is it?" As soon as the words left his mouth, he knew what she was going to say.

Alanna stared at him, grip tightening in anxiety. "I have no idea." Her voice cracked. "And I've heard her voice six times now. James, what the hell is going on?" She sounded like she was about to cry, and James could absolutely understand why. The situation was sowing seeds of panic in his chest, and he wasn't sure what to do.

Long term, he might not have had a plan. But in this moment, there was one thing he knew he could do. Setting Lily down on the bed next to him, he leaned in and wrapped his arms around Alanna, pulling her into a hug. She jerked in surprise at the physical comfort, but after a second, she returned it, almost crushing James's spine in her steel embrace.

The two of them sat like that for a couple minutes, with Alanna catching her breath and James just trying to not freak out any further. "Okay," he finally said, leaning back. "Now is probably a bad time to remind you I'm not wearing pants."

Alanna let out a wet snort, cutting off a sob, which quickly turned into gasps of laughter. After a minute, she pulled back, wiping at her nose and eyes. "Yeah, good timing, Romeo," she said as she sat back down on the end of the bed. "But seriously. What . . . what the fuck do we do about this?"

"Well, step one is easy," James said, and Alanna raised her eyebrows at him in disbelief. "We go through more conversations and see if we can profile this girl. We also need to decide if this is someone real who we forgot, or if this is just one weird file fucking with us. Because, let's be honest here, the dungeon isn't exactly light on the bullshit, right?"

"Right. Right!" Alanna's mind grabbed onto the life preserver that James threw her. Of course this could be a trick, just another trap from a place that was already full of the things. Though she felt in her heart that it wasn't true, and James would have agreed, they both kept that to themselves and let it stand that this could be the dungeon's idea of a prank. "So. Um. Do you want to hit the button next, or should I?"

James toppled backward onto the bed, letting his muscles go limp. "Uggggh. You do it for a minute. If I'm not sleeping anyway, then I'm going to put pants on and go get magical coffee."

"Before I do, I wanted to ask. Why aren't we abusing the shit out of that coffee when we go delving?" Alanna asked him.

"Oh, I thought you'd have guessed already, considering how last week went," James told her as he shuffled around on his floor with the blanket still covering him, trying to find a pair of sweatpants. "It's because it's still coffee. The literal-actual-magic part doesn't change the fact that if you drink a thermos of that, you're gonna need a bathroom within half an hour. And, as noted, we literally cannot find our way back to the bathrooms."

Alanna rolled that thought around her head. "Ew. But since you *have* a bathroom in this apartment, can I have a cup too?"

"Sure thing," James said with a smile.

As he walked out into the hall, he half closed the door so the noise wouldn't wake Anesh. Behind him, he heard a conversation start playing as Alanna didn't bother waiting for him. As he went to brew coffee, he hoped that he could get his hands to stop shaking before he got back. The last thing Alanna needed to see right now was that he was probably just as afraid as she was.

"Hey, Secret," he muttered under his breath. "Anything you can do about that?" he asked the empty, cold air of his living room.

But there was no answer this time.

Anesh woke up normally. He got up ten minutes before his alarm, stood out of bed, and did his now-normal morning stretching routine. After a short set of push-ups and squats, putting on reasonable clothing for the early days of spring, and a trip to the bathroom, he got his bookbag together and made for the front door of the flat.

Given that it was seven a.m., he was a bit surprised to see James and Alanna at the living room table. There was a laptop open with nothing on it but an audio file, with a set of headphones running out of it, the two of them splitting the earbuds.

"At the table" was kind of a generous description. They were on the couch that took up one of the long sides of the table, both of them fast asleep, half leaning on each other. He was kind of amazed they could sleep through each other's snoring.

The table itself had most of the stuff he'd been working on pushed to one end, and a new set of notes spread across it. Anesh peered over at it, letting his curious nature keep him from breakfast for a minute. A lot of the papers were what looked like short conversations, with one party in each one underlined. The rest of the paper was spread out and composed a brainstorming web. At the edge of the table, left specifically for him, was a note with his name on it that just said 99%.

"What are you two pets working on?" he muttered to himself as he read. "Sarah Moyle, eh? Is this a . . . character creation project?" He looked over the web; they'd done a good job emphasizing keywords and then going into greater detail off those, but a lot of the descriptions ended in reference numbers. It didn't take him long to connect them to the conversation logs he'd looked at first, but that also didn't answer the question of what was going on.

He didn't want to wake the two lovebirds, though, so he settled for trying to solve the puzzle while eating a Pop-Tart before he had to run to class. "Someone naturally cheerful, someone they both like . . . can't be a character, then. Is this how they plan to ask someone out? What a madcap plan," he muttered. "At least they're not asking me out this way."

After five minutes of poking through the files, he felt like he was no closer to knowing what the hell they were doing. They were also no closer to waking up and telling him, and he still didn't want to be the guy who kicked James awake at 7:30 a.m. Anesh *was*, however, much closer to being late for class.

A mystery for another day, then.

Before he left, though, he wrote James his own note, reminding him to make damn sure to record the color, tone, luminosity, and every skill he got out of the football-sized orb when he cracked it. Not to mention whatever Lily finally identified it as.

He was pretty sure that they wouldn't get up to any trouble without him, but Anesh was savvy enough to know that he couldn't exactly trust James not to instantly jump on the chance to use another skorb when it was available. Not that he blamed his friend, honestly.

It was only Wednesday, and he was already looking forward to going back in.

If Anesh wasn't careful, he'd end up like James: just constantly wanting to throw himself into danger so he could laugh about it afterward. He smiled as he walked out the door. Well, maybe it wasn't too bad a way to live. James at least had finally found the motivation to work out that he needed. And the constant upward progression of personal knowledge didn't hurt either.

There were worse fates, Anesh thought as the door swung closed on his two friends.

CHAPTER 42

Sunlight falls on a young woman, filtered through slatted blinds. It casts sharp shadows on her face and fills the room with a clean and fresh feeling.

She's young, but no longer a child. Twenty-six years old and pushed into a role of responsibility years prior, she's been acting like an adult for a while now, no matter how much she wants to pretend otherwise. Dull black hair flows from her head; she would tell you that she keeps it at precisely shoulder length, but everyone knows that she has neither the time nor the money to spare on haircuts, and so it currently sits at just past the nape of her neck in length. It gets in the way more and more these days, and she's been keeping it in a small ponytail, emulating James a bit. No one calls her out on it, though. Partly because it looks good on her, and also partly because Alanna actually has some serious muscle on her.

It's a point of pride for her, and has been for a while, that she be stronger than anyone around her. Even though that cost her friends in high school, on account of her being "the weird girl," it also gained her the attention of James and his friend Scott, the two people in their school who didn't seem to care that their friend towered over them and could probably one-arm fling them into the stratosphere. Scott had moved away, but Alanna never really got out of the habit of being in James's social circle.

At present, James was being drooled on by Alanna. The two of them had fallen asleep together on the couch in James's living room, having discovered firsthand the side effect of drinking too much magic coffee. Turns out, if you drank too much of it, it didn't just wear off; you hit some kind of floating-point error and went from *wired as all hell* to *dead asleep* in a single sip. Their hair was about the same color, making them look like one big mop with their heads tilted together. But James stood out with a skin tone a few shades lighter than Alanna's. While her ancestry was a complicated and mixed bag, James was all too aware of who he was descended from. The French. And pretty much *only* the French.

Alanna was just starting to drift back to consciousness when the wailing of a ringtone cut through the apartment. Shocked awake, she jolted upright at about the same moment James did, the two of them knocking their heads together in a painful collision. It took a second for them to realize who it was they'd actually hit, and then they both jerked backward away from each other. Not out of embarrassment or regret, but because they had no idea how they'd fallen asleep together on the couch, and neither wanted to offend the other.

"What the fuck . . ." James grumbled, digging his phone out. Alanna just looked around and saw the daylight pouring into the room. While James answered his phone, she checked her own and saw the time. Four fucking p.m.? Also two missed calls from work, and one from her mom. She was just getting a nice panic attack going when James hung up and turned to her. "Welp. My boss is glad I'm not dead, but less glad I'm not at my desk right now." He was supposed to be in early today.

There was a pause while James stood up, maneuvering around the table. It took Alanna a minute to clear her throat of all the gunk that had built up over the last nine solid hours of sleep, but when she did, she spoke up before James could leave the room. "What the hell happened?"

James just shrugged. "We fell asleep, I guess? Fucking hell, my shoulders are sore. Never fall asleep sitting up again." He rolled his neck around, trying to loosen up the muscles. "We were working on the thing, and then . . . I guess the coffee wore off?"

"Or the coffee decided it was sick of our shit," Alanna replied.

"Or that, yes." James nodded. "The good news is, I feel amazing. I don't think I've slept that well in years. We should probably make a note about this, but right now, I really need to use the bathroom." That comment got a vehement agreement from Alanna, and the two of them briefly made eye contact before bolting toward the bathroom door. Alanna lost their improvised race, as she had to scramble over the couch to get there, but the sting of defeat was dulled a bit by the fact that the apartment had a second bathroom in it.

Half an hour later, after both of them had a chance to take a quick shower, they were back at the table eating leftover pizza in companionable silence. James was checking the notes spread across the table, while Alanna was texting back to the missed calls.

"Fuck." Alanna broke the silence. "Fuck! Fucking fuck!" Her voice escalated to a yell, making James look up and worry a bit about his friend.

"What's up?" he asked.

She took a deep breath before snarling out, "I just got fired over text message. Piece-of-shit job."

James hummed a sympathetic noise. "That's pretty shitty, yeah. But, um . . . is it a problem?"

"Excuse me?" Alanna glared at him, and James felt a brief moment of fear before he got his explanation in.

"I just mean, we make more than a week's pay on every delve, right?" James said. "I have to keep my job or we lose easy access. But, like, you? You don't need a job. You just need an hour of looting."

Alanna set her phone down and cocked her head. She opened her mouth as if to say something, then closed it again, looking up at the ceiling as if she were lost in thought. James watched her do this in silence, taking a few bites of pizza while waiting. After a while, she finally looked at him. "Why didn't I think of that?"

"I mean, it's prudent, for one thing. You make more money if you have multiple income sources, and I know you're taking care of your mom, so, yeah. But you've also only been in twice, and it's high pressure. Really easy to miss stuff, forget a lot of things." James shrugged. "Don't feel bad for, you know, acting like a normal person."

He spoke from a place of personal experience. For the last month, it hadn't been more than an hour between each time he thought about quitting. It would be so easy, he rationalized. They could bribe Frank, or just sneak in. It was no big deal.

But then, every day, he found himself getting up and going to work. Moving on momentum. He had a job, because humans had jobs, and he kept forgetting that he probably could just leave at this point. Or he'd make up some reason about stability or dungeon access. But all of it, really, was to cover up his own personal fear that the dungeon would just not be there one day. That he'd wake up from the dream and see that everything had gone back to normal. And that, more than anything, was James's biggest fear: that his life would snap back to being mundane, and that if he did anything too out of the ordinary, reality might notice and take away everything cool he'd stumbled onto.

Alanna shook her head, accepting the explanation, but still a bit jarred from so suddenly having her financial lifeline cut off. Thinking a topic change might help her keep from going off and murdering her manager, she pointed over at the notes James was going through. "So how far did we get? I'm kinda fuzzy on it."

"Well, we've got a name, at least. Also, I think this is your handwriting? What does 'fucking Bill Murray' mean?"

"Oh!" Alanna said quickly. "It means we ruled out time travel."

James hissed air through his teeth. Part of him felt like he should have gotten the joke. "Because . . . because *Groundhog Day*, right? Right." Alanna nodded. "Okay, we have . . . a lot written here. I guess our reason is in this pile. But still. No time travel means it's not from the future, I guess? And that's becaaaaauuuusse . . ." He trailed off, flipping through pages. "Ah, here. She references your twenty-fourth birthday coming up. Okay."

The two of them kept sorting through the pile of paper, trying to understand notes written under the influence of no sleep and extra caffeine. Getting a better picture of the person they were trying to grasp, and their own theories from last night. The short list of theories that Alanna didn't veto as soon as James read them out were that the audio file looked into an alternate reality, the person was actually the dungeon trying to talk to them, it was someone who had been removed from reality, or, most worrying, it was someone who was still in reality but none of them could remember her.

Her name was Sarah. She showed up as far back as high school for both of them, and even further back for Alanna. Though it was hard to prove, as voices changed too much to always recognize her when the conversations were from when the parties involved were eight years old. She liked ice cream and hated very little. Every time she spoke, it was bright and cheerful, the kind of person that James tended to shy away from most of the time. But from the way she spoke, she was good friends with him in the world of the conversations. She couldn't drive, but that was fine since she loved to bike and everything was close by anyway. She was employed somewhere, but they never found out the name of the place.

As far as James could figure, she had a massive crush on Alanna. As far as Alanna was concerned, she was into James. They agreed to disagree on this point, before it got too overly enthusiastic. Or violent.

Well, *agreed* was a strong word. They were sitting on opposite sides of the table, pointedly glaring at different transcripts and not talking to each other, when Anesh walked in.

"Hey!" He cheerfully greeted the pair. "You guys are awake! I was worried."

"If you were worried, why did you just leave us there?" Alanna asked with a laugh. "Wait, you . . . um . . ."

Anesh grinned, teeth showing through as he chuckled. "Yeah, I didn't want to disturb you two with your whole—" He was cut off as a pizza crust bounced off his head. "Dammit, James, you wanker! I'm trying to have a moment of smug amusement here!" He sighed, deflecting the second crust lobbed at him by Alanna. "Well, the moment's gone now. *Thanks*. Anyway, if you two are up, do you want to head to the hardware store with me?"

James was on his feet in a flash. "Yes!" he shouted. "Yes! Pick me! I'll go!"

"Calm down, mutt." Alanna stood up herself. "I'll come along. I'm guessing we're building something for the dungeon?"

It was difficult for James to contain his excitement, but he managed long enough to let Anesh answer the question. "Yeah, we're going to make a few things. Well, we're going to make a couple of weapon things, and then a bunch of explosives. James is over there having an excitement seizure because he's tipped to get to take advantage of his indirect-fire skill."

"I've given up being surprised by these things, but that one is silly," Alanna said with a wry tone as she threw on her coat and the trio headed back out the door.

The closest local hardware store was a place called Hammer Time. Well, one of the local hardware stores. There were others, obviously, all of them massive box stores owned by national chains. None of them had puns for names. And so, naturally, they were here, having open conversations about delving because they were certain no one would guess they weren't just talking about a game or something.

"Did you ever use that green?" Anesh was asking Alanna while they waited for James to google the exact width of pipe they needed to make a harpoon gun.

She shook her head. "I've been trying to think of the right place, you know? I know that 'at home' seems like a safe bet, but if they're all good things, then I want to actually use it somewhere valuable. Somewhere it'll make a difference for a lot of people, like how you guys used yours on the hospital."

"Fair enough," Anesh said. "Just make sure you let me know when you do. Still . . ."

"Tracking skills, yeah, yeah." Alanna waved a hand, not dismissing him but reminding Anesh that they'd had this conversation a dozen times, and she knew the drill. It hadn't taken long at all for her to fully adopt the mind-set of the delving lifestyle. "So, what do you think about this mystery person?"

Now it was Anesh who didn't have a good answer. "I have no idea," he said. "It seems like she's just a ghost. But every time I say 'ghost' when James is paying attention, he shoots that down." They glanced over at James, who was still engrossed in his Wikipedia research. "Right, so, really? I think it's a ghost. I don't know what kind yet, but . . . maybe it's someone who could have been part of our lives, but wasn't?"

"Creepy," Alanna said.

"I don't know if I'd call it creepy, just weird. But yeah, so far, we haven't seen anything to suggest the dungeon can actually do time *travel*, just distortion. So maybe the file plays conversations that could have been just a tiny diversion from reality?" He shrugged with his arms out and palms up in a helpless gesture. "I don't know. I do know it's probably not a dungeon incarnation trying to talk to us, because it's not creepy *enough*."

Alanna let out a whoosh of breath. "No kidding. That place can get deep into fucking nightmare fuel when it wants."

Anesh nodded. The dungeon was, at times, incredibly peaceful. The strolling pace through the cubicles near the edge was a walk through a calm silence, the feeling of sitting under the LED branches of the decision tree was pacifying, and the creative flavors of food it came up with were thrilling, but in a way that satisfied without scaring. But in contrast to the childish glee one could feel when watching a flock of paper sheets overhead, there was so much that could horrify. Pretty much everything that had tentacles of any kind bothered Anesh. There were death traps with trigger conditions that kept him on edge at every moment. And then there were even more outlandish monsters; not just life forms or creatures, but real monsters. Like the molten glass bird, or the camraconda.

Camraconda. That was the name. Alanna was wrong; there *was* a pun in there.

"So hey, changing topics." Anesh broke the silence. "You own guns, yes?"

"No," Alanna flatly declared.

Anesh looked at her sideways. "What? What are you talking about? That was a rhetorical question, I know you own firearms."

Alanna turned to glare at her friend. "I mean, 'no, not in the dungeon.' I'm with James on this one. The noise is too much of a risk. When we get in a fight, it's one thing. I think the sounds of active combat keep most of the more easily scared creatures away. But gunfire? No way. That's gonna alert everything with a green orb within ten miles."

"I don't see . . ." Anesh trailed off as he processed her words. His pattern recognition kicked into high gear as his brain ran through the last two months of delving operations. "Oh bloody hell, the green ones are actively trying to kill us, aren't they?"

"Probably?" Alanna said with an expression of uncertainty and a small shrug. "I've only seen one. But you guys have told me enough that I know they're way more aggressive. Anyway, the point is, gunfire seems like a good way to attract unwanted attention. Either too many tumblefeeds or another swarm of striders."

James came over, pocketing his phone and dumping a few lengths of pipe into the cart. "Okay, got it. What're you guys talking about?"

"You really zone out when you're on your phone," Anesh said glibly.

Alanna spoke half over him. "Do you think we could kill a swarm with guns?"

"Screw you, and hell no," James said, addressing both of them in order. "Guns are the worst idea. That's why I don't bring mine. Do you seriously think we could even hit a tiny, fast-moving target? Maybe Alanna could, but the rest of us? JP would shoot his own foot. Dave would shoot JP's foot. It's a terrible idea."

"What about a firing line of shotguns?" Anesh prompted as they moved down the aisles of tools and supplies.

James hummed as he thought about it. "Probably not. Because we'd need to line them up, right? And the only place there's enough open space for that is either a break room or Fort Door. Both of those are terrible spots, because one compromises a fallback location and the other one is in tumblefeed territory."

He looked over to see Alanna standing there with a raised hand. James cut his monologue short to point at her, like he was a teacher in a classroom. She said, "I had a question about that. Why are the tumblefeeds hanging out in the break rooms? That doesn't make sense. Shouldn't there be a server rack or a breaker room that they live in?"

"I thought about that, but we haven't found any. Maybe it's because anywhere can have a mess of cables in an office? I dunno."

Personally, he was willing to just chalk it up to the mystery of the dungeon's random number generator. There was a lot of stuff that he threw into that part of his brain, the part that told him not to worry about it, because they had the dungeon, and maybe they'd figure it out sooner or later, but it wasn't a big deal. The money-versus-giftcards thing was in there. So was the fact that none of the food was ever poisoned or tainted. So was the existence of friendly creatures, like Rufus. Ganesh wasn't in there, since it was pretty clear that Rufus had made him, but if James were a little less good at putting the pieces together, he'd probably have put that tidbit in the same place.

Anesh and Alanna were less willing to let it go. "Maybe it's a hunter. Or a sentinel or something," Alanna offered. "The break rooms are where it's ordered to guard?"

"Almost makes sense." Anesh rubbed his head as James tossed a gas can into the cart. "Please be careful with that. But yeah, nah. I can't really get why the dungeon would put one of those in a break room."

"Are we talking about the dungeon like it's a person now?" Alanna asked. "I thought we agreed the fucker wasn't able to screw with us like that. Or does this go into different territory than the audio file?"

"That audio file puts us in some deep epistemological shit. Frankly, I'm not a fan," Anesh grumbled. "There's really no good outcome for it."

James and Alanna wanted to laugh, but it was a pretty grim thought that Anesh brought up. There wasn't a good outcome to their investigation, not really. No matter what happened, they weren't getting ahead. The best possible option was that Sarah was someone who never existed. And ... that was a shame, wasn't it?

They kept moving in silence, Alanna and James looking off to the sides and throwing up a wall of silence around Anesh. It was a few awkward minutes of quiet before Alanna broke the silence. "So, um... while we're here, can we get the stuff to build me a shield?"

Grateful for the reprieve, James let out a relieved sigh. "Yes! Yes. We can do that. There's a bunch of other stuff on the list that we should pick up while we're here. Anesh, you have anything you want?"

"I wanted to build a chemical ballista. We're pretty much getting that done, so you rubes can get whatever you want. The First Delvers United petty cash account can handle the expense."

Alanna looked over at him. "Can I know what's in that account?" she asked. "Actually, wait. Are you actually doing accounting for this? Did you name our party? Is there an expense fund for payroll?"

Anesh looked over at James, who had opened his mouth as if to say something. But after a small thought, he closed it, then reopened it. "I'm actually curious about those things too. Are we splitting the money the same way we do the orbs, pirate style?"

"I trusted you to get me out of this." Anesh frowned at James. "But yes, I'll actually set up a bookkeeping system, and... why the hell am I the one doing all the paperwork? Wait, is *this* why you brought me in, James? You bloody—"

"No, no!" James cut him off. "That's impossible. That would have required forethought and planning on my part. Which, I think you will agree, is not a thing that happens."

It was true, and Anesh couldn't deny that. So he let it drop for now. Though in the back of his head, he did honestly consider using some of their newfound mild wealth to hire an accountant. Or a college student. No need to go overboard. He considered whether the costs of using an intern would outweigh the benefits of not paying for someone with a degree. After that, he considered whether he'd been in America for too long.

Lost in thought was how Anesh passed the rest of the time while the others picked up the materials to make Alanna her shield. He was only shaken out of his train of thought when they came up to the register to pay. Fortunately, everyone in this damned city seemed to be apathetic to everything suspicious, and the clerk had no trouble selling them the materials to make an artillery piece and the nail bombs to go with it.

That . . . was something else they should probably address. "Does anyone find it weird . . ." Anesh started to say as they loaded up the back of James's car.

"Yes," both of the others chorused.

"But," James said, "before you ask, I don't think it's a dungeon thing. I think it's just because people aren't naturally suspicious."

Alanna put a hand on his shoulder. "Someone helped him make thermite," she said, simply. "That is not normal," Alanna declared. It was a pretty simple chain of thought for her: thermogenic weapons weren't something that people *helped you make* in their off time.

"You've never met a chemistry student, have you?" James asked.

It was evening when JP and Dave walked into the apartment, the door bouncing off a chunk of sheet metal on the floor.

"Hey! Watch that!" James called out from the table. The smell of sawdust and glue hung in the air, and the sound of a power drill cut through the room when Dave tried to respond.

The two newcomers looked around, Dave worried that he was going to step on something pointy, JP concerned about something totally different. "Hey, friends," he said, "are you at all concerned with the hole in the wall you've created?"

"Not really!" James cheerfully called back. "Because it means the spear gun works!" He looked down at the pile of unsecured piping on the table. "Almost," he amended. It had almost worked, but it had also fallen apart on the first test. The first accidental test.

"Why are you doing this inside?" JP asked in a patient, fatherly way. It was a voice that said *I am not angry, but I am disappointed in you*. Which was probably worse, as far as James was concerned. It was the sort of voice that JP pulled out when he was more curious than angry and trying to inflict comical guilt on his friends. Still, it was a pretty reasonable question.

James answered it as best he could. "It's still kinda cold outside, and our back deck is tiny. Also, we can patch the hole later. We've got some extra cash set aside anyway, even with the extra bills this month."

While that was true, it did raise an interesting question. While Dave and JP came in and got comfortable, the thought sat there. While the others set their work aside and they started figuring out what they were going to eat that night, the thought festered. And after the pizza arrived and they rearranged the living room for anime night, it finally made it out.

"Hey, quick tangent," Dave said, addressing the group. "If you guys had your bills go up, why don't you just rent out the other bedroom?"

The room went quiet. Every head turned to look at Dave, with James frozen, his finger over the play button for the night's selection.

"At the risk of sounding stupid," Alanna said, "what other bedroom? Have you seen this apartment?"

There was a round of agreement. The apartment had two bedrooms, Anesh's and James's. It was why they didn't have any other roommates in the first place. But Dave didn't seem to have grasped that. "I've seen the apartment, it's got . . . three bedrooms? Doesn't it?"

"Noooope," James said. "That's part of why our rent is so offensive."

"Then how have you been affording it for the last three years?" Dave asked, irritated. "Besides that, what about Wes?"

JP leaned over and stage-whispered at his friend, "Who's Wes?"

"He was the roommate before . . . Anesh . . ." James said, trailing off. "No, that's not right. He was a roommate, though, I definitely remember him. He moved out when . . . um . . ." James racked his brain. He knew Wes had lived here. He knew that the guy had moved out at some point. He hadn't been part of their social circle, but he hadn't been an enemy or anything. But beyond that, there wasn't anything. In fact, it felt like his thoughts were running up against barbed wire when he tried to remember anything concrete. "Uh-oh," he said sharply.

Alanna leaned forward, her larger frame bowing the couch as she shifted her weight on it. "If we're asking dumb questions, well, your place does have two bathrooms. That's *kinda* odd for a two-bedroom place, but I figured that was part of why the rent was high."

There was a thud as Dave tried to roll over the back of the couch and collided with the floor. "Hang on, I'm gonna go check. I could have sworn you have three bedrooms." He started taking long steps down their hallway.

"Dave, wait!" James's voice betrayed actual fear as he saw his friend head out of sight. On the other side of the living room, Anesh echoed his sentiment with a barked-out "Stop!" But Dave wasn't listening, intent on proving himself right. James rolled to the floor and bolted after him, with Alanna and JP standing up and moving after them.

The hallway was short, because it was only a two-bedroom place, but James wasn't fast enough to catch and stop Dave, who was now counting off doors. "One, two, bathroom, and . . ." James caught up but was too late to stop it. "Three. Right there. Or is that a closet?"

"That isn't a closet," Alanna muttered. James and Anesh were frozen in place, rigid as statues. "That isn't . . . supposed to be there," she said, grim confusion on her face.

Of course it wasn't supposed to be there. Because this was a two . . . bedroom . . . apartment. Wasn't it? The thoughts fought against each other in their minds, battling for dominance. Two or three? How many bedrooms? How many roommates? Other thoughts were consumed as ammunition in the war. Why were there two bathrooms? Why was the rent going up? Why did no one remember why Wes moved out?

Dave was oblivious to all of this. He hadn't really paid enough attention for any one thought to be firmly rooted in his mind. So it wasn't that hard for him to reach out and open the door.

"Hey, it *is* a bedroom!" Dave said cheerily. Behind him, JP stepped through the others and looked through the door, while James, Alanna, and Anesh just locked up.

"That's... uncomfortable. Do you guys..." He turned around and saw his friends, unmoving. "Okay, I have new concerns." JP leaned over and poked James in the cheek. "Hello?"

Inside James's mind, two thoughts went to war.

One was the truth: there were three bedrooms in his apartment, and there always had been. It was a thought that was reinforced with scraps of evidence and the genre savviness that he'd built up over a lifetime of books, anime, and the last few months of having an actual dungeon to test his trope knowledge on. The other was the truth: there were only two bedrooms in the apartment, and there always had been. It fired molten shots of doubt and anxiety, of the knowledge that he was always short on rent and the explanation that he was misremembering timelines.

But James knew. Part of him knew all too well what that second truth was made of, what motivated it. And that part of him, while it may have just been a gut instinct, was enough to call for help.

Secret! Help me! his mind shouted. And with no preamble, Secret was there on the battlefield. A weaponized meme: it was a shotgun to the swords and spears of James's errant thoughts. James himself wasn't unarmed either, able to focus on the dreamlike state with clarity. He and Secret tore through the evidence and structure of the false truth, exposing its core. Exposing something that, to James's senses, felt a whole hell of a lot like Secret himself.

What the fuck is that... A resonant echo of his thoughts called across the scorched waste of his dreamscape. The answer was, it was a monster. Something he couldn't quite put into human thoughts but was forced to occupy a human mind. It was too many shadowy limbs and too many single red burning eyes. It lashed out at him, exposed and unwilling to go back to the confines of the ruse.

James blocked the first strike, and his perception of self cracked. Someone who may have been James tried to deflect the second imperative aimed his way, and their conscious control of themself started to slip. The third madness would have killed him outright if it hit. There was no universe where James would ever be equipped to kill this thing.

Fortunately, he was just the bait. Secret was the one doing the killing. A razor-sharp directive, burning white around the edges with righteous rage and indignation, cut through the invader, severing it from its connection to James's mind. And just like that, he woke up.

He stumbled forward, caught by JP, who wore a concerned expression. "Are you all right? You all just stopped moving."

James whipped his head around. Anesh and Alanna were still frozen in place. "Secret! Kill!" he commanded. Terse, but not cruel. The words were important to expose Secret, so he could move; the actual conversation about the course of action took place in a split second inside his head.

Something that looked like the angry ghost of one of the ancient leviathans that once roamed Earth's oceans burst forth from James's skull. It trailed blue-and-white flames as it dove forward from him, splitting into two fragments and striking into Alanna and Anesh.

A startled "What the fucking fuck is that?" came out of Dave, now watching the events in the hallway, as he slammed the door shut again, while JP could only bring himself to ask James, "Why was it wearing your coat?"

James couldn't answer. He was too busy falling forward into comfortable blackness.

He woke up some time later, which was a pleasant surprise. "Ow" was his first word, and it alerted JP.

"Hey, he's coming around. I think we're okay," he called to someone else, who James couldn't see.

"How long?" James rasped at him.

JP checked his phone. "Two minutes, forty-eight seconds," he said. "Are you okay? What the hell was that?"

"Something in our heads," he said. "Not in yours, I guess? Or maybe it wasn't as bad because... reasons. Ow. Fuck." James kneaded his forehead with the palms of his hands. "I need water. Or a lobotomy. Or... fuck, where's Secret?"

"What secret?" Dave asked. "Did I miss something?"

JP slapped him on the knee from his crouched position on the hallway floor. "He means the glowing shark monster. It went back into you, that's why we're concerned, and Alanna has your gun. So please don't try anything."

James looked up, his vision swimming for a second before focusing on the image of Alanna towering over him, with his nine-millimeter pistol aimed at the floor in a comfortable grip in her hands. "Oh. Please don't shoot me?" Looking to the left, he also saw Anesh with a Nerf gun. "Really, please don't shoot me with *that*."

"James, what the fuck was that?" Alanna asked

"Which part? Also, can I have some water?"

"The part with the glowing shark, James," JP said, polite and almost monotone. A voice like he was giving a lecture. Or conducting an interrogation.

James nodded. "Okay, so, I get the suspicions, but it's actually fine. Secret is the name of the independent thought that was preventing me from talking about the dungeon. Anesh, yours got hungry and died off, which is why you got out of it. But mine had a whole other life to feed on. So I made a deal with it. Him. He likes being a him. It's a lot like the comfortable symbiosis with Rufus, actually."

"And the neon reenactment of *Street Sharks* inside our heads?" Alanna demanded, not loosening her grip on the weapon.

"There was something hiding there. When Dave opened the door, it compromised it, and it tried to kill me. I saw you two frozen and panicked. Thought it was after you, too. So I sent Secret in as backup." He looked around, worry starting to reach his eyes. "Guys, it's not any weirder than our average Tuesday," he said, shaking. "Also, are you okay? Did it work?"

Anesh shrugged. "No idea. The only reason I know anything weird is going on is that Dave insists that we've been missing a bedroom for months, but I can't remember a time when we didn't have three bedrooms. But then . . . but then, whose room is that, right? Bollocks. This is weirder than an average Tuesday." He sighed and set the dart gun back on his desk in his own room before returning to the hall. "Alanna, I think we're okay here."

The woman just grunted as she unloaded the pistol and checked it carefully with practiced motions before replacing it in the carrying case. JP helped James up to his feet, and everyone clustered around in the hallway.

"So now," James said, taking the lead. "The question is." He reached out to the doorknob, and everyone unconsciously held their breath around him. "Who was it?"

CHAPTER 43

The door swung inward, and dust long left undisturbed danced in the light of sunset pouring through the window: golden specks of matter floating in a room that looked like it hadn't been lived in for a long time, but when it had, oh, what a life it had held.

There was a small alcove for the door, with the rest of the room in that simple, apartment block ten-by-ten square past it. A loft bed took up the back left corner of the room, dominating almost half the space with the dresser at its foot. What was underneath the bed was obscured by a purple blanket with white fabric stars on it, and what was on top of the bed itself was out of sight, though James could spot the front half of a bright pink stuffed unicorn poking over the side.

The walls were lined with posters. Peering in from the door, James and Alanna started to put together a picture of the kind of eclectic person who lived here. They were the kind of nerd that would have framed posters for *The Fifth Element* and *Akira*, right next to one for *Twelve Angry Men* that looked like it might have been an original theater advertisement that was just taped to the wall. Album foldouts for Zebrahead and AC/DC coexisted alongside Alanis Morissette and Fiona Apple. There were ornate metal candle sconces by the head of the bed, flanking a dream catcher that, to James, looked for all the world like it was an ancient kindergarten art project.

To the right of the bed was a desk. Well, something that had started out as a desk at one point in its life. Anesh much preferred his own desk, which was mostly just a flat box, but in contrast, this thing was a bit of an amalgamation of shelves and cabinets. All painted different colors, and none of them looking manufactured, giving the desk an appearance of having been added to by hand over the years, every time the person needed a new place to hold their collection of knickknacks. The hydra of storage space reached up from the original desk, almost all the way to the ceiling, showing the weight of a life spent collecting everything from old Game Boy games to what looked like a row of jars of sand.

And the floor was covered in loose articles of clothing and empty soda cans.

"What. The hell. Am I supposed to take away from this?" James asked rhetorically.

Alanna pushed past him, kicking a hoodie out of the way to make a space on the floor to stand. She looked around, hands on her hips and deliberately not touching anything. "It smells fucking awful in here," she declared, still sweeping her vision over the room. "Oh. There it is." She took another careful step in and poked at something on the desk. It was a paper plate, with a thin layer of dust on it settled over a thicker layer of something that was once pizza. "Gross."

James took a half step in himself, pushing aside the curtain on the underside of the bed. It was a small half couch, some kind of cushy smooth material, and a small TV screen with a couple game systems hooked up to it. "This place is, I will not lie, totally rad. I wish my room were this cool. Though I'm not a fan of all the trash."

"Yeah, should we, like, clean this up?" Dave asked from the door. "I can get a garbage bag."

They looked around, everyone having essentially the same thought. They could clean it up, and probably should, if only to make sure there were no more category X health risks like the thing-that-was-once-pizza. But then, there was the flip side. This was a place that shouldn't be here. It was a third room in a two-bedroom apartment. It belonged to someone they'd never met. James and Anesh could remember Wes, their old roommate; there was no gap in their memory about the kind of person he was. He was just wholly forgettable, and not anyone worth remembering. This was not the kind of room that screamed "boring" to them. There had been someone else here in the meantime, and they had done some really sweet stuff with the place. If they were going to clean it up—and Anesh was quickly falling onto Team Clean the Place as he caught the smell of it—then they should make sure not to disturb anything that could give them a clue as to what happened.

"It's a crime scene," James said. "A weird one, but still. Yeah, get the bag, but we're going to document this first and go over everything before we throw it away."

"Even this?" Alanna asked, holding up a Tupperware container with aggressively unpleasant remnants of chicken in it.

"Even that," James replied. He looked at the fine white fuzz of spores and swallowed hard. "Okay, no, not that. Good god, what *was* that, chicken?"

Alanna looked into it. "Hard to say." She lobbed it underhand into the hall, where Dave held open a bag to catch it. "Moot point now. I don't think it's gonna tell us anything. Let's get the rotten food and soda cans out of here and then start going over stuff, yeah?"

They set about it with careful hands, partly to keep from disturbing anything, but also to keep from touching anything too much. The place really was a total mess, with a thin stratum of debris on the floor: food wrappers and tissues along with the clothing and books and scattered sports gear. James almost tripped over a baseball bat at one point and spent a good minute swearing at the worn aluminum stick.

It wasn't hard to identify stuff that was clearly trash, but it also wasn't easy to pick through stuff piece by piece, making sure that it wasn't a hint. They got caught up in the work, and no one really noticed when JP wandered off to take a call. The group chattered as they worked, James and Alanna talking about the posters on the wall, Anesh asking if the food wrappers were actual food you could buy in America.

JP came back to the group while they were about halfway through cleaning up, shoving his phone back in his pocket. "Okay, you guys have fun. I need to head out. Let me know if you find anything, okay? Also, Dave, you're my ride, so I need you to head out as well."

"Dammit, man, we had a rhythm going here," Alanna said, stacking a bunch of opened mail on the desk. "Specifically, a rhythm where I had someone else to sort out the recycling."

"Yeesh. Well, you've got maybe five bucks in cans there," JP responded with a grimace, looking at the two bags in the hallway already stuffed with cans and bottles.

James wiped the grime of dust and sweat off his forehead. "Also we've been using Dave to run down the garbage. It's really helpful to have someone else do the heavy lifting. But yeah, you guys go. Everything all right?"

"I just need to take care a family thing. No big deal." JP gave an easy shrug. "Anyway, I leave this in your hands, as you three are the masters of the ransack already." He made a small bow and headed down the hall toward the door. Dave gave a shrug and a quick round of goodbyes before leaving the garbage bag inside the door and following.

Anesh shook his head. "Okay, well. It's no big deal, we are almost done here, yeah? No one's found *anything* weird here?" Alanna and James both froze, turning to look at him. Alanna was currently going through that sheaf of opened mail they'd gathered from the floor and the nooks and crannies around the desk, while James had, for convenience, finished folding up all the clothing that had been lying around.

James shot a blank stare toward his friend. "Are you joking? Man, literally everything about this is weird by definition."

"I found a bag of sex toys, does that count?" Alanna asked with an equally straight face.

"Ew," James and Anesh said together. James continued, "Also, no, it doesn't count. That's a reasonable thing to have. But, given how much of a mess this place is, maybe don't touch them." He sighed. It was getting kind of late, and the crisp night air had filtered in through the open window of the room enough to make taking a deep breath a tolerable idea. "Honestly, I was hoping that we'd find something more overtly helpful. It kind of annoys me that none of these posters on the walls are obvious dungeon motivation posters."

Anesh stood up from his spot on the floor. "Okay, I'm gonna get a drink. Also . . . I have a concern based on that, James."

"Based on your drinking habits?" James snarked.

"Based on the dungeon thing, you ghoul." Anesh scowled. "So we have an actual, literal dungeon on our hands, yes?"

Alanna threw an envelope folded badly into a paper airplane at him. "Stop recapping. We know."

"Okay, well," Anesh continued as he stepped out into the hallway, "all I want you two to consider is that we may need to look into the fact that literal magic is real, and there's more to the world than the dungeon." He shrugged, shaking dust off himself from the doorway. "Think on that." And he walked off.

James and Alanna shared a look of concern, an exaggerated frown on James's face. They had not thought of that.

Both of them started to talk at once and then cut themselves and each other off. James motioned for Alanna to go ahead, and she said, "Ten bucks says your roommate was a witch, and this is some kind of curse backfiring."

"Fuck, I was going to say that one," James said. "Okay, ten bucks says that she got abducted by aliens."

Alanna nodded vigorously. "Oh! I'll put another ten on her being a mythological creature in disguise, returning to her people!"

With a snap of his fingers, James countered, "My money is on 'literally just a vampire' for this one!"

"Teleportation spell misfire!"

"Shadowy government agency!"

"Anything that's the plot to an episode of *Buffy the Vampire Slayer*!"

"Okay, that's not fair at all . . ."

Anesh stepped in before James could finish whining at Alanna's blanket coverage of pop culture. Opening a soda with a *hiss*, he asked pointedly, "Can I bet money that it's the person you've been trying to research who shows up on the conversation .mp3?"

"Anesh, stop ruining our fun," Alanna griped.

"Yeah," James said, "besides, just because we know it's her doesn't mean that it couldn't have been something else as well, right?"

Swallowing a sip of his drink, Anesh clicked his tongue and aimed a question at James. "Wait, you know it's her?"

It was with a sheepish look on his face that James answered, "Oh, yeah. We read the name on the mail. Sorry! I guess you were out of the room when we were doing it." James stood up, stretching muscles stiff from sitting on the floor folding laundry for an hour. "But man, come on. You just said it. We've tunnel-visioned in on the dungeon, really hard, and that's maybe a huge problem. Like, think about it. The dungeon . . . isn't normal?"

Alanna snorted loudly behind him, while Anesh just gave him a short, deadpan "Really."

"Really!" James said. "I'm serious here! It's not something that's supposed to be part of the world!" He took a breath, trying to keep his anxiety under control. "Look, I'm pretty genre savvy. But this is a ridiculous thing, right? It's not normal, it's not supposed to exist. The real world doesn't work this way. But it's here. So, like Anesh said"—he nodded at his roommate—"if this is real, what else might be?"

"Vampires," Alanna answered without hesitation.

James nodded, pointing at her. "Exactly, vampires!" He paced around the cleared floor a bit, waving his hands as he talked. "Wizards? Maybe! Dragons? Alanna, we could get a pet dragon."

Alanna's face lit up like it was Christmas Eve. "Really?" she said, forgetting her stoic and deadpan attitude for a second.

"Probably not! We'd probably get eaten!" James said, quickly smashing her hopes and dreams, and her expression dropped back into a glum frown. "But, like, this just can't be the only weird thing in the world."

There was a pause as Anesh took a minute to look around the room. "I want to agree with you, James. Especially since you're agreeing with me, and it makes me feel like a clever lad."

"Well, that," James replied, "but also because we didn't find a shred of evidence that this person ... Sarah, I need to call her by her name ... was ever once exposed to the dungeon."

Alanna chimed in. "Yeah, no otherworldly candy wrappers. No conspicuous weaponry lying around. We went through all the paperwork in her desk and just learned that she went paperless with most of her stuff. A few bills, voter pamphlets, credit card offers, nothing that looks like what we do. She's got that bulletin board on the wall, but..."

"Sorry, the what?" Anesh asked.

"Um ... corkboard? That thing." Alanna pointed at the brown board with dozens of small mementos pinned to it. Movie tickets and postcards, mostly. "The kind of thing that someone like you would use to make one of those creepy string-webs of information that looks like a conspiracy theorist gone mad?"

Anesh let out a small "Ah," looking over the board. "Right, okay. But this one is just personal stuff." He stepped up to it, moving around a pyramid of stuffed animals that James had stacked up. "Plane tickets, though. Actually, a big chunk here from a vacation. Maybe we can look into this, see if they ... she ... was visiting anyone. Might give us a lead." He reached up to pull several of the pins out and start taking things off the board. "I'll look into this. It'll give me a break while you guys keep tossing the room."

He walked out with the material, balancing the files and his soda as he propped the door open. "Have fun!" James called after him before shaking his head and turning back to Alanna. "I really want it to be the dungeon, you know?" he said.

"Why?" She leaned back in her commandeered desk chair, and James propped himself against the loft bed frame. The two of them were tired: tired of cleaning, tired of searching, and tired of not spending their day off relaxing.

"Because the dungeon is ours. It's special, it matters," James said. "I also just kinda have a feeling about it. Like, I know we're sorta-not-kidding, but I really don't actually believe in vampires. But I do believe in tumblefeeds and skill orbs, and I'm worried." He shrugged slightly, trying to find a way to express how he felt.

It was sort of simple, but also sort of not. He could see the path that had been taken to get here, so very clearly. The dungeon had claimed someone, and that someone had been someone he'd known. It was simple, but also not. It didn't answer any questions, it just reinforced what he already suspected. Though he didn't have any proof, he was, in his gut, certain that Sarah had been swallowed up by the same place he'd been casually farming for history classes and martial arts skills.

Maybe it was strange to believe that the dungeon was the only supernatural thing in the world. But, despite all he'd seen, despite the creatures and the orbs and the life form in his head that was becoming a friend, James just couldn't imagine living in a world with werewolves. He wasn't ashamed to admit that back in high school, he'd legitimately tried to find a way to become a wizard and had come up short. And he was sure enough that he wasn't the only one who imagined, on a long enough timeline, that someone would have stumbled across an actual spell and posted it on the internet.

So he was left with this thought that the dungeon was special. And that it was his. His and his group's. Perhaps that was a bit arrogant, or self-centered, but this whole empty room was just a bit too close to home, literally, for him to think anything else.

Alanna got it, though. She and James had stayed up for hours, listening to hundreds of conversations, looking for ones with a person they couldn't remember. And after hearing her own voice, over and over, talking to someone she'd never met, it started to hit her that this was someone she *did* know now, in a weird way. It was someone she wanted to be friends with, wanted more of in her life.

And that someone was gone. Not that she didn't exist, but she'd been taken away. And there was one very obvious culprit. It lived in the east stairwell of James's office building, and it had a giant fucking bull's-eye drawn on it.

"I get it," she told him, with a small and difficult smile. Seeing the twisted and uncomforted, but understanding, look on her face, James bowed his head to look at the floor. The comfort of having someone else who got what he meant was huge to him, and Alanna felt about the same way.

They sat that way in companionable silence for a little while, mostly just giving James a chance to compose himself. After a few minutes of quiet, he cleared his throat awkwardly and said, "I feel like going on a walk. Do you want to come along? Maybe go down to that coffee place that's open until two a.m.?"

"Yeah, sounds good." Alanna agreed instantly, eager to get out for a bit and enjoy the cool night air.

James pushed himself up from his leaning position, shuffling his socked feet across the clean carpet. "Cool. Let me just grab my phone. You want to go see if Anesh is interested?"

She made an assenting grunt and hauled herself up, while James ducked back across the hall into his own room. Throwing himself across the comfortable expanse of his bed, he extended his arms in an exaggerated fashion to reach out for his phone. Well, one for his phone, the other one just to give Lily some scritches. The iLipede had been doing good work scanning the massive orb that he and Anesh had brought back what felt like a lifetime ago, but she'd been stuck at ninety-nine percent for a while. James wasn't too worried—he knew sometimes that last percent took longer than it should—but he was impatient. Didn't want to let Lily see it, though.

Grabbing his actual, non-bug-shaped phone, he checked it really quick before standing up. His normal wallpaper image was covered by the *missed call* notification. "Ah, crap," he announced as he walked out into the pleasant, soft lighting of his living room. "I missed a call from my mom when we were cleaning."

"Oof. I've met your mother; you have my condolences," Anesh told him. He was throwing a coat on, apparently planning to come along with them. Alanna was nowhere in sight, and James assumed she was already outside.

"Yeah, it's a whole *thing*. When was this, anyway?" He opened up his call log. "Hm. Three hours, that's . . . huh." James trailed off, looking at his phone with a concerned expression, scrolling through the call log.

Anesh looked at him from by the door. "Huh what? Also, you coming?"

"Yeah, yeah. I just … have more missed calls than I thought." He poked at his phone. "These are all from the same number. How did I never notice these before?"

A contemplative noise from Anesh. "When were they?"

"Over the last two months," James responded. "And some of them aren't missed! What the fuck?"

"Okay, that's easy. It was just something you couldn't think about, like the room. Now you got your Pokémon to kill off the hostile memes, and you can see it again. Easy."

"That's not easy," James snarled. "That's insane. Hang on, I'm going to call this person back."

"It's pretty late, are you sure you should call now?" Anesh asked.

James had already dialed. Holding the phone up, he flopped back against the couch and tapped his foot on the end of it. "Don't worry, I'll just leave a message. Also, stop calling Secret a Po—"

The ringing cut out, and the call went to voice mail. "This is Detective Madden," the voice on the other end said. It was a deep voice, the kind of thick growl that came from a lifetime of smoking, or being punched in the throat. "If you have information relative to a case, or are returning a call, leave a message. If this is an emergency, hang up and call dispatch." There was a quick beep tone to let James know that he was supposed to say something.

"Detective. Um. Hi. My name is James Lyle?" he stuttered out, not prepared for this. "This might be weird, but I don't know if we've spoken before. I found a lot of missed calls from this number on my phone, and I was hoping to figure out who this was. Um … if you still need to talk, I'm available most evenings, I guess? Thanks. Bye." He hung up.

Anesh grinned at him from the door. "Why did you thank him? Is that an American thing on voice mail?"

With a snort and an extension of his middle finger, James pointedly refused to answer his friend. He let out a small hum before saying, "It is still kind of weird that a detective was calling me. It didn't say if he was with the police, or a private investigator, but, well..."

"Probably looking into Sarah, right?" Anesh asked.

"Maybe," James replied. "It just feels weird," he said as he got his shoes and coat on. "He can't be police right? I mean, if he was actually investigating a missing person and I missed eight calls, someone would check on that, right?"

Anesh nodded. "I think that's how the police work. Anyway, let's not keep Alanna waiting." James grumbled, but agreed. He needed a break from all of this anyway. A nice walk under the stars and enough caffeine to incapacitate a shark. It would be great to just enjoy some time without panicking about what the dungeon would throw at them next, or how it seemed like it wasn't contained to its own little stairwell. Those were problems for Future James. Present James was going to go get a mocha.

"All right," he told Anesh with a steady breath and a smile. "Let's go get some coffee." Anesh returned the smile, genuine and happy, and reached out to open the door to the cool night air and a clear, starry sky.

Standing in the doorway was a human-shaped figure, wearing a white button-up shirt and black slacks. It had only a blank expanse where its face should be, and the texture of cardboard where a person should have eyes and a mouth.

"Ja—!" was as far as Anesh got before it backhanded him into the kitchen counter.

The stuffed shirt stepped over the threshold of the door, into their apartment. James stood stock-still, frozen in fear. "Secret..." he whispered to himself. "Is this a nightmare too?"

There was no response from inside his mind. The hollow employee stepped closer, deliberately and in a strange jaunted walk that still made it look like it was limping, or not fully in control of its legs. "Commmm-panny proPERty must **not** be removed froM the OFFice."

It spoke in an alien voice, the words formed of scrap paper and pencil shavings. They washed across James and stole away his willpower. He couldn't move, he couldn't *react*.

This wasn't supposed to be happening. This *couldn't* be happening. The dungeon was supposed to be contained; it wasn't supposed to come out!

As the thing stepped closer, James found his mind racing but his survival instincts kicking into high gear. Forget about what it was "supposed" to do. It wasn't fucking *allowed* to do this. His eyes narrowed, and his heart beat faster, but it wasn't out of control. This thing came into his home, hurt Anesh—again—and now it was moving in for him? No.

This bullshit would not do.

James slid his foot forward into a combat stance, just as the thing strode closer and reached out a hand, twisted into a grim claw, for James's throat. His martial arts training kicked in, and he slapped the arm away with a sharp blow from the blade of his hand. The employee frowned before reaching out again, and James again slapped its arm away.

It kept moving forward, forcing him to shuffle back to keep a small distance between them. James was quickly running out of living room space, and back into the hallway of their apartment. The empty man was moving faster and faster, ramping up the speed and frequency of its attempts to seize him, but James was keeping up. For every hand it tried to snake toward his throat, he had a block, a counterstrike, and a slight shifting of his feet to keep himself out of threat range.

It was almost enough to make James grin. But he couldn't. Because while he was hitting it, over and over, and he seemed to finally have the physical ability to stand up to its insane speed and strength, as long as he fought smart, James knew a painful truth. While he could have worn it down fighting this way, he would have to do it perfectly, and it would take an hour, maybe more, to injure it enough to bring it to rest. And James, well . . .

He was running out of hallway.

Another step, another block. He deflected its hand, and it struck the corner of the hallway entrance. The hand closed and a fist came away with a chunk of drywall in it, making James gulp. The blank face of the thing advancing on him was wrinkled, as if in an eyeless scowl; he was making it angry.

"InDUSTrialll esssspionage is A punishAble *Offense!*" it screamed at him.

Behind it, James saw Anesh staggering to his feet, clutching at his arm. And at the door, left hanging open, Alanna appeared, gasping for breath and covered in dirt. Backup was coming, help was on the way, but it was too late. He lashed out in a short kick, connecting with what should have been a knee and buying himself a second. Another smashing counterblock that would have left a human opponent gasping in pain, but here just kept James from losing the structural integrity of his bones. And then, it happened.

James had run out of hall.

He almost pressed his back against the wall at the end of the hallway, but then, a small moment of hope opened up to him. The door to his bedroom was closed and it would take precious time to get into, but the door to Sarah's room was left hanging open. Five more seconds was all he needed to let his friends get to him and help him kill this fucker.

He pivoted, ducked a grab, and tried to jerk backward while landing a hard punch on the abdomen of the monster in front of him. But then it did something unexpected. It kicked him right in the stomach. Hard.

James had been in a few fights when he was a kid. He'd been bullied, he'd briefly lived with a physically abusive uncle, and he'd once fallen off his bike on the side of a hill. But he had never once felt a singular hit as hard as the one that struck him now. He felt like his whole body caved in around it as he was lifted off the ground and flung backward, his feet catching on the desk chair and sending him toppling to the floor against the wall.

As the ultimate insult to injury, the bulletin board was knocked loose from its moorings and landed on his head.

But the hollow one didn't stop. It just strode in, pulling a purple orb out of its pocket and holding it up to eye level, as if aiming it at James. "*No more stolen secrets,*" it wailed.

James tried to lash out with a foot, but couldn't untangle himself from the chair legs. Tried to roll, but couldn't find the energy to move. Tried to scream, but couldn't even find the air in his lungs to do more than cough.

Then the gunfire started.

A cracking staccato echoed through the apartment, through James's ears, and through the air for the surrounding four blocks. Over and over the noise barked out, and each time, a plume of dust and confetti sprayed out over James to accompany the new hole in the un-man. James tried to count shots but lost track after five as his vision swam and his ears burned. Finally, after what seemed like forever, the noise came to an end, when the paper pusher toppled forward onto its face, sprawled out over the floor.

Alanna stepped into the room, James's pistol held in her bleeding hands. She said something as she walked in, and James cocked his head at her, trying to shrug or tap at his still ringing ears.

"*Do you have any downstairs neighbors?*" Alanna shouted at him. Not angrily, just loudly, to make sure that the words were clear and heard.

James shook his head.

She nodded and planted a foot on the shoulder blades of the human-shaped nightmare on the floor. Then she took aim and emptied the rest of the magazine into its head.

After James pulled himself into a sitting position and made sure he wasn't going to vomit up the remains of his internal organs, he tried to ask Alanna what happened.

"Fucker went right through me," she said. "I didn't even realize I wasn't being mugged, except I got thrown into the fucking stupid fucking blackberry bushes outside your fucking apartment." She was shaking as she talked, adrenaline receding and fear coming back. "Anesh is okay. He cut his arm open on the countertop. That thing made a beeline for you, which is the only reason that we're alive."

James tried to nod and found that his neck felt like one giant bruise. "It makes sense," he croaked out, still not really able to hear his own voice properly. "It said . . . it said no more . . . I think it was specifically trying to kill Secret." He coughed and tasted the coppery tang of blood in his mouth. "Thank you," he said. "I don't think it planned on stopping with him."

Alanna carefully unloaded the magazine of the pistol, set both it and the gun down on the desk with trembling hands, and then sat down gently on the couch under the loft bed. She leaned forward, holding her head in her hands. James reached out with his arm, trying to pat her knee and reassure her that everything was okay.

"You saved my life," he said. "You saved Anesh, too. Thank you." It was a quiet, true thing, and he meant it more than he ever had anything in his life.

"I've never shot a person before," Alanna said in a small voice. "I don't like it."

Anesh walked into the room, a bloody bandage on his arm. "Technically you still haven't." He rolled the paper man over to show off the blank face that Alanna hadn't seen. "Not human. No blood either." It took a while for this to sink into her mind, but James had another question while Alanna processed the information.

"Hey. What the hell?" He pointed at what was hidden under the corpse. It was an orb. But not, as with the other one, a massive yellow orb. This one was bright neon green. It was the size of a melon, and its glow was bright enough to cast its color onto the walls. "Why'd it change color settings?" James asked the group.

"I'll do you one better," Anesh said, reaching down onto the floor next to James. "What do you make of this?" he said, pulling up the fallen corkboard. A half-dozen pins had fallen out of the front when it fell, showering James in a flurry of airplane tickets and birthday cards. But that wasn't what Anesh was showing them. On the *back* of the board, where they hadn't bothered to look, was a separate tableau of information.

"I've seen notes like that before," Alanna said, her voice regaining strength. "I've helped you *make* notes like that."

Anesh looked down at the two grimly. "Okay, no gods or wizards. Just one dungeon that took our roommate and is pissed that we know about it."

"Looks that way," James said, meeting Anesh's eyes before sweeping his gaze over to look at Alanna.

Anesh examined the map a bit. "It actually looks similar to ours. They use a different north, but looks like they got to the bathrooms too. That's where the map ends, though."

There was a minute while the three of them sat there in silence. It was a quiet, contemplative moment, with all of them wondering where they went from here. James was trying to decide if he should take time off so he and Anesh could move somewhere that the dungeon didn't know about. Anesh was trying to decide if he even wanted to keep delving if this was going to be their average Wednesday night. And Alanna, well.

"Who gets the orbs?" Alanna asked, breaking the spell of the glum mood. James and Anesh pointed at her in unison, smiling. "What? No, I can't take both of them."

"Fucking take the blighters," Anesh said. "I think you earned it." To which James nodded his agreement.

James reached up, handing her the purple orb that had rolled into his leg when the paper man fell forward. "Look. Here's the thing," he said. "I don't know if there are rules to this little game we're playing with the dungeon. But it doesn't get to do this." Alanna reached out a still slightly shaking hand to grasp at the orb. "It doesn't get to come to our home," James said, his voice steadying and intensifying. "It doesn't get to take our roommate, whether they were the one we liked or not." He raised his voice a bit more. "I'm pretty fucking pissed at it right now." He pushed off the ground, grunting a bit as what felt like a cracked rib got jolted a bit. "So take the orb," he told Alanna. "And next week, when we go in again, and we *will* go in again, we take everything from it. We dredge for every scrap of useful ability we can. And we use it to kick the shit out of that place. We're going to the damn bathroom, as stupid as that sounds now that I say it out loud, and we're going to see what's past it. And, if there's anyone human left in there, we're going to drag them out and kill *anything* that gets in our way."

Alanna felt a swelling in her chest as James spoke, and as he finished, he made eye contact with her and closed his hand around hers. She gave a single nod and focused on the orb in her hand, bursting it in a flash of purple dust.

[Shell Upgraded : Surface Fracture-Energy Value, +2,250 Newtons]

"I'm using the green on the elementary school down the road," she said. "We can stop by on the way to get coffee. And then, yeah. Let's fuck that place up."

Anesh cleared his throat. "You know we have to wait until next week, right? Unless we want to crawl through the vents. Also, are you going to ask Dave and JP about this?" he asked James. What he meant was *Are you going to ask* me *about this?*

James got it, though. He saw the worry and the fear in Anesh's face. "Yeah, I'll ask them. And are you okay with this? I know it's not what I invited you into this nonsense for. But . . . I don't . . . No, I mean, no excuses. If you're not in, I won't push it." James felt like he wasn't expressing himself clearly, but he knew that above all else, he wasn't going to try to force his best friend into a life-or-death fight.

And, with a small nod, Anesh understood and agreed. "I just wanted you to ask, that's all," he told his friend.

"Great." James sighed. "Now, *now* can we go get coffee? And maybe some medical attention. Someone check that thing for blues while I go lie on the couch and moan in pain."

ABOUT THE AUTHOR

Argus got started writing sci-fi short stories a decade ago, and has spent the majority of that time trying to capture within narrative the feeling of simultaneously not knowing what is happening, and overexplaining what is happening. He lives in the Pacific Northwest, where he studied and worked at a number of unconnected things before becoming an author. He did not know if this biography should be in first or third person, and as with all uncertainty in his life, has decided to turn that fact into a joke.

DISCOVER
STORIES UNBOUND

PodiumAudio.com

www.ingramcontent.com/pod-product-compliance
Ingram Content Group UK Ltd.
Pitfield, Milton Keynes, MK11 3LW, UK
UKHW041304180426